Sander Jakobsen is the pseudonym [ ] Winther and Kenneth Degnbol. [ ] *Birmingham Post & Mail* and the European Commission in Brussels before becoming a teacher at a Danish High School. **Kenneth Degnbol** has a Master's degree in Music and History, and spent four years as a consultant before he began teaching philosophy and music alongside Dagmar. He is a skilled musician and father of three. Both authors live outside of Aarhus. *The Preacher* is their debut novel, which they translated into English themselves. They are currently working on their next book.

www.sanderjakobsen.com
@sanderjakobsen

The Praise is building for *The Preacher* . . .

'A deceptively clever thriller that bears thinking about . . . *The Preacher* holds its own among the Scandi-crime competing for our attention, and is, I think, ahead of the pack when it comes to the quality of the prose and the subtlety of the themes'
Killing Time blog

'A classic thriller with all the quirky characters from a small-town society . . . *The Preacher* is well-crafted with elegant details, credible dilemmas between motive and opportunity; it's simply a really good – in places even thought-provoking – thriller'
Alt for Damerne Magazine

'A skilful crime thriller debut . . . with sharp images and dialogue that linger on the eyes and the tongue. A sure hit for the commuter's bag – just remember to get off the bus!'
Liv Magazine

The Preacher

SANDER JAKOBSEN

sphere

SPHERE

First published in Great Britain in 2013 by Sphere
This paperback edition published in 2014 by Sphere
Reprinted 2014

A CIP catalogue record for this book
is available from the British Library.

ISBN 978-0-7515-5237-9

Typeset in Sabon by Palimpsest Book Production Limited,
Falkirk, Stirlingshire
Printed and bound in Great Britain by
Clays Ltd, St Ives plc

Papers used by Sphere are from well-managed forests
and other responsible sources.

MIX
Paper from
responsible sources
FSC® C104740

Sphere
An imprint of
Little, Brown Book Group
100 Victoria Embankment
London EC4Y 0DY

An Hachette UK Company
www.hachette.co.uk

www.littlebrown.co.uk

He cries to the sky: 'Give me enough, and more than enough. My heart is bared to thee now, and I will not let thee go except thou bless me. Drown me if you like, but kill me not with caprices.'

Karen Blixen, *Out of Africa*

PROLOGUE

The day they released his wife's murderer from the East Jutland State Prison, Thorkild Christensen was ready outside.

It was a September day in Denmark, blue but surprisingly cold. He was wearing an oilskin coat and had found a pair of mittens from last winter in its pockets. He could see his own white breath in the afternoon light, he had stood there for such a long time.

This was the day his wife's murderer would be released. He'd been able to discover the date from the newspapers, but not the time. So he had brought food with him in the car, which lay untouched in the old ice-cream container he used as a lunchbox, and a thermos of strong coffee. He'd been parked at Enner Mark from eight o'clock in the morning, his eyes fixed on the prison which, he thought, looked like a typical Danish high school. It had, together with the harsh September sun, given him a violent headache.

A taxi pulled up in front of the main entrance at 16.12, and he knew that the moment had come. Hurrying across to it, he got in the back seat and asked the driver to wait. He registered the shadow of the person he was waiting for emerging from behind the prison doors. A black silhouette approaching. He was backlit. Thorkild Christensen squinted, focused, but had to give up and turn his eyes downwards. Damn headache.

When the man opened the door of the taxi, Thorkild noticed an almost imperceptible hesitation, a faltering in the elegant motion with which the man jumped in next to Thorkild. The man's gaze was relaxed, with a hint of amusement.

1

And Thorkild was filled with regret. Regret that he now provided his wife's killer with this pleasure. He cursed himself for not having anticipated precisely this reaction. But then he resigned himself to it – it could not be otherwise. He had waited a year for this. Finally it would happen.

Here they were. Two strangers, yet very connected.

There was a long pause, one that Thorkild Christensen deliberately prolonged. He would do anything, anything he could to make the man beside him lose his composure. He failed, with the exception of a small glimmer of impatience in the other's voice.

'Where to, Thorkild? I suppose it's your taxi, even though I called for it. You sat here first.'

'Århus. If that fits with a free person's travel plans. I've something I want to show you.'

'As long as it involves a cup of coffee. I need one.'

He's not afraid, Thorkild thought. Not in the slightest. He's not bothered about being in a car with me. The blood rushed to his brain, making the headache pound twice as hard. Nausea. He breathed deeply. It's just provocation, he reminded himself. Nothing more. Everything this man says is calculated to provoke. I mustn't rise to the bait. Maybe inwardly he's trembling with anxiety.

The idea gave him strength. He handed the taxi driver his depleted credit card in advance. The man beside Thorkild shrugged his broad shoulders.

'Suit yourself. It's a long trip to Århus. I was only going to Horsens train station.' He paused, then continued: 'Aren't you supposed to wave a Danish flag when you pick someone up from prison? I saw it in a film once.'

Thorkild turned his head and looked the man straight in the eye. 'You find this amusing? Really?'

Again the man shrugged his shoulders. 'Why not? As I said, it's a long trip to Århus. You're not looking too good, Thorkild.'

'That's quite possible. And I might say the same of you, by

the way. A year in the shadows has leached some of the colour from you.'

The man chuckled. 'There wasn't much shadow, I'm afraid. The prison is divided into five living quarters they call villages. I mean, for God's sake, the most beautiful green areas. Wonderful light in the textile workshop. Brand-new community centre – you could almost smell the wet paint. Not to mention the cultural events; there was a trio from the Århus Academy of Music who played Arvo Pärt every Thursday evening. It was positively ludicrous. Karen would have loved those concerts. It's part of the Prison Service's idea of a so-called normalisation principle. It's a vision, a beautiful vision. Or mission, I can never tell the difference between such consultancy concepts. Can you? One is what you do. The other is what you dream about doing.'

'I believe I've read,' said Thorkild, suppressing his anger over hearing his wife's name mentioned, 'that you spent some time in the section that they use for the *negative* inmates. How was the light in isolation?'

The man's face closed up. He looked regretful, his voice sounded almost disappointed: 'I wanted to experience it, simple as that. That particular part of the world. It's the first time I've been in prison. And it will be the last. This is what you have not quite accepted, Thorkild. I suppose that's why we're here.'

Thorkild thought it over, considered his options and decided that the truth and genuine, raw emotion would be the best strategy. He had spent each day of the long, hard year that had passed contemplating this meeting. He'd played the various scenarios out in his head, one by one, deciding on one and then rejecting it for an alternative. Formulated a game plan, staging what would happen. And somehow he had still wound up here, in the plush seat of a taxi with pounding heart and temples, speaking the truth that was right in front of him.

'Yes. That's why we're here.'

He chose a café in the inner city, letting the taxi drive them straight to the door and signing the credit-card receipt without registering the staggering amount. Then they stood in front of the doors, both men staring at the tables inside, the steaming glasses of coffee, the candles in heavy, painted glass holders. There was soft jazz playing.

It felt like a date. Thorkild started giggling almost hysterically and for the first time he sensed uncertainty in the man next to him, emanating from his body. The discovery was like a soothing poultice on Thorkild's sore head. It felt so good that he stopped with his hand on the door and took a deep breath, liberated.

The other man noticed and asserted control.

'And if I don't want to come?'

'Then you don't come. Then you get the hell out of here. *Auf Wiedersehen.*'

'What is it that you think I owe you?'

'Not a damn thing. Apart from the coffee. And half of the taxi fare, if we're being fair. But fairness sure as hell doesn't count when you are involved, does it?'

The glimmer of amusement returned to the man's eyes.

'Ah, the quest for justice – that's the Thorkild I remember. When did you start to swear? You are still a vicar, aren't you? So I owe you nothing, huh? But all of this is about debt, isn't it? That's what you want from me, right? Honestly, I can't be bothered with an embarrassing scene—'

Thorkild stepped close to the man and hissed: 'You are coming with me. And you are coming with me now. And you will do so because ten wild horses could not drag you from the pleasure of seeing me suffer and lose my temper. Because you have nothing better to do at this moment. Because you need a decent cup of coffee. And because I'm not about to sit here and plead with you. You think I've underestimated you. I have not. I know exactly what you are willing to give. And you are damn well going to give it to me. You are coming because it interests you. Because I interest you. And because it's cold as hell out here.'

4

The man laughed. 'OK, yes. But let's get moving, eh? People are starting to stare. I bet there's a reason why we have come here. What is it, Thorkild? Was it Karen's favourite café?'

Thorkild nodded towards a table. 'Even better. This was where I first met her. And this is where I proposed to her. I thought you would appreciate the pathetic irony in me bringing you here.'

The man looked at Thorkild as if seeing him in a new light. 'Certainly, Thorkild. Certainly.'

The man drank his coffee, a full glass, revelling in long gulps of the boiling liquid. He gestured for another with a sigh of contentment. 'Lovely. Really nice. You were right, Thorkild, I needed this. And to see people around me who are at the upper end of the normality scale. It would certainly make the good people in Prison Services happy to see their clientele here. Well chosen, I must say. And for courting, too! I can just picture you two back then, comely Karen and yourself in one of those velvet jackets people wear at the Divinity School. Did you get down on one knee?'

Thorkild glared at the man, making no attempt to disguise his anger. 'That's too cheap. To make fun of the people we used to be? I didn't expect that from you. Obviously I've overestimated you. You're nothing but a sadist. Are you trying to provoke me into attacking you? Fine, say the word. But I'll be damned if you get to sit here and make derogatory remarks about her. You took her life.'

Thorkild stood up. The man waved, a deprecating gesture.

'You misunderstand. And I apologise. Listen to me, Thorkild, for it's probably the only apology you'll ever get from me. I meant it affectionately. With respect. I didn't despise Karen. But I realise that it could be misunderstood. It was . . .' he searched for the words, 'badly put. Clumsy.'

Thorkild sat down again. They drank coffee in silence until the man started to fidget with his fingers, drumming on the white paper tablecloth.

'You brought me here, Thorkild. What is it you want? Do you have more questions?'

'More questions? Such as, why did my wife have to die? Why did they all have to die?'

'Like that, yes.'

Thorkild shook his head. 'I suppose it's too much to expect, that a single year in the ambient surroundings of prison would give you the insight that you might owe me an explanation. That there are many explanations owed.'

'That's not fair. You were given ample explanation the last time you and I saw each other. So no. There is nothing more to add. If you cannot accept that, it's your problem, not mine. Unfortunately.' He opened his hands with a gesture of regret. His eyes seemed sincere. Thorkild held his gaze for a long moment, the other didn't blink.

'Aren't you afraid that I'm going to kill you?'

'No,' replied the man.

'But I will.'

'No. You won't. So I ask you again: what is it you want?'

Thorkild emptied his coffee cup. 'I want to know what you're going to do next. Where will you go? What are you going to work on? I want to know how your life will be from now on.'

The man looked surprised, then he laughed, heartily. 'Is that so? My dear Thorkild, how sympathetic of you, even though your motives are hardly sympathetic. I probably don't need to tell you that that's not going to happen.'

'A lifeline,' whispered Thorkild, suddenly desperate. 'Something. An address. A telephone number. You cannot simply disappear now.'

They looked at each other.

'I don't get it, Thorkild,' the man said. 'What I do has no meaning for you now. None whatsoever. Close your eyes and sleep tight.'

'Are you leaving?'

'Am I leaving? What difference does it make if I'm leaving?'

'I want to know. I just want to know.'

'Are you sure it is . . . wise, so to speak? Good for you? Move on with your life now. Forget me. I have received my punishment, I've served my time.'

'Served your time? You should have served twenty years!'

'Nothing I have done justifies that kind of punishment. I have the court's word for it. The system you believe in so strongly. State of the evidence.'

'That trial was a farce.'

'I agree.'

'But you don't want to be forgotten,' said Thorkild. 'And you don't want to disappear. You want me to know where you are. Don't waste our time. Give me what I'm asking for.'

The man sat there for a while. Nodded slowly. Then he wrote a phone number down on a coffee-stained napkin.

'And who do I get if I dial that number? Alcoholics Anonymous? A call girl? Your local pizzeria?'

The man looked put out. 'You asked me not to waste time. Dial the number.'

Thorkild fished his worn, old-fashioned mobile phone out of his pocket and dialled laboriously. A chirping ring tone sounded from the man's breast pocket. 'There, you see? A lifeline. A strange choice of words, Thorkild. Preferably during normal office hours, OK? Can I go now?'

'Yes. You know what I'm going to say.'

'Probably. So don't say it.'

There was a long pause during which all the café's sounds concentrated around the two men. Then Thorkild spoke, slowly and distinctly, as to a child. 'You must leave her alone. All the fear you have created. Don't pursue her any more. Do you hear me?'

'Her?' the man said and got to his feet. 'I will hunt her until I have her.'

He stood up, neither slowly nor quickly, put on his overcoat and disappeared into the darkness, an imposing silhouette against the glittering city.

Thorkild sat there for some time without moving, his head throbbing again. It dawned on him that his car was at the prison, way out in Enner Mark. It was a long way home.

Only when he got up and grabbed his jacket did he see the man's mobile phone. He had left it on the table.

PART 1

PART I

1

It takes a while before the shooter approaches the woman on the ground.

It was quick. Fortunately.

The shooter's eyes were closed when the shots were fired. Now they can see that they hit where they should. The woman on the ground is bleeding heavily from her chest. She's already far away, barely breathing, her gaze distant.

The shooter comes up to her and breathes with a shiver, gives a wild shake of the head, knowing there's no time to lose. It's only half-light, but in theory someone could come walking down the trail at any minute. Panic and nausea lodge in the throat. This was not where it was supposed to happen. But this was where they had come face to face. The shooter and the woman who now lies on the ground.

The blood seeps into the dust on the trail, and the shooter hurriedly kicks a little gravel over it. But it is futile.

Away, away – hurry. The shooter grabs the woman's army green jacket, which is open. Pulls. It is unreasonably heavy, heavier than the shooter could ever have imagined. This isn't working. There are bubbles emerging from the woman's chest and from her mouth, which is half open. Her eyes flicker. The shooter lets go of the coat, startled. But grabs it again, spins the woman around, into the reeds and the tall dewy grass beside the path.

The shooter lets the woman lie and runs, sweating with exertion. Returns with the car, which is too wide for the narrow path. Tows the body and hauls it into the car. When the woman is turned around, her eyes are closed.

The shooter plunges both hands into the blood-soaked soil, which is turning into ochre-coloured mud, scoops it up and throws into the car on top of the woman until there is no blood left on the ground.

The sun is almost up.

The construction site is abandoned, and the shooter brakes hard, gravel spraying from the tyres, and parks behind a bulldozer. In front lies the creek. Is it deep enough?

The shooter's every fibre is taut with strain, listening for sounds, fighting the rising nausea, sick with fear. As the woman is hauled from the car, her head hits the sandy ground with a crunch that makes the shooter moan out loud before setting off down towards the river, the body trailing behind. Finally the body is rolled into the water.

As she hits the water the woman opens her eyes again in a last breath. Her face trembles in a cramp. Then she closes her eyes again.

Shaking violently, the shooter puts a gloved hand on the woman's shoulder and pushes. The body slips out into the water with a sigh. It's supposed to be sinking. Why doesn't it sink? Instead, it settles at the water's edge, rocking gently in the current. The woman's body is like a small dam; the water rises up along her belly. And now it flows over her with a delicate little trickle. The caking of blood and dust in the woman's hair loosens and dissolves in wine-coloured swirls.

She rocks back and forth. Is she dead?

Not a breath of wind. Then, a wood pigeon cooing.

The shooter looks up and sees the figure, standing on the far side of the creek. Two pairs of eyes lock for a few endless seconds. Then the outline of this other person fades in the mist. Gone.

The shooter bites hard into their lip to keep from crying out loud. Their hands will not stop shaking.

2

At first it was just a feeling. A feeling and an image on the retina. An image formed before consciousness took over to give it a more sensible explanation. Maybe it was his holiday reading – crime fiction – that led him to see it that way. Maybe it was the Danish late summer's heavy rain that clothed everything in gloom, causing the soil to send out fumes and odours, making things appear strange and full of foreboding.

The creek in Roslinge, which was normally emerald green with pondweed, glittering and friendly, suddenly came sliding out of the mist all quiet and pale. The raindrops were scattered but heavy, making holes in the grey surface. It looked deeper than it was.

Thorkild Christensen saw something in the water. He'd popped out of the house to get a breath of morning air, clearing his thoughts for Sunday's sermon. And what he saw reminded him of a human arm. A summer-brown arm with the elbow sticking out of the water, the ends bent downward. He quickly dropped the image. Decided that it was probably one of the brown PVC pipes used in sanitary installations, the sort of thing that sometimes landed down here with other debris from the construction site up on the hill. Thorkild shrugged, inwardly at least, and went inside to resume his writing. It was only six a.m., he was a morning person. The vicarage was silent.

It was not until some time later that he noticed the conspicuous silence. Not that she ever made much noise. But this was a new silence. He called out for Karen. Unconcerned at first.

And then, with the process that we all follow when we find that we're missing something important: keys, wallet, sunglasses. We look in the obvious places. We abandon the search, deciding that the item will probably turn up, and then we go back later when we think of a place where it might be. As the possibilities are exhausted, we become worried. Maybe we will save the most obvious place for last in order to maintain hope. And so it can take a long time before we admit to having lost something.

And that is what happened to the vicar, Thorkild Christensen, on the fourth weekend in August. It was not until Sunday afternoon that he allowed himself to feel fear.

The last place he checked before he systematically began to make phone calls to friends and acquaintances in the town was the bathroom that had been hers since the children had grown up. Went in there, feeling lost, and looked at the small signs of her. A space of understated femininity, much like Karen herself. Her favourite, practical soap, which she always rinsed after use to get rid of leftover foam. It used to amuse him. The room was tidy. A jar of hair accessories, a small woven basket with a single mascara, lip balm with only a hint of colour. Crisp and clean white towels neatly hung up, so unlike his own, always scattered over the floor.

It was ridiculous to suppose that she would have stayed here for that long, but he had avoided the room in order to have a place for hope, a place that would keep the creeping sense of anxiety away. Reluctantly he phoned Michael and Nadia, trying to sound casual. Instead, his voice was stiff and his words clumsy. They hadn't seen their mother, and it was pretty much the one thing Thorkild had been almost sure of from the start. The trips to Copenhagen to visit their grown-up children were one of the few things he and Karen had continued doing together, enjoying together.

The last person he called was the local police officer.

When a death is suspicious, it is always a noisy affair. Detective Thea Krogh stood on the sidelines and took in the scene. A few technicians were helping the local police officer, Bjørn Devantier, to retrieve the corpse from the water. They had done their best to cordon the area off. The entire marsh area surrounding the creek, which was a continuation of the parsonage garden, was surrounded by red-and-white plastic tape. No wonder people are drawn like flies when crime-scene tape is the same colour as sales signs, she thought. It seemed a shame. Because even when death resulted from a crime, it was still a person who had passed away, a life abruptly ended, and that should call for silence and respect.

She lay on a white tarpaulin beside the creek.

The local police officer's latex-clad hand lifted the woman's arm.

'Look,' he said, his face colourless.

Thea was one step away. The body had been distorted by the lukewarm river water. Everything expanded into a slightly larger version, bloated yet without being grotesque. Eyes, fingers, toes, skin characteristics. The bullet wounds, jagged flesh around tissue, were white at the edges and decay was already working its way inside.

Bjørn Devantier let the arm fall with a thud on the tarpaulin. 'Shot. Three times, as far as I can see. And the bullets have gone through. Where did your technician go? I suppose she wants access? She's strong as an ox, that one, I doubt I could have hauled the body ashore without her. What's her name?'

Thea nodded. 'Alice Caspersen.'

The crime technician approached with her little suitcase. She stopped and pulled something from her inside pocket. Only then did Thea register the smell.

The woman's unruly hair, stained with mud from the river bed, gripped like fingers on the white plastic. Her skin's summer tan had been transformed by death to a white transparency, cold and distant, round and voluminous from the water penetrating every pore. Limbs like a rag doll, painfully bent and twisted. The policeman shook his head.

'Where is the vicar?' Thea said.

'He hasn't shown himself since I arrived. He's up in the parsonage, I expect. He . . . I don't think he came too close, fortunately. Good Lord, it stinks.'

'Yes,' said Thea. 'It's probably better that way.' She looked down at the broken remains.

The local policeman sighed. 'It's not clear-cut, I can assure you – the vicar's wife. I have nothing on the family, and water is the worst. It washes everything away. The techs say they hate water bodies. But then again, who doesn't?'

Alice Caspersen stood up and blew a red strand of hair away from her mouth with a snort.

'No bullets in her. So you know at least that. For starters.'

Bjørn Devantier rose from the tarpaulin and walked up the hill.

The slope down towards the river was the perfect arena. The stage at the bottom, then the stalls filled with curious people – mostly women – from the village, and at the top behind the fence, as if in a theatre box, the vicar suddenly appeared. Thea looked at him and felt sorry for him.

He stood there in isolation. He, who had probably taken part in quite a few people's grief, standing all alone. Once the body was taken away, the crowd would dissolve and turn around. And it would only make him feel even more alone, Thea predicted.

She sighed. Before long, it would be her job as lead investigator to cast aside pity and approach him as a possible suspect. Most murders are committed by those who are closest. Spouses kill each other, enemies and lovers kill each other, we're all capable of killing when whatever had existed between us is killed. And that Karen Simonsen was killed was beyond doubt. Three shots had penetrated the torso.

Thea squinted to get a better look at the vicar. Greyish hair, deep furrows in his face that indicated not only had he passed fifty but he'd endured another kind of life experience that went beyond mere age. Black clothes that resembled neither mourning apparel or pastoral everyday wear. It was smart black. Urban trendy. He stood out, in one way or another. Deviating from the small town's standard repertoire of cheap jeans, fleece gilets, overalls, Icelandic sweaters, mouse-grey old women's coats, scarves over grey hair. In the midst of all this stood the black-clad vicar, looking out over the field with eyes that sparkled, Thea could tell it from a distance. His shoulders drooped, he looked lost. As if that way of carrying himself was ingrained in him, as if he was a man who throughout life had felt too high in relation to the surroundings.

She lowered her eyes and began to systematically memorise the various individuals who had been standing along the cordon. This was her workplace for the forseeable future, here in Roslinge. There was probably no other setting that would cause the villagers to gather in the same way and offer her the same overview. Not the church. Possibly the local grocery shop on a Saturday morning. There didn't appear to be any other significant institutions. But she probably wouldn't even make it to Saturday morning before the crime was solved. On the contrary, these things were usually concluded quickly. Reality is not as fancy as the novel's twisted universe. Reality is full of men who go down to the local post office in clogs with a toy gun in hand and rob 550 kroner and a toy mailbox made of tin for their grandsons, only to be caught twenty minutes later, at home, on the couch. This would probably turn out to be the case here, too. The easiest way to kill is with a gun. It's not difficult, requires no muscle or special expertise. You can almost look away while you do it, and thus it is the easiest way to get yourself to do it if you're not an experienced killer. One who aims for the torso is probably an inexperienced shooter who chooses the safe bet. Three shots is security. One or two shots in the head is the work of a professional. Four or five shots or more, distributed over the body, is an act of aggression. Three shots in the torso is the first-time killer who needs to be sure that he will succeed. The trickiest part is obtaining the gun. And for the same reason, shootings are the easiest to solve, because it really is all about finding the gun.

Thea Krogh had a plan ready in her head. The technicians would search the area for the murder weapon, the doctor would do the autopsy, her investigators, together with local officers, would question most of the town's inhabitants, while she herself would interview the vicar. Wednesday morning they would meet and paint the picture together, and the same afternoon hopefully – no reason to believe otherwise – arrest the vicar's wife's murderer.

3

The first thought that occurred as the calm fell over him was that Karen would be sad to see what they had done to the garden and the house.

The second thought was that he felt lonely.

It was only in his third thought that he registered that Karen had died. Thorkild Christensen stood at the window in the living room, gazing out over the garden. He stood there for a long time. And saw nothing.

There was enough to see, though. An uproar of voices shouting and calling out foreign names. Squeaking voices in mobile phones, voices shouting out of windows, in through doors and up and down the stairs. Voices that searched, agreed and coordinated. Voices that changed the house. And because the heavy hall carpet had been rolled up to make room for equipment and dirty shoes and dusty suitcases, there were new sounds, harder sounds, long sounds. Humans and the stuff they brought with them. Machinery and bodies moved around each other in a subtle choreography, making discoveries, conclusions, establishing facts for the investigation, finding traces of anything. Outside and inside, the garden and the house had been invaded. Nooks that were not used to seeing sunlight were bathed in the cameras' flashes. Garden paths that Karen had recently raked were torn up by busy boot heels. Corners that had never seen dust filled up with gravel and sand that was hauled in but not removed.

Then, once again, calm spread its wide blanket over the vicarage. At the end of the day it lay messy and disturbed, but silent. Only the red-and-white police tape that stretched across the garden was still somehow noisy.

It was Sunday night. The same day they had found Karen in the water.

Thorkild stood there. Dizzy, confused and with an inferno of sounds and impressions that violated his senses. But without a single thought in his head. All day, he had been asked to find things, move, explain himself. Not questioned outright – they had avoided that until now. He'd stood there, like an immovable tower, seeing it all. His body had sensed and recorded it, the distance to reality dulled by death itself.

Slowly he began to move. He moved around the house with heavy, laboured movements. Gradually he regained his ability to think, his mobility, the pull of his emotions. And while the heaviness lay upon him, Thorkild tried to comprehend.

The mobile phone in his pocket rang. He dug it out and refused the call, then fiddled with it for a while to put it on silent; he was not great with technical stuff. One rash push of a button and he managed to open a list of his outgoing calls. He wondered about the latest – Michael. He could not quite recall their conversation, but the display showed that it had taken him just four minutes and forty-three seconds to inform his son of his mother's death.

Michael had offered to call Nadia, his sister, himself.

Throughout the evening Thorkild wandered around the house. He didn't eat or drink. He walked around a lifetime's collection of things that appeared both animated, when he thought of the living Karen, and as treasures in a museum, when Karen's death in small incomprehensible bits invaded and claimed him.

He held in his hand the flowered vase they had been given as a wedding present and which had stood on the dining table for twenty-two years. More often than not it was filled with the flowers that Karen bought. Always too expensive, finished bouquets. Thorkild spilled the flower water as he stood with the vase between his hands. He didn't notice the water that formed a lake on the table runner but wondered why it held no flowers just now.

He sat at the desk. Looked at letters and envelopes and floral cards from Outer Mission, which Karen had intended for family or some of their few friends on birthdays and other special occasions. He opened the small pearl-studded box of stamps. Inside the lid was a damp pad to moisten stamps. Karen had bought it during their first real holiday, a vacation in Mallorca with the two children while they were still very young.

He opened her little calendar. *Thorkild*, it said somewhere in the month of April. Thorkild considered the sober message. Their wedding day. No red heart, no pet name. Just like Karen had always been. Matter-of-fact. Thorkild looked up the month of August, added Karen's name and entered the date of her death. It occurred to him that it was a strange thing to do. But it felt good. Like a small ritual.

An angry buzz made him flinch. The mobile phone was dancing furiously on the coffee table. He grabbed it and read the text message from Michael:

N and I on the train now. Get in at 00:22. Will take a taxi.

His children were on their way from Copenhagen. He smiled. Michael was very practical, he had without a doubt arranged for pre-printed tickets for both of them and remembered to bring water bottles for the train journey. His son didn't happily part with his money, would not dream of paying the extortionate train menu prices. It was hardly a coincidence that he had informed his father of the train's exact arrival time.

Should he go and pick them up from Århus? Yes, he should. But the thought of it made him squint with incomprehension. A scene at the station? Was he expected to cry and hug both children? And the ride home, Nadia in the back seat. What should he say to them?

No. Everything had changed, and the kids would simply have to take a taxi. He could pay for it.

The absurdity of his thoughts made him groan and bury his head in his hands.

Then the urge to do something struck him.

He opened all the cupboards and drawers, turned on all the lights in the kitchen and let the porcelain and pots bask in it. He took his time, looked at every single item in what was actually Karen's domain, and solemnly assigned each thing time and attention. When he had finished dwelling on each item and trying to summon Karen from each of the cake forks she had painstakingly collected, and each of the dishes she had stacked by size, he left the kitchen with the lights on and cabinets open.

He congratulated himself on having done something. It was probably healthy.

Moving on! He looked at the frames in the hall where Karen's fabric prints were exhibited, from a brief period in her life when she attempted such projects. She'd referred, with a touch of humour, to these periods in her life as the textile-printing period, the calligraphy period, the origami period. He'd always liked her introspective quest for something to devote her time to. It struck him that he didn't actually know what she was doing at the moment, or what she would call this current period, if she could. In fact, he could not remember having properly noticed anything since the era of the fabric prints. He looked at the date in the corner of one of them. They were three years old now. Strange and abstract, bright colours.

Later, Thorkild woke up in the rocking chair by the garden window. Apathetic and weary in every muscle in his body. He didn't remember how, but he had fallen asleep. It was the middle of the night and he was suddenly wide awake. He remained seated. It was as if the night hours allowed him to rest. Karen had never been part of his nights when he meditatively paced around and tried to dig a sermon out of his head, or when he read and tried to keep pace with the latest research in the dialectical theology which had been his thesis topic at the theological faculty. As he sat there, he was in a familiar world where Karen didn't belong.

For the first time he took her with him into his night. He wondered about Karen. What had she done all those hours when he was buried in his work?

He pictured her, always introspective and busy, working in the house and garden, preparing food, tending to weeds, polishing the old brass handles on the doors – she was obsessed with making them shine – or tidying the bathroom where she changed the towels every day. Or reading, or every now and then writing at her desk. Content.

But was this really how she'd spent her time when Thorkild worked? He wondered. Struggling to override the feelings and think clearly instead, he pursued clues. Wondered who she actually considered to be friends and who she socialised with. Were there others, besides the few from the parish that they occasionally saw? He knew a few. Asger, with whom she discussed the fiction she read. Isabella, her childhood friend. He tried to see connections. Make sense of it all. There was a certain satisfaction in thinking this way, but nothing revealed itself. Nothing suspicious, nothing unusual, nothing that could explain anything. Nevertheless he kept wondering as he stood up, walked into the hall, opened the bedroom door and fell asleep on the bed with all his clothes on.

4

'When your children have left home, does that make you old?' she asked into the darkness and felt his lanky body respond to her voice. He turned towards her and Thea enjoyed the comfort of knowing that even now, after so many years, he always woke up and listened when she said something.

Because of course, time had left its mark. It was no different for them than for others who are in a relationship. Even secret lovers.

All the times they had left and returned to each other through the years, rediscovering the intensity and sinking back into the safety of their old habits. The first year, she would sleep with her lips pressed against his shoulder, which was sweaty and salty. A taste she could recall at any time and took with her into all the beds she slept in. They rarely did that now, when they had a night together. Now, they tore themselves loose from each other's grip, settled in, wrapped themselves into their own blankets, trying to get a good night's sleep.

In a way this was almost better, the homeliness of it. And Kristian still made an effort to answer her, even in the middle of the night, if she asked him something.

She let him wake up, knowing that the answer would come. The street lamp outside showed the contours of his face in the dark. It had taken him a long time to get used to the light at her place. She had bought blackout curtains, he had put them up.

And although he never complained about it, she knew that the city's constant mumbling annoyed him. He was never fully rested when he was with her. Even on those rare Sunday mornings when she liked to sleep in, Kristian woke early and looked tired, so she wondered if he was wishing he was back at the house in Brabrand. A thought that she was reconciled with.

You can put up curtains, she thought. Keep the light out. But some things never change, like the sounds. They penetrate everything.

Then he was there. Placing a warm hand on her back and stroking her blonde hair.

'I guess you are.'

Kristian Videbæk was forty-two years old, married to a woman named Mette, who was a high school teacher when she wasn't on sick leave. He had a Peugeot 405 station wagon in the garage and two car seats in the back for their dark-haired girls, Emma and Victoria. Both times Kristian had become a father, Thea had been surprised with their choice of names.

'Beautiful,' he whispered. 'You are far away. Are you in Roslinge?'

'Yes, I suppose I am.'

'Don't you think you should get some sleep? You came back late yesterday. And we have to get up soon.'

Kristian also worked for the Århus Police. They had known each other a lifetime, long before Mette came into the picture. They'd attended the same class at the police academy. He had been two years her senior at Samsøgade Elementary, had hit her in the eye with a caramel on his last day of school. In a way he had always been there, near her.

'Kristian. Are you asleep?'

'Yes. In a minute. Shall I fetch some water for you?'

'I'm going to question the vicar in Roslinge today.'

'Do you want me to go with you?'

'No, that's not necessary. But I was watching him yesterday at the scene, where we found his wife. It really is a beautiful place.'

'It is.'

'He's fifty-one, he has two grown children who have left home. He's old, right?' She turned towards him and cuddled up, rested her head under his chin. 'Someone who has finished a major part of his life. Children and all that.'

He smiled in the darkness, she could feel it on his chin.

'All that,' he said.

'Kristian, do you think I'm getting old?'

He kissed her bright hair.

'Thea, I think you're just as pretty and youthful and incredibly wise as you have always been in all the years I've known you. You aren't the least bit old.'

'Youthful. What a way to put it.'

He chuckled and yawned.

'I never had all that.'

Her voice, as always when they discussed the topic, matter-of-fact, devoid of emotion. And as always, his was filled with tenderness.

'Again, sweetheart?'

'Again.'

'OK. You made the choice many years ago that it wasn't what you wanted. I wanted children. But you didn't. No way.'

Kristian laughed.

'You've always been like that. Then and now. Stood by your choices and fought for what you believed in. You wanted to be free, Thea. Bury yourself in work, do whatever the hell suited you. Work your way up.'

She always listened intently at this point, although she knew his words by heart. They had been said so many times between them.

'And you succeeded. Already a seasoned detective, everyone I know in the force has great respect for you. And you're still only thirty-nine. And youthful.'

'You feel sorry for me. It's so obvious.'

'Yes. Maybe I do.'

She nodded in the dark.

'I can't have children.'

'I know.'

'I couldn't then.'

'I know that, too.'

'I guess I'm just—'

'—Telling yourself. Yes. I know, Thea, I know it all. For the millionth time: You don't need to explain yourself to me.'

She turned, squeezed herself into his arms.

'You're the one who's doing the explaining. Because I asked you to.'

He waited for the tears that always came at this stage of their shared narrative. It never failed. Three little shivers, his arm turned damp against her cheek, which rested on it. It was always quick, over before it had begun.

'You didn't want to go the long way the doctors recommended. You mourned over it for a while. But I was so proud of you. You never allowed it to become a negative story about you. You discovered the positive possibilities of your life instead. Without all that.'

'Without all that. And without you, Kristian.'

'I had to do something else.'

'Yes.'

Thea looked up at him and kissed him.

'I wonder who I am these days,' she said and stood up, walked into the bathroom while he looked after her. The semi-long blonde hair fell to her shoulders. Her pale body, strong and slender, neither tall nor short. The way she walked, strangely stout, always focused. And yet so feminine, he had always thought so. Her breasts, he knew them so well. At meetings at work, he could picture them behind the light blue shirts and black jackets. Large without being heavy, always firm and yet soft when he held them in his hands.

In all the years he had known her, Thea had never talked about dieting, exercise and fitness, and he found this very attractive. Never the feminine way of picking on herself. She did that so rarely, even now when she was pushing forty.

She had one of those bodies that stay in shape with everyday activity. She was not overly active, although she had a little red carbon-fibre kayak that she took out into the bay in summer, and she enjoyed skiing in winter.

Kristian and Mette had taken her with them on a Swedish farm holiday one summer. Thea had Victoria and Emma out fishing and canoeing, sleeping in tents, while Kristian and Mette had been able to relax and read books. It suited Thea, Kristian thought. Sweden was just like her. Beautiful without being showy, natural without being foot-shaped. Neither flat like Denmark or steep like Norway.

She brought him a glass of water when she came back. Gave it to him without a word.

'Do you remember the personality tests those consultants made us take a few years ago?' he whispered as she lay down again and wrapped the quilt around her. The street lamp was switched off, the grey dawn came creeping. He pressed himself against her.

'Yes?'

'We all had our quirks. Fluctuations here and there. Some were at one end of the scales, some were at the other.'

'Yes.'

'But you – you were bang in the middle of it all. A great balance. As common as any of us.'

'Is that supposed to be a compliment?'

'It's who you are. My dream realm. Swedish, in fact.'

As if that was enough of an answer, she relaxed in his arms.

When he had gone, she drifted around the apartment. Drank the rest of the coffee. Watered the peace lilies she thought belonged in any home. Dressed and packed a bag with clothes, enough for a couple of days.

Before she zipped her toilet bag she applied mascara to her eyelashes. Just a hint. Not too much.

5

She looked around, breathed in the gritty air and turned towards the local police officer, who stood on the stairs looking sceptical.

'It's fine. Absolutely fine, Devantier.'

It was Monday morning.

'Well, there you have it. Again – I apologise for the state it's in. I don't really use this room. And cleaning . . . I'm divorced. It's only women who clean the rooms they're not using. If I'd known you were coming, I would have tidied up the place. But everything's moving so quickly – as you well know. Yesterday, I have my first-ever murder in Roslinge. Today, I have twenty-odd police officers running all over town. And a house guest.'

The room was small and had been used for storage. There was a shelf with old children's books, a small laminate table and an old-fashioned ship couch. A strip of dusty golden sunshine came in through the skylight and gave the room a peaceful colour.

Thea Krogh smiled at him, already comfortable with the thought of the hours she could spend in this room. Which was on the first floor of Bjørn Devantier's residence in Roslinge.

This was how she preferred to do it. To go and live in the environment that she would investigate. Just for a few days. Usually it was a hostel or hotel, a couple of occasions she'd had an acquaintance in the area, and other times it was private accommodation with local police. As in this case, the local police station generally had a guest room available upon request.

It was easy for her. There was no one she needed to notify except for her colleagues at the station. No pets to be cared for. And the bag lay ready in her apartment, filled with everything she would need for a few days when, as in this case, she was summoned by her boss Anne-Grethe Schalborg with no time to prepare. Eight years at Århus Police, blessed with never having to feel guilty about letting anyone down.

The first time Thea had taken up residence in one of the towns during an investigation, it had been by accident. She'd sent Kristian home with the car while she stayed behind processing data at the makeshift workplace they had established in the no-frills local hotel. She'd offered to take a bus home, since Kristian was already running late and suffering an attack of bad conscience. That was when Emma, his eldest, was quite small and Mette was constantly on the phone to him; Thea remembered it clearly.

She'd lost track of time and place and of course the bus schedule, and had to stay at the hotel. She ended up staying there for five nights until they had finished their work. It was her first real case, and she'd been praised for her efforts, as she'd worked hard and set aside personal needs in the interest of solving the case.

Since then, she had made a virtue out of necessity.

Not because of the somewhat undeserved praise. But because she believed it made her think in a different way. That even in anonymous hotel rooms, the town came creeping, covering her like a layer of sounds and smells. In many of the villages she visited, it was probably a bit optimistic to talk of a *pulse*. But a breath. A certain mood or tension in the air. Perceiving that breath made her better, sharper. Of that she was sure.

Thea had always been fascinated by people. She devoured novels as a child, and as an adult she found herself studying literary history at university, simply because she loved the stories, the tragedies, the great epics with heroes, victims and villains. When, many years later and mostly by chance, she found herself in the police homicide department, she was very aware of that fascination and went out of her way to nurture it. In the course of her work, she gained access to all the personal stories that were interwoven in whatever crime they might be investigating. On returning to her room each night, she would sit thinking about the people she'd met.

As did most of her colleagues. Reviewing statements and drawing conclusions was part of the job.

But Thea reckoned her working conditions were more conducive, because she'd spend her evenings in a room where she was free to think without distractions from the TV, other people, laundry and chores. It was a method her mother drily referred to as *never taking time off*.

The appeal of living in whatever random places an investigation might take her had long since faded, and yet she carried on doing it. No sooner had she returned from one expedition than she'd pack a bag with toiletries, two sets of practical clothes, something warm and something rainproof, and a more stylish outfit for special occasions, so as to be ready for the next. And always there was the familiar, fundamental pang of relief when she took in her new quarters for the first time.

As she shoved her bag under the bed, Thea heard a rattling of cups and a coffee maker in action downstairs. She'd arranged a short meeting with the local officer, Bjørn Devantier, so he could give her an overview of the town.

She should have sat down and written the preliminary report on the case to Anne-Grethe, but she didn't have the energy. Writing reports had never been a favourite task of hers, especially since her boss subjected them to such close scrutiny that a lot of time and thought had to go into every line. For the time being Anne-Grethe would have to settle for a text message. They were settling in and everything had gone according to plan thus far. That was all there was to say, really. She dug out her phone and browsed through a considerable number of missed calls. She checked her voicemail and heard her boss's familiar, matter-of-fact voice inviting her to call as soon as possible. Three journalists, one local, one from a larger newspaper and one from the Danish news agency Ritzau, all of whom had good sources within the police, had left messages asking for a statement. Hungry as always on a Monday morning. And then a message from Anne-Grethe yet again, instructing her to refer all calls from journalists to the relatively new department of communications. And to call said department at her earliest convenience.

Instead, she called Kristian and heard his hurried voice amidst a clamour of background noise.

'I'm at the shop. It's Victoria's birthday party tomorrow, I have a massive shopping list. Can I call you later?'

'Sure, but it's nothing important. I didn't call for a reason. Just wanted to let you know that I'm all settled in Roslinge. I've got a room at the local station.'

'There's no hotel?'

'No, there isn't. There's hardly anything here.'

'Didn't we once look at a house in Roslinge? That old dairy – needed at least a million kroner worth of restoration? You thought it would be so lovely.'

Kristian tutted, the beeping grew louder, he was probably approaching the checkout.

'God, yes. No, wait – that was in Vilå. But it's pretty close to Roslinge.'

Kristian snorted at the other end of the line.

'Good lord, look at that line! I have to make pizza for sixteen kids, can you believe it? Is it cheating if I buy them ready-made?'

She smiled, picturing him there.

6

Thea Krogh would rather have gone alone. It went against proper procedure, but there were many situations where she believed that she would get further by speaking in confidence, establishing an understanding with the individual. And that was best done person to person and without the mp3 recorder's red eye, which served as a constant reminder to the interviewee that they should choose their words very carefully.

Fortunately, her current rank meant that the officers who accompanied her on assignments remained in the background, leaving her to steer the conversation. It was a tacit agreement, honouring the strict hierarchy that exists in every workplace. She could not, however, escape the mp3 recorder, but eventually she'd learned to appreciate it. More often than not she would invite a colleague to listen to the tape before drawing her own conclusions. Usually it was Kristian, who was always willing to help, although he'd recently been assigned to the new task force dealing with biker-gangs.

He was her preferred source for a second opinion. Nine times out of ten he had no comment to offer, but when he did it was worth hearing. Moreover she enjoyed their time together in his office, with him perching on the edge of the desk and listening. As if this was the real police work: listening intently to what had been said, picking up on subtle nuances. Kristian's ear was so finely tuned that he could make out the person's body language from shifts in their tone of voice, an ability that was all the more admirable given that his keen hearing was usually wasted on Pop FM.

Refusing to carry out the interrogation at the local police station, Thea had summoned Bjørn Devantier to accompany her to the vicarage on Monday afternoon. A person's home said more than a thousand words. On the drive over, she pictured the process. She would mix standard questions with the questions she thought were needed to open up this particular man. Her approach was, she realised, based on some very stereotypical views of villagers, vicars, men, black-clad fifty-year-olds. Then again Thea's homespun psychology generally proved accurate. It was depressingly rare for one of these stereotypes to surprise her, for the outcome to be anything other than the one she'd predicted.

She discovered that she was looking forward to seeing Thorkild Christensen again with the same avid anticipation usually reserved for the latest episode of one of her favourite TV series. The next chapter of this man. She wondered where in the grief process he found himself. In shock, reacting, or already going into the repair phase? How far along the arduous path towards reorientation that awaits mourners like an oasis on the horizon? Visiting the bereaved usually made her stomach clench, knowing what she was about to put them through, her questions forcing them to confront the very things that are the most painful to recall. Not the drama – what happened – but the mundane. The everyday routines that she always asked about. Those were things that made relatives sob with longing, recalling the one who used to walk the dog, the one who brought flowers home every payday, the one who remembered the Christmas gift for grandma, the one who was absolutely impossible when she was having her period. For some reason she had a feeling that the visit to the vicar would be different. Perhaps because grief and misery and furious demands for justice and reason were hardly new to him. In his line of work, he must have been bombarded with desperate appeals from people demanding to know *why*.

She parked the car, a nondescript black Ford Mondeo, at the kerb. It was a pretty vicarage, an old building made from red brick, worn but well kept. A large house that sprawled over the plot and probably contained numerous rooms, garrets and crawl spaces. The yard was gravelled, two big pots of evergreen topiary stood by the front door. And behind the house she could just make out the garden that sloped down towards the meadow and creek, glittering in the bright sun. There were people at work, probably the forensic techs, squatting by the creek as if they were collecting mud samples. It was windy, and the large apple trees that surrounded the vicarage whistled majestically. Bjørn Devantier was already there, standing on the pavement, smoking.

'You just missed the kids,' he said. 'Michael and Nadia. They've driven up to Randers to see their grandmother. She lives in a nursing home there, she hasn't heard yet. Apparently they're not sure whether they should tell her. She suffers from dementia.'

'Are they coming back? We need to talk to them as well. Today. You should have stopped them.'

'I'm sure they will,' said Devantier, looking as if it hadn't occurred to him that the children might do otherwise. 'I'm sorry, but their mother just died and they wanted to go tell a relative. They'll probably want to be with their father.'

At that precise moment, the vicar opened the door.

Thea shook Thorkild Christensen's warm hand, sat down in the deep burgundy sofa in the living room. She set up the recorder without thinking, it was a routine task. She tried to take in the room without being too obvious. The most obvious thing was the smell, she thought. An aroma of sweetness and spice and something strangely artificial – like a squirt from a can of ant poison in the middle of a rainforest. That was often the way. The other senses generated so many words, they would quickly settle into certain patterns. This was not the case with smells. She remembered reading once that infatuation is mostly brought on by odours, because we have no defence against those particular sensory impressions.

The vicar emerged from the kitchen with teacups and a steaming pot on a tray. He looked directly at her with a smile, as if he was amused by her judgmental eyes, and with a certain confidence, as if he meant to impart some truth with that. Again, he was dressed in black; or at least the shirt was black but softened by a pair of loose-fitting jeans, which struck her as suitable for a vicar on his day off. He looked clean-shaven and plausible, his hair was damp and displayed the furrows of a comb that had recently passed through. The eyes were tired, but alive and kicking.

'Here you go, have some coffee.' And then, in the same breath: 'Much as I enjoy impaling worshippers on Sundays, I'm not a killer.'

He looked down, was silent for a while. Bjørn Devantier's eyebrows rose disapprovingly, he found the comment inappropriate. Thea suddenly felt acutely alive and present. She ignored the buzzing phone in her pocket.

Thorkild looked up again. The lines in his face were very deep, the eyes glistening from their sockets. I wonder if it's fire or tears in there, she wondered.

'Pardon my sarcasm. I've seen so much sorrow, I know so much about grief. But it's as if I have trouble dealing with it now. I keep judging myself. What am I doing, what am I feeling? Do I miss her? Do I miss Karen?'

He looked into the room, facing the well-kept garden's sturdy trees.

'Do you?' she asked him, her voice neutral.

Thorkild Christensen considered his answer.

'In moments, she's present. There are sounds, sensations, moments where I forget everything and think it's just a dream. And then there are times when the horror of it all is abundantly clear to me. I'm so confused. I would like to have loved her. But do you know when I am most aware of the fact that she's gone? It's when I notice that some of the things she does – or did – are no longer there to annoy me.'

Thorkild looked up: 'So. Did I love her?'

He looked at Thea, as if she had the answer to that very question. She understood him, and she didn't. Is it always so simple that you can simply respond to that after a whole lifetime of ups and downs? Listen, Vicar, did you love your wife? She followed his gaze out to the elm trees and the empty clothes-line. The idea of the hardworking, brave little vicar's wife wearing wellies and a scarf over her hair flickered past her mind's eye. This was a place where industrious, brave wives hung their wet clothes out to dry.

The vicar smiled wryly.

'Thorkild,' Devantier broke in impatiently, 'what the hell happened here?'

'You're probably going to ask me whether she had enemies or anything like that, right?'

'Yes. Well, not in those words,' said Thea. 'We usually ask if anyone might have had reason to do her harm. There can be many reasons. More than you would imagine.'

Bjørn Devantier nodded, poured some coffee.

The vicar was still smiling. 'You'd really like me to say no, right? Everybody loved her. Everybody loves me. Everyone loves us. But we're so damn alone. As human beings, that is. You make a point of being your true self, and then people don't like you. You come together to escape the loneliness, but then you forget yourself.'

There was smouldering passion in Thorkild Christensen's voice, but he stopped himself. Caught Thea's eye.

'There were many who didn't like her,' he said soberly. 'But I think I loved her because she did things her own way. As if she was liberated from the constant preoccupation with whether others liked her. People don't care for that. Not needing the company of others is like poison – especially in a small place such as this. Nor am I free of it myself. She was so introverted that I would often ask myself what I meant to her. Do we ever know whether others truly love us?' Thorkild looked up with the last word. 'We just have to trust it. Then suddenly someone kills her, and what is left to trust any more? Except for the fact that she must have mattered enough to another human being to be worth killing.'

'Was she? Worth killing,' said Thea, surprised to realise that she'd never put that question so directly to a spouse during an interrogation.

Thorkild laughed in a way that Thea believed contained both an element of bitterness and genuine warmth.

'I don't suppose she mattered to me to the extent that I would ever do anything . . . so violent. When she did something nice for me, I was happy and bought her flowers. The last time was in February. Hyacinths, actually. I thought we were the ones who meant the most to each other. But suddenly it turns out there's someone who considered her worth killing.'

'Do you suspect anyone?' Thea had to clear her throat. The vicar looked remote.

'When some of the women wouldn't say hello to her in the supermarket, she said that they were hurting her. She'd talk about it calmly, as if it was irrelevant, yet I always knew that this was indeed how she felt. So who could have killed her, if not everyone?'

'Who did she socialise with here?'

'Not many. Some through my work, of course, but nothing significant. More like courtesy visits. Asger Jørgensen – she met up with him to discuss literature.'

Thea took note of the name.

Suddenly overcome by emotion, he got up and threw open the patio door, letting cold air in. For a while he stood there in the doorway, then he took off, striding away into the garden.

'Excuse me, but we need to get moving,' Devantier said to Thea. 'Bring him in later, you can go over his love life in all the detail you want. Right now, we need something to go on here, something to work with. My phone won't stop ringing.'

'Neither will mine,' said Thea, annoyed at his criticism, but also aware of the legitimacy of it. 'I realise the urgency of the situation, believe me. But this is crucial. Letting him set the pace here might help me win his trust, convince him that we're not looking for easy answers.'

She struggled to find the right words to explain. 'This man either knows something or he doesn't. But look at what he's told us in a matter of minutes, at the very beginning of our interrogation. He goes straight to love, their love for each other, their relationship. What we decide to reveal to others is just as important as the things we try to hide. Every choice he makes tell us something. Trust me: the extra minutes we spend with him now could well pay off later on.'

Devantier pointed towards her buzzing pocket. 'Not everybody agrees with you on that.'

Thea ignored him. Began to look around instead.

It's so easy to see the conformity. What fits and confirms everything. The heavy bookcases with heavyweight literature, tables and chairs arranged so it seems that people are expected to engage in conversation when they're in the same room. Paintings and art posters that speak of tradition, history and modern religious art.

Thea always tried to see the things that were slightly out of kilter. It didn't take her long to identify them. A coloured sculpture of a French clown. Some children's drawings. A book entitled *The History of Pornography*. A festive picture of revellers with drinks, caught in the glare of a flashbulb. A giant television, its screen the same size as a modern flat-screen, but with a cathode sticking three feet out the back and with a collection of Quentin Tarantino videos scattered across the tiled table. A star chart for astrologers. A primitive calendar hanging on the wall, homemade on a computer with two columns – one for Thorkild Christensen, and one for Karen. Most entries had been done on the computer, but in Karen's column a few things had been written by hand: 'K out' every Tuesday evening and 'B' every Thursday. Thea noticed it automatically, she had a gift for memorising weekdays, dates and times.

She stood up, went across to examine the grainy celebratory shot. Two women, three men, smiling from a café table with raised mojito cocktails. She didn't recognise the men, but one of the women was definitely Karen Simonsen. Her dark hair was longer than the pageboy hair she'd seen on the dead woman, and tied into a bun at the back of her head. Her cheeks were flushed, the blue eyes looking in an excited, almost reverent way at the photographer. She was wearing a sleeveless but very becoming top. The café table hid the rest of the relatively slender body. The other woman was laughing at the camera, her eyes closed from the flashlight. One of the three men had red, drunken eyes, the other was laughing at the third, whose neck was the only part of him that was visible, filling most of the foreground. It was not a good photo in any sense: overexposed, badly composed. Why was it on the wall?

Thorkild Christensen materialised behind her, apparently reading her thoughts.

'Who are the mysterious people in the picture?' he asked, then continued: 'These are some of Karen's classmates from Århus. It's from before I knew her. I found it in a drawer of her old pictures, back when we moved to Roslinge. I'm the one who put it up. Karen couldn't for the life of her understand why I would want it on the wall.'

He stood there for a while.

'I think it's a great picture,' he said, rocking indecisively on his feet as if waiting for Thea's next move. She waved her arm and invited him to sit again. A faint shadow of fatigue slid over the vicar's face.

Thea pointed to the wall calendar, but Thorkild was way ahead of her.

'Yes, I thought you would ask. "K out" means Karen out. She always put it like that. Even when she got a mobile phone a few years back and learned to text. If I wrote and asked where she was, she always replied *Out*. But on Tuesday nights she would usually attend something. She sang in a choir for a while. Then it was the gym – they have different things on. Karen went there sometimes. She also went to night school in Århus a while back.'

'Are you sure? That she actually went to those places,' said Bjørn Devantier. The vicar fixed him with his gaze.

'No, I suppose I'm not. I've never checked, if that's what you mean. Never had a reason to. Besides I think it's important that people have some space. That it isn't always anybody else's business what you're doing. But I've no idea what "B" is every Thursday. She drove to Århus on Thursdays. She said. Drank coffee, took a walk in the pedestrian precinct. She loves Århus.'

Bjørn Devantier's phone rang again; he got up and went outside. They sat quietly for a while.

'I studied astronomy, back in the day.' Thea pointed at the star chart. 'It was the first thing I studied. But it didn't stick.'

'Why not?' Thorkild asked.

'Natural science seemed too remote. There was no room for interpretation, only logical proof. It never really engaged me, because every time I tried to understand the meaning of it all, I was told that I was going beyond the boundaries of my field.'

Thorkild nodded, suddenly alert and encouraging. 'Logical proof. It sounds remarkably like police work.'

She smiled. 'So I switched to literature. From one extreme to another. With fiction, nothing was ever carved in stone. Everything was up for discussion and individual viewpoints.'

'What happened, then?'

'It was coincidence that led me to the police academy. I saw an advertisement in the cinema, and I had a friend who spoke well of it. It's a long way from the academic disciplines. But I soon found out that it suited me. You know . . .'

She looked up enquiringly, decided to continue.

'. . . detective work is a mixture of positivism and hermeneutics. Things are as they are once you've finally proved them, but to get there you go through many interpretations of the same events.'

Thorkild Christensen smiled at her. A bright smile and, she thought, relieved. He offered her more coffee. Bjørn Devantier came back in, wiping his feet carefully on the mat in front of the terrace door.

'We need to go now, Thea. As in right now. Anne-Grethe Schalborg would like you to call her back immediately.'

'A breakthrough?' the vicar asked.

Bjørn Devantier sent him a look, not unkind. 'When I know, you'll know, Thorkild.'

'I suppose,' said the vicar slowly, 'it's a matter of everybody else working this case wanting to know what I've told you. Whether you think I did it. How best to investigate. I expect you'd better go tell them, then.'

Afterwards, in the dry heat of the Mondeo, Thea couldn't help wondering what had happened. She didn't know what kind of conversation they had had, but she felt wiser. They had actually talked. In some ways, though it hadn't fit with her preconceived notions, it hadn't offered up any new stereotypes either. It had been strange.

Thea shook her head. This had indeed taken longer than planned. And time was crucial, everybody needed to start ringing doorbells and piecing things together.

She hurriedly made arrangements with Devantier concerning the rest of the day's work and grabbed her phone.

7

It was Tuesday afternoon, just two days after Karen Simonsen's body was pulled from the river. Thea Krogh was wearing her uniform jacket over the blue shirt.

She'd called a meeting of the investigation team so that they could hopefully draw preliminary conclusions. The conference room belonged to Bjørn Devantier and was located in the basement of the A-shaped villa that housed Roslinge's local police station as well as Devantier's private residence on the ground floor, and the first-floor guest room where Thea was staying.

The conference room was cramped and showed obvious signs of Devantier's hasty efforts to clear up five minutes before his colleagues arrived. Piles of paper had become one big pile, two foam mattresses had been hurled out into the hall, a damp cloth had left tracks in the dust on the heavy wooden table, made from lacquered beech. The chairs had been ripped from a stack and looked unmistakably like old classroom chairs: uncomfortable and worn. There was a bulletin board with outdated phone numbers for the Emergency Room and doctor in attendance, as well as an impressive collection of framed certificates and newspaper clippings with pictures of Devantier and a German shepherd.

Fortunately, his first priority had been to put the coffee on, and the aroma went some way to alleviate the claustrophobic atmosphere in the room. Colleagues shook hands as they arrived, and the roll of plastic cups was passed round with a clacking sound. The dog could be heard barking furiously from the upper floor until Bjørn Devantier, embarrassed, ran up the stairs and shouted a command so the animal went silent. Thea sent him a measured nod.

'OK, good morning, everyone. It's good to see you. We have quite a task ahead of us.'

She paused and held up a newspaper headline in front of them.

Police without a clue in vicarage murder: Karen's killer is out there.

The accompanying picture was a gloomy, dark shot of the crime scene shrouded in a thick fog, where you could just make out the police tape. Thea had been expecting derisive snorts – the usual reaction when police officers were confronted with journalists' sensational headlines. But they didn't come.

'The paper is basically correct,' she noted. 'At least, we have no decisive clues. It's almost forty-eight hours since we started. We need something on the table today. You all know it. We need the breakthrough now, otherwise it's going to get difficult.'

She'd intended it to be a pep talk, but it came out sounding like a criticism of her colleagues' work, and that wasn't fair. She changed her tone.

'Nevertheless we're somewhat wiser. Let's begin with the victim.'

Søren Edvardsen took over. He had a habit of commanding everyone's attention by getting up slowly, while meeting all eyes around the table. With superb timing, the dog upstairs erupted in furious barking at the precise moment Edvardsen opened his mouth to speak.

'For God's sake,' Devantier yelled and left the room again. This time his voice rang out loud and clear from upstairs. Thea listened in amazement with the rest of the room and signalled for Edvardsen to wait.

'Er, Devantier . . . is your dog named Mouse?' Alice Caspersen asked when the irritated officer returned.

'Uh, no. It's called Moos – after Jørn Moos, you know, the one who tracked down Blekingegadebanden. My ex-wife thought after tracking down Denmark's only terrorists, Inspector Moos deserved to have a dog named after him. And also the guy on TV – Morse. It was the kind of thing she considered funny.' He looked beseechingly at Thea, who didn't have a clue what he wanted her to say.

'People never get it,' Devantier continued, embarrassed. 'So now, everyone in Roslinge thinks the police dog is called Mouse.'

Alice laughed heartily, and the other colleagues gratefully joined in. Thea smiled disarmingly at Devantier.

'If I may continue . . .' said Edvardsen, in a tone that implied he found the dog's name far from amusing. Thea nodded.

'Karen Simonsen was forty-eight years old. Married to Thorkild Christensen for twenty-two years. They didn't share the same last name because she was too independent a woman – in his words – to want to take his name, and he did not want to end up with the same name as the old Århus mayor. She was from Vejen –' Edvardsen gestured, an indefinite southward wave with one hand '– and met Thorkild whilst studying theology, but she never completed her studies. She became the vicar's wife and lived as such. Lived for the home, the children and herself. Solitary. The common impression is that nobody in town had anything against her. And that they didn't know her. The two grown-up children are both studying in Copenhagen. Thorkild Christensen doesn't think that she would have had enemies. No vices, no inclinations, nothing really. She usually did something on Tuesday evenings, probably a choir, although Christensen doesn't know what choir it is. Then there was a "B" marked on her calendar every Thursday; her husband has no idea what it meant. She had some friends she socialised with, but they can't come up with any animosities or anything out of the ordinary. The vast majority of the couple's acquaintances, fellow church workers and even neighbours have already been checked for alibis.'

'And you, Bjørn, received the call Sunday afternoon from Thorkild Christensen,' said Thea.

'At three o'clock, yes. By then, the vicar had called everyone he knows. And I have personally talked to all the people in Roslinge.'

Thea stopped him.

'The children, Søren?'

Edvardsen looked annoyed.

'Yes. That was unfortunate, to say the least. They went back to Copenhagen yesterday. We haven't had the opportunity to interrogate them.'

Thea looked at Bjørn Devantier: 'I thought they were with their father?'

'We thought so, too,' said Edvardsen. 'But they went to Randers yesterday morning to inform Karen Simonsen's mother. From there, they appear to have travelled directly to

Copenhagen. They've not even spent twelve hours in the vicarage. I think that in itself is interesting. But I understand that Devantier did speak with them. Apparently he neglected to inform them that they should make themselves available for questioning.'

Bjørn Devantier looked defiant. 'I assumed they would come back. I've asked Thorkild to get hold of them and have them come back here, but he says they can't make it until the day after tomorrow. Michael, that's the oldest, has an important exam tomorrow. Apparently that's why they left. It's some kind of a re-take examination that you cannot afford to miss.'

'I'm not sure we can wait,' said Thea. Thanking Søren, she moved on to Alice Caspersen. The tech was quicker to take the floor and shot the words out in rapid succession:

'Cause of death: three shots, 9 millimetre. One of the most common types of pistol ammunition. Often penetrates the entire target. In this case, the bullets passed straight through and haven't been found yet. We don't believe that the victim was shot at the creek. She was probably shot somewhere else and transported there. That should ensure plenty of clues, but we've found nothing. No trace on the body pointing to any location, probably because it has been partly submerged in water for two days. And so far we've found no blood in the vicinity. There are many traces of vehicles, due to the building site further up the creek. We have taken prints, but haven't had time to run them against the databases. The victim probably died after the first shot. And we're talking Friday night as the time of death. Difficult to be more precise at present.'

'There are no neighbours in the area who heard or saw anything out of the ordinary on Friday night,' Bjørn Devantier added.

Alice Caspersen did not appreciate the interruption and resumed almost before Bjørn had finished talking.

'The body could have been unloaded at the construction site – no one has seen anything, as I was about to mention –

and it could have floated down to the vicarage. There's quite a bit of water in the creek at this time of year. No signs of violence, rape, sex or anything of that sort.'

'She probably didn't have sex at all – at least not with her husband. It took him until Sunday to notice that she'd gone. An entire night went by without him giving her a second thought.'

It was Søren Edvardsen who raised the question, one that Thea felt she could answer with a certain degree of authority after talking with the vicar.

'No, Thorkild Christensen says that they led very separate lives and frequently went about their business for some time without seeing each other. It may sound strange, but there are many ways to live together, and there's nothing to suggest that he's lying. Were you finished, Alice?'

The technician nodded.

'As Alice and Bjørn have already stated, we've learned nothing of significance from the anyone we've talked to in town. But we'd better hear a summary of that, too. Sorry, Jørgen, was it?'

The large, burly guy with the red beard who'd been sitting next to Bjørn Devantier spoke up. He had a comical high, effeminate voice that stood in sharp contrast to his rugged exterior. Like a biker who'd got something stuck in his throat.

'Jørgen Schmidt. Also a local officer – just from the other side of the municipality, Vilå. We usually give each other a hand in the neighbouring districts. And since there's not been a damn thing happening in my town over the summer, I've been making the rounds in Roslinge. Bjørn and I have spoken with half the town, I reckon. Everyone's busy protesting that they couldn't have done it. It's as if there's a collective suspicion cast over the town, because nobody really cared for Karen. Typical,' he chuckled. 'It's exactly the same in my town. Once I had a young girl who disappeared, and they'd already managed to write *scum* on the door of the local suspected paedophile and the lynch mob was already forming when we found the girl – she'd gotten on the wrong bus. Well, whatever! Some say they heard construction noise from the site on Friday, but not after four o'clock, supposedly. The only car that has been observed nearby that is not a work vehicle is the construction manager's private four-wheel drive. He's a complete moron, by the way. Not from this area.'

Bjørn Devantier signalled to Schmidt that he was eager to take over, and the big man duly made way for him.

'The last person to have seen Karen alive is her neighbour. Karen had dinner with Thorkild at seven o'clock on Friday. He doesn't know what she did later on, but the neighbour saw her standing at the bus stop at eight. The neighbour was walking her dog, but wasn't on sufficiently friendly terms with Karen to initiate a chat. They just said hello. Quarter past eight the bus to Århus arrives and drives off, heading south. No one saw whether she got on the bus or if someone got off. The bus driver we talked to, he thinks she got on, but he seemed pretty unsure about it. We suspect he was only saying what he thought we wanted to hear. No ticket was issued at that time, but the vicar says she had a bus pass. Otherwise, we know nothing.'

Devantier looked at Thea expectantly.

'Right . . .' Thea hesitated. She cast her eyes around the table with what she hoped was a firm, reassuring look.

'You've done a lot of good work. We've done everything completely by the book and we've learned a lot. The problem is, what we know doesn't give us any useful leads to pursue – yet,' she added. The group responded with silence.

In need of some time to think, Thea handed out a few specific duties, asked the group to grab some lunch and then reconvene in an hour.

In the meantime she went for a walk to think things through. Up and down Roslinge's lacklustre main street in a quick, angry trot. She was fuming.

She would have liked to invite someone to join her. Someone she could share her thoughts with, but as usual there was no one in the group who could take that role. They were skilled drones who could do their jobs to perfection, but not one of them had shown any ability to think creatively in this phase of the investigation, she thought, frustrated. Or was it her? Was it Thea who was at fault, having no insights to share with the confidante she was missing?

She tried to call Anne-Grethe but went through to voicemail. Instead, she sent a text message asking whether Kristian Videbæk could be borrowed from biker crime and assigned to the Roslinge case.

'OK . . .' Thea hated herself for starting the session with such an empty a word. They were back in the conference room, most of them clutching bags bearing the local baker's pretzel logo. Bjørn, who had been asked to contact the bus driver again, had a sandwich in hand. Someone had pushed a paper bag with four greasy pastries into the centre of the table; they were apparently for anybody. Thea, suddenly aware that she had not eaten, reached across and grabbed one.

'. . . we've done the groundwork. Now it's time to go deeper. Most murders are committed by people close to the victim. We need to dig up everything we can about Thorkild and Karen's relationship: who were they, where did they meet, who cleaned the house, how was their relationship with the children, how much does Thorkild inherit, how often did they have guests, who took care of the garden, how often did they have sex, what were their habits, their hobbies, their temperament, their bad sides. Everybody has bad sides. I want to know everything. And I want to know what other relationships of importance Karen had. There must be somebody. The hidden connection – a lover, a friend, a doctor, a confidante on some level or another.'

She took a bite of the pastry.

'And we continue asking everyone in town, and when we've

been through every last one of them we start all over again. Søren and I will go to Copenhagen and talk to the children. We need to get to them before the funeral. Before everyone coordinates their stories and begins to tell the same story about Karen Simonsen.'

'Well . . .' said Søren Edvardsen, managing to make it sound like an objection. She ignored him.

'Good luck, everybody.'

To Thea's relief, no one had any questions. They got up slowly and left the room, all except for Schmidt, who took a pastry and started to read one of the articles on the wall, about the police dog Moos, who for the second consecutive year had won the Danish Kennel Club's Best in Breed for obedience.

'He knows the stuff,' said Schmidt. Since he was standing with his back to her, Thea couldn't work out whether he was talking to himself about the dog, or to her about Bjørn Devantier. Either way, she was inclined to agree.

8

Thea grabbed her phone and the list of internal phone numbers. It was Wednesday morning, three days after the body was discovered, she had to drive to Århus to collect Søren Edvardsen, and Bjørn Devantier needed to be put to work.

A local woman, who was on the Roslinge parish council, had called the police wanting to tell them something. At the beginning of a murder case there were always lots of tips that had to be painstakingly followed up, usually only to be filed away as worthless. But Thea couldn't help wondering why this woman had phoned the nationwide police service number instead of contacting the local officer whose station was within ten minutes' walk of any residence in town.

Devantier answered after the fourth ring, sounding a little breathless. A stiff wind roared into the microphone.

'Hey, Bjørn, where are you?'

'Hi, Thea. I'm on my way home. I was trying to grab a bite. What can I do for you?'

'I have another interview for you and it's one of the locals, so I think you should do it.'

'OK. But I thought I'd spoken with the whole town already. And I haven't had anything to eat yet.'

'It can probably wait until you've eaten. I doubt there's much to it.'

'What's her name?'

Thea was startled.

'How do you know it's a woman?'

'Because otherwise you'd probably have done it yourself,' said Bjørn. Then, sounding as if he could have bitten his tongue off, he went on, 'I mean . . . you have a way with men. Oh, damn, that came out wrong. Well, you did such a great job with the vicar. The chemistry between you.'

Thea was stunned. Had they been trading jokes about her questioning of Thorkild? She could do without that kind of talk. Her tone was aloof.

'It's someone by the name of Anika Svendsen. Ring a bell?'

'Yeah, I know her. That's fine, I don't need any more info.'

Bjørn paused, as if he wanted to say more, but Thea hung up.

Anika Svendsen had insisted that they meet in the church. For, as she'd anxiously whispered on the phone, 'When the organ is playing, no one can hear what we say.'

Bjørn Devantier figured she'd probably seen too many spy

movies with hidden microphones and that kind of thing. Nevertheless he'd consented, and they sat down, each in their own pew, while the organist practised the upcoming Sunday postlude.

She was a small lady, dishevelled and wrinkled and entangled in a huge scarf. The only remarkable thing about her was her lustrous black hair without a hint of grey. She sighed and squirmed uncomfortably on the bench, cleared her throat, trying to get started, then stopped herself. What came out was a whisper.

Bjørn interrupted her impatiently: 'You'll have to speak louder if I am to hear anything above this noise. Could we go outside? Or into the church hall?'

Anika Svendsen flinched and pulled herself together.

'It's because I've seen something.'

Then she stalled, at a loss as to how to continue. Trying to conceal his irritation, Bjørn took a deep breath and prompted:

'It's all right, Anika. What is it you've seen?'

'I think I saw Karen Simonsen's murderer. The vicar's little wife.'

Bjørn glared at her. Her eyes filled with frightened tears.

'Why have you left it until now to come forward, Anika?'

'You already knew she'd been shot. And I can't say much more, I'm afraid.'

'Is that so? Maybe you could tell us where? And when? Maybe even who did it?'

The old lady's lower lip quivered like a child's.

'Yes, it was out on the trail – the path that goes down to the mill. Anton and I have lived there for thirty-two years. Karen took a walk there every morning. And I don't appreciate your attitude. I'm trying to help, I'll have you know.'

'How can you be sure she took a walk every morning?'

'Because I do too. We met most mornings. And this was on Saturday morning. I read in the newspaper that she was killed on Friday night, but that's not true. And then I thought I probably needed to talk to you.'

'What time and where, precisely?'

'It was certainly early. I couldn't sleep. It was where the path runs alongside the creek. Down towards the meadow. A nice walk, it is. It was. I've not gone there since, but Anton says it's nonsense.'

Bjørn recalled the spot. Was that why they hadn't found it? The soil was so moist in that spot, especially when it had rained, as it had in late August. The water hid all traces. On one side was the creek. Or rather, the bog – that could easily have sucked up the two stray bullets without them ever being found. On the other side of the path was a dense thicket where it would be easy to hide. And beyond the bushes was a paved cycle track to the school. There'd have been hardly anyone about on a Saturday morning and the track was wide enough to allow a car to drive in and pick up a body. It could have happened like that. It probably had. Adrenalin surged in him: finally they had something to go on.

'What happened that morning, Anika?'

Anika looked down at her lap.

'Yes, I heard some shots. I took no notice of it, for it was from a long way away, and there are always hunters out there – although Anton said afterwards that the hunting season hasn't even started yet. The grocer, he hunts ducks. Once I found a bullet hole in a tablecloth that I'd hung up to dry outside. But I got a new one in the supermarket for free. And you know what? It was better than the old one. Anton said it was the least they could do.'

'Anton, yes. How many shots?'

'Two. I walked along the path and saw a woman coming towards me, I hadn't seen before. I hid behind a tree, yes, I did. I don't know why, I think it was a little scary. I'm not sure whether she saw me, but she began to run. Right there, no track suit or anything, and she ran straight past me, hiding her face. It sounded as if she was crying.'

'Did you see Karen afterwards?'

'No, I wasn't going any further, that's for sure! I took the path up to town. I was so beside myself, I didn't know what to do.'

'You should have called the police, Anika – that goes without saying!'

'Yes, I thought so, but I had to go home first, and when I got home Anton said I was seeing things because I'm taking some new medication at the moment, and it's really been giving me grief. And then we went out there again. I'd rather not have, but Anton brought the hunting rifle with him. When we got there, she was gone and there was nothing. And Anton said that I shouldn't go making a fool out of myself.' She looked down at her knees. 'I don't like being laughed at.'

Bjørn dug his nails into his thighs and counted to ten.

'Why didn't you call us when you found out that she was dead?'

'Yes, well, you found her in the creek by the vicarage. That's not where I'd seen her. And then I decided I'd give it some time. Anton always says that, before you say anything, you'd be wise to consider your words.'

Bjørn decided not to pursue the matter any further. Experience had taught him that people's actions were sometimes dictated by the oddest reasons, and he knew that, for Anika, as she sat there wringing her hands, the prospect of being laughed at was probably the worst-case scenario she could imagine.

Moreover, her description was vague at best. He needed to check out the place before he went any further with her statement. It was doubtful that they would find anything out there after all this time. Damn, they had combed the area shortly after the murder. Almost the entire town. He'd spent what felt like a week wading slowly through the pouring rain at the other end of the creek. That was the way the stream travelled, so that's where they had devoted the most resources. But he knew that they'd also had people out checking the trail to the mill. And then the damn bullets – those had not yet been located.

'Anika, I need you to think carefully about this. You said two shots?'

'Two, yes.'

'Can you say where?'

'Yes, I know where I met the woman who ran.'

'And how long after the shots was that?'

'Probably only ten minutes.'

'Ten minutes! In that time one can cover the whole of Roslinge.'

'Well, maybe two minutes. I really don't know these things.'

'Could it be less than a minute?'

'Yes. Do you think that was it?'

To hell with it. Just typical, Bjørn thought, finally a witness comes forward, and it turns out she has no sense of time. That wasn't going to help much in terms of pinpointing the scene of the crime.

'The woman you saw – what did she look like? What clothes was she wearing?'

'Yes, there's the matter of that, too. I saw her face before she hid it. It was someone I know, I think. And she was wearing dark clothes. Maybe green, some kind of pattern?'

'What? Someone you know?'

The organ stopped, so Anika's voice suddenly sounded loud in the room.

'It was Elisabeth.'

Anika lowered her voice into a whisper. Bjørn had to lean all the way over the back of his pew to get close enough to hear.

'Elisabeth? Elisabeth Jepsen? The grocer's wife?'

'Yes, it could have been her. But I've never seen her wear such colours. She mostly wears red. And sometimes orange.'

'Did you not say,' said Bjørn, slowly and clearly, 'just two minutes ago that it was a woman you hadn't seen before?'

'I said that I'd not seen her *there* before,' snorted Anika, as if it was self-explanatory.

54

'How sure are you? Anika, it's very important that you are certain if you are accusing someone of something like that.'

'I'm almost sure, I think. Or at least, it was someone who looked like her.'

Bjørn sighed. He asked Anika to come down to the station later in the day so he could file an official report. Then he went up to the altar and called Thea Krogh.

'Thea? This is Bjørn. I don't think this is worth pursuing. Anika's not sure what it was she saw. She says a woman came running along the mill trail at an undefined time, not long after she'd heard shots on Saturday morning . . . Where are you? I'm having trouble hearing you.'

'Yes, sorry, I'm on my way to Copenhagen, the connection isn't great on the ferry. In the morning, you say? How does that fit with what Alice says?'

'She said Friday night. But she also said that it was hard to be specific. I'll bet that if you were to ask her, she could just as easily say Saturday morning.'

Thea knew he was right. TV shows had made the work of pathologists and technicians appear to be a very precise science, where it was possible to determine an exact timeline for anything a person had been exposed to, based on weird factors such as stomach contents, chemical analysis of hair follicles, insect reproduction and decay, blood vessel contractions in the iris, the salt concentration in blood plasma . . . The reality was there were an infinite number of factors that would hinder or completely disrupt the task of arriving at such conclusions. Humidity, the body's overall condition in the moment of death, the injuries the bullets had inflicted, and not least the rainwater composition and stream water temperatures – all would have had an impact on the body and thus on the task of estimating time of death.

Yes, Alice would say the same. The best they could offer was a guess, even though it was an educated guess.

'And, Thea . . .?' Bjørn lowered his voice. 'Anika points the finger at a specific person: Elisabeth Jepsen. She's married to Mugge – Mogens Jepsen, the grocer here in town. The local king, so to speak. But I don't believe it, I'm afraid.'

'Because?'

'Because when we get down to the details, Anika is not at all sure what it was that she saw and heard. She says two shots, not three. She's been struggling with various illnesses, real and imaginary, ever since I came to this town, and she's heavily medicated. She comes forward four days after the event, she cannot say anything about the time and even doubts herself. Plus I've already spoken with both Mogens and Elisabeth. I didn't get the feeling that there was anything suspicious there.'

Anika was still sitting on her pew, glancing anxiously at Bjørn as if she'd started the third world war.

'OK. Obviously, we need to examine the trail again,' said Thea. 'And take Anika Svendsen back to the station and get her to make a formal statement. But it doesn't sound as though we have a decisive new direction to go in, if I understand you correctly?'

'I think not. But we'll look into it, of course it's worth investigating.'

The young organist came down the stairs from the gallery. It was not someone Bjørn remembered having seen before, but he made a mental note to question this kid next.

'Hey, you startled me. I thought I was alone in the church. What's going on?' he demanded.

Bjørn waved him away.

'Hey, pal? We can't have people walking around the altar.'

The young man was advancing up the aisle towards Bjørn, looking protective.

Bjørn turned, clasped one hand over the receiver so as not to yell into Thea's ear, and shouted at the top of his voice:

'This is the police and I'm on the phone. Shut up, *pal*!'

9

Michael and Nadia Christensen sat beside each other. Thea had made arrangements with both of them separately, but when she and Søren Edvardsen arrived at Michael's apartment in Istedgade, his sister was there as well.

'We thought it would be easier for you,' said Nadia Christensen with a friendly, sad smile, which immediately reminded Thea of Thorkild.

On the whole, the Christensen children resembled their father. They were tall, almost lanky, sleek and handsome young people. They had inherited their mother's brown hair and dark eyes, but otherwise the cheekbones, the symmetry of the faces were their father's. Obvious siblings, and apparently they were close. There was a familiarity and casualness in their movements, a silent coordination in the way they set the table for coffee. Nadia moved familiarly around her brother's apartment. Michael lived alone, while Thea could see from her notes that Nadia lived with a boyfriend somewhere in Vesterbro. She studied biology, he studied religion. They looked like a pair of smooth, well-functioning young people, neatly dressed, well-groomed. Thea felt strangely comfortable, yet at the same time she was intrigued by these two, Vicar Thorkild's children. Nadia's eyes were swollen and red, her nose too. Michael however, looked calm and collected.

Søren Edvardsen had been in a bad mood ever since they boarded the Mols Line, and Thea left him to it.

'I have to get back soon,' said Michael. 'Study group meeting. I've got an exam this afternoon at quarter past two. What would you like to know?'

Not unfriendly, but brief and to the point. The two children had settled down beside each other on the couch, Thea sat opposite, and Søren stood at the window looking out, but Thea could see that he was focused and listening.

'They'd probably like to hear about Mum. You know, what she was like?' Nadia asked, her voice was small, velvety soft and delicate like a Disney heroine. Latent tears lay in the corner of her eyes.

'In that case, I guess you'd best tell them,' said her big brother. Turning to Thea, he added: 'Nadia was closer to Mum. If you can put it that way. Where I'm concerned, she's always been a little distant.'

'Distant?' Thea began, but Michael interrupted her.

'I'm going to stop you right there if I may. There's nothing unusual about our relationship. She was a little remote, end of story. I have long since dropped the mother fixation. I don't know much about Mum, except that she was Mum. And a good mother.'

He smiled. Thea looked at him, heard his father's formulations in the boy's way of speaking; she found him strangely charming.

'I think,' Michael added, 'that every human on the far side of, shall we say twenty-five, should make peace with their parents. Acknowledge their mistakes, their humanity, review them and see what you yourself would do differently. Draw a line under the whole thing. So I'm done with Mother in that way. I loved her, but I'm done with her, I've drawn a line, all that's finished. She lived in Roslinge, I'd go home for Christmas, she and Father would pop over here now and again and we'd go for a meal at Café Sommersko. That's fine. It is what it is.'

He met Thea's eye, his tone unequivocal. 'You're welcome to ask away, I will be happy to answer. But I just think we will in any case end up where we are now.'

There was no challenge in what he said. Although the categorical way of speaking, so soon after his mother's death, surprised Thea. Was it a bulwark against sorrow? Thea was not sure. He seemed sincere, what he said seemed thought through. Accepting him at his word, she turned her attention to Nadia, who gazed at her brother with her big Disney eyes and looked, Thea thought, desperately unhappy.

'You know her better, Nadia?'

'I don't understand what you're saying, Michael,' her voice pleaded. 'You don't just draw a line under someone and be done with them. Your own mother. Dad and Mum were not finished with each other. And I certainly was not finished with Mum. Do you even realise . . . what if you have children, Michael?'

There were tears in her eyes. Michael looked at his sister.

'Dad and Mum were so distant, I'm not sure Dad even regarded Mum as a real person. It would surprise me if it makes any difference to him that she isn't around any more. In the real world.'

'Michael! What a thing to say!' Nadia buried her head in her hands and began to cry, and Thea wondered if the young man was all that *finished* with his father, to use Michael's own phrase. 'Did you see the state of the kitchen? Dad had taken everything out of the cabinets and just left it.'

Michael placed a hand reassuringly on his sister's arm.

'We're quite different, Nadia and I,' he said. 'In many respects Nadia probably has a more healthy approach to the world. She's sweet and kind.' The warmth in his voice touched Thea.

'Mum was a wonderful mother,' said Nadia firmly, looking up and wiping her eyes. 'Mum has always been there for me. And you, Michael. She baked cakes and looked after us when we were sick, read us stories. I know you didn't think she was all that present since we were teenagers . . .'

'You're right, I don't think she was. She'd never ask about us. Your basic *How was your day?* – that sure as hell wasn't Mum.'

'No, but it was Dad, Mike. All the time. Talk, talk, talk.

I'm not sure Mum could ever get a word in,' said Nadia, thoughtfully. 'But you can't go saying that it doesn't matter to Dad. We don't know anything about it. You can never know these things. What people really mean to each other.'

Thea carefully observed the two and was no longer annoyed that they would not be questioned separately.

'When do you know your mother, Nadia? When does she stop being the idea of *mother* and becomes an ordinary human being, a woman even, whom you must respond to differently,' said Michael.

'People's roles change along the way. Sometimes I had such good talks with Mum. She told me about her childhood and stuff, Grandmother and Grandfather. I'm named after my grandmother,' Nadia explained.

'That wasn't my experience,' said Michael. 'But lately, I've started to question whether parents should even do that.'

'Do what,' said Thea.

'Turn into people.'

'I don't understand what you mean,' said Thea.

'I do,' said Nadia. 'I agree with you, I think, Michael. I don't want Thorkild and Karen. I want Mum and Dad.'

'You're grown-ups,' said Thea, surprised.

'Oh, we are, of course. But I just don't believe that the role of mother and father is something you put away when your kids reach a certain age. And then let loose with all your shortcomings. You are still Mum and Dad to someone, it must be taken seriously. I don't think Mother did.'

'I think she did,' said Nadia. 'And I think you should consider what you say, Michael. She's dead, and you will not sit here and speak ill of her.'

'What kind of inadequacies are you talking about?' said Thea.

'Michael,' said Nadia warningly. 'Think about it. What you say makes no sense – you claim to be oh-so finished with Mum and Dad, and yet you're still angry with Mum because there was some mother-role you don't think she lived up to.'

'I'm not angry, quite the contrary. I'm not all that involved, frankly. I don't want to spend the rest of my life trying to define myself in relation to them. Or, in contrast to them. These are minor considerations.'

'You sound exactly like Dad,' Nadia sighed, and Thea smiled inwardly.

'You were in a hurry to get home yesterday? Your father said you arrived Sunday night by train. Then home again Monday?'

Nadia looked anxious. 'We'll go back again tonight. Once Michael has finished his exam. That's why.'

Michael looked at Thea, for the first time with hostility.

'We rushed home to be with Dad. He couldn't be bothered to pick us up in Århus, he was asleep when we got there, and he hadn't even called Grandma, for fuck's sake. So we decided to go and tell her. And you know what? It wasn't all that much fun. So when we were finished in Randers, where Grandma lives, we didn't have the energy to go back to Roslinge again. Plus I have exams today, I think I mentioned that? Not just any exam, either. If I fail, I'll have to re-take the entire semester. And Mum always used to say that if there was anything that could make her depressed, it was people who brought their entire lives to a halt because of . . . grief. She'd say it was hurtful to the dead. Mum would have wanted me to take the exam and pass.'

His eyes grew distant. They sat for a while. Nadia took her brother's hand and looked discreetly at her watch.

Finally, Søren Edvardsen interrupted with his question:

'Have you any idea how your mother got along in Roslinge?'

'Roslinge,' Michael Christensen said quickly, 'is a fucking little piece-of-crap town.'

10

Bjørn only had one antidote to a frustration of that magnitude. Food, decent food. Or as close as you could get to that on a Wednesday, late in the day, when you had no energy to climb in the car and drive around for decent groceries or perhaps even eat out. He wanted to give himself that much, especially after such a lousy week, but the energy wasn't there. The vicar's wife was a nightmare, although he was doing his best to keep cool. The detectives they'd drafted in from Århus were OK, really; the lead detective Thea seemed competent, and they hadn't turned out to be quite the smartasses he'd feared, indeed he'd been almost certain they would be. Yet he was conscious of all the looks and the unspoken questions at the team briefings. This murder had occurred on his patch. Hell, practically in his backyard. He was supposed to know his community, it should be a simple matter of who and why.

And normally, he had a pretty good idea.

Bjørn Devantier knew who could be found on any given Saturday night driving in his Ford Cortina with a dangerously high blood alcohol level, despite having lost his licence. He knew which of the local eighteen-year-olds were able to supply amphetamines, pot of a decent quality and occasionally a few of their mother's prescription opiates. He knew where the nearest brothel was located – about five miles outside the town limits in a dilapidated barn with poinsettias in the windows. He knew that the Q8 petrol station was selling beer to minors after 10 p.m. That the local pub's cola bottles were imported from Turkey, and that the owner had replaced the less-than-happy smiley sign from the National Board of Health with a home-fabricated one in much higher spirits, in order to continue serving French toast and his wife's home-made spaghetti with meat sauce for customers when they were hungry. He knew where he could go and recover the PH-lamps, silver heirlooms and flat-screen TVs after a series of weekend burglaries, assuming the local gang hadn't yet managed to get it picked up first. Last time he'd arrived just ten minutes after Palle's North German acquaintance had called by with a van and rushed the stolen goods off to Hamburg. The jubilant Palle had almost invited Bjørn in for a beer to celebrate his victory.

So he needed food. And for lack of a better option, Bjørn went down to the local supermarket that he would have preferred to avoid. He usually frequented the Netto in Vilå, reserving the local supermarket for the occasional errand to prevent people condemning him for not shopping locally. Not only was the Netto slightly cheaper but he could shop there without being subjected to the sort of comments that came with the job – the half- or whole-hearted attempts at humour that locals indulged in whenever they were in his presence. Indeed, he'd barely entered the shop when a local prankster roared, 'Oh-oh, the sheriff!' and turned his coat pockets inside out.

Smiling dutifully, Bjørn grabbed a cart and was starting to evaluate the sell-by date on a packet of bread when she tapped him on the shoulder. A small, red-haired lady, probably in her late sixties, with heavy red lipstick and green duffel coat, holding a sponge cake up in his face.

'Now, I'll buy one more. And then I hope you will come. They don't keep that long, you know. Even though it says so on them, you can't always go by that.'

She blinked behind the pair of huge glasses that perched on the end of her nose.

'It's the third one I buy.'

There was no mistaking the accusation in her voice. 'They really are delicious, fresh out of the package. Just don't put them in the oven, they fall apart completely. I like a little whipped cream with it. But now, I also have to buy more cream.'

'I don't quite follow,' said Bjørn, trying to sound as dismissive as he could.

'You don't follow,' the lady repeated with a sigh. Then, apparently mobilising her entire reserve of patience, she announced, 'I'm Lily.'

Bjørn looked at the sponge cake, waiting.

'You've probably heard of me in the bookstore? Lily. No?'

She looked at him in astonishment.

'I'm writing my memoirs. Obviously I've alerted the bookstore. It's about my upbringing. Not far from here, actually, on the farm where I grew up. With two siblings, my mother and my father. The book is mainly about him, actually.'

She turned her eyes on Bjørn, a significant look. 'He hit me.'

Bjørn stared at her, unable to find the right facial expression. The lady's face turned dark.

'Perhaps you don't find that to be an interesting story?'

'Oh yes. Certainly, of course it is. That's a given. But I'm not sure . . .'

Bjørn left the sentence open, accustomed to being helped along. Lily, however, had no intention of supplying the necessary prompt. The silence was long and awkward, until Lily threw the sponge cake into her basket, took it up again, inspected the damage and swapped it with a new one from the shelf. Then she gave him a big smile.

'Do you have time right away?'

'I'm not sure what it is I'm doing?'

'Good Lord, have you already found out who killed Karen Simonsen? It must have been today, then. There wasn't any mention of it in the newspaper. But then you probably won't mind telling me who it was?'

She looked expectantly at Bjørn, and it dawned on him what the errand could be. Just another crazy old lady, for Christ's sake.

'Did you say your name is Lily? Do you happen to know who did it?'

'I know something.' Lily suddenly sounded so secretive that Bjørn had to smile. He tried to contain it, but it was perceived and fortunately not taken amiss. She smiled herself, this time disarmingly, and pushed up her glasses.

'I rent the first floor at number 30,' she said, as if stating the obvious, 'with the Espersens. Sweet family. Especially the youngest, he's adorable – a real charmer. But she lets him have his way a little too often, if you ask me.' She lowered her voice to a whisper. 'And they've had money troubles since she became unemployed. Yes, I don't mean to gossip, but you *are* the police. And so they decided to rent out the first floor. They simply dragged everything down to the ground floor and now they just live there, all of them. Cramped, but like I said to her, it's nothing compared to what some of us have had to endure. They even offered a little discount on the rent if I'd look after the kids now and then.'

Lily looked at the officer as if she expected a reaction. When he failed to oblige, she delivered it herself, laughing out loud.

'Me – a nanny! But I said to her, no, I said. I'm writing my memoirs. Anyway, one can easily see over to the Christensens' from number 30. And you've also been talking to the Espersens. And then I thought: Now, he must come and ask me soon. So I rushed down and got cake and whatnot. But you didn't come. Have you been busy?'

She looked reproachfully at Bjørn, who scratched his head and recalled the not particularly informative chat with Adam and Louise Espersen. Until Lily let out a loud gasp.

'Good grief! You don't mean to say . . . My goodness! You probably didn't even know I live up there! I've completely forgotten to put the name on the mailbox. My niece has made such a neat little name tag at work, a sticker of sorts. But it isn't there, is it?'

Lily laughed, it echoed throughout the store.

'And there I was with sponge cake and whipped cream and whatnot. I'll be damned!'

She put her hand to her mouth, horrified. 'And now I'm swearing. I do beg your pardon. But isn't that just the darnedest thing? So the mystery is solved, at least. Perhaps we can do it immediately?'

Bjørn tried for a loophole.

'If I were to conduct a formal interview, someone else must be present. It must be recorded on tape. It's not something you just do. You're welcome to come down to the station tomorrow, if that's OK?'

'Nonsense! It's not an interrogation. I just have something I must tell you. A tip.' She waved the shopping basket. 'I need to get some cream.' And then she stomped off to the dairy counter, while Bjørn wondered if he had a can of tuna somewhere in his closet for when he finally made it home. Then decided that no, this mysterious Lily would have to wait until he'd had a decent meal.

And then he changed his mind again, fed by his curiosity. So he waited at the checkout, while Lily paid for the cream and cake. She didn't buy anything else.

'You probably think I'm crazy,' she said, almost indifferent, as she fished for the obligatory piece of paper that older ladies have in their handbags with the code for their credit card, and paid for the goods.

Bjørn felt slightly silly as he trudged after the little lady into the driveway of number 30, a large, rundown house in red brick, which seemed to be teeming with life on all fronts. A ladder was leaning against the half-plastered wall, there were colourful plastic toys on every square metre of the lawn. Two cheering children, a boy and a girl, were jumping up and down on a big blue garden trampoline, while a plump, short-haired woman was hanging laundry on a clothesline. As they walked up, the woman waved happily and the children, both short of breath, shouted, 'Hi, Lily!'

'He finally made it then, Lily? Hello again, Devantier. Look,

Kalle, now the policeman has come again! I actually have some bones I've used to make stock, would you like them for Mouse?'

The youngest child, a blond curly boy, immediately stopped bouncing and studied Bjørn with a puzzled look and a few fingers in his mouth.

'If you could possibly make sure they don't yell and scream too loudly, Louise,' Lily said, bristling with self-importance. 'I'm about to have a chat with the police.'

'That I will,' the woman chuckled. 'Enjoy, Officer. Finally someone gets to hear Lily's secret. She won't tell us. And the kids are dying of curiosity.'

'It's definitely not for children,' Lily said, adamant. 'And I don't hold with gossip, Louise, you know that perfectly well. It's another matter when it's the police. Investigating a murder.' She started up the stairs with Bjørn following her.

'Lily, can we have the cake again, if the policeman doesn't want it?' called the girl from the trampoline.

Bjørn sat down on a high-backed sofa, trying to signal that he would soon be off again. Lily began to whip cream with an old-fashioned hand whisk, tirelessly.

'My mother could whip egg whites stiff with a fork,' she said. 'But I think this one here is clever, actually.'

'I'm a tad busy. I have an important meeting I need to attend.'

She raised her eyebrows inquisitively.

'At police headquarters in Århus. We cannot let them wait, Lily.'

'No, of course,' she said and placed the cup and cake plate in front of him. She'd cut a big slice of sponge cake and arranged whipped cream on top in a neat twist. There was a nice cake fork made in silver on the side. Bjørn sent his missed dinner a thought and then put the fork in the cake with a sigh. Lily took note of it, happily.

'The grocer's Elisabeth has a friend,' she said bluntly.

Bjørn raised his eyebrows. Elisabeth again?

'A friend?'

'A friend. Who is not her husband, if you understand what I mean. A . . . boyfriend – or whatever the term is nowadays. Anyway, Mogens Jepsen is certainly a cuckold. You still say that, I'm sure?'

'Hmmm, how about that. And you think there's some connection with Karen Simonsen's murder?'

'Well, the boyfriend was also Karen's friend.'

That woke Bjørn up.

'Is that so? Who is he?'

'Like I said, I don't hold with gossip. Far as I'm concerned, people can keep their affairs to themselves,' Lily said, in a way that suggested the opposite. 'But you're the police. It's Mr Jørgensen. He lives down at Pilevej. The teacher. Well, he's not a school teacher here in town. He visits Karen a lot. And he's also seeing Elisabeth Jepsen, that's for sure. I've even seen her sneak away early. Three times.'

Bjørn frowned.

'I do hope he won't be in any trouble,' said Lily, almost wistfully. 'Jørgensen doesn't need to know that you've heard it from me. Two married ladies. He gets around, that one.'

'Are you positive that Karen Simonsen and Asger Jørgensen had an affair?'

'Why, yes. He came into her home.'

'That doesn't have to mean they were lovers. They may well have been friends.'

Lily shook her head emphatically.

'Have you seen Jørgensen hugging Karen? Kissing her? Something like that?'

Again, she shook her head.

'Karen Simonsen was friends with Asger Jørgensen,' Bjørn said. 'They read literature together, as far as I know.'

Lily snorted indignantly.

'Literature! When an unmarried man visits a married woman's home. And always when the husband is out. It sure looks that way. And mark my words, Mr Policeman. These so-called friendships, there's always more to it. Men and women. Put them together, sparks fly. I don't know much, but I know that.'

Bjørn looked at her, tired.

'Anything else, Lily?'

Her cheeks turned bright red.

'Perhaps the school teacher wants to read my memoirs if he's interested in literature. I think I will ask him. How did you know, officer? About Ms Simonsen and Mr Jørgensen.'

'Someone else told me. I don't believe it's a secret.'

'Ha! Anika Svendsen, without a doubt. That old fool. Frankly, she's ridiculous. And she's never been able to mind her own business. Always parading around the vicarage, as if she has something to do there.'

Bjørn smiled.

'In fact, the vicar told us himself. That his wife met with Jørgensen now and then. You know, Lily, sometimes there's nothing underhanded going on.'

'The poor man! Doesn't want to think ill of her. Take it from me, she was as unreliable as a cat, I can always tell. She never greeted anyone. At least, not in a way that you would think that she meant it. I certainly hope he finds himself a nice new wife. One that fits in here a little better.'

When Bjørn left Lily, he was thoughtful. When was the last time they'd had a case like this here in town? Karen Simonsen, whom he didn't really know much about. And apparently no one had much to say about her. His question-and-answer sessions with the neighbours had given him almost nothing. Except of course that it spoke volumes there was nothing to be said. It was unreliable gossip, like Lily. And Anika Svendsen, whom Lily was talking about. Gossip that made him feel weary because he still had to go through the charade of checking it to see whether there was something somewhere with substance for the investigation. Bjørn remembered well the vicar's wife from his own childhood – long and lanky, friendly and always on her bike, following in her husband's footsteps with baskets of bread, bibles, used baby clothes when there was a need for it. She was dry but well liked. A proper vicar's wife, that's what they all said.

Times were different now. Perfectly acceptable for a vicar's wife to live her own life, take care of herself and even reserve the right not to participate in her husband's church services, preferring to hold court in the vicarage with whoever happened to suit her. Often when her husband was home, but sometimes when he was not.

Thorkild Christensen had himself explained that Karen had a friend in Asger Jørgensen, one of the local commuters, a school teacher. A divorced man in his late forties, whose car was now and then parked in front of the vicarage. He recalled Søren Edvardsen's unexciting summary of the interrogation of Jørgensen.

Was there something there? He felt his pulse quicken and sent a silent thank you upwards because crimes are always so predictable – one lover here and there and a jealousy drama. He fished the phone out of his pocket.

Bjørn's optimism deflated like a balloon when he and Jørgen Schmidt, who fortunately didn't have far to drive from Vilå, arrived at Asger Jørgensen's. They were welcomed with no drama and offered coffee in his tidy house. The man seemed the personification of reliability and there was a glimmer of amusement in his eyes when Bjørn went fishing for a possible love affair with the vicar's wife.

'You've got it wrong, Devantier,' Asger Jørgensen said in a tone that almost automatically freed him of further suspicion in Bjørn's mind. 'I understand that you have to ask. And that maybe it looks weird. But an affair with Karen is something that never crossed my mind. She's not the type you have an affair with. Too unapproachable, in a way. As if allowing you to be in her company is a big enough favour in itself. I liked her a lot. But that's different, right?'

'Well . . . what did the two of you do when you were

visiting?' said Bjørn and suddenly felt both sheepish and primitive, because the question made it sound as if it was an enigma to him what an unmarried man and a woman might find to do together if it wasn't sexual. Schmidt looked like one big question mark.

Jørgensen noticed it, and his eyes sparkled with amusement again.

'Collector's book club, as a matter of fact. I once took the bus home from Århus and sat next to Karen. She wasn't very talkative. But we got chatting eventually. And when we started talking books, she woke up. We're both collectors, you see. The book of the month was some Swede, I remember. Excruciating, unoriginal, Karen felt the same way about him. And it was a wonderful talk. I was quite uplifted. And Karen said, just before she got off the bus, that I should stop by the vicarage now and then, so we could have a chat about literature. So I did. It's not exactly the kind of conversation you get at the town festival in Vilå, right?'

The last remark was delivered with a contemptuous snort, which did not go unnoticed by Vilå's local officer. Schmidt looked insulted.

'Why did the literary talk have to take place while the vicar wasn't home?' Bjørn tried. But he'd already given up.

'Well, initially I didn't know when he was around and when he wasn't. So the first few times, Thorkild came and sat with us. But it wasn't really the same when he was there. Not because the vicar is unintelligent, not at all. A very well-read gentleman. But Karen was just different when he was there. It's hard to pinpoint. But the mood was not the same.'

'Was she insecure when her husband was there?'

Asger Jørgensen considered it.

'No, that would probably be to simplify it. Karen was, in many ways, an insecure person, I think. Especially towards others. But she didn't seem insecure around her husband. You know, performance anxiety or that kind of banality. I think almost it seemed as if his presence irritated Karen. But it was very odd – because she had no great familiarity with me. I mean, Thorkild might as well have been there when we met – there was nothing improper or intimate about our conversations. But it was still nicer when he was not there. So I started to plan around it.'

Bjørn looked into his coffee cup, embarrassed without quite knowing why he felt embarrassed. Asger Jørgensen's kitchen, which they found themselves in, was tidy and spotless. On the table beside the stove lay a book, open but with the pages facing down. Bjørn glanced at it to see what it was. Asger Jørgensen beat him to it.

'It's an American novel. In fact, it was Karen's recommendation. She was convinced he was due a major breakthrough. While I have little difficulty in seeing it. It hasn't been translated into Danish.'

Bjørn got up, put his cup in the sink and said goodbye, Schmidt had already gone outside. An unfinished thought struck him as he stood in the doorway.

'Will you miss her, you think?'

Asger Jørgensen looked nonplussed.

'What do you mean?'

Bjørn shrugged and didn't quite know what he meant. That was how they parted.

At home, Bjørn started writing reports of the interviews with both Lily and Asger. He was always careful to get everything written down as soon as possible, so he could remember exactly what he'd heard. Details, even those he immediately dismissed as gossip. An investigation was a puzzle to be gathered in an unpredictable way, and pieces that at first didn't belong to the game, often turned out later to carry the central motifs. He looked for a long time at one of the pieces that Asger had given him.

It said:

An affair with Karen is something that never crossed my mind.

She's not the type you have an affair with. Too unapproachable, in a way. As if allowing you to be in her company is a big enough favour in itself.

He could not grasp what it meant. He gave up. Put the leash on Moos. He couldn't get to grips with Karen at all.

11

The darkness crept over Roslinge, starting from one end. It had a funny way of sneaking up, like a twilight that came oozing out from the woods and slowly made its way into town.

Summer evenings. Chilly, so people find their hidden cardigans, hoodies and other thicker fabrics from the closets.

Too chilly to see real summer-night children playing outside, way too late. Too late in the year for the scents of freshly cut grass and charcoal. Late summer evenings have a wistful sound and smell of overripe fruit and warm soil, a little hint of the great process of decay that is underway. The initial manoeuvres of autumn. A strange moment in time, until the harvest arrives with new wealth and until the combine harvester starts rolling around in the fields.

Bjørn Devantier liked these late summer evenings. On the whole, they were quiet. It was pleasant to walk around in Roslinge at dusk and know that everything was at peace, and that the nights were usually uneventful and without interrupted sleep. He liked to go there. Patrolling, guarding his town.

But although most of the three years he'd been married to Marie had been hard work, with books flying through the air, he actually missed her for the evening walks. There hadn't been much in Roslinge she'd bothered with. But she'd liked their evening walk. It was as if the town's silent breath and lilac-scented idyll, the dogs barking in the distance, even the birdsong and the muffled sounds of steady traffic on the nearby highway had had a calming influence on Marie. When he thought about his failed marriage, it was precisely those moments he thought they had been happy. Side by side on Roslinge's main street, they would rarely walk hand in hand, but still very together. A time-out before they would return home to the police station, and the fighting could resume.

Bjørn trudged down the main street. He was tired and still starving after his visit with Lily and Asger Jørgensen, and had begun to consider making the long trip to Århus to find a McDonald's when his phone rang. It was Jørgen Schmidt, whom he'd just said goodbye to at Asger's.

He'd always enjoyed working with Jørgen, his longstanding colleague. Jørgen was the hardboiled type of policeman with tough-woven muscles, a bushy red beard and a height that Bjørn envied him. It was an eternal fight to maintain authority when you were alone out here in the country. It was Bjørn's belief that when you were over 1.95 and weighed as much as Jørgen did, you would never have problems imposing your authority. At least as long as you didn't need to talk in that oddly high-pitched voice.

'Bjørn? Why aren't you answering your phone? I'm in front of your house. The red-haired technician from Århus called. And Thea Krogh.'

Bjørn could tell by Jørgen's thin voice that something important was coming even before he'd started his explanation.

'I was just taking a breather. I've fucking slaved away all day. I haven't eaten yet. What's happening?'

'Alice Caspersen says they're pretty sure that a body has been transported down to the river from the construction site. They've finally found blood remains up there, so it's solid.

Karen wasn't shot down by the creek. Up at the construction site, right where they've dug up the blood trace, they've also found tracks.'

'I thought there were tons of wheel tracks up there.'

'These were apparently left in the mud, out where it's soft. The car was driven thirty centimetres outside the gravel. Which is lucky, because it's hard as concrete, the construction site, but it was enough for it to leave an imprint. Apparently. Caspersen says it was left at the weekend. It has something to do with how solidified the print is and the composition of the mud and . . . what do I know. Anyway she's certain that the prints come from a big SUV. Oh, yes, they're quite capable, them Århusians.' Jørgen used the same tone he would have adopted if he'd called them crazy.

'But it's not definite that the tracks have anything to do with our case? There are people on the site at all times.'

'No, but hang on, now.'

Jørgen's voice became even more fragile when it got excited. He held a powerful dramatic pause.

'Well, I drive down your main street and I spot a grey Suzuki Grand Vitara, which is totally covered in mud! So I stop and grab a picture of the tyres with my mobile and send it to Caspersen, right? And she cannot say with a hundred per cent guarantee, but she says it probably is our car from the site. And what's more, it has probably been in contact with blood. And so she checks the licence plates.'

Bjørn felt his mood sink. He knew very well who drove a silver SUV in Roslinge.

'The car belongs to the grocer. Mogens Jepsen,' said Jørgen. With disbelief in his voice, yet a large exclamation mark. Mogens Jepsen's integrity was unassailable. He was the hub of the town's confidence. People bought on credit, you could even get money back with the goods at the end of the month for a very reasonable rate, and people invested their deepest secrets with Mogens too, confiding in him when there was no one else in the store. Schmidt wasn't aware of this, but he understood how small communities operate. Here, the grocer is not just anyone.

'We have been asked to go and pick him up. But dammit, Bjørn, we can't just walk in the store and grab him in front of all the customers?'

'They're closed. I'm there now. I can see the damn car from where I stand, Jørgen. Drive up here, we'll take a look at it.'

Jørgen was there in four minutes, and Bjørn got into his Toyota and took over the wheel. They drove a few car-lengths away from the Suzuki and waited. The supermarket was closed, but the light was turned on and a young, scrawny guy was sweeping the floor inside the porch.

'Mugge is settling accounts and closing the till,' Bjørn explained. 'He never leaves it to his employees. I don't think he and Elisabeth have been on vacation for the entire time I've lived in Roslinge, and rumour says it's because he will not trust that job with someone else. He's a skilled businessman, but paranoid as hell. He once came down to the station and asked for police protection. It was when they had that robbery in the Netto over at yours. It made Mugge nervous and he wanted me to be standing up here every evening at half-past nine, when he comes out with the money.'

'Get out of here!' Jørgen muttered.

'When Netto was robbed a second time, he asked again and threatened me with fire and brimstone. I was actually contemplating doing it for a little while – stand guard here. But then Marie said that if I had to sit up here and babysit every night, I shouldn't count on her being there when I got home.'

'Get out of here,' Jørgen said again, his thoughts elsewhere. 'Hey, someone's there!'

They had been waiting for about twenty minutes when a guy rushed out through the porch, past the sweeping staff member and sat behind the wheel of the Vitara in one smooth move.

'It's not Mogens,' Bjørn managed to say, but before they could react, the Suzuki was out on the road and accelerating. Bjørn and Jørgen went after it.

At the outskirts of town, Bjørn put the siren on the roof. It didn't make the Suzuki stop. Rather, it accelerated even more. Bjørn looked at Jørgen – would they pursue? Jørgen's face was steadfastly focused on the car in front of them. Bjørn handed him the microphone of the police radio and then concentrated on his driving.

Both cars had accelerated to a hundred and fifty on the straight and narrow road. Bjørn and Jørgen slowly gained on the Suzuki, both men tense and without exchanging a word. When they were right up behind it and had to run left of it, it slowed down. Bjørn tore at the steering wheel to complete the left turn, so they avoided a collision. The Suzuki swung a sharp right down a dirt road while the police car had to brake and ended up facing the opposite direction. Bjørn had to make a three-point turn before he could enter the narrow road and follow.

'Hell no,' cried Jørgen, excited. 'Go, go!'

On the dirt road they had no chance. The Vitara was superior to the terrain, and it was obvious that the driver knew what he was doing. Jørgen sat with the radio and the map and tried to orient himself, while the Toyota jumped and danced, and Bjørn seriously feared it would break an axle.

The Suzuki was far ahead in a cloud of dust.

'Where are we going?' cried Jørgen.

'Vadstrupgård. It's a dead end. He can't go any further!'

The Suzuki was approaching the impressive wooden gates of the Vadstrupgård Estate at the end of the road at breakneck speed, when a white car slowly emerged through the gate. The Suzuki was caught between the two cars that were moving towards it from opposite directions. Snorting with excitement, Bjørn pushed on, full throttle.

As the Suzuki passed the last poplars of the avenue, now dangerously close to the gate, they saw the white car brake sharply, then it skidded out and came to a halt across the road, blocking everything. They saw a man, presumably Steen Vadstrup, throw himself out of the car to avoid being caught in the inevitable collision. But instead of ploughing into the obstacle, the Suzuki held its course and speed, and executed a turn through an open barn door. Bjørn ran past the estate owner's car, avoided the man in the ditch and went after the car. The Suzuki wheel width fitted with the two slurry trenches inside the barn, while Jørgen's car was neither wide enough or tall enough. They drove up and down the two slurry trenches while the chassis dragged along the cement floor. At the end of the barn the Vitara slowed down, turned 90 degrees and snuck out of the other stable door, which barely fit the width of the car. Everything was going so fast. By the time the Vitara emerged from the yard and set off in the other direction, Bjørn was bogged down in the slurry trenches.

The Vitara had a big advantage on them.

When Bjørn and Jørgen made it back on the road and managed to get out of the yard, they saw the Vitara's rear end swing as it came to the curve and shoot into a new road on the other side. If the driver knew the area, he could very well disappear from them now.

'Hell and damnation,' Jørgen moaned. They roared back up the road, while the farmer yelled something at them and held his arms in front of his face to protect him from the gravel spray.

Halfway towards the highway they heard a big bang. Up on the highway they could see down the other road. There was a tractor with a trailer, which was parked. The Suzuki had tried to go around it, but had hit a poplar tree at the side of the road and was now wrapped around it.

'Now there's a kiss,' Jørgen noted, drily and bright. 'It's been a while since I've been in a car chase.'

'I think I hit a cat in Vadstrupgård,' Bjørn stammered, while the adrenalin in his blood bubbled and made him dizzy. Behind them, Steen Vadstrup came galloping, gesticulating wildly.

12

The driver of the Suzuki was not the grocer, Mogens Jepsen. His name was Torben Jepsen, they discovered, when he finally came to his senses in Bjørn's office an hour later. Neither Bjørn or Jørgen knew him. He was a grumpy-looking guy in his late thirties with tousled black hair that covered his forehead. He'd suffered a blow from the Vitara airbag and was somewhat groggy, but since they'd pulled him out of the wreckage, he'd said nothing. After they'd given him a glass of water and put him in handcuffs, he'd looked up at Bjørn and Jørgen with a vicious glare that was hard to decipher. Bjørn wondered if they should stop by the emergency room.

Meanwhile, Jørgen was having a heated argument over the phone with the owner of Vadstrupgård.

'You can get fifty, Steen. Anyone who has a cat worth seven thousand kroner can damn well afford to insure the thing. And I've no time for this. No, you cannot speak to Devantier! We have our hands full. I don't know if you happened to notice what we were doing when we hit your prize feline? Well, why don't you go right ahead and do that.' Jørgen slammed down the receiver and pressed the record button on Bjørn's old-fashioned tape recorder. 'And now spill, pal. I should warn you, I'm in no mood for games. Name!'

Jepsen snarled something.

'You want a lawyer, how about that? You have the right to remain silent. But you are obliged to provide your name. And you'd do well to tell us right about now.'

The man sneered again.

'Torben Holm Jepsen, I see. Got any ID? A driver's licence, perhaps? Even if your driving didn't seem like that of a man who's passed a driving test,' Jørgen thundered. He was brusque and in a bad mood, while Bjørn couldn't help smiling at the thought of the chase down the road. It had been cool, adrenalin-pumped; a car chase was not an everyday occurrence in Roslinge.

'I have nothing on me. It's at home with my cousin. Mugge. Call him. My cards are in the outer pocket of my duffel bag.'

'You can be assured that we will, so no bullshit.'

'Relax, will you? Call him.'

Torben Jepsen scratched a phone number down on a napkin, and Jørgen stuck it in his pocket.

Bjørn took over.

'Did you park the car last Friday or Saturday at the construction site on the other side of the creek?'

Torben looked nervous. He spoke into the water-soaked cold cloth that he held against a bump on the side of his head.

Without speaking, Jørgen waved away the cloth and pointed to the tape recorder. Torben spoke again, this time more clearly:

'I have nothing, OK? That's why I'm here in your piece of shit town. To get back on my feet.' He sneered it out so that the officers knew that the revival was not his own project.

'You know, otherwise I wouldn't fucking be here. I've had some . . . personal problems. I lost my job and the house in this recession. Not that it's any of your business. Mogens and Elisabeth have said that I could stay with them for a while. He's even given me a so-called job. I fiddle about in the shop and take care of the recycled bottles. Then Mogens can really feel like he's rescuing me.'

His voice was thick with contempt, but it was uncertain

whether it was directed against the well-meaning cousin or Torben Jepsen himself.

'I borrow the Vitara every now and again. Mogens doesn't like it, doesn't want me driving it. But sometimes Elisabeth says I can take it. I did on Friday.'

'How long did you have it?'

'I drove to the shop mid-afternoon. At three, I think. I'd promised to sweep the floors. I think it was like that.'

'Again: how long did you have it?'

'I was supposed to stay until closing time.'

'When? Give me a time of day.'

Torben said nothing.

'Torben, we have reason to believe that the car you borrowed has been used to transport Karen, the vicar's wife, dead or alive, to the place by the river where she was dumped. Our technicians are checking it as we speak. But they can already confirm the overall picture: there is mud from the construction site, the wheel print is similar to tracks left at the construction site, where Karen's body was dropped, and finally there are traces of blood in the car. Karen's blood.'

The latter was not entirely true, the blood hadn't yet been matched, but Bjørn felt very confident about the outcome. Alice Caspersen had already done the initial sweep of the Vitara's trunk and quickly spotted the few black spots in the dark felt. Blood mixed with dust. Someone had cleaned the trunk, but it had been rushed.

Torben remained silent. Through the door, Bjørn could see Thea Krogh parking her Mondeo.

'Torben Jepsen, you are under arrest. You should get a lawyer, you don't have to answer any questions before you are properly represented. Do you understand that?'

Torben continued to look at the floor. He shook his head.

'Torben, did you murder Karen Simonsen? Have you driven her or otherwise helped someone who did? Do you know something?'

'I haven't done anything. And certainly not –' he tasted

the words with disbelief '– murdered someone. It's . . . it's crazy. This can't be right. You don't know what you're talking about.'

'This is bloody important. If you don't have anything to do with it, say so for Christ's sake, so we can move forward!'

'Yes, well . . .' Torben Jepsen hesitated. 'I haven't told Mugge this. And you're not going to believe me anyway. But the car was stolen.'

'Stolen. Aha! How about that.'

Jepsen's gaze was empty with fear as the reality of it all dawned on him.

'Yes, I borrowed the car on Friday. And when I came to pick it up on Saturday morning, it was parked somewhere else.'

'What do you mean?'

'I know I parked it right outside the supermarket. At the kerb on the main street. Hell, I was only supposed to be in there for a couple of hours.'

'Five hours. The supermarket closed at eight.'

'Yes, yes. But when I came back to get it, it was parked like a hundred metres down the road.'

'Why didn't you take the car home on Friday night? Wasn't that why you borrowed it? What is it we're supposed to believe here?'

'Well, I finished up in the shop . . . Don't say anything to Mugge about this.'

Jørgen Schmidt snorted.

'How old are you, seriously? Don't tell Mugge? Don't count on it.'

Jepsen flinched.

'I called a pal of mine from Århus. He came out here, and so we sat and drank some beers in the store. Like a beer tasting.' He smiled distantly. 'Mugge has a nice little selection. Especially the Belgian beer, the brunettes and the blondes. He's arranged a corner of the store, have you seen it? With an old wine barrel he uses as a table and a large collection of beer mugs and a few posters from Oktoberfest on the walls. The funny thing is that I can remember when he had it made. It was back when he thought I was worth something. So he invited me and my ex-wife for dinner, steak and béarnaise sauce and little hostess gifts, the works, and then we went into the shop and tasted some of the stuff he'd ordered.'

Torben Jepsen paused, as if he'd given enough explanation.

'You had your own little celebration. Is that what you're saying?'

'Well, things disappear all the time. Who's to say the beers weren't stolen from the shop by some teenager, right?'

'And then?'

'I wasn't going to drive home drunk, of course. I tell you, if anything happens to that car, Mugge will go to his grave.'

Torben looked up with a rascal smile to Bjørn.

'This is serious, Torben. Who is your friend?'

'Leif. Leif Birkerød. He's a bartender in Århus. But listen up, Leif went home before me, around midnight, he had to work. I sat for another hour. I showed him out and had a fag before he drove off, I saw him go. And the car was right where it should be.'

'OK. We'll check it, of course. Not least how a bartender who's been sat drinking out in Roslinge can make it back to Århus at that time without driving drunk. But how the hell would someone take the car?'

'Well, the keys were in it, I guess.'

'And you haven't told anybody about this, because everything is a bit too embarrassing. Drinking beer, stealing from your benefactor, leaving his expensive car open and up for grabs all night while sleeping on his couch – and you act like it's nothing!' Bjørn deliberately used the word 'benefactor' to provoke Jepsen. He recalled one of the courses in interviewing techniques he'd attended; it was a so-called trigger word.

It had the desired effect. Jepsen raised his voice several decibels.

'Yes, yes, it's probably something like that! Hell, I'm just trying to survive, OK? I don't have a damn thing and two kids I'm paying towards. And I've been blacklisted by the unemployment fund because I've screwed up some ridiculous form. I didn't even know you could fill it out wrong.'

'It sounds like an old wives' tale, mate,' said Jørgen. 'And now you seriously want us to believe that someone stole a car that happens to have traces of mud and blood in it? What did you have against Karen Simonsen, Torben? Were you in love with her? Did you see her that night, drunk and furious? Are you missing your wife? Did you take it out on Karen?'

Torben looked at him, calmly.

'You know something, officer? I didn't even know her name was Karen.'

Thea Krogh was just on the other side of the door, Bjørn could see her silhouette, she was listening attentively.

'Back to Friday,' he said. 'Did you go directly to Mogens and Elisabeth's from the supermarket when you were done drinking?'

'Yes. Probably quarter past one. I didn't meet a soul. It's so disgustingly quiet at night here in town, not a sound, I usually listen to my iPod, but I left it at home. The silence out here is worse than the worst neighbourhoods in Copenhagen at night. I was drunk and frightened, I ran the last stretch home. And so I slept it off on the couch. All night, until I went to get rolls from the baker the next morning. Both Mogens and Elisabeth were at home, and her parents were there as well, for fuck's sake – they visit on weekends. That's why I slept on the couch, right? That shit couch all night with the dog on top of me because her parents must have the guest room. You can ask them. I couldn't even risk going to the toilet in the night because I didn't want that stupid mongrel waking the whole house.

You know Bisse, right, Officer? Runs off all the time. Angry little bastard. It barked like mad when I got home a little after one, and Elisabeth came out in her dressing gown and asked if I could get it to shut up. That would be what you call an alibi, right?'

'No, actually it's not. If it's true, then it offers an explanation as to your whereabouts for only a portion of the night. Not all of it,' said Bjørn, as he recalled the infernal sound of the little devil of a Pekingese.

'Before one o'clock, I was with Leif – talk to him! And Saturday morning I went to the bakery, but if you think I can commit a murder and buy rolls on the way home in fifteen minutes, I'm fucking Flash Gordon! I haven't killed anyone, you must believe me. Dammit, I didn't even know who died.'

The voice was suddenly husky with anxiety. 'Listen, Saturday morning I get up early to get the car home before Mogens realises it's missing. I go to the bakery. I see that it isn't parked outside the supermarket, as it should be. But just as I start to panic, I notice it's a hundred metres further down. I run over there and check it, it looks good, although it has muddy tyres. It's probably some boys, I think to myself. They've seen it parked with the key in and they've been out driving in the ploughed fields. There's no harm done, I drive it home, end of story.'

The man in front of them looked very tired.

'Why did you run from us, Torben, if you have nothing to hide? What was the whole race thing about?' said Bjørn.

'Well, I wasn't thinking. I just drove, I had to make the pharmacy in Vilå and suddenly you're there behind me with the siren and everything. And then I thought immediately that it was something to do with the car, right? That I'd probably done something wrong. Mogens had found out somehow, or maybe about the beers, and he'd called the police on me. I don't know, I didn't think much. Everything has just been so rotten and I didn't want to end up in the clutches of the police, OK? I didn't think it would be a problem to slip away from you, when I had an SUV.'

'It's too thin. Torben, we'll check your alibi, we'll check your explanation. But on the basis of what you've told us so far, you are under arrest.'

Torben Jepsen lowered his head.

'How bad is the car?'

'Totally smashed. I hope for your sake the grocer has good insurance.'

The man smiled.

'I'm sure he does. He's insured up to his neck. But I feel sorry for Elisabeth. Boy, I really do. She was the one who said I could take it. Even though I wasn't allowed to, thanks to Mogens. I'd actually thought of buying something for her. For some of the bottle money.'

'Fuck off, Jepsen. Don't push your luck,' said Jørgen.

Torben Jepsen sent him another rascal look from under his fringe.

'I'm just kidding.'

'You shouldn't be kidding right now, joker. You're in Roslinge, not at home at Nørrebro. And as far as the grocer's wife is concerned, this would be a good time to start pulling the chestnuts out of the fire and promise her flowers from the Q8 petrol station. She's out in the front office and would like to speak with you. I'll be damned if she doesn't look like she's worried about your sorry ass.'

Jepsen's mouth twitched a little. Bjørn looked at Jørgen, who thankfully didn't comment.

13

There was a cool breeze over town. Maybe it was the east wind that brought coolness with it all the way from Århus bay. It felt like a warning of autumn. The breeze scattered the clouds that had hung over Roslinge as a constant blanket for several days now. Scattered rays of sun fell on the roofs. It was a cold light. A departure from late summer's normal soft glow. Thea stuck out her tongue to see if she could taste the salt in the air. She knew the North Sea weather, and now what she longed for was a salty west wind that could cleanse the pores. There was also an atmosphere permeating the town that needed to be cleansed. The breeze was merely a reflection of what she wanted. So East Jutland, undramatic. As the sun fell, the roofs of the town seemed different. She watched them from the skylight in her room at the local station. For her, tiles were a symbol of Denmark. The red roofs were famous both on Bornholm and Skagen and everything in between, and the red-brick buildings were known throughout the country, unlike in other parts of the world where it was all whitewashed houses in different colours. In recent years, it was as if the distinctive trademark of the tile roofs had come to signal how much diversity there was. Here and there were black glazed tiles with sharp reflections of the sun, while the old red roofs soaked up the sun with their green algae growth. There must be many pig farms nearby, she thought, with the algae. I wonder if it's pig farmers who can afford glazed brick? She didn't know much about farming or the residents of this small town. She sighed. She'd been six days in Roslinge – travelling to and fro, admittedly – but six days nonetheless.

Roslinge sat on a river bank. Main street and the creek ran parallel courses north of the river as it meandered on towards the Bay of Århus. The town formed a long axis, with main street stretching between the old village school at one end and the modern gym at the other. At first sight it seemed an odd choice of priorities: a small school and a large fitness centre. But the school catered for the area in conjunction with the municipality's other schools as part of a carefully conceived plan. The fitness centre, however, was the only one of its kind for miles and therefore had a large customer base. In the middle of the main street was a square with a supermarket, and, a little set back from the road, the whitewashed village church dating back to the Middle Ages – the era when church-building reached its peak. The combined vicarage and parish community centre was on the other side of the church, towards the creek.

The creek flanked the town. True, new houses were being built on the far side, but Roslinge residents were sceptical of whether the area could ever be integrated. So far, there wasn't even a bridge. Until now there had been no call for a bridge. The carpenter in Roslinge, who was a subcontractor for the new estate, drove out to the highway to cross. Running along the creek on the Roslinge side was a path. It went past the vicarage and carried on in the direction of the school until it reached the old mill outside of town. Along the way it connected with a path that led up to the school. The school's official access was the entrance on main street. Most children, however, took advantage of a separate paved cycle track enclosed by tall privet hedges that extended from the town square. On the main street was also an old inn, a local bank, a bakery, a bookshop and a small branch of one of the big chains of estate agents. In addition there was a hobby shop that specialised in model trains, and a pizzeria run by the town's only immigrant family. Clearly at one time there had been many more shops. Main street was dotted with shop windows that were covered with faded sheets, with partly eroded inscriptions still visible in the red stone. You could still make out words like 'Draper' and 'Perms'. Part of the town's commercial life revolved around the petrol station out by the highway, which boasted the town's second highest turnover, after the supermarket. Finally, there was the scout house out in the woods and the local heating plant, whose connection fee was so high that it kept house prices well below the average for the surrounding towns.

The forensic pathologists had completed the autopsy and the police had given permission for Thorkild Christensen to bury his wife, which was why the lone bell of the white-washed church tower was tolling at this moment. And in front of the supermarket, newspaper placards informed passers by of the arrest of Torben Jepsen, the new suspect in the case.

The Death Driver of Roslinge: Karen's blood found in car.

It was an insensitive display, given that the funeral procession would follow this route.

As she studied the placards, doubts surfaced in Thea's mind. The blood in the car. The thin alibi. The grocer's unflattering testimony about his cousin's character. Was it a breakthrough?

Torben Jepsen had no criminal record, no previous offences. But he was listed at RKI as a defaulter, had been through a bitter divorce and lost his job – had basically lost everything. And to lose everything could, in principle, drive people to do anything if they were desperate enough.

She recalled her own interrogation of Torben Jepsen. Had she been faced with a desperate man?

Later in the day she got a call from her boss, Anne-Grethe. Thea had been expecting the call. A quick congratulations and seeking assurance that the case was drawing to an end, so resources could be channelled elsewhere. Thea kicked off her boots, lay down on the room's uncomfortable little couch and thought of other matters while the boss spoke. And this did not go unnoticed by Anne-Grethe.

'Tell me something, Thea, where are you?'

'In Roslinge. I'm in a room at the local station.'

'You've moved in there?'

'It helps me think. Understand this place.'

She could almost see Schalborg rolling her eyes through the phone line. But at the same time there was a hint of reluctant admiration in the boss's voice.

'As I said, I need you to understand the place a bit faster. It's the silly season. We've been on the front page of the tabloids six days in a row, Thea. We can't have that. I very much hope that you see the matter as finished now and will be back here on Monday.'

Thea surprised herself by letting her amusement show in her voice.

'No, I realise we can't possibly have that – people breathing down your neck. Journalists are complete and utter *vultures* –' she exaggerated the word on purpose, then in a regretful tone continued '– but it's not as if the killer has walked into Roslinge station and turned himself in. We're working out here, Anne-Grethe. And we need to pursue this. There are still leads to be followed up, and in any case we need more info on Torben Jepsen. I'll be out here at least until Monday. Plus there's the annoying little detail that he refuses to admit that he did it. It's not a confession. There will never be a confession. You might as well prepare yourself for that.'

The phone went silent.

'If I didn't know better, Thea,' said Schalborg slowly, 'I'd say you were enjoying yourself. You like it out there in Roslinge.'

'Honestly, Anne-Grethe, I just don't get the point of these phone calls where the boss rings up, pushing for a breakthrough. As if it's merely a question of us doing something differently or better, and then we'll have our man. Someone's been shot and killed, presumably by an individual who has gone to a great deal of trouble to prevent us finding out who he is. You cannot order the case closed. You cannot tell me that I am handling this case incompetently. And yet you call me. I suppose it's all part of the game, so I'm just playing along.'

Schalborg sighed. And then came the bombshell:

'I don't necessarily think it's helpful when the entire police squad is seen trotting along the main street in Roslinge armed with paper bags from the bakery.'

That took Thea by surprise.

'You are joking. A lunch break! And someone phoned and told you about that? So who was it, Anne-Grethe, an outraged taxpayer? Or one of my "loyal" investigators?'

'Don't be paranoid, Thea. Good heavens, I don't have a mole hidden in your troops. I happened to be driving past. I have a grandchild out in Vilå. As a matter of fact, I waved at you. I simply feel you could be a little more discreet in this regard.'

'What regard? Lunch? Am I supposed to take this seriously?'

'Save it, Thea,' Anne-Grethe cut her off. 'Your righteous indignation is apparently also part of the game. We'll deal with it another time. In the meantime, I'll send Kristian Videbæk out. Purely to wrap things up – I can assure of you that. All the best.'

Thea put the phone down. More than anything she was angry with herself for letting Anne-Grethe get her all worked up. She sat on the window sill and gazed out at the rooftops again. Put her forehead against the window and felt the first tickling in the throat, the beginning of a cold.

Then the phone rang. It was Alice Caspersen. She had located the crime scene.

14

The investigation had established a permanent base at Roslinge local police station. Thea had insisted that, if she could stay in Roslinge, the other members of the team could find their way there, if only to hold group meetings. It had been six days since they had found Karen.

It was evident from the walls that Bjørn's office was now the team's headquarters. The articles on Moos' excellence in various competitions and selections had been sacrificed to make way for schedules, scribbled notes and black-and-white charts, photographs of various individuals that had been annotated with names and data, each graded on a scale of one to ten depending on their relevance to the investigation. The one with the highest score was obviously Torben Jepsen, the fleeing driver of the grocer's, his cousin's, Suzuki. The waste-paper bins were overflowing with pizza boxes and fast-food packaging from hastily snatched meals. And then there was the coffee, whose aroma was again the one bright spot in the gloom. Today Bjørn had baked a cake to go with the coffee. He was not accustomed to his Århus colleagues' taste for takeaways, which seemed to him extravagant. *Out here, we try and save the tax payers' money* was one of his favourite sayings, to which his colleagues responded by laughing and drawing little halos over their heads. In the corner, Jørgen Schmidt was going over the details of the car chase for the umpteenth time with Søren Edvardsen. Søren was his usual silent and moody self, but that didn't prevent Jørgen from making sure that the most important points were spoken out loud and in Thea's direction. For example, he made a point of saying how it would have been nice if the police invested in vehicles that could handle terrain such as slurry trenches.

Today, however, there was a feeling of closure in the room. Torben Jepsen was on remand in Århus Prison. The blood in the grocer's car was a match for Karen Simonsen. And although the case hadn't formally been closed, it was considered a given that these long days in the basement room broken only by snatched naps on foam mattresses in the hallway were drawing to an end.

Thea kicked off the meeting by asking Jørgen to brief the team on the arrest of Torben Jepsen. Everyone at the table looked at Jørgen. Conscious of this, his voice squeaked even more than usual as he retold the story, accompanied by dramatic outbursts and gestures, and dry interjections from Bjørn.

Kristian Videbæk had arrived. He remained in the background, studying the papers of the case so far and rarely looking at Thea.

Thea informed them that Torben Jepsen had been through the preliminary hearing and would be held in provisional custody for eight days while they set about proving that he should be prosecuted for more than reckless driving.

'. . . And the cat homicide,' Bjørn added. Thea smiled.

'But we must not let our investigation focus blindly on Torben Jepsen. Let us bear in mind what else we have,' she said.

Alice Caspersen took over.

'The time of the murder we estimate at roughly – and here, let me emphasise the word roughly – early Saturday morning. It's in the late end of the range of possibilities my research pointed to, but still quite possible.'

'And since she was the one who gave us the scene of the crime, that means we're now paying a bit more attention to Anika Svendsen. According to her statement the shooting occurred on Saturday morning,' Thea added.

'Exactly,' said Alice, satisfied. 'You are all aware of the crime scene, right? I've conducted practically archaeological excavations the length of the entire path, and now it's finally paid off. The murder took place on the winding stretch that runs along the river towards the mill. It was a well chosen location, not overlooked from either side. The only way the killer would have been seen was if someone came along the path. And that makes early morning the ideal time. When you think about, it was the only logical place. We found Karen's blood there. Someone has made an effort to remove it, and the rain has done its best to eliminate traces. But it was there.'

'No bullets, though,' said Edvardsen.

'No, no bullets yet. And it's proving extremely difficult to locate them, or give you a precise idea of the murder weapon. We've been doing our best. But when the body is moved, it's hard to know where to look, especially in a bog. However we can tell you that Karen was transported to the building site in Mogens Jepsen's Grand Vitara, and then she was dumped in the creek. Presumably, the murderer hoped to hinder our investigations with that manoeuvre.'

'He succeeded,' observed Edvardsen.

'He did,' Alice admitted. 'We have blood and dirt and everything else in the car, so there is no doubt that it's been used in connection with the killing. Unfortunately, we don't have much else. The car is full of prints: Mogens', Elisabeth's, Torben Jepsen's. But nothing useful in the trunk. And the steering wheel is a veritable goldmine of bacteria and fingerprints. Any half-decent lawyer will see to it that we can't get a conviction based solely on that.'

Now, Jørgen Schmidt spoke up.

'It's fairly obvious, isn't it? Torben Jepsen shot Karen, probably a crime of passion. Or he did it in collaboration with the lovely Elisabeth, who seems determined to fight his corner. She insists that he came home on Saturday evening, she backs up his alibi. And he's her alibi – she was also seen down at the creek, remember? It's obvious that Jepsen will do anything for her. But she has plenty of motives. Just think of the lover – Asger Jørgensen. Virtually all crime is about sex or money.'

Bjørn joined in.

'Asger Jørgensen may just be the link we need. Elisabeth and Karen could have fought over him. Elisabeth is seen down by the river, crying, shots are heard. It's a few too many coincidences, I reckon. And Torben Jepsen's explanation is too far-fetched. A classic. My car has been used for a crime? Oh yes, it was stolen, I forgot to mention it.'

Thea nodded.

'It's possible. But at the same time it's still too vague. All we have is an elderly, confused woman who makes a questionable identification. I agree that the evidence we have so far points in one direction. But there are also a number of dead ends. Traps that we need to avoid. For example, the grocer says he slept next to his wife all night, and that they got up together on Saturday – and he's hardly likely to be involved in a conspiracy to benefit his wife's alleged lover. They had guests, her parents. They ate bread rolls. Torben's drunken friend Leif confirms the story in almost every respect. I think it's thin ice.'

Thea walked over to the board and the photograph of Asger Jørgensen.

'According to you, just three days ago Asger Jørgensen was not a person of interest. Neither was Elisabeth. You were confident of this, as was Schmidt.'

'But it all fits,' Bjørn said.

Thea paused.

'We mustn't be blinded, that's all I'm saying,' she said. In a voice that made it clear there would be no argument, she went on: 'We have no evidence. Let's not ignore our initial gut feelings when we interviewed these people. Your sense of Asger was that he was not sexually involved with Karen. And that he appeared to be telling the truth.'

She caught Kristian's gaze and tried to interpret it, but failed.

'A liar is a liar,' he said. 'And the brightest ones can easily fool a police investigator, no matter how competent he is. Torben Jepsen, Elisabeth Jepsen, Thorkild Christensen – they could all be lying through their teeth, they all have motives. I don't know enough yet.'

Thea drew a deep breath.

'To sum up: Torben Jepsen is on remand. He's our prime suspect for the murder of Karen Simonsen. But we have no motive as yet. You may well be right in assuming that he's our man. There's much to support that theory. But we don't know for sure. And until we do, all options are to be kept open. I agree that Torben's explanation is pretty thin, but that doesn't necessarily mean it's untrue. People have the strangest reasons to do the strangest things.'

'Indeed,' said Edvardsen drily, clearly addressing Thea.

Bjørn felt uncomfortable with the atmosphere. Mindful of his role as host, he passed the cake around.

'Banana Cake. Marie's recipe. Help yourselves, there's plenty.' He fumbled for the cake forks in the cutlery drawer, which made a noisy contrast to the plastic cups being passed out from beside the coffee machine.

There was silence while the cake made its way around. Thea seized the opportunity.

'Torben Jepsen is a prime suspect. All other options are kept open. We continue with the same tasks as before. Karen's life and activities, her calendar with the mysterious "B". Asger – we need fresh eyes on him. Alice, we need to re-examine the scene. Bjørn, everyone in town needs to be questioned about the car – who has seen it and where it was seen. Then we have to review every piece of evidence – that'll be your top priority, Alice. Søren, you're the anchor man on Torben and Elisabeth and Mogens and the whole family. I want you to talk to Elisabeth again. Kristian – we need someone at headquarters to run comparisons with other cases, weapons in the area, etc. We have eight days to get something on the table before the remand expires. As for Thorkild Christensen, I will talk to him again myself.'

15

Local news, parish of Vilå.
The World According to Men of Letters

Finally Roslinge has been hit.

Accidents happen only to the neighbours. Not a neighbour in specific terms. But accidents, violence, evil – these things are not to be found in our own pond. These are things we read about in national newspapers, things that happen elsewhere, in places we think there is something wrong with. High levels of crime, too many immigrants, unemployment. Here, where we call home, there are no such atrocities.

A week ago, the vicar's wife was killed in Roslinge. What will it do to us? What will become of Roslinge?

In order for something to have an identity, it must remain true to something. When people are loyal, they're predictable. You can trust what they're going to do. There is an immutable core, a little dog in all of us that is steadfast. It makes people, communities, towns recognisable.

Has Roslinge now become unfaithful? Suddenly it's impossible to tell what each new day will bring, what surprises the town and its people will throw up. Roslinge is no longer true to its small size, its reputation for anonymity, tranquillity.

'It's going to affect real estate prices negatively,' we'll say in the bank. 'We're stuck in Roslinge,' we'll say in the houses on the other side of the river, even though no one has moved out of the area in recent years. 'Imagine what others will say about us,' we say to our fellow parishioners. We'll notice an increase in Sunday-afternoon traffic on main street. 'To think, we've finally become a tourist attraction,' we will rejoice in the Chamber of Trade. No doubt Roslinge will soon surrender to Sunday shopping in order to capitalise on its newfound infamy.

But amid all this, we've lost someone. I had the great pleasure of knowing Karen Simonsen. The most peaceful woman I've ever met.

Evil is not true evil because of its ability to hit the places we expect. True evil is the fact that it hits randomly, in the places we least expect it. In Roslinge, in the vicarage garden, in Karen's life. In the midst of peace itself. Therein lies our reason to fear evil.

Asger Jørgensen

16

She has never cared much for people. For all that she has longed for them, thought about them, dreamed about them.

That she would be freed from this loneliness once and for all by a man who would take her in and love her, and he would be the one she would let in.

She imagined it so many times. She would lie in bed at night and dream of his arms around her, feel his breath on her neck when he lay close to her and slept. Imagined his kiss on her shoulder when he awoke.

Through the passing years she held on to the belief that he had to come one day, even as she grew older. Because that's the way things are supposed to go. Even in the darkest solitude, you will meet someone some day, a person you want to let in.

And then you will, magically, find the courage. To talk to

him, reach out for him and hold him close and be allowed to. Him, she will let in.

When he showed up, it was stronger than she'd ever dreamed.

The nights she'd used to dream became sleepless, ecstatic. Joyous and painful. It was better than she'd dared to imagine. And much, much worse.

But she'd let him in, she had dared to. That was the most important thing.

Her life has become one long round of waiting for him, she feels like a big, quivering nerve. Listening for her phone, endlessly checking her messages, looking out the window in case he shows up unannounced, as he sometimes does.

But it doesn't bother her that much. After years of waiting for nothing, her life is all about waiting for him. She lets herself be wrapped up in the feeling. Happiness, when he's there. Grief when he is not.

For grief is what tortures her, paralysing her and making her a stranger to herself.

Yet she has let him in. And she has a lifetime's worth of accumulated, unused feelings to indulge in her love, her luck and her tragedy.

She's his. She loves to be his. And he's hers.

She sits on her sofa with the TV on and waits for the phone's dark display to light up. A candle in the window to show him the way, if he comes. He's said he might, but maybe he won't. And she feels happy, indeed this is when she's happiest, because it can go both ways. Either he comes, and everything is wild and fierce, magnificent and frightening. Or he doesn't, and she goes to bed with a broken heart. But then come the text messages, making it up to her after the disappointment of being let down. She deletes them always, faithfully, but grudgingly. And smiling through her tears.

She *feels*.

She laughs at herself when she hears steps on the stairs

and feels the warmth in her stomach. Such a wonderful feeling! She imagines being married to him and waiting until he comes home from work. Will she ever stop feeling butterflies in her stomach when she knows he's on his way?

There's a knock at the door, and she remembers to stroke her hand through her hair and lick her lips wet before she opens it.

But there is no trembling of the hands here. The person before her takes a deep breath, levels a weapon at her and charges ahead, chasing her into the apartment.

PART 2

17

Thea hurried into her living room leaving a trail of wet foot-prints. She turned on the television just in time to see the camera zoom in on the news reader, and then began shedding layers of sodden clothing, drenched from the autumn downpour.

Fifteen days after the murder of Karen Simonsen and she was back in her own apartment. To everyone's surprise the investigation had ground to a complete halt. The press, the leadership as personified by Anne-Grethe Schalborg, the investigators working the case – they had all thought the detention of Torben Jepsen marked a real breakthrough. Jepsen remained in custody, and the judge had granted them another three weeks to hold him while they continued their inquiries. But the fact was that, over the past week, the investigation hadn't budged an inch. They just kept pursuing the same leads, feeling all the while that the trail was growing colder. They'd gone back and re-interviewed witnesses, conducted repeated interrogations, only to deliver the same results but with less clarity. People's memories could be astonishingly short when it came to the crucial details. And repeated questioning seemed to have the effect of freezing the image in the mind, so that no fresh details came to light. It was a phenomenon Thea had come across in the past and she'd done her best to prevent it by insisting that they must not narrow their focus, but it had happened regardless. It was too much of a struggle for the imagination to keep coming up with alternative lines of questioning, so gradually they resorted to asking Torben Jepsen, Asger Jørgensen, Elisabeth Jepsen and of course Thorkild Christensen the same old questions. For his part, Torben Jepsen continued to defend his statement down to the smallest detail. Far-fetched as it had seemed in the beginning, not one part of it could be proved untrue.

The press had taken to using metaphors of decay and stagnation to describe police efforts. A few politicians who were premature in believing that an election was imminent had begun politicising the case with demands for increased resources and stricter control of the police. Anne-Grethe was constantly on the phone to Thea. But the most frustrated and annoyed of them all was undoubtedly Thea Krogh herself. She'd worked the case relentlessly, whipping everyone into shape. She'd kept abreast of every last detail in order to maintain an overview of the case – which thus far had generated almost 200 interviews with Roslinge residents and others, who, for various reasons, had known Karen Simonsen, along with 37 forensic reports detailing findings of soils, clothing fibres, tyres tracks and everything else. She'd committed these details to memory so she would be able to compare any given detail with the whole picture. But to no avail. It was as if Autumn had hit the case, and there was nothing she could do to prevent the clues getting colder and dimmer and darker.

So, after a two-week stay at the police station in Roslinge, she was home again. There'd been a slight stirring of homeliness when she opened the door to her apartment in northern Århus. Not with the sigh of relief that many people feel when they step over their own threshold and let clothes and possessions fall to the floor with a thud. But a welcome hint of herself, a fragrance that soothed her, and not least a warm bed that was welcome after fourteen nights in a sleeping bag in the cold room at the station. Her mother had once said that the apartment was like Thea herself. An apartment like any other. Neat but not flashy or otherwise remarkable. No unnecessary decorations, stucco ceilings, bay windows, Jacuzzis or other frivolities. Above all practical, functional. Back when Thea was in her late twenties and mired in an over-ripe rebellion against her mother, the comparison hurt her feelings. Now, at the age of thirty-nine, it amused her somewhat and she was comfortable with the image. She liked the apartment, the bright furniture mixed with large, bulky heirlooms in black mahogany. She thought that her mother was right, and that it was a compliment. And when she occasionally bought new kitchen utensils, a plant, or put a picture on the wall, her mother's words would come back to her. So any addition to the place was an addition to herself. Which was why she was careful in choosing what – and especially who – was allowed over the threshold.

She'd heard the news on the radio on the way home, and now focused intently on catching the rest. Wet and half-naked with her soaked trousers down around her ankles.

'Last night, a forty-two-year-old woman was found dead in her apartment in Vindbygårde, north of Aalborg. Police have concluded that it is a homicide, but are refusing at this stage to comment on the investigation.'

Thea didn't catch the local reporter's name because her head was momentarily stuck in the wet T-shirt she was peeling off. The cold struck her skin, unwelcoming, and she turned up the nearest thermostat.

'. . . Unconfirmed reports say the woman was shot sometime over the weekend, and had been lying dead for three or four days before her brother discovered the body. Police have no immediate suspects and there have been no arrests. We will bring you further developments as the case unfolds.'

Thea made a mental note to contact the police in Aalborg.

She listened to the rest of the news broadcast, distracted, while she dried her hair and had some dinner.

Next day she went to headquarters to catch up on paperwork.

'Care for company?'

Kristian Videbæk was edging his way towards Thea with his tray of cafeteria food. She'd spent the morning organising her email, overcome by a sudden urge to get the Roslinge case out of her head completely, just for one morning. And it had proved successful. She'd switched off her brain while she waded through her inbox, sorting emails, archiving most of them under the category 'out of sight, out of mind': some as spam, others under 'read later'. Seeing the 'unread messages' count dwindle had given her a huge, slightly embarrassed sense of satisfaction. A few she'd dealt with straight away. She'd rejected three invitations to participate in cyberspace social networks – a friend from high school, a former colleague and one of her mother's friends. She'd jotted down the names of two journalists who wanted her to call back. Studied a bank statement and said yes to a birthday invitation from her little nephew.

Refreshed, she had gone to the canteen at lunchtime, hoping to run into Kristian Videbæk. Although they'd seen quite a bit of each other during the investigation, they'd had remarkably little private time together. Thea missed his presence, missed the intimate moments. Things other lovers took for granted, like a night together, were rarely an option for them, so even a conversation with him over lunch felt like a blessing. And rare that they shared lunch outside of formal office meetings, because Kristian was very concerned that their preference for each other's company should not be too obvious.

He looked tired, she noted. He was still working biker crime, although Anne-Grethe had seconded him to the Roslinge case. Cases involving biker gangs were incredibly frustrating; although they seldom delivered on their threats, the bikers were keen on sending menacing letters to investigators and journalists, often in the form of clumsily spelled notes delivered to people's private addresses. It was intimate and uncomfortable, even for seasoned professionals like Kristian. Thea often thought to herself that much police work was best suited to those who did not have other commitments. She thought of the wives who occasionally turned up at police headquarters in the small hours wearing nightclothes and boots, sobbing with a child in their arms. In search of the remnants of the reliable man they had married, their children's father. Instead, they found over-worked, distracted investigators, high on caffeine and adrenalin, who called for taxis and sent them back home. Police work is draining. Despite the recruitment pamphlets' promises of teamwork, excellent training and career opportunities, it seemed best suited to individualists, lone wolves, zealous watchdogs and those with Asperger's syndrome. The ones who could sink their teeth into a case and bury themselves in it without fear of letting their loved ones down. People like her.

Thea had hoped that they could forget about work, but Kristian wanted to discuss the new murder in Vindbygårde. The one that had been mentioned in the news the day before.

'Have you looked at it, Thea?'

'Yes, I've looked at it. I heard about it yesterday. Today, I read everything I could find. Forty-two-year-old woman, killed north of Aalborg. Shot. Also gunshot wounds to her hands.'

He smiled. 'Stigmata, according to the journalists. They're milking it for all it's worth, trying to suggest that there's a hidden message in the MO.'

'Doesn't seem to have anything to do with our case.'

Kristian bit his lip and went to war on his pasta salad.

'No, you'd probably know, if you've looked at it.'

'I've looked at all there was to see. It's not much, so far.'

She looked into his face, searching for something new, but didn't find it. She welcomed Kristian's input, and experience had shown that they were worth taking seriously. He wasn't in the habit of asking questions without good reason.

'They're both women,' she said. 'They were shot. But the similarities end there. Different methods, socially they had nothing in common, and no one in their respective circles ties them together. It's probably a complete coincidence. There's nothing to suggest otherwise.'

'Yes, but I just wanted to make sure. That's fine, Thea. Too bad we've hit a dead end with Roslinge. It's hard with those little ingrown communities.'

They both fell silent. Thea moved the chair so her knees

touched his. He looked up and gave her the look which meant he missed her.

'How's Mette, Kristian? Is she back yet?'

'No. Not yet.'

'It takes time. To get back on your feet.'

'Yes, it takes time.'

Thea regretted the change of topic. Kristian's wife, Mette, had been ill for a prolonged period after an otherwise not too serious car accident. Stress, depression, back pain, an intense and inexplicable cocktail.

'There's progress, though,' Kristian said quickly. He got up and walked away with his tray. He had two cups of coffee with him when he returned.

'I think we should give it some time, the murder in Vindbygårde. Let them do their job up there, get on with the basics.'

'A week?'

'If they don't have anything in a week, we'll drive up there, OK? Have a chat with the deceased woman's brother.'

'He's the one who found her?'

'Yes. Frank Andersen is his name.'

She hesitated.

'I don't know, Kristian. I think there should be something more specific to go after.'

'Listen, Thea, your database searches of other unsolved murders of women, what have they told you? There wasn't much in the database, right?'

'No, not unsolved. Not recent cases. I limited the search to gun murders, the last fifteen years. There's the old case from Aabenraa – two unsolved murders of women back in '99. You remember, don't you?' Thea blew on the scalding hot coffee.

'I do, yes – "The Shadow". Any similarities?'

'No.' Thea put the coffee down.

'So?'

'So this is what I'll do. I'll go up to Aalborg, as you suggest, in a week or so. And maybe Aabenraa. Routine checks. Long shots. After all, we haven't got much else to go on.'

He sat for a moment. Then he stood up suddenly, taking her cup with him and depositing it on the trolley on the way out.

'Good luck, Thea.'

Too late and too loudly, she shouted 'Say hi to Mette' after Kristian Videbæk's retreating back.

18

A full stop concludes a sentence. The small dot marks the end, it means that there's nothing more to say. A little drama, an episode, an arc that starts somewhere, rises, falls and finishes. The meaning cannot be deciphered until the dot is in place. Only then is the arc finished, and one can conclude on its form: how high did it soar, how long was it, did it promise more than it delivered, did it surprise in the descent?

The full stop that completed the sentence Karen Simonsen was a black hole. A bullet entry wound in the body. Not a dot with a richness of ink, but the sentence contained in its ending. Karen ended with a hole. An absence.

Even the longest and most important sentences end with the same small dot, like a subordinate clause. Karen was no subordinate clause. But the hole that ended Karen was, in its absence, a provocation for Thorkild. His wife, his distant companion, his children's mother was finished with a piece of nothing two and a half centimetres in diameter.

A reverse vanishing point, Thorkild thought. As she stepped into the painting on his inner eye and emerged towards him to this point in time we call the present, she should have left the vanishing point in the background. Instead Karen simply dissolved at the point of absence.

This provoked him to think back on the richness that had been. He tried to make Karen bigger somehow, as if to compensate for the absence she had become. But it was difficult. She eluded him, she disappeared. The secret of her death made an impact. It's not unimportant how a person dies. Death marks the life. Who was Karen?

Thorkild began to seek out places that had belonged to her life. Unconsciously, he would suddenly stray into shops he knew she used to visit. Bookshops, the one in Vilå and a much larger, more specialised one in downtown Århus. He went to the hairdresser in Vilå she used to frequent, bought a tremendously expensive shampoo, bewildered. Trudged around in the tea aisle of the supermarket – Karen liked her tea. He went to the library's small reading room where he bought a cup of indescribably bad hot chocolate from a vending machine and wondered if she'd done something similar. Suddenly he didn't have the energy to ask the librarian if he could remember what Karen used to do. It felt so strange. The sort of thing he, her husband, ought to know. What she used to do. Without having to consult with librarians, hairdressers, the police, for Christ's sake!

He began, in his dark speculative hours of the evening, to use her bathroom. He'd stand for a long time gazing into the same mirror she'd spent hours in front of. In the living room, he'd remain motionless in front of the picture on the wall, as if waiting in vain for the young Karen to notice him standing there.

When he drove, he took all sorts of detours that led him past the places she'd liked or where they had been together.

He became more and more aware of these tendencies. And gradually he began to plan how he would explore every corner of her life. To hell with what others thought. When he remembered a book she'd read and talked about, he'd write down the title so he could dig it out and read it. When he recalled people who had at some time meant something to Karen, he resolved to pay them a visit. And he went back to the library and questioned the librarian, who didn't recall anything particular about her.

In their shared calendar in the kitchen were her plans.

He brooded over the B on Thursdays. There it was, right in front of him, Thursday after Thursday. It stung his heart and cried to him from the paper: *You have no idea what I am.*

Tuesday evenings she'd devoted to some interest or another that she wanted to practice alone. Last season, a new and very popular discipline had reached the town gym. *Goddess! Discover your body awareness through oriental belly dancing.* She'd never told much about it. Probably because she knew all too well Thorkild's antipathy towards "guru-isms", as he called them. Now it made him sad; he wished he'd asked her about it.

Thorkild rang the gym, and through persistence managed to obtain the private number of the owner, Sonja Kjeldsen. There wasn't much of the goddess in her sober voice when he got hold of her. She didn't remember Karen, but her name was on the list of participants, so she had paid her subscription. Thorkild could remember it: 1265 kroner for a half season as a goddess. It was as if the amount had been written in neon print on their bank statements, which he'd always kept track of. The owner explained that there had been many people in the class whose names she didn't know, and attendance was very varied. But, eager to help Thorkild, she invited him to come along the following Tuesday evening with a picture of Karen.

It took Thorkild a long time to choose which picture to take with him. Ideally, he would have picked the festive picture off the wall because he liked the young woman, almost a girl, he saw there. He had a hard time letting go of the idea. But it wouldn't work, it was too old, so he had to find a newer one.

He went through Karen's drawers and found nothing. When had she last had her picture taken? When do adults have their pictures taken, once the school photographer stops documenting changing hairstyles, polo shirts, baby teeth? Thorkild himself featured, smiling and paternal, on the parish website, and he'd also posed for a professional photographer in Århus for a portrait that was used in the church newsletter and as an attachment to the letters to the editor he occasionally wrote. But Karen? There were no photos of her, or at least nothing new.

He rang the children and got by Nadia to send him a digital photo taken at Christmas three years ago which featured Karen wearing a wry smile and a kind of grey jumpsuit. And he took that one with him.

On his visit to the gym that Tuesday, Thorkild managed to find the room used by the dancers only because of the smell of incense that lingered in the lobby. It was a melange of very different styles all in the one place: white plaster walls, a click-parquet floor and signs with technical explanations about house rules and emergency exits, along with advertising for various events that had no common denominator. Dotted about in between these were pictures of colourful Hindu deities, bad photographs of more contemporary gurus, and in the middle of the floor stood a Ganesh sculpture in white plastic, half a metre tall.

The guy who was the instructor of the goddess discipline came to greet Thorkild with as much of an authoritarian step as you can manage in loose linen trousers and with a stiff gaze that never left Thorkild's eyes.

'Welcome. My name is Gayatri. You have something I'm supposed to look at? Kjeldsen called me. I'm in a hurry, we start in about ten minutes.'

Thorkild showed him the photograph. He shook his head.

'She has not been here?'

'I can't say.'

Thorkild was nonplussed.

'What do you mean? You don't want to tell me? Is there some kind of confidentiality clause here?'

Sarcasm was wasted on the instructor, his eyes grew distant.

'I really couldn't say. There are many people here. I rarely notice their physical manifestations.'

'You look at their aura, perhaps?'

'Exactly!' said the instructor, and Thorkild, who had meant it as a joke, was not sure whether to laugh or cry. The guru looked at him impatiently.

'OK. Well . . . there must be something you can tell me?'

'Your aura,' said the guru, 'could do with finding an expression. Dance is an excellent tool. As I say, we start in about ten minutes. Men are welcome.'

But instead he accompanied Thorkild to the engineering room, where they found a janitor who was the guru's complete opposite in every way. Between the two of them, they managed to run Karen's magnetic card through the system so they could track her comings and goings.

'Here we have her,' the janitor said happily. 'Picture and all. Look here, Christensen.'

The most recent picture of Karen he'd come across appeared on the screen. An unexpected longing for her knocked the wind out of him. Her grey eyes looked directly at him. A distant smile that reminded him of the Mona Lisa lay across her lips. Karen! There you are.

'Here, you can see her activities. I can grab a print, if you'd like? Is it someone from your class, Gorm?'

'Gayatri,' the guru corrected him, annoyed. 'And I cannot spend more time on this. My class is about to begin and I have to make the room ready first.'

'Faggot,' said the janitor to the guru's back.

'I'm pretty sure that Gayatri is a girl's name,' said Thorkild.

'I don't see the point in that,' said the janitor.

'Me neither,' Thorkild admitted.

He left the gym with the knowledge that Karen had gone there the first two Tuesdays last autumn. Then she'd attended a lecture on a Thursday afternoon. She'd not been back since. The lecture was called *Mental Images to Train Your Inner Strength* and was conducted by a therapist named Ivan Geertsen. Thorkild wrote it down, intending to look him up later. Perhaps he had written a book, maybe Karen had been interested in him, maybe he could get closer to her?

Was she vanishing again? Thorkild searched for Karen, but she kept disappearing. Where had she been all those Tuesdays? Her absence drew its shadow back over her life.

Karen had been dead for three weeks.

19

Frank Andersen had just sat down with a fresh pot of coffee, a large chocolate éclair and his screwdriver when the phone rang. He gave an annoyed snort. The phone had barely stopped ringing since Sanne, his sister, had died. He'd had more phone calls over the last week than he had in the whole of last year. First it was the undertaker, then it was a moronic journalist from *BT*, then it was Question-Jørgen from the local newspaper. One of his old comrades had called, asking how he was in a strained voice. And their aunt Agnes, but Frank had hung up the phone before she managed to get beyond the pleasantries and down to business: Sanne's money that she had inherited from their parents. Agnes felt that a part of it should go to her. Although she was not entitled to anything. *It's a matter of decency*, as Agnes used to whine bitterly every time she managed to get hold of Sanne.

A few others had also called about money. Two men, one of them a local and one who presented himself as an international business genius, had called to present an idea that would make a fortune but lacked investors.

Frank told them to go to hell. He said the same to the next person who called: the leader of a local lodge, the Denmark Sisters, who claimed that Sanne had come to them for spiritual and existential guidance, and who was certain that Sanne had wanted to donate a part of her fortune to them. New tables for the living room, specifically, and they had already been ordered, said the leader indignantly.

But all these stupid vultures were barking up the wrong tree. Thankfully, Frank was man enough to get them to back off. That Sanne would have gone to a lodge, he strongly doubted. She seldom left home. And they sure as hell weren't getting any money.

Angrily, he marched over to the phone, ready to send another vulture packing. He barked out his name.

'This is Majbritt – hey, Frank. My condolences. Did you get my card?'

Bloody hell. Majbritt. One of Sanne's old girlfriends from school, she saw her once in a while. Majbritt lived in Copenhagen and made lots of money, and when she occasionally visited her parents, she would occasionally stop by Sanne's apartment.

And Frank knew because he'd asked Sanne about Majbritt's visits. Because even if they weren't really an *item*, he still liked to know what she was up to. Because nearly three years ago they had ended up in the sack at his place after the local festival, Majbritt having suddenly showed up and got blind drunk, even though she never used to be home at that time of year.

Next day, Frank had felt guilty because he'd gone to bed with her when she was that drunk – not exactly gentlemanly behaviour. Something Majbritt had also been aware of when she woke up in his apartment the next day with red-rimmed eyes and a bad hangover. But she'd not really blamed him. She was all right, Majbritt.

And a lovely girl – round and lovely curves, expensively styled curly hair and trailing the scent of an unfamiliar perfume that remained in his bedding for a long time afterwards. Exquisite underwear with all sorts of lace and such. He still conjured up her image whenever he fantasised about women.

Whether she was married or not, he wasn't actually sure. He'd not wanted to ask Sanne about it, because that Sanne didn't know – and she was never to know, he'd promised Majbritt. No one knew, apart from a couple of the guys in the bowling club to whom he'd occasionally mention a mysterious ex from Copenhagen, because it was such a pleasant thought.

Right now he was a little mad at Majbritt because she hadn't come to the funeral. He'd looked for her, but she hadn't shown up. Not cool.

He cleared his throat.

'Hello. Yes, I got it. It was nice of you.'

'Come on, Frank. I'm sorry I couldn't come to the funeral. My daughter had a fever of almost forty.'

'And your husband was busy?'

He winced, realising he was pushing it. A lengthy silence followed, but then she laughed, thank God. She was all right, really, Majbritt.

'All my men are terribly busy. How are you, Frank?'

'OK. I'm fine . . . I am. And you, how are you?'

She didn't answer that.

'Frank, I'd like to help. I take it you haven't emptied the apartment?' She didn't wait for an answer. 'I'm home for the weekend. Coming in on Friday. And then I thought we could get some of her stuff packed up, right?'

He was a little overwhelmed by a feeling he didn't recognise. And it surprised him that she would bother. She and Sanne hadn't been all that close. Had Majbritt cared more about his timid sister than he gave her credit for?

'I thought I could take some of her clothes. We're the same size. I might as well take the stuff rather than you giving it away to a second-hand shop, right?' And then she added: 'She has a rabbit-fur coat I've always admired.'

Aha. Another vulture. But an honest one. And he could certainly use a hand.

They agreed to meet on Saturday afternoon.

Majbritt looked like her old self when Frank saw her standing there in front of Sanne's place, squinting in the bright sun. The curls were a little longer and hung down over her shoulders, held off her face by a pair of sunglasses. Although she was wearing jeans and an anorak and a pair of practical shoes, he thought she looked good.

After standing in front of the mirror agonising about it for a bit, he'd decided not to give a damn about the whole thing and just wear the clothes he always did: jeans and a sweater. He'd shaved, but that was it. Why should he dress up? He was going to Sanne's apartment to cart her stuff about, so it wasn't exactly an occasion for a tie and cologne.

When she caught sight of him she waved, and as he drew level with her she gave him a hug, which was long enough that he managed to poke his nose into her curls and get a whiff of the perfume. It was the same, he noticed. His entire body seemed to respond to the scent, so he hurriedly released her and cleared his throat.

'Why, hello, Majbritt. And thank—'

'Don't mention it,' she cut him off. 'You look good, Frank. Given the circumstances. Shall we go?'

She took a few energetic steps up the stairs, but when he made to follow his legs refused to obey. Overcome by a disinclination ever to set foot in the apartment again, he stood rooted to the pavement. Feeling lost, he looked at Majbritt, who had turned around with one hand on the cold iron railing was staring at him, questioningly.

'Uh . . . we could grab a cup of coffee first. If you'd like? There's a café just around the corner,' he suggested, desperately trying to forget the sight of his sister's lifeless body, which now for the first time seriously encroached on him. Eyes pleading, he looked at Majbritt.

'I don't have all that much time,' she said impatiently, shuffling in her running shoes.

This provoked an anger in him that sparked his legs back to life. She was an insensitive bitch, that Majbritt. Damned if he'd ever sleep with her again. He stomped past her, unlocked the door and toiled up the stairs. But now it was she who hesitated.

'They've cleaned up, right? Got some air in, or . . . whatever it is they do? There won't be any of that red police tape you have to crawl under, will there?'

There was no such thing. No red tape. And he was pretty sure there was a window open because the paramedic had said something about that when they came to get Sanne.

But he told Majbritt that he had no idea, enjoying the uncertainty in her eyes as she apprehensively walked towards him.

The apartment was tidy as always. As if Sanne might come home any minute. Only the icy air revealed that something was dead. Frank quickly went over and closed the open kitchen window.

'She was lying in the kitchen,' he said over his shoulder to Majbritt, mostly because he figured she would probably ask. Or at least want to know.

There were lots of things in Sanne's apartment. Everything well organised, but all the same the rooms seemed overcrowded. She was fond of ornaments, figurines, multicoloured glass bits and pieces that adorned every surface – on top of the TV, shelves, window sills. She had a bookcase in dark pine, which had belonged to their parents, filled with magazines. Frank knew they were sorted by date. He had once asked her why she didn't throw them out, for even though she had many things, Sanne wasn't one of those fanatical collectors who saved every yogurt cup. But for some reason she'd kept the magazines.

'Maybe some day . . .' she'd replied, absent in tone. Frank never did find out what 'some day' meant. It was hardly a sentimental dream of husband and children, he thought, because in that case a decade's worth of *Se & Hør* was not the most obvious thing to save. Still, Sanne seemed to have the idea that someone would enjoy them.

As he stood and looked at the orderly magazine holders, it struck him Sanne had liked to hide in a pile of magazines when they used to visit their grandmother's apartment as children. He'd never thought of it before. Perhaps Sanne had dreamed of a little girl who would want to sit and look at the colourful pictures. A child, or even a grandchild.

His head felt heavy. So he went to Sanne's small kitchen and put water in the kettle.

Majbritt voice sounded neutral:

'There's nothing to see.'

'No, someone's been here and cleaned up. The undertaker took care of everything.'

She came forward and stood with her arms crossed and looked at him.

'Was it bad, Frank?'

'It wasn't much fun.' He rummaged in the kitchen cupboards for some Nescafé, but found only a few teabags of different flavours. He held them up in front of her. She paid no attention.

'You could tell me about it.'

'Or not. Blackberry it is.'

Her tone irritated him. Although he had never in his life been to a psychologist, he imagined that was how they sounded. Infuriatingly calm. Yet, in the next breath, he told her about it.

'I'd look in on Sanne every now and again, right? And then I was going to stop by Jem&Fix in Aalborg on Saturday – that is, the day after, right? And then I wanted to ask Sanne if she wanted to go, I thought we could go window shopping perhaps, get something to eat. So that night, when I was coming home from bowling, I thought it was strange that she hadn't answered the message I'd sent. She always has her phone nearby. So I thought I'd stop by her place on the way home and see.'

Majbritt made the tea and handed him a steaming cup.

'There's light at her apartment, right? And when I go in, the door is open. And it was strange, because the door to the building itself, that was locked. But her apartment, wide open. And it's completely quiet, and that's strange, I think, because she used to have the TV on most of the time. And all the lamps are lit throughout the apartment, which is bright as a summer day. Even the little lamp in the cooker hood. Lights everywhere. And I call out for her . . .' Frank stopped.

Majbritt sipped her tea, burned her lips and looked at him.

'So, she's on the floor, curled up on her side. Like a tiger, sleeping. She's bleeding from both hands. There's blood on the floor, but it's all black and congealed, and it smells . . .'

Frank was looking for words to describe it, but gave up.

'There's under-floor heating,' he said, simply. Stood there for a while, then looked up at Majbritt.

'So that's it,' he said in an indefinable tone. Then he gulped the hot tea down. 'Should we take a look at it, then?'

They spent a couple of hours sorting the things on the shelves and kitchen cabinets. It soon became clear that it would take longer than a day to get the job done. But actually, Frank thought, it was OK to be here with someone. He was not the type to be sentimental about things, not even Sanne's stuff. It was only when Majbritt disappeared into the bedroom and came out again, dressed in a white rabbit-fur coat, which she posed in, that he hurt a little bit, even though he laughed. He'd had no idea that Sanne owned such a coat. She never went anywhere. What had she wanted with it?

'Is it OK that I take it?' Majbritt asked. It suited her and fitted the perfume. She stroked the white fur.

'I think it's a shame if it ends up at the second-hand shop.'

Suddenly she walked over to Frank and gave him a hug. He buried his nose into the rabbit fur like a little boy and stood there for a few long moments before his desire took over and he began to fantasise about being with her right here, in Sanne's apartment.

When she let go of him and looked into his eyes, it was as if she momentarily thought about it, too. Then she shook her head a little, said, 'There, Frank.'

It had been so good to hold her. The warmth flowed through his body. When she released him, it was as if the cold in Sanne's apartment hit him with double force. And the rest of the day, he knew in a split-second, would be just as cold. The crappy weather outside his own cold rooms. He closed his eyes tightly and grabbed her again. Hugged her hard and fumbled after something with his hands, fingers stinging like a leg that's gone to sleep. He kissed her neck and got her down on Sanne's sofa before she came to her senses. She raised an elbow and gave him a jab in the chest. He got off of her, not daring to look her in the eye. Not so much out of shame, but because he thought he might try to grab her again.

She snorted and sat up and stared at him, dumbfounded. 'For fuck's sake! Frank, you gotta . . . for fuck's sake!'

He had expected that she would storm out of the apartment, but she stayed on the sofa until she caught her breath. Then she got up and poked him in the chest, right where her elbow had hit him. He mumbled and moaned.

'That . . .' She paused. 'What the hell was that? What was that about?'

Frank tried to look offended. As if it was nothing special. They had been together before. But the fear was biting into him. He'd never grabbed a woman like that. Perhaps he'd thought that she would want him too, if they got started. But even so . . . This was messed up. He cleared his throat.

'Sorry. I'm not sure . . . what I thought. Sorry, Majbritt.'

She brushed a hand through her curls.

'What were you thinking?'

'I don't know. I swear, I don't know what came over me.'

'You don't know what came over you?'

'That's what I said, OK?'

He strode into the kitchen and put the kettle on again, not knowing quite why. They probably weren't going to drink more tea. But the everyday sound of it bubbling on the stove helped a little with the awkward silence.

Majbritt had followed him into the kitchen. She had put her anorak back on and the rabbit fur was draped over her arm.

'You were going to rape me,' she noted drily.

'Rape!' he spluttered, trying to sound indignant. 'Slow down, now. Of course I wouldn't. I'm not a criminal . . . And I said I'm sorry. Honestly, come on, right?'

She glared at him and would not take her eyes away.

'It's Sanne,' he tried. He didn't know what to do with his hands. He stuffed them in his pockets.

'You need some help, Frank. OK?'

He couldn't think of a reply. Actually, he had always thought it was nonsense, the idea of getting 'help'. Who would help him? What would really help? Should he sit with some psychologist and talk about his childhood? Yet, there was Majbritt standing in front of him, and he had almost attacked her. It was possible that she had a point.

'OK?' she insisted.

'Yes, yes, dammit. I . . . I'll get help. Or, I was planning to. There is some kind of group counselling thing, I'll join that.'

'I think that would be a really good idea, Frank,' she said. Then she giggled and gave him a slap with the rabbit fur.

'I'm taking this, Frank. Just so you know. Holy shit, man.'

20

Thorkild continued his search for Karen. Her places, her life, all the unknown quantities.

Having resolved to sort out the photographs in Karen's drawer, he had bought an album and made a start. At first he had felt a little uncomfortable, as if he was rummaging through things that were not intended for his eyes. On the other hand, Karen had never shrouded anything in their home in outright secrecy. The drawer with the photographs was there in her dresser, she had never asked him to stay away from it. It had probably never been necessary.

So he went through the pictures, grainy, half bad, mostly taken by him. A whole life he had taken snapshots of when there was something he wanted to remember. He documented Michael's birth, a holiday in Austria, their celebration dinner the day he graduated from the Theological Seminary. Nadia's birth. Both kids' first day of school and confirmations, the day Michael won a mountain bike, Karen on the day she had a disastrous perm.

He was seized by a restlessness unlike anything he'd experienced before, a very real grumbling and feeling of unrest in the stomach, dizziness. Suddenly he feared that it was a heart attack. Or a panic attack. He closed his eyes, concentrating on his breathing, fled into Karen's bathroom and lay down flat on the floor. He pressed his cheek against the white tiles, feeling the floor heating his whole body. He lay there for a long time and felt both comforted and ridiculous.

The phone buzzed in his pocket and he fished it out. Saw his daughter's name on the display and didn't have the energy to answer. They rang often, the children, every day or every two days. Always taking turns, so he suspected them of having agreed on a kind of schedule. It seemed as if they were managing OK, both of them, and moving on with their lives, full speed ahead. Or maybe they had made a virtue out of keeping up appearances, so that he would not have to worry about them. It would be typical of Michael and Nadia. Always caring, overly responsible. Both of them. It touched him and it irritated him. Irritated him because, in a way, it felt fake. As if they were hiding something from him, caring for him in a manner that stood in the way of his really talking with them or understanding how they experienced the loss of Karen. And at the same time he had to admit to a feeling of relief. That it was liberating, good, not having to carry the children's grief on top of his own.

He understood that the way to understanding Karen better would soon have to go via Michael and Nadia. He would have to meet with them and ask about Karen as they saw her, Karen as a mother, their version of her. But not now.

He felt ill prepared for that talk. As if he had desperately little to offer when only by asking his children could he put the pieces of their mother's puzzle into place.

Instead, he searched the phone memory and called up someone whom he suddenly felt an urgent need to talk to. She replied quickly

'Thea Krogh,' she answered. A little tired and hoarse, as if she had been sleeping. It dawned on Thorkild that it was late, a lot later than when it would otherwise be considered reasonable to call someone up.

'Thea. Hi, it's Thorkild. Thorkild Christensen, Karen's husband.'

'How did you get this number?'

Not unfriendly, but Thorkild could hear the reservation in her voice and knew he had crossed a line. He hesitated.

'You gave it to me. Or maybe you didn't. You called me from this number last time you came to see me. I saved it, thought it might be nice to have. I'm sorry for calling. I didn't mean to . . . And it's way too late, I know. I didn't actually realise how late it is.'

'It's OK.'

'You were asleep?'

She didn't answer that, remained silent on the line. Thorkild cleared his throat.

'I guess I just wanted to . . . see how it went. The case. It's been three weeks.'

'There's nothing new. You would have heard if there was. We're working as hard as we can. But I don't think I can tell you anything you don't already know.'

'I doubt it,' said Thorkild and thought his voice sounded pathetic and despondent.

'What do you mean?'

He heard concern in her voice. And interest, genuine interest.

'I don't know, Thea. I'm just trying to find out who the hell I was married to. There are so many closed doors. I sit and look at old pictures. And talk to people. And I don't feel like I'm getting any closer to her.'

He heard Thea suppress a yawn.

'I'm sorry. It's actually late. It's not because I'm bored by you.'

'This Jepsen guy, Torben Jepsen, he's still in custody?'

'He is. Have you thought of anything that connects Karen with him? Anything, even the smallest detail, can be of importance.'

'No. And, Thea, it makes no sense to me. As I understand it, there's absolutely no reason why that man should have done what you say.'

Thea's voice was suddenly alert and alive.

'And what are we saying he did?'

'That he ran into Karen that morning and just shot her. Without any reason, not even rape or anything like that. That you meet a woman you don't know and execute her, close range.'

He paused, then said: 'Elisabeth was here yesterday. Elisabeth Jepsen.'

'I see. I understand, then. Thorkild, we're not saying anything. We're working on different theories. We know that Karen was in that car, we know the car was in Jepsen's custody.'

Thorkild sighed.

'Yes. Of course, you must investigate. I can see that . . . it's just that you and I, Thea, we're in many ways in the same line of business. We sit with people through their toughest moments. We try to understand the individuals we're dealing with. We hear their confessions and excuses and defences and coping strategies. And Elisabeth – I've sat with her. Just as you have. She's not a strong person. She says Torben Jepsen was home that night, and I believe her. Do you believe her, Thea? Are you sure you have the right man?'

'I'm not sure of anything,' she said quietly.

'Thea,' he said, pleadingly, feeling as if he was laying himself bare. 'I'm wondering if you've . . . have you found out something that you won't tell me? You've gone through every aspect of Karen's life, I wondered if you had found out anything? Will you please tell me? I know you're investigating, and that I'm a part of it, or whatever. But I don't think you really believe I've done this to Karen. So won't you just tell me? I need . . . peace. In my head.'

She held a long pause.

'What am I to tell you?'

'Have you found out that Karen was seeing somebody else?'

'I thought you were certain that she wasn't,' Thea said, surprised. The trembling voice was far from the stoic vicar she pictured in her head.

'I'm not sure of anything any more. It's probably crazy. But I feel so . . . cut off from reality, in a way.'

'We've spoken to all the people we can come up with, the people Karen knew. And no, we haven't found another man. Or anything pointing in that direction. Although we haven't yet charted her entire existence. She's difficult to figure out.

But no secret lover so far. If you think it helps you to hear that.'

'Yes. I think it does.'

'Was there anything particular that got you thinking that way?'

Now she sounded like an investigator again, professionally attentive.

'Only the fact that I can't find my way around Karen's life. And the B in the calendar. I don't know . . . it's like a nightmare that won't let go of me, not knowing where she went on those Thursdays.'

'Well, I think I can help you with that.' Thea put the phone down, and he could hear her rummaging through some papers.

'Here – Thursdays. Now, obviously there's a possibility that this isn't true, Thorkild, you need to keep that in mind. But according to a memo written by Detective Søren Edvardsen, it appears that Karen spent a few Thursdays in the company of an old friend from Århus. Name of Isabella. Does that ring a bell?'

'Yes, that rings a bell.'

'It says here that . . . I can't go into details, Thorkild. I really can't . . . but according to my colleague there's no reason to believe that this Isabella is lying. She approached us a few days after Karen's death, according to this. In order to help us if she could.'

'What did Karen do with her? Can you tell me?'

Thea hesitated.

'Thorkild, do me a favour and visit her yourself? I can't sit here and read a colleague's report aloud. There is a confidentiality between a witness and the police. Call her, OK?'

'I understand. I will do.'

They were both silent for a moment. The conversation felt somehow unfinished to Thorkild. He didn't want to hang up, wanted to hear more of the calm, objective voice. She was a link to Karen. And another person, one who behaved towards him in a way he really liked. Perhaps it was her curiosity.

'Can I just ask. What I said . . . Is it true? Do you believe that it wasn't me?'

He heard her sigh, but could not tell if it was with fatigue, resignation or just an afterthought.

'Does it matter? What I think?'

'It matters. Most definitely.'

Then he added: 'You are investigating the murder.'

She was silent, then she put down the phone. Even though it was the first time it had happened to him – that someone simply hung up without saying goodbye – it seemed to Thorkild to be the right thing to do. To disconnect without phrases and goodbyes. What was there to say?

21

Isabella lived in the Øgade quarter in Århus. Karen's old friend. And probably Thorkild's as well, although it had taken him a long time to consider her a friend. He liked her, he always had, ever since he met her and Karen, a close-knit pair of friends, at the university. He'd had his doubts for a long time whether the feeling was mutual. Karen and Isabella went to the same sixth-form college and had stuck together as they both moved to Århus, Karen to study Theology and Isabella Political Science. And although he was occasionally invited to their movie nights and dinner clubs, and though Isabella often visited their apartment when he and Karen moved in together, he was still unsure whether she liked him. She was never hostile or curt, and she usually chatted about his interests and activities in a friendly manner. Yet he could never quite shake the feeling that she was amused by him, found him a bit comical. The emotion provoked him to go out of his way in an attempt to win her over, until one day, with some relief, he dropped his efforts. It was after they'd moved to Roslinge and Karen became pregnant, and he remembered feeling a strange sort of victory; now he and Karen were settling down and establishing a family, he was an inescapable part of Karen, while Isabella had never been married or even dated anyone significant. A self-proclaimed single girl who occasionally came to visit, though usually they got together alone, Karen and Isabella.

She still lived in Samsøgade. In one of the old apartments in a narrow street just north of the centre of Århus, on the way up to the university on what used to be the gallows hill in the Middle Ages. An idyllic renovated piece of Århus, coveted by students of means and otherwise populated by middle-aged bohemians who'd bought their way in when it was still cheap.

Isabella was the bohemian type. The apartment was full of books. Organised like a library. One shelf held the academic literature – her political tendencies were clearly left of centre. The second bookcase housed the humanist books, a preponderance of literature on alternative religious and paranormal phenomena. And then there were the novels, everything from feminist authors, a complete collection of Hermann Hesse, who also was part of an ordered sequence of Nobel Prize recipients, as far as Thorkild could see. Then there were the classics – especially German and French – and a number of Soviet dissidents: Solzhenitsyn, Sakharov and several others. In the window, which was lined with heavy curtains, sat a large statue of a fat buddha; the furniture was heavy, draped and antique.

Isabella asked Thorkild to sit on the Rococo sofa by the window.

She had been up when he phoned from the car, even though it was after midnight. He'd jumped in the car immediately after the conversation with Thea, he didn't feel it could wait even a moment. Found the number in Karen's address book. And

Isabella hadn't sounded surprised, just invited him to drop by when it suited him. And yes, right now would be fine.

He'd been curious to see her, it had been a long time and as far as he remembered, she hadn't attended Karen's funeral. Or had she been there? He couldn't recall. But there was certainly nothing familiar about Isabella, he thought. Her red hair hung in a long braid down her back. A candle flickered on the window sill. She had been a beautiful girl, but now she looked old, with a weariness in her features.

But although it was late, there was plenty of life in Isabella's grey eyes. She poured black coffee, which was already on the table in a thermos.

'I think, Thorkild, that maybe I was the one who knew Karen best. I'm so very sorry about what happened.'

Isabella folded her legs up under the long purple skirt and looked straight into Thorkild's eyes. She used her Social Science degree to do some kind of consultancy work; Thorkild wasn't sure exactly what it was. Once, he remembered, the three of them had been walking in the university park and tried to guess what people studied, based on their clothes. Judging by Isabella's clothes today, she should have studied Spanish, he thought.

But he said nothing, simply looked at her with encouragement, and it seemed as if she understood his errand without him needing to put it into words.

'We spoke on the phone a lot, as you know, and she often came here to visit. As if she needed to get away for a while. We always met here. Even though I offered to come out to yours to visit. It's nice to get away from town every now and again, I think. Karen felt the same, just the other way round.'

Thorkild sipped the coffee, it was strong and bitter, as if it had sat there for some time, but still scalding hot.

'You said on the phone that you were afraid she was seeing another man,' said Isabella, calmly. 'She wasn't. I'm sure. She would have told me, we had that kind of intimacy. But she was doing many other things.'

Isabella got up and walked to one of the shelves. She took out a stack of books that were piled on top of each other and stood out from the otherwise neat order. Thorkild opened his mouth to say something, but Isabella waved him off. The grey eyes signalled that, for now, he should just listen.

'Karen was increasingly interested in certain things. You know, psychology, her own individual development. She read books and wanted to discuss them. These books belong to her. She took them home one at a time, so you've probably seen a few of them, but she preferred to keep them here.'

'Why?' said Thorkild, his voice sounding vague.

Isabella sat down again, folded her legs, unperturbed.

'Thorkild, Karen felt as if the two of you were growing apart. Not sharing anything of importance. She had no confidence that you could follow her in this.' Isabella looked deep into his eyes as she pointed to the books.

'She would ring me up wanting to talk about a lot of things, but she never mentioned you. It was as if you guys lived together without making much difference to each other. I don't know, that was just my impression. She wrote a lot and participated very actively in some forums online. I'm not sure what kind of forums. She read a lot. And then she saw a therapist. But I suppose you're already aware of that?'

Thorkild shook his head.

'I got the impression that it was a regular thing. Weekly, I think. It must have cost you a fortune.'

Thorkild shook his head again. He'd gone over the bank statements and had kept track of such things. An expenditure of that magnitude, he would have known about it. And Karen had no other accounts, he knew that much, as he and their bank manager had gone through their financial affairs.

He must have looked lost, because Isabella reached out and patted him on the hand in a motherly way.

'Don't look so alarmed, Thorkild. Karen was approaching fifty. It triggers something. You develop a need to think things over, look at your life and decide how it should be lived from now on. Some get divorced, go travelling, buy a dog or a Harley Davidson, start a bed and breakfast, whatever. All of us have a need for such reflection, a journey into oneself. One wonders: Am I done here? Should the rest of my life be lived in comfort and convenience, or do I have more, other things to offer? Can I be somebody else, do something else? I myself had such a trip a few years back. I think it's more worrying when people don't make that kind of experimentation.'

'May I see the books?'

Thorkild reached for the pile. He looked at the covers. Colourful covers and titles, all promising a lot. These were not books he was familiar with.

'You should not interpret from the titles alone, Thorkild. I think you need to understand that it's part of a certain culture to label things *Find Your Inner Heart With Hypnosis* and stuff like that. Some of the books are interesting. It's not entirely superficial. Although some are, of course.'

Thorkild looked at the quiet woman in front of him, feeling lost.

'I don't understand . . . why she hasn't told me about any of this.'

Isabella smiled, not unkindly.

'Do you understand how to listen, Thorkild?'

'I'm a vicar, of course I do. I cannot remember ever having rejected Karen when there was something she wanted to talk about. It was just so rare.'

'There are many ways of listening. And many things to listen to, not just what is being said, when you live together.'

'Did she want a divorce?'

'No, Thorkild, frankly I don't think your marriage mattered enough to her that it was worth changing.'

Thorkild was silent. Filled with anxiety and fear, his stomach clenched.

'She had lots of respect for you. She often spoke about what you did as a vicar. Always with respect.'

'But not about what I did for her?'

'No. What are you thinking?'

'I don't know. That's the problem.'

Isabella studied his face. She looked serious.

'Respect is an important thing, Thorkild. And I'm sure that you both lived good lives. Just separately. It's not the worst thing that could happen. It's much worse when people eat each other up.'

'Is it? At least then it makes a difference. Then I would have made a difference.'

'Thorkild, a lot of things are going to surprise you right now. But I'm confident that you will eventually see the same thing and you'll come to recognise how that type of relationship also makes sense in its own way. I think you should take the books with you. Maybe you'll want to flip through them.'

Suddenly Isabella got to her feet, changing the subject.

'Thorkild, why don't I make us some food? I have some things for a casserole for two and you look as if you need to eat.'

'What? No thanks, I don't think so. I'll probably stop by some other day. Would that be OK?'

'Sure.' Isabella smiled.

He remembered something.

'You saw each other on Thursdays, right? In Karen's calendar, she called you B. Why would she do that?'

'I really couldn't say. Every now and again she'd call me Bella, because Nadia did that when she was little. Couldn't pronounce the 's'. But then again, she might have had her own little code language. Or she needed for you not to know what she was doing. Maybe she wasn't ready to share it yet. And yes, it was always on Thursdays. We grabbed a bite here or went to a café. Talked. Are you sure you don't want to stay?'

'No, I'd better get home. Thanks, anyway. There are just so many things, you know.'

Thorkild went out into the hall and took his jacket. At the door he turned around.

'Who was the therapist she was seeing?'

'I don't know, Thorkild. I honestly don't know. She never said a name, never told me anything about the method. It was another world for her. Do stop by again whenever you feel like it.'

Isabella smiled at Thorkild again. Closed the door. He suddenly stood alone on the stairs with ten books, hundreds of unknown feelings and a thousand questions.

22

Thea had decided to give Frank Andersen a try.

That afternoon she had received permission and information from Aalborg Police, who were investigating the murder in Vindbygårde. And the head of the investigation had officially given her the green light to try one more time with Frank, who was, off the record, no longer a suspect in the murder of his sister Sanne.

'It's hard to say quite why, but I simply don't believe Frank did it,' said the homicide detective in his sing-song North Jutland accent, which had made Thea smile on the phone. 'There's no motive. We haven't completely dropped him, but it's not where we're using our resources. It's a tricky one, Vindbygårde. She was a real loner, so it's a case of anyone could have done it. No one heard the shots. And it's bizarre – shot through both hands. That's pretty unusual.'

'Nothing to go on,' Thea mused, instantly regretting the judgmental undertones of the question. She herself had very little on the Karen Simonsen murder. She admitted that to the detective, who fortunately became even more forthcoming as a result.

'Stop by to see Frank if you think it might help you. Let me know if you get anything out of it. Perhaps I should go with you, if you're such an interrogation oracle.'

'I'm in no way an oracle. Far from it. I don't for one moment believe that I can do something you can't. Mostly I'm just hoping to hear something that will give me the inspiration to kickstart my own case. It's been three weeks and we're completely stuck. This is a long shot, but worth a try.' But all the while she was speaking Thea was wondering if it was from Kristian Videbæk that the detective had gotten the idea of an oracle.

The murder was initially dubbed *The Millionaire Murder* on the front pages of the papers, because unnamed sources had revealed that the victim, Sanne Andersen, was filthy rich. So the first attempts to find a motive had – in the absence of any better ideas – focused on her fortune. But as it turned out, there wasn't any, according to the police investigation of the victim's finances. There was money, but not an overwhelming amount, it said in the report. Which painted a picture of a woman who lived isolated and alone. She didn't even own a computer, and her mobile phone had not been found. The only piece of technology they had uncovered was a GPS in her outdated Toyota Carina, which the technicians were now working on. Later, the papers took to calling it *The Stigmata Murder* because the victim was shot in both hands, a discovery that had got the news mill spinning again. But now the media interest had died away, as that kind of story invariably did after a week without news.

The picture of Sanne showed a pale, blonde woman who looked younger than forty-two. A small abscess on the side of the nose was the only distinct feature of an anonymous face.

Thea drove alone. She'd decided against showing up in a police vehicle and uniform, hoping a more informal approach would work on Frank Andersen.

The brother resembled the victim. That was her first thought as she stood facing the man on a doorstep in the suburb of Vindbygårde. It was late afternoon and too dark for Thea to have an overview of the city. All she could make out were the early autumn imprints of any Danish city: black, wet streets, a mass of fallen leaves on the sidewalks, orange-yellow streetlights. A Fakta supermarket, an Irish pub with a dark wood facade, street after street of unimpressive bungalows from the seventies. Frank Andersen lived in a development of new townhouses, deep in a quaint maze of closed roads, playgrounds and deserted petanque lanes. His house was small and lit by powerful lamps that sent a ray of light far into the quiet road. He was tall and sturdily built, the blond hair was short and coarse, his opaque blue eyes were sceptical. He wore jeans and a large, light blue sweater.

'Thea Krogh from Århus Police. Are you Frank Andersen? We have an appointment? I called earlier.'

'If I'm the one you have an appointment with, I'll have to be Frank Andersen, won't I? Shall we do this on the stairs? Or would you like to have coffee and small talk?'

He looked annoyed, as if she had interrupted. Thea was surprised by this, because Frank Andersen had sounded, if not friendly, then at least not quite as dismissive over the phone.

'I'd like to come inside. You don't have to serve me anything. Is that OK?'

Andersen emerged, stepped into a pair of black clogs, closed the door behind him and set off down the garden path. He opened another door and turned to her.

'Did you want to come in, or what? The back door is the quickest way into the kitchen.'

Thea followed. Without waiting to be invited, she sat down on one of two white perch chairs at the dining table.

'You'll have to live with that monster there.'

Andersen pointed to a large remote-controlled car, which took up most of the table. The rest of the space was filled with all kinds of parts that belonged to the car he was in the middle of assembling.

'You're a salesman, Mr Andersen?'

'Just call me Frank. The coffee's going cold, by the way. And yes, I sell for a living. Copiers, faxes, other office equipment. We service, too. You guys aren't short of anything in Århus, by any chance?'

He handed Thea a half-filled cup. Instead of sitting down on the vacant chair in front of him, he opted to remain standing by the sink. Apparently he had decided to get the visit over with as quickly as possible. In the weary voice of a man who is bored to death, he continued:

'Yes, I'm Sanne's brother. This is what I assume you want to talk to me about. I didn't murder her, and I don't know who did – I honestly haven't a clue, because Sanne never went outside her door and no one knew her. But if I get hold of him, then I might be guilty of murder. Although one probably shouldn't say such things nowadays.'

Thea waved him off.

'Frank, I'm not here because I think you've murdered your sister. I came because I'm following up leads on another murder. One that happened some time ago in the Århus area. Also a woman. There are probably no connections, but I just wanted to be sure before I close that door.'

Thea spoke gently and carefully. She was conscious that Frank Andersen was doing everything he could to create a distance between them. It was as if he was protecting himself. Thea couldn't decide whether it was grief or whether he was afraid of her, or what the reason might be. The reaction was so obvious, almost physical, and it made her pity him.

But now he looked at her with a little more openness in his eyes. Surprised.

'I have an mp3 recorder here, Frank, but I'll put it away.

I have no pad to write on, nothing. I just want to listen. Will you tell me about your sister? Then I'll let you know if there's anything I need to hear more about. I'm not going to use any of this.'

Frank sipped his coffee a few times as if it was hot, took his time and then put the cup down on the table, letting his shoulders drop. He looked into Thea's eyes.

'Sanne and I only had each other. And she's always been a bit of a loner. It wasn't that we saw each other often, but there was like this invisible bond between us. That's probably what made us both carry on living in this town. Close to each other.'

'What did she do for a living?' said Thea, although she knew it from the report.

'Sanne was originally a trainee accountant. It feels like a hundred years ago now. I don't know why, but suddenly she stopped. And she's never worked since. Disability pension or rehabilitation allowance or whatever it's called nowadays. The name is always something new, right? She's on welfare. It would drive me nuts, never to see anybody, but Sanne liked it just fine. She went with me every now and again, when I drove around the country, yeah?'

Thea nodded. 'So she lived off the welfare money?'

'She didn't spend much. You probably know that she had some money. The newspapers have managed to make it sound more than it was. We both inherited some when our parents died. I got the summer house out by Saltum Beach. And she got some money. It wasn't a fortune or anything like that, but I think she's been good at saving it. Never used a krone. So the money just sat in her bank account. She even saved up a bit of her welfare money, I believe. But to call her a millionaire would be exaggerating.'

'No boyfriends, friends? Interests?'

Frank Andersen smiled. It was a smile tinged with sadness, but there was derision there too, thought Thea.

'No, she was always home. Watched a lot of television,

read magazines, had a few girlfriends from her schooldays who sometimes came to visit. I'd drive past her apartment every day. The light was always on up there, so I think she was always home.'

'She never attended anything?'

The big man thought about it.

'I can only recall one night when I happened to ring on her doorbell and she wasn't there. I remember it because it was the day we celebrated the anniversary of the city. I was running a relay race with my colleagues from work and we'd won. It was a sort of town festival with a lot of stuff going on. And free beer. That was why I wanted my sister to come out and join us. Not that she would have come out. She wasn't into that kind of thing.'

Frank pointed to a newspaper article on the bulletin board. *The Heating Plant Brought the Heat to the Relay*. Thea noticed it was from back in spring. Beside it was a list of forthcoming meetings at the Samaritans in Aalborg. Otherwise, the board was empty.

'I thought you were in sales?'

'I'm also down at the plant.' The man looked embarrassed. 'You can't make a living only by selling these days. And I have no wife and kids or anything like that.'

He used a new, firm voice.

'Some of us actually like to work and earn money. And I'm crazy about cars, right? I drive a BMW. You can see it out there. Costs an arm and a leg.'

He nodded proudly towards the kitchen window where the outside light illuminated the little carport and the shiny car that stood out there.

'But the night of the town festival – did she say where she'd been?'

Frank thought again.

'She said she'd started singing lessons. But I've never heard her sing, so I didn't buy it. Then the following week she was away again – I remember, now that we're talking about it.

So I thought it was probably true that she was taking lessons. It really doesn't sound like her, though, believe me. I've tried to get her to go out since for ever. There was a time I suggested she tried something like salsa. I've heard that it kind of injects a little life into people.'

Thea gave up on the cold coffee and put it down. Looked around what she could see of the man's home. The kitchen was tidy with a silver kettle, which according to the logo was a Porsche. A glimpse of the living room showed the back of a sofa in black leather and a television of considerable size, which was on with the sound muted. There was nothing on the walls, but each wall had an uplight in blue glass, throwing zigzag shadows on the ceiling and keeping the room from looking empty. A large weeping fig stood in a copper pot with small flowers around the base. It did not fit in.

'It was my mother's. It's easy enough to look after. It just needs a little water once a week. Mum always said that I could kill a cactus if you left me in charge of one. So now there's a bit of sport in it for me, keeping it alive, right?'

'How did your parents die?'

'Car crash. Out on the bypass. The first winter night with frost. It's been almost ten years. Sanne stayed at home a lot with Mum and Dad while they were still alive. It was Mum who eventually kicked Sanne out, said that it was time for her to leave home. But it was also Mum and Dad who bought the apartment for her.'

Thea bit her lip. There wasn't much to go on. But it struck her as strange, hearing this woman so undramatically, almost unexcitingly described. After all, she had been killed, and in the same violent manner as Karen Simonsen. Both had lived secluded, solitary lives. But that seemed to be the extent of any similarity.

'Do you know why she never finished her training or found a job?'

'No. I think she suffered from a form of anxiety – not

that she talked about it. I don't know why I think that. But there was definitely something amiss. Every now and then, Mum would come out with things like, "We should let her do things at her own pace." Stuff like that. But Sanne wasn't stupid or retarded or anything. She suffered from some kind of depression, I'm sure. I suggested she should talk to someone about it.'

There was disgust, almost contempt in Frank's voice. But also an unmistakable love, an affection for his sister.

'Did she? Get help, talk to someone?'

'Not that I know of.'

Frank moved restlessly back and forth as if it was an uncomfortable topic. Peeked over at the clock above the door to the pantry.

'So . . . Anything else you wanted to know?'

'Aalborg Police say that Sanne had no computer. Is that true? They didn't find one, or an internet service provider with a listing for her address.'

'Sanne never wanted one. She didn't like the idea of people chatting or emailing any time of day. As if she had anyone to chat with.'

'Most people have a computer. She never used an internet bank or Facebook or purchased music, that sort of thing?'

'I've never heard her talk about anything like that. I'm certain she never used online banking, because she often got me to transfer money for her, pay her bills and stuff. So she'd bring the bills over, right, and I'd do it for her. And then she brought cash for me. She wouldn't do that if she had a computer, now, would she?'

'I think it sounds a little cumbersome. You pay her bills online, and then she takes out money for you? Why not just go to the bank or the post office?'

'You don't know Sanne. Everything that is bothersome or involves PIN codes and bar codes and postal numbers and stuff, it would make her completely exhausted. She liked doing things this way.'

Thea considered this.

'Could she have used a computer somewhere else? At the library, for example?'

'Well, she could have, I guess. But I can't see it myself. If she had something she needed a computer for, she would probably have bought one, right? She had enough money, like I said. But she did sometimes go to the library in Aalborg. And I know she had an email address, but she hadn't sent me an email in years. You can have it, if you want.'

'Who will inherit your sister's money?'

'We had a will drawn up many years ago, when we inherited from Mum and Dad. The money is to be distributed to a variety of charities. No big portions. A lot of animal welfare facilities – she liked animals. But she wasn't allowed to have any in the apartment. So . . . She wasn't a millionaire, like they wrote, the assholes. And not into some religious bullshit, either. That stigmata nonsense is completely off.'

'Frank, have you any idea who might have murdered your sister?'

'Nope.'

He gave her a look that signalled he was tired of being asked that question. And tired of her. If the door to Frank Andersen had ever been opened, it was certainly closed now.

'OK, then. Thanks for your time.'

Thea went to the door. As expected, there was nothing new here that could move her case forward. A wheezing sound caused her to turn and face the man again. Was he crying? She couldn't see his face. Just the silhouette of a big man and the toy car on the table and the fluttering light from the TV in the living room. Her pity came back, full strength.

'And what about you, Frank? Are you talking to anyone? I understand that it was you . . . who found her. It's hard, that. There are groups, professionals . . .'

'I manage.' Said with the proud masculinity she'd heard from God knew how many other desperate men.

'There's nothing wrong with that – needing help under those circumstances.'

In that moment she couldn't recall seeing a man who looked as alone as Frank Andersen. Except the vicar of Roslinge, maybe.

'I don't need anyone to rummage around inside my head. A psychologist is just someone who's read a lot of books. They don't know what it's like to suddenly have someone shoot your sister. People who don't know what they're talking about should just stay away from me.'

She paused hesitantly in the doorway, as if his angry voice demanded her compassion and another attempt. 'I see you have a number on your board – the Samaritans, Budolfi Square. By the cathedral, right? There are people other than psychologists you can talk to.'

Feeling she'd intruded too much, she hastily said her goodbyes and hurried off to the car.

23

It was quite simple. But still, Frank didn't believe it.

On TV, people brought in geeky experts to break passwords, track money transfers and hack websites. Young guys, overweight, surrounded by buzzing monitors. He'd seen a lot of that kind of TV, enjoyed it. But that was the reason he'd been quite intimidated when he tried to log into Sanne's email account. He'd hoped she might have some photos saved there. Of herself. Some newer ones. He only had the one, from when she was about fourteen years old, a school photo. All of a sudden he wanted to see what she looked like. Not that the image of her was fading in his mind, he could still picture her clearly. But it wasn't multifaceted. It was just Sanne in her apartment, Sanne behind her plate at the dining table, Sanne in front of the TV. Sanne wearing the usual jeans, generic black T-shirt and the long blue cardigan. Sanne on the beach in her white skiing jacket, her shoulder-length blonde hair tucked behind her ears, never a hint of makeup. Not pretty, not ugly, not really anything.

When Hotmail asked for a password, he first entered her name, her date of birth and their parents' names. The tenth attempt was simply *frank*, and he was startled when it gave him access. The inbox manifested itself in front of him.

He had gone to the Central Library in Aalborg. That was where Sanne had sometimes gone, so if she had sent emails it would have been from here. That much he remembered from the time he had helped her create the email account. They had done it at his place, and he had offered her to go out and buy a computer with her if she wanted one. She had said she would consider it. And a few days later, he got an email from her. He still remembered the words: *Hey Frank, bet you hadn't seen that one coming? Greetings from Sanne.* He called her up to ask if she had gone and bought a computer without him, but fortunately she hadn't. She had taken the bus to Aalborg and found her way to the library to send him that one line. And since then, she hadn't really talked about getting a computer.

The Central Library felt like the place to do this, even though he might as well have tried it at home on his own PC. Somehow it felt like he was doing right by Sanne, that he had made the journey here, as if it justified breaking into her account. What the hell, he thought, it's no different than cleaning out her drawers in the apartment. He sent a thought to Majbritt. You'll always uncover secrets when you clean up after another person. This was surely no different.

He straightened up in his chair and looked around. The Central Library had been completely renovated since the last time he'd visited. The atrium reminded him of a courtyard. Raw brick, a few stories tall, with small windows in concrete frames. Rustic, almost medieval. The round information desk had a green light fixture above it, almost like a halo, he thought. All around there were entrances to the themed spaces. Such as *Crime Scene* with crime novels and thrillers. *Children's Library* with a variety of weekly activities such as reading clubs and homework help. A mother's group had convened on a sofa with noisy babies, somewhere a radio was playing 'A Little Less Conversation' by Elvis Presley. The days when the library was a place you shushed people were long gone.

He focused on the screen in front of him. Sanne's email was sorted into neat folders, no new mail, nor old messages that cluttered the inbox unsorted. The inbox was empty. He carefully looked through her folders and suppressed a small pang of guilt. It looked as though she used the account mainly to save her own information. Surprisingly, he found a folder entitled Budget. There was another folder with funny little video clips that Sanne had downloaded. One with a funny kitten, one with a bride who tripped and fell into her wedding cake, a couple featuring talented Chinese children who stacked cups at lightning speed.

The last one was a folder she'd labelled Misc. The most recent emails had been sent by www.dateinyourcity.com. It startled him. Sanne? Or was she just saving junk mail? He quickly scrolled down through the first few pages of messages. There were a few old messages from him, five from a couple of her girlfriends. But most were updates from www. dateinyourcity.com. He clicked on a direct link to the site via one of the messages. And to his surprise found himself logged directly on to her profile.

Oh, Sanne, what were you doing? And it was so easy!

He felt another jolt when his sister looked out at him from the profile dkmiss_S. An image of her that he had never seen before.

It had the exact proportions that self-portraits have when taken at arm's length with a digital camera. He didn't know where she'd got the camera from. Her ancient Nokia mobile certainly had no camera. Yet it was undeniably Sanne, poorly lit in her black T-shirt, but without the cardigan. He could see the door and a little of the bookcase in the background; he knew exactly where in the apartment the picture had been taken. She was smiling, though the smile was slightly crooked and detached, as if she couldn't quite take the smile seriously. But with her eyes, she had tried, really tried, to flirt. The opaque blue irises were complemented by both eyeliner and a discreet shade of grey over the eyelid. They were big, bigger than usual, probably because of the angle of the camera. The hair was overexposed by the flash and shone in a freshly brushed way

It was, given the circumstances, a very good picture of Sanne.

Stunned, Frank absorbed the image of his sister and then rummaged frantically around the profile inbox. Horrified, he discovered dozens of emails, but as he clicked through them he calmed down. Most were of the 'hello sexy' type, standard letters from men in Portland, USA; Dresden, Germany; Redditch, England. The mail system showed the correspondence as a conversation, and Sanne hadn't replied to any of them.

But she had opened and read them all.

The site was geared towards locating a partner who lived close by, preferably in your own town. To his relief he saw that Sanne hadn't revealed either her home town or her phone number. But there were emails from a couple of Danish guys. A Jeppe in Copenhagen, Alex in Roskilde, Jan on Lolland. As far as he could see, Sanne hadn't answered them. What on earth did she want with the site? How did she even come up with the idea?

He glared angrily at the three Danish profiles that had written to Sanne. And stumbled across a fourth. Steffen. From Vindbygårde. And a very familiar face, smirking on the picture, taken in profile, bare-chested and without any irony. Frank blinked and read the email from Steffen to Sanne, which she hadn't answered either:

Heeey beautiful! You look cute, just my type. Haven't I seen you somewhere before? ☺☺ sorry bad joke. Write to me at steffenrules@hotmail.com. I'll teach you the rules. Xx

Steffen Hou was a trainee bricklayer in town, he lived no more than half a fucking kilometre away. Frank thought he remembered having been drinking with Hou in several pubs because he knew his boss.

He drummed his fingers on the tabletop and stared. Then he carefully went through everything in the Misc folder and retrieved Sanne's total mail correspondence, which was now supplemented by the library's delivery service, TDC customer support, Aunt Agnes, Amnesty International's newsletter and Steffen Hou.

A quick search brought all emails from Steffen forward. He found six. There was no consistency, so she might have deleted some. The first one he read was dated six months back.

Hi Sanne. Great seeing you. I must say it fulfilled all expectations. Would like to see you again. xx S.

No reply from Sanne, not to any of them, thankfully. He read on.

Hello beautiful. Wednesday is fine, same time same place. Kiss from Steffen.

Hi, I've been thinking about you, are you interested in some more? Same conditions.

Have not received anything from you, could you check again? You were great. S

And the last one, three months old:

Hi, it's gone through OK. See you next Wednesday? Hugs from S.

And later that same day:

I almost feel guilty. How about 500 next time? It should be the other way round. Kisses from your Steffen.

While he read, Frank realised in horror why Sanne had kept them. The inane pet names and phrases had meant something to her. *Would like to see you again, beautiful, kisses. I've been thinking of you.*

He gasped for breath, opened the browser again, went into an online directory and checked Steffen Hou's address, then he rushed back to the car while angry tears burned in his eyes.

It was Steffen's mother who opened the door. She was obviously both nonplussed and frightened by the big man who appeared on the doorstep at dusk and with a brusque voice demanded to speak with her son.

'Steffen? What's this about? Henrik,' she called over her shoulder.

'You'll get him right now, I need to talk to him.'

'Henrik,' the woman yelled, louder. In the living room the TV was turned off, and a sleepy-looking man emerged from inside, while Steffen Hou, twenty-three years old and with boyish blond wax-smeared hair came up the stairs, which obviously led into his basement domain, judging by the loud rap music playing down there. It ignited Frank's rage further. A fucking puppy who lived in his mum and dad's basement, had been, had dared . . .

'Who are you?' the father tried, but Steffen Hou squeezed in front of him, full of youthful bravado, and repeated his father's question, higher and in a more superior voice.

'I'm Frank. Andersen,' he added, when the boy raised an eyebrow.

'Do we know each other?'

'I think you know my sister. Sanne?' Hysteria trembled

beneath the surface of Frank's calm voice, and Steffen Hou's face gave a nervous twist before he regained his composure.

'Want to go for a walk, Steffen?' Frank suggested calmly. Steffen Hou looked around, perplexed, and glanced at his worried mother. 'Or should we discuss it right here?' Frank, too, fixed his eyes on the mother.

'Uh. No, I'm coming,' muttered Steffen. He slipped his feet into a pair of battered running shoes that stood behind the door.

'Good call, Steffen,' said Frank, and marched down the garden path with the boy skulking behind him. In the background, they could hear his mother yelling at Steffen's father.

'Listen here, pal . . .' Steffen managed to say when they got out on the sidewalk, before Frank grabbed him by the collar and with full force threw him into a white picket fence. The neighbour's security light came on, illuminating Frank's contorted face.

'Have you been with my sister? Sanne? Have you, you nasty little fuck?'

Hou stared at him in shock until adrenalin and righteous indignation kicked in, prompting a belligerent comeback.

'What the hell do you care if I have? Why don't you just chill?'

'YOU CHARGED HER?' Frank screamed.

'That's my business. And hers. Mind your own business, you nutjob!'

Frank slammed his fist into Steffen Hou's jaw and sent him crashing into the sidewalk. But Hou was both strong and fast. In an instant he was on his feet, slamming his head into Frank's belly, making him double over in pain. The two men gasped for breath and stared at each other.

'She's dead, Hou. You killed her!' Frank wanted to bellow his accusations into the face of the boy so that his eardrums would burst, but he was too winded and the words came out in a gasping wheeze.

'What are you talking about? She's dead? Like hell she is. I just saw her.' Hou hesitated. 'Is she dead?'

'She was shot. One month ago. Where the hell have you been?' demanded Frank, his surprise at Hou's reaction taking the edge off his anger.

'I don't read newspapers. Sanne's dead? I'm sorry, man. Seriously.' Hou rubbed his cheek. 'But I didn't kill her, if that's what you think. Shot? Holy shit, man. I really liked Sanne. You can believe that or not.'

Frank gasped for breath, the rage returning.

'What were you doing with Sanne? Tell me!'

'I wrote her on this website, thought she looked cute. We met once in the Aalborg, but the chemistry just wasn't there. She didn't have much to say, I thought she was a little boring – sorry. She was *old*,' said Hou, with contempt. 'She looked younger in the picture. But Sanne wanted to see me again and I thought, why not? I came to her apartment a few times. And the money, that was her fucking idea! It's not like I demanded payment. But she offered it the third time I was there, and I thought, why not? I don't know why she offered. Maybe she could tell that I wasn't really interested in something more and didn't reply to her messages and stuff. I'm sorry, but that's gotta be fair enough, man. She wasn't my type.'

Frank admitted something to himself for the first time and yelled:

'She was lonely, goddammit!'

'And that's my problem, because . . .'

Frank stared incredulously at Hou. 'It's *my* problem, you twat. My sister is my problem.'

'Look, if it's any consolation, I don't think she was lonely. She probably was when we first met, yeah? But I haven't seen Sanne for several months and she was the one who didn't want to get together any more. She wrote a text saying that it wasn't a good idea. She didn't need it any more, she wrote. I thought she must've met someone.'

'And why is that?'

The boy smirked.

'Sanne was crazy about me. I did well. No reason why she suddenly wouldn't want it any more, unless she got it somewhere else. Or the money ran out.'

'Because you . . . went to bed with her and demanded money for it! You little whore! You're disgusting. Man whore!'

'Fuck you, pal,' said Steffen Hou, loud and full of himself. He turned to go back to his house.

Frank came at him from behind, knocked him down and pressed his head on the pavement. Hou whimpered, his parents came running down the road.

'I'll press charges! For violence,' Hou shrieked when Frank removed his hand from the boy's head. Blood ran from a solid bruise on the handsome face. His mother gasped and kneeled down at her son's side, the father stood nonplussed, waving a mobile phone.

'Call the police, Henrik,' cried the mother. 'You bully!'

'I think you should do just that,' shouted Frank. 'I actually have something I want to talk to them about. About young Steffen here. You must be damn proud of him!'

'Hang up, Dad,' Steffen mumbled, getting to his feet. 'Go back in the house. It's OK. Just a misunderstanding.'

The mother put her arm around him, and together they went down the garden path. Then she turned her head and looked at Frank through tears.

'Get some help,' she said.

Frank looked at his bloody hands and thought he would do just that. Get some help.

24

Who do you call? Frank stared at his message board, the pamphlet of forthcoming meetings at the Samaritans on Budolfi Road. He'd been to one of those sessions once. A friend of his used to go there and had lured Frank into coming with him. Sympathetic, kind people, Frank recalled. Not at all holier-than-thou but the kind who *know* something about life. All the same, he didn't think he fitted into that category. Alcoholics, drug addicts, homeless. Goddamn it, you had to be a category? What was he? Alone, abandoned, aggressive? He sighed, and gave up on the idea of the Samaritans. Moved on to Budolfi Church, the Aalborg Cathedral. He'd never been there. At least not inside. All those times he had passed by it. It seemed a little far-fetched to call on one of the vicars there. But then what? He'd long since written off therapists and psychologists. No one was going to make money off him.

The vicar at Sanne's funeral had been very nice. A woman. She had even phoned and asked which hymns they should sing, and if he had some things about Sanne he would like for her to say in church. He'd chosen 'The Sun Rises in the East', because it was the only hymn he knew, and he had replied that Sanne was a good sister. And that's what the vicar had said. Using the same words.

Frank postponed it. Put the kettle on for coffee, sighed, missing Sanne's silent company. If she had been here, they could have gone down to rent a film. Or gone out bowling. Or whatever they wanted.

He needed to do something. He couldn't run around beating

other people up. And although the thought of the little man-whore Steffen Hou still made his blood boil, the last thing he needed was an assault charge. He just wanted to stop thinking about it. It had to go away, one way or another.

But then what? He thought of Thea, the nice cop.

He sat down by the computer. Wanted to find out more about her, but he couldn't remember her last name. He googled the Roslinge murder. And suddenly it was there, both the last name Krogh and the idea. Thea had spoken of the vicar in Roslinge. Could he call him? Somebody who knew what it meant to lose a loved one? He found the number and wrote it down. He didn't have to decide right away.

He poured the coffee, feeling angry with Sanne. Everyone had to die and at least she wouldn't suffer from that dementia-thing, where they run around and threaten each other with knives and unable to remember their own names. She had the life she had created for herself, end of story. How much more would she have done in this life? It felt as if you could have turned the clock twenty years forward and she would still have been living there, reading the same magazines and avoiding the same people. Thank God she hadn't had time to squander any more of her inheritance money on magazines, he thought, feeling angry and a little ashamed.

He wanted something more for himself.

Frank Andersen would not go on living for another twenty years without making a difference. He just needed to get through this, maybe get a little help in doing so, come to terms with the fact that Sanne wasn't there any more, and then the world would open up for him. Or he would find a way to open it.

He dialled the number on the piece of paper. It rang and rang.

Well, he's not home, Frank thought. At least I've done something. No one can say I haven't done anything.

'Yes?'

The voice sounded calm and friendly. Suddenly Frank didn't know what to say.

'Yes, hello. Are you the vicar whose wife was murdered? Thorkild Christensen?'

'I beg your pardon – I'm sorry, who is this?'

'My name is Frank Andersen. I'm calling from Vindbygårde. My sister has been shot. Maybe you've heard about it? I thought I'd try to talk to someone, and psychologists just aren't for me. Not that there's anything wrong per se. The world's not going to stop, is it?' Frank babbled on nervously, not knowing where he was going. He needed something concrete to ask the vicar. 'But then I thought, you know, you have to find something to write on her tombstone, and I thought someone like you might know what to write?'

The vicar at the other end of the line chuckled.

'Who is someone like me?'

'A vicar. And I guess you also need some kind of sculpture.'

'Oh, I see. You can write the name. The full name and then the dates of her birth and death. That's all you need. And then you can write a few words that have meaning for you. "Thank you for everything," for example. Many people write that.'

'OK, what have you written?'

The vicar hesitated. 'Loved and missed.'

'So I could just write that?'

It sounded as if the vicar was enjoying himself. 'It is perhaps not the most obvious choice, considering you were not married to her?'

'No. Of course. But I was wondering, also . . . What do you do at night when you lie in bed and think of her?'

Frank had never meant to ask the vicar that, but Thorkild Christensen's calm voice was pleasant to listen to, and suddenly it felt good to ask.

'Frank, was it? I'm sorry about your sister. You can arrange to talk with your vicar, if you are feeling sad. There are many who do so and it's perfectly OK. It may help. You could try it.'

Frank felt rejected.

'Yes, but I don't have a vicar. Everyone has one?'

'What about the one who buried your sister?'

'Well, I'm not sure about that. She mostly talked about hymns and stuff. It's not as if I *know* her, just because she buried Sanne. Is she my vicar? How do you find out? Who is yours, by the way? Vicar for the vicar.'

'Frank, you said Vindbygårde, didn't you? I have read about it in newspapers. I have a meeting in Aalborg on Thursday, so I can stop by – if you'd like me to?'

'Yes. I'll just check to see if Thursday's free.'

Frank took his time and pretended to fiddle with a calendar. Suddenly, this felt so very unfamiliar. But he badly wanted to speak with the man at the other end of the line.

'Yes, it's OK. I have nothing on that day. So just stop by, I'll be here.'

'And where is *here*, Frank?'

Frank gave him the address, said a proper goodbye – it was the most formal word he could think of – and hung up.

That Thursday, Frank bought a big Danish at the bakery. He vacuumed the house and threw the dirty clothes into the closet, let the dishwasher run with the few things that stood in the sink and took the newspapers out. He took a Bible from the shelf and threw it nonchalantly on his nightstand, and then shaved and found a shirt and a blazer from the closet.

As the doorbell rang, Frank stood ready in the hall, but he waited until the doorbell had rung a second time before he opened. But first he put the Bible away, shaking his head.

'Good morning, Vicar – welcome. Sorry you had to wait, I was on the phone. I'll take your jacket. What was your name again?'

He felt a little silly asking that, as he clearly remembered the vicar's name, it was on the piece of paper with the phone number he had scribbled down. But he needed something to say, he was not accustomed to welcoming vicars into his home. And he was surprised by the tall, clean-cut man on the doorstep, elegantly dressed in a well-fitting woollen coat and a trendy cream-coloured scarf of the kind he knew was really expensive. He'd expected a small, stocky guy with curly hair and a beard.

'Thorkild, my name is Thorkild.'

They shook hands, and Thorkild stepped inside. He hesitated at the entrance to the kitchen.

'You don't have to take off your shoes or anything. Just come in and sit down. I have some cake.'

Thorkild went into the kitchen, folded his scarf and placed it on the table. He looked at Frank.

'How are you?' he asked.

'How are *you*?' Frank replied. Quickly.

Thorkild shrugged his shoulders and smiled.

'Well, how are we.'

Frank felt better. Now they seemed more equal. Both were men who had lost someone. This wasn't just some vicar who had come to take care of him. He cut the cake and shoved the coffee pot in the vicar's direction.

'It's strange that two women die within such a short period of time. I think it's strange.'

'I don't know. People die all the time. I bury two every week.'

'Yes. But shot in that way?'

'Yes, that's . . . odd, as you say. It doesn't happen that often in Denmark. I read that Sanne was found at home? And it was you who found her?'

'Yes. She was in the kitchen. I didn't think she had any enemies. Did she – your wife?'

Thorkild looked embarrassed.

'My wife's name was Karen. I don't understand it either. From one day to another. Then she's gone, I don't know why, I hardly know how. Suddenly everything's changed.'

'I hope they find the bastard, he'll hang for—' Frank looked uncomfortable. 'I'd decided not to swear in front of you.'

'It's OK, sometimes it's the one thing that helps.'

'I'm afraid I often need help, then. We can help each other, I suppose.'

They dug into the coffee and cake, then Thorkild continued.

'I'm a vicar, Frank. I do funerals, often several times a week. I'm forever talking about death, I speak with the relatives. It's so strangely absurd. Now it's me who's bereaved. If you want to talk about Sanne, go ahead. I can listen, give advice, help and support, comfort, be a shoulder to cry on. It's perfectly OK. I'm a professional, to the manor born. But if you have approached me because we're in the same situation, I don't know if I'll be of any use to you. That's a role I'm not accustomed to.'

Frank thought about it.

'I'm jumpy, I become enraged, angry, I take it out on others. On my old friends – Majbritt, for example. And several others as well. I need to be angry with someone. Do you know the feeling?'

'Does it help you, Frank? To be angry?'

'I just wish that whoever did this could feel . . . the same. That's my religion, Vicar. Quid pro quo. That's the way it is. An eye for an eye, it says so in the Bible somewhere. That which is evil, the good guys have a duty to fight it.'

Thorkild looked at him with puzzlement in his eyes. Or maybe it was admiration, Frank wasn't sure.

'My religion is that the good will survive by being good,' the vicar said, thoughtfully. 'Or rather, there are no good and bad people, but good and evil deeds, and so we must each find a way to be good. Meeting the bad with the good. That is what your – our – job is now, I think.'

'Excuse me, Vicar? That's why the good guys always lose. They lie down and let themselves be run over. Oh, no, no hitting or spitting. In your religion there, Thorkild, is there a difference between being good and being . . . maybe should I say *correct*?'

'Maybe it's more a question of propriety. People have to stand up, speak out, mark out their boundaries. But in a proper way. Otherwise we lose respect.' Thorkild's eyes were distant.

'I have no respect left for a murderer, and you mustn't delude yourself into thinking that you have,' exclaimed Frank, striking his fist on the table so hard the cups danced. Thorkild shook his head.

'Respect for yourself. It's a well-known statement in war that you so easily end up resembling your enemy. Don't resemble your enemy here, Frank. The question is, who are you?'

'I'm certainly not a murderer. If I get hold of that bastard I wouldn't like to think what would happen. But no matter what I do, I demand that he be punished. In front of a judge or in a different way. It's always been like that. We think we're so civilised, we have people to judge everything, but we'll hardly scold a child who has stolen cookies. It's not right, though.' Frank spoke with passion and it felt good. 'You need to make things happen. Get things done. Just look at rapists – they get a holiday in the barred hotel, including meals and visits and dessert and all, and they barely have time to turn around in the cell before they're out again. Bunch of wankers, the whole lot of them. A slap on the wrist, and then they're out again, making life miserable for the rest of us.'

'Frank, my first job was working as a prison vicar. That's not the way it works.' The vicar looked at him calmly. 'But, regardless whether punishment is just or not, what difference is it to you? Sanne will never come back, you can never punish *enough*. Small-minded people require punishment. You must make yourself bigger than that. Think of Sanne. She's the one who matters. How you think about her life, how you allow yourself room to be upset. Sorrow – it takes time.' Thorkild had also spoken with passion and looked at Frank, earnestly.

'Right now you're filling the emptiness with anger, I think. It's like a big container. You have shut out Sanne and the good things you shared because it's too hard to think about those things at the moment. And in order to keep it out of the container, you must fill that space with other feelings. Anger, revenge and stuff.'

Thorkild paused and bit his lip. Frank's gaze was like a laser, going straight through him with a clean cut.

'What about yourself?' Frank said. 'Do you practise any of the things you're preaching?'

Thorkild fell silent. It was a simple question, but he had no answer.

Frank continued: 'Then by all means, please tell me how to grieve, properly.'

There was silence in the room.

'I don't know,' said Thorkild.

Then it was Frank's turn to be silent. Thorkild sighed, slumped a little in the chair.

'Frank, when I talk about it this way, it's in order to protect myself. Do you understand?'

'No. Not really.'

'Something has to stand when I'm about to collapse. I have lots of opinions. I could open a shop with them – and they're so authentic, like a gallery that sells only originals. I really should sell them, so I wouldn't have quite so many. I'm sorry, Frank. I should probably just shut up sometimes.'

At that moment, the TV changed programme. The sound was muted, but the new flickering in different colours captured both men's attention. It was sport, a summary of the day's premier league matches. Frank turned it up a bit, and then they sat and watched for about fifteen minutes. They joined in a common chorus of boos and recognition, the men's universal language of Ahh and impressed chuckles. When the programme was over, Frank turned it off and sat for a while, looking at nothing.

'Sanne, my sister, she was shot. She was shot in the stomach, it was what killed her. But she was also shot through both hands. And that's bizarre. Like something you see on film.'

'Yes, I've read it. Stigmata, isn't that the word that the newspapers used?'

'Yes, the journalists have given it a lot of names – The Stigmata Killing, The Millionaire Murder, stuff like that. But the police have not mentioned it once. Isn't it incredible that I have to read stuff like that in the newspapers?'

Thorkild thought of Thea. 'I think the police are very cautious about labelling a case that way. The danger of staring themselves blind at an angle. But if you want to know what stigmata is, it's the Greek word for mark. I think it has to do with identification. The murder must mean something.'

'Such as?'

'It can be identified with some of the things you associate with the crucifixion, or Christianity in general. The victim on the cross, salvation, suffering. That kind of thing.'

'It leaves me none the wiser. That wasn't Sanne. She wasn't religious.' And then he remembered Steffen Hou and thought how little he knew of his sister. 'But then again,' he added, 'what do any of us know about each other?'

That made Thorkild nod.

'I can't seem to decide whether it was a good idea that I came,' he said, rising from his chair. 'Or a bad idea. Somehow, I think we should talk again. But right now I need to run.'

'Well, what the hell. At least I have enough cake for my evening coffee. I think it was OK, this.' Frank gestured at the table. 'Just so you know.' Then he got up to follow Thorkild out.

In the hall he looked into Thorkild's eyes.

'OK, I'll refrain from doing something stupid.'

'And maybe I should try to do something stupid. For once.'

They smiled, and Frank thought the occasion warranted some kind of seal, so he stretched out his hand to formally greet Thorkild. Thorkild pressed it hard, gave Frank a more informal pat on the shoulder and walked away.

25

'I understand you have spoken with my parents-in-law.'

The grocer stood, mighty and imposing, in the doorway to his house, effectively blocking the way to Thea and Kristian. 'Don't you think it's time this came to an end? I'm on my way out.'

Mogens Jepsen's house was recently built, Thea guessed it was ten years old at most, and obviously designed to showcase the grocer's status. The Jepsen family had run a business in Roslinge for over half a century, and Mogens Jepsen's childhood home had been a relatively modest red stone bungalow with brown-painted woodwork, which stood alongside the co-op supermarket. It now served as a retirement home for the grocer's parents, who were alive and well, while Mogens Jepsen had bought himself one of the municipal building sites, which with a little good will could be said to have a view. There, he had built a bungalow, approximately 400 square metres and architect-designed, yet Thea could see nothing special about it. Although twice the size, the place reminded her of her parents' home. It sprawled over the site with great lamella-clad panoramic windows, a landscaped garden with a huge gas barbecue grill and a colour-coordinated theme of rhododendrons in neat flower beds. There was a small pond with a pump-powered fountain and a few goldfish, the carport had room for two cars, and behind it stood a caravan covered by a huge tarpaulin. His taste was both expensive and, it seemed to Thea, pretentious. She glanced at Kristian, recalling his scorn for this provincial version of luxury back when they had been looking at homes together. He was wearing a crooked smile that remained in place as the grocer grudgingly allowed them to cross the threshold, while he used one foot to keep the viciously barking Pekingese at bay.

Thea had been in the Jepsen family house before, but the immaculate order within still amazed her. She and Kristian had arrived unannounced, in part because they wanted to see if it was for real, or if the grocers had made a big deal out of tidying up before the first visit. But the house was, in spite of the dog, cat and three boys, completely flawless. Not a speck of dust, not one stray toy. Its perfection was reminiscent of an old-fashioned hotel. Potpourri and candles on the window sills, large candles with bows on them, looking as if they'd never been used. The potted plants were bedecked with beads and artificial butterflies. The bathroom, which Thea used, featured big rustic tiles, and there were neat piles of cream-coloured towels and an unused fragrance soap in a bowl next to the washbasin's bronze tap. It was a thoroughly neat house, her mother would have loved it.

'I'm selling the car,' said Mogens Jepsen, as they stood in the large kitchen. He gestured for them to take a seat at the big Ellipse table. He remained standing, emptied a cup of coffee and put it into a dishwasher that was camouflaged behind a cabinet door. 'Elisabeth doesn't think we can keep it any more. I'm going to lose money on it. It's a bad time to sell big cars.'

The expression on his face was inscrutable, a strange mixture of irritation and solemnity. 'But I'm glad to hear you've talked with Elisabeth's parents. I assume you will stop treating my wife with this unbearable suspicion.'

'We've spoken to your in-laws, yes,' said Kristian. 'I apologise if you see it as unbearable. It's a difficult case for everyone involved.'

The grocer nodded impatiently. 'I've said what I have to say, but I may as well say it again. Torben is a failure and a disappointment, and I don't trust him any further than I can throw him. But Elisabeth did not go out Saturday night or

Saturday morning. And if she says Torben came home and lay down with the dog, then that's the truth. There you have it, finished.'

He stood with his back to the table, looking out over the fields.

'You're probably asking yourselves, why did I let Torben work in the store. And I'm sure he's told you all kinds of rubbish. But it was what Elisabeth wanted. And Elisabeth . . .' He shrugged his big shoulders. 'It's not often that she asks me for anything.'

Like a shadow, Elisabeth slipped into the kitchen. The grocer nodded to her.

'I'm off to the store,' he said. 'Perhaps you'd like to call in advance of your next visit, so I can make time for you? But really in my opinion our participation in this investigation is done.'

Kristian's gaze was firm. 'I think that's for us to decide, I'm afraid.'

'I just meant that there's a limit to how much more we can contribute,' said Mogens Jepsen, hastily trying to smooth things over. 'We've had so many conversations already. We will cooperate, naturally. We'd like nothing better than a successful conclusion to the case. To summarise: It is our conviction that Torben was careless with the car and left the keys in the ignition. Someone then took it and used it for this atrocious crime. My wife was at home, Torben likewise. My in-laws have probably confirmed it?'

Thea nodded. 'We're here about something else. We're trying to get an idea of Karen Simonsen's life in this town. Among other things, a series of lectures that were held in the gym. We understand from Sonja Kjeldsen that Elisabeth has attended a few of them. We're trying to find out if anyone saw Karen in the company of others at any of these lectures.'

Mogens Jepsen granted permission with a sweeping gesture of the hand. 'Go ahead. Maybe Elisabeth can put some coffee on. Have a nice day.'

Throwing a coat over his arm, he left the house. They heard a car start up.

'It's my car he's taking. Mogens always drives. Even if it takes ten minutes to walk to the store.' Elisabeth Jepsen began to put the coffee on. 'But I don't think he could drive around in the Vitara.'

Elisabeth Jepsen was tall, skinny and colourless, but with beautiful blonde hair tinged with a hint of red. She had dull green eyes and was wearing obviously expensive clothes in the style Kristian liked to call suburban chic: linen in pastel colours with sewn-on motifs in lace and sequins, a necklace made from dark moonstones and sturdy mary-jane shoes in leather. She was not unattractive, but there was a tired, washed-out look about her. Thea wondered whether the spotless house was her main task in life. As if to confirm the notion, Elisabeth slid a washcloth across the kitchen table with an absent gaze. It slipped over the granite, in and out among the numerous bottles of olive oil, balsamic vinegar and herbal schnapps. It occurred to Thea that maybe she was drunk.

'How is Torben?' said Elisabeth, and then, in the same breath: 'Do you take anything in your coffee?'

Kristian shook his head, Thea could see that he was subjecting the woman in front of them to close scrutiny. Elisabeth placed a couple of cups in front of them, stood there a moment, a little insecure, and ended up sitting down.

'Torben Jepsen is fine,' said Thea, keeping it friendly.

'Won't he be out soon? As I understand it, there's no concrete evidence against him.'

The uncertainty was gone. Elisabeth was now firm in voice and gaze. 'My mother and father – you've spoken with them. We were together, here, that morning. Torben went out to buy rolls. That gives him less than an hour to do what you say he has done.'

'We're not saying he's done anything,' said Kristian. 'And you need to hold on to that, Elisabeth. We're here because we want to talk to you.'

'Yes. OK. About the lectures?'

The thing about the lectures was partially true. They were really here because Thea wanted to speak to Elisabeth again, and she wanted to Kristian to see her, evaluate her.

'Karen Simonsen attended some events down at the gym. I believe you did as well?'

'A few, yes. No more than that. Mogens thinks it's important that we support local initiatives.'

Elisabeth's voice revealed that, left to her own devices, she certainly wouldn't be supporting anything. 'So I had to attend some of the lectures. But I wasn't a member of the gym – that's where I draw the line. And I think their dance instructor is very odd.'

He had seemed odd to Thea as well. But Gorm Gayatri had already been excluded as a potential suspect because he had been in Copenhagen the weekend of the murder, hired to lend an exotic touch to a hen party in Holte. She smiled at memory of the guru's indignant retelling of the event, which had apparently been attended by a bunch of champagne-drunk upper-class cows who had been far from *receptive*, giggling hysterically throughout the session.

'I went to a soiree one evening in April. There was a girl from the music academy performing songs from musicals – *Sound of Music*, that sort of thing. Then I went to the lifestyle lecture with the brooch man, but I left after fifteen minutes because I wasn't feeling well.'

'Brooch man?' said Kristian.

'I just noticed that he wore a big, strange brooch. It looked like a large flower in silver with a lump of amber inside. Not something a man would typically wear. And then there was a writer's reading. This young poet from Århus who calls himself the Aros Poet. That's the only time I remember seeing Karen. She was speaking with Asger Jørgensen.'

Elisabeth looked directly at Thea.

'I don't read. It's not for me. But I went to the lecture anyway because Asger is interested in literature. I sat with him and Karen at one of the front tables. He didn't know I was coming, and he didn't look as if he thought it was a good idea. I'm not sure why I did it. Asger's very worried that people will find out about me and him. That people will start talking. The worst thing about this town is how people talk.'

Thea followed her voice attentively, listening for nuances. When they'd questioned her on previous occasions, Elisabeth hadn't exactly tried to hide her affair with the schoolteacher, but she hadn't gone into any detail about it. This time around Thea could see the woman's pain, more obvious and desperate.

'To summarise, as Mogens likes to say: I have not done anything to Karen Simonsen. I was not anywhere near the mill on Saturday morning. The witness you have is mistaken. My husband and my parents and Torben can confirm it. Why would I do such a thing? Why would Torben?'

Tears welled up in the green eyes, Elisabeth wiped them away with a weary swipe of her hand. 'I've thought and thought about how this could possibly be, what it is you're thinking. I wanted to help Torben because he was going through a rough time. I would never do anything that could put him in greater trouble. I simply can't understand why he would have done anything to the vicar's wife. Or why I would have helped him get away with it.'

She sniffled, blew her nose.

'So I'm thinking that you probably suspect I did it myself. I crept out of the house Saturday morning without waking either Mogens or Bisse, went down to the mill path and shot Karen. And you're assuming this is about Asger. But you're wrong, and I don't know how to convince you that you're wrong. You must speak with Asger. Have you spoken with him?'

Kristian nodded. 'We have, of course.'

Elisabeth was silent for a while, composing herself. They let her fill the silence.

'Asger,' she said, 'is my way of surviving.'

As if unhappy with her choice of words, she went on: 'By surviving, I mean . . . I don't know what I mean. Take a look around –' She waved her arms, indicating the gleaming kitchen, as if the explanation was there. 'I bet Asger has told you it's nothing special between us. And he's right, he really is. We don't see each other very often, and it's not champagne and red roses when we do. I enjoy his company, I do. And I would like to have roses from him. But that's not what we're there for, and I've settled for that. Asger doesn't love me.'

'But you love him,' said Kristian.

'Love and love,' the woman said, soberly. 'I'm not so sure any more. In the beginning, you know, when everything is so exciting and forbidden, you might start to believe. But we're just lonely, Asger and me. My boys are getting so big, they pull themselves away from me, they reject my caresses. They don't want their old mother any more. And when nobody touches you, ever, for years, then that first touch is . . . intoxicating. So, you seek consolation. And to be touched. That's what Asger means to me. Is that pathetic?'

Thea didn't answer, and it surprised her when Kristian did. 'No. I don't think it is, Elisabeth.'

'In light of that, you must think that I saw Karen as a threat because she had a friendship with Asger. And I won't sit here and pretend that I wasn't jealous – I was. Because she found it easy to connect with the part of his world that is so important to him. I've tried, I've read some things he's recommended. But it's not for me, I can't get through a book. I simply stop.'

She looked away. 'Talk to Asger. He didn't have a relationship with Karen. I'm certain of it.'

'What about your marriage, Elisabeth?' said Thea.

Elisabeth Jepsen shrugged. 'What about it? I live here. I have a nice house. I have three wonderful sons. Jonathan is going to have his confirmation next spring.'

Then it dawned on her what else lay in Thea's question.

'My mum and dad have undoubtedly told you about their

weekend with us. We dined together Friday night, Torben was in the store and didn't show up until much later. He should have been back by eight, but he wasn't. Then Mogens went down to see if the store was locked, and it was. He came home and was angry that the Vitara was parked outside – I'd said that Torben could borrow it. And I thought it was embarrassing that Mogens pointed it out, about the car, while my parents were there. As if I'm not allowed to lend it to someone.'

Thea nodded. It was consistent with what Elisabeth's anxious parents had told them, independent of each other.

'My father then suggested that we play a game of bridge, to lighten the mood – Mogens loves to play bridge. And so we played. When we were done, Mogens and I went to bed, Mum and Dad a little later. My mum likes to sort out the kitchen before she goes to bed.'

Thea nodded again. Her own mother liked to do that as well.

'At about one in the morning, Bisse starts going crazy in the hall, and I hurry out so that he won't wake Mum and Dad. It's Torben coming home, drunk and stupid. I ask him to go to bed and take the dog with him, and he does. Then I go back to bed. Neither Mogens nor I went anywhere during the night, and it makes no sense. Karen makes no difference to what Asger and I have together. And Mogens – why would he hurt Karen?'

She took a deep breath, then continued, her voice shaky:

'Mogens doesn't know, about Asger and me. At least, I think not. And if he did, he would probably choose to harm one of us – not Karen. If you think it's necessary to tell him about it, do so. I cannot see what purpose it would serve. I have no plans to leave Mogens and the boys. Why would I? But if you tell him this, he'll kick me out for sure. He'll just have to do that.'

Outside the grocer's house Thea paused to listen to her phone messages before she and Kristian climbed into the Mondeo.

They drove, for lack of a better alternative, out to the petrol station on the bypass and ordered a couple of French hotdogs.

'I don't know, Thea, whether you need to confront Mogens with the affair. I have trouble seeing the motive. And this strange threesome are each other's alibi, they're in complete agreement that someone must have stolen the car. Anika Svendsen's identification of Elisabeth – I wouldn't go to court on that. And the connection to Karen is weak at best. I see nothing here that justifies a conspiracy between Mogens, Torben and Elisabeth. If that's the explanation there must be something we've overlooked. Besides, it's a huge risk to take: using his own car to transport the body. I don't know.' Kristian shook his head.

'Do you think she's lying?'

'No, not really. Probably mostly to herself. But I follow her reasoning. Who called?'

'Anne-Grethe, who was kind enough to point out that it's almost been a month. And Søren. He's talked with the manager of the gym, Sonja Kjeldsen, about the lectures. The only slightly interesting thing is that the one Elisabeth called the brooch man is called Bo Zellweger, like the actor. She could in fact also remember that brooch. The title of the lecture was *Insist on Yourself* and was something in the self-help line. The odd part is that they have no personal information on him. He'd called Sonja Kjeldsen, offering to give a lecture and referring her to a nice website with good reviews. He said he had been earning a fortune as a motivational speaker in the United States, speaking at corporate events and stuff, and now he wanted to try out a Danish audience in a small venue, see if he could get people going when he spoke Danish. And Sonja remembered because his Danish was absolutely flawless – no uncertainty or accent. He received the fee in cash, and the website has since closed, it's impossible to track down who hosted it back then.'

'Was Karen present at the lecture?' Kristian asked.

'Sonja Kjeldsen is convinced that she was. He was probably

just another one of these prophets who need to start over with new health theories. But it's worth looking into.'

Kristian ordered another hotdog. 'What a house, huh? Completely bereft of charm. All those knick-knacks and orna-ments, Monet reproductions, fragrant candles. As if the whole thing was put together by someone incapable of having a single independent thought.'

'It's not like you to say so.'

'It's not?' he said. 'Of course it is. I've always had a hard time with that kind of thing – the fake suburban idyll. And a spineless woman who sits in the middle of it all and appar-ently sees it as her mission in life to guard her reputation.'

Thea looked at him, stunned.

'What now,' he said. 'That's not like me, either?'

'No, it's not. One of the things that makes you such a good investigator is that you always have such a keen eye for the subtleties, Kristian. You rarely judge. It's strange to hear you speak so categorically about that woman and her home.'

'Isn't this our lunch break? I'm not speaking as an investigator now. But as your . . .' He didn't complete the sentence, but gave her a look. She thought she saw an allegation in it.

'Your what?'

'Goddamn it, Thea. Can't I talk about something off the record? Can't I say anything to you without it immediately being processed and analysed?'

'Let's go, Kristian. I don't want to talk when you're being so belligerent. Unless you want to tell me what this is really about.'

To her amazement she saw him turn against her, his face distorted and every muscle tense.

'Have I disappointed you, Thea? Have I not lived up to your expectations? Kristian Videbæk takes twenty minutes off and says something that doesn't fit into your picture. And immediately, you drop the hammer.'

He tugged on his jacket with angry jerks. 'I don't know if you've noticed, but I'm struggling to keep it together. I take care of the kids, I do everything around the house, I shop and

I cook, I'm working overtime to afford all the things that Mette thinks she needs. Therapy, a cleaning lady because she can't do anything. Right now she has this idea that some fancy pillows with magnets in them is the way to go. Are you aware of what these things cost? And still, I make the time to see you.'

'OK. I was not aware I was a stress factor in your life.'

'That was not what I said. But maybe you're not the only one who is disappointed. When was the last time you asked me how I feel?'

'I ask. All the time.'

He shook his head.

'Maybe it's not always that easy for me to hear, Kristian – have you thought about that? Having it spelled out in minute detail how your life is at home?'

'Wow. We've known each other for years. Don't pretend that suddenly you can't handle it.'

'Just because we've known each other for years, just because we've chosen certain things, that doesn't mean it doesn't hurt. I thought you knew.'

'I can't believe you think that you're the one who has it hard. Given the circumstances.'

'Should I feel sorry for you? Is that it? Do you need a pat on the head?'

'I didn't say that. But maybe a little compassion. The sort of thing people can usually summon up when it's someone they're supposed to love.'

'You don't see Elisabeth Jepsen. You see Mette. And now you want an accomplice – but it's not me, Kristian! We made our choices. If you don't like the consequences any more, then make some new ones.'

'Oh, how easy. How easy it is, Thea. Thanks for the wise words.'

Kristian got up and stormed out so fast that the petrol station's glass doors barely managed to open in time. Thea sat and watched him walk past the car and down the road with long, almost running strides.

26

They were an odd bunch, as they made their way to the vicarage. They arrived with determined steps, as if they had pulled themselves together. Which probably wasn't too far wrong, Thorkild thought, when he spotted the uninvited guests from his kitchen window. He had been granted a six-week leave from the church by the dean, while his colleague in Vilå covered for him. In the month that had passed since Karen's death, he hadn't seen many members of the congregation. But he had, in general, seen few people. And of the delegation of three self-appointed VIPs from the parish council, two had been involved in the police investigation. Anton Svendsen, the short-legged local missionary whose temper was known far and wide, making his wife, Anika, the subject of collective pity from the whole parish, was flanked by the grocer, Mogens Jepsen, and the cantor, who looked uncomfortable. That Anika Svendsen claimed to have seen Elisabeth Jepsen at the scene was known all over Roslinge, and as a result the atmosphere between the two men was tense. Actually, Thorkild could well understand that it was awkward for them to show up in the vicarage.

But here they were. Anton rapped on the door with a firm knock, and Thorkild pulled himself together and opened the door. First, however, he glanced at himself in the mirror in the hall. He looked just about OK. He'd lost weight, but he'd managed a few good nights' sleep, and that had done him good.

'Hello, Thorkild. We're here on behalf of the parish council.'

'Yes, I can see that. Welcome. Come on in.'

The three men wiped their feet on the mat in a laborious way. Thorkild wondered where they should go and sit. The kitchen was the place where he always had his meals now, and he was beginning to enjoy it, thought it was nice to be near the simmering pots and the gurgles of the coffee machine – he was constantly putting on coffee. Yet he showed his three guests into the living room, where he discovered that some of Karen's long-since withered flowers were still standing in a vase on the bureau. He grabbed them while Mogens Jepsen handed him a bouquet from the supermarket's little flower stall: pink peonies wrapped in cellophane. Embarrassed, he accepted it and stood with the withered flowers in one hand and the fresh in the other.

'Yes. We thought it best that we don't all disturb you. I mean, in your grief. You probably have lots to do. So we've come on everyone's behalf. We extend our condolences,' said the grocer.

'Yes, we extend our condolences,' repeated the cantor, meekly.

He was a small, pale man with a liver-pâté-coloured moustache, known only as The Cantor. Everyone in Roslinge spoke of him as The Cantor, and he and his wife were collectively known as *The Cantors*. Karen would always object to the term whenever Thorkild announced: 'I've been to see the Cantors about Sunday's hymn—'

'Who's that?' she'd reply. 'Why don't you use their names – they're surely called something. At least give her a name.'

Thorkild had always thought it a sweet custom. And he'd liked the idea that he and Karen together had comprised *The Vicars*.

He went into the kitchen, put the coffee on and poured the biscuits he had purchased for condolence visits on a platter. They looked dull and prosaic. Actually, he wanted a beer and smiled at the thought of what the missionary man Anton would say if he were to place four cold bottles of Carlsberg at the table. A proper wake! But he could not quite remember whether Anton was a fierce teetotaller or just moderate. Until he was thirsty enough.

Thorkild threw the withered flowers in the rubbish bin and put the peonies in the empty vase, struggling to get them to stand up nicely. When he returned to the room, the three men were still standing.

'Please, have a seat. Make yourselves at home.'

'We don't wish to intrude.' The cantor was hesitant.

Then Mogens Jepsen pulled a chair over to the coffee table and sat down resolutely. The others followed suit.

'Yes, it's so very sad,' Mogens said, before the silence took hold of them. 'Very strange, the whole business. I don't think I have to tell you, Thorkild, that this matter affects us all deeply. The entire church council – indeed, the whole town, for that matter.'

Anton cleared his throat and followed this with: 'And Karen. Little Karen, who never harmed a soul. Imagine that. Anika and I, we appreciated her. We always thought she kept everything so nice up here. A good wife doesn't make a fuss.'

That one was directly addressed to Mogens.

'No, Karen minded her own business. That's what a good wife does, too. In my opinion,' he replied. Thorkild had an urge to giggle; he rubbed his nose in an effort to avert it.

The cantor looked thoughtful. 'But you know it, Thorkild – the sorrow. It is perhaps an advantage?'

Thorkild shook his head. 'No, it's . . . very different when it's like this. It's difficult to use my experience from funerals in this situation.'

'Of course it is,' said Anton Svendsen. 'It's obviously quite different. None of us can imagine what it must be like. A murder, it's terrible. And your spouse. His one and only.'

'Has the vicar ever buried . . .' the cantor was struggling to find the right words, '– a murder victim before?'

'No, I have not,' said Thorkild.

'Of course you haven't, Thorkild. Such things are rare,

thankfully. That's why it's so unbelievable with Karen,' said Anton.

They all lapsed into silence until Mogens Jepsen cleared his throat:

'We sincerely hope you have someone who can help you. Your children are probably a reliable support during this . . . difficult time.'

'Yes, it's difficult for us too,' supplemented the cantor, 'maybe we should—'

'But we pray for the vicar. You must know that. And you must put your faith in that, Thorkild,' said Anton.

'So many people read the headlines in the store when there's news on the case. I think that shows an interest from the people in this town. I sell twice as many newspapers when there is something about the case. No, there is certainly no lack of interest,' said Mogens.

'Yes, everyone is thinking of you,' said the cantor. 'Everyone asks about you in church. They come up after the sermon, as if I know something.'

Thorkild smiled. 'Not that there's much to know. Is everything going well with my substitute?'

'Yes, for a Vilå vicar she's not half bad,' said the cantor. 'Although there are probably different opinions on that.' He looked sternly at Anton, who had not appeared in church for any of the female substitute's services.

'You just take all the time you need, and we look forward to welcoming your happy face back to the church,' said Anton. 'I think we should go and let Thorkild have some peace.'

Mogens stood up, as resolutely as he had sat himself down. 'Yes, and do come to the store if you need something. I have some ready meals in the refrigerators, they're actually quite good. You probably don't have the energy to cook. And Elisabeth is great at baking. If you need anything . . . We're terribly sorry for everything that this matter has brought on.'

'Now, the daily bread we pray for is not simply a question of what fills the stomach,' said Anton.

The three men stood up. Thorkild opened the front door for them, noted an incipient headache, brought on by his mournful grimace. 'Thank you for coming, it means a lot to me.'

'But of course,' replied Anton Svendsen. 'We're happy to tell the rest of the parish council that, given the circumstances, you are doing well.'

27

Birgitte had come to visit Thorkild.

Or Birgitte had moved in with Thorkild. What's the difference? In this case, the limit had imperceptibly been crossed.

Birgitte Hjort was one of Thorkild's old girlfriends from the university. She had been in love with Thorkild back then, and had swallowed her disappointment when Thorkild got together with Karen, in order to still be able to see Thorkild. They had kept in touch the first few years after Thorkild was married, with a few visits and a few dinners. When Michael was born, it faded away.

He remembered Birgitte's infatuation clearly. He was deeply surprised. And very, very flattered. Had for a brief moment wondered whether he should discontinue the relationship with Karen to let himself be engulfed by the feeling Birgitte's admiration aroused in him. And quickly abandoned the idea. He was not in love with her. And he told her so, in a café back in what seemed like another life. His university years, his optimism, all the prospects, the pleasure of Karen – his first real girlfriend. All the thoughts that he had about the life he wanted. *He*, rather than *they*, he had to admit, but that was only natural, wasn't it?

It went OK at the café. Birgitte was not the type to make a scene. And there was nothing to end, really, just a hope to extinguish. He was to meet with Karen in Magasin afterwards, he recalled. And he also recalled how he had felt oddly at ease when he left the café. The idea of being wanted, courted, having had to say no to one woman in order to say yes to another. The greatness of the moment, the importance of it had engulfed him, made his steps heavy and dignified. But since then, he had rarely thought of Birgitte.

A month after the death, she had arrived. One bright sunny morning she had suddenly barged in with her suitcase and five bags of groceries from a Føtex supermarket. Red-cheeked, smiling, with wind-swept hair, she stood on his doorstep, woke him from a stupor with an energetic knock and laughed delightedly at his perplexed expression when he opened the door. He recognised her immediately because of that laugh.

'What the . . . Birgitte, is that you?'

'I forgot onions and I just couldn't be bothered to run all the way into Føtex again. So I've been to your local store. Good God, the prices! I hope you make a lot of money or supplement it with the collections.' She smiled disarmingly. 'Didn't you get my text?'

'Your text? Uh. It's just that . . . I don't check the phone that often. You've written?'

She put the bags down on the doorstep and gave him a hug.

'I have. And I'm going to cook. I seem to remember you like Italian?'

She let go. Studied him.

'Don't you want some company, Thorkild?'

He stepped aside and let her in.

Birgitte and Karen were as different as night and day, and though he'd married the one type, the second type – lively, overbearing, immediate – always held a massive attraction for him.

She was blonde. She was jolly. She was energetic and capable, found an extra blanket in a long-forgotten chest, aired it and put on fresh linen. She picked flowers and put them in vases. She cut the overgrown plants in the pots in front of the rectory into shape. She cleaned with an unknown brand of detergent, which made the whole house smell differently. She cooked and sang in his kitchen with the radio on, full volume.

She stayed.

It was a little awkward. It shouldn't be like this, Thorkild thought, he ought to be by himself, facing the grief head on instead of just letting the void be filled. And when he received well-intentioned condolence visits, he thought he owed some explanation as to why Birgitte apparently lived there, and it seemed so artificial. But dammit, had he not promised Frank Andersen during his strange visit up north to be a little less correct?

And the distraction, he enjoyed to the full. He let the photo album rest. Didn't stop to wonder how it was possible that she was there. Had she taken leave? How was her life otherwise? She said nothing, he made a virtue out of not asking, of just being in this woman's company, enjoying her cakes, her red wine, her ears that listened to his concerns. She slept in the guest room and had the morning coffee ready when he got up.

But one evening, Birgitte grabbed his hand. Just after Thorkild had closed the front door on the parish council chairman and his mouse-grey wife after yet another condolence visit. She pushed him back against the closed front door, in the narrow hallway, so he could not escape her gaze. He was taken by surprise. It was the first time that Birgitte had touched him beyond a friendly hug.

'Thorkild,' she said firmly, 'you're a fucking parody of a vicar. And this show is getting boring.' He stared at her, stunned.

'You have comforted so many people, you've helped them in their grief, and then you have created a picture of how grief should be. Deep, silent, introverted. And now you think you have a hell of a lot to live up to. Every time we have guests you put on your mournful face, the vicar who is supposed to be quiet, soul-searching and becomingly sad. But the rest of the time, you walk around, almost whistling. Why can't you let grief have its own expression instead of playing that role?'

Her gaze nailed him to the wall. A rush of anger surprised him. A breach of their implied contract, their roles so far. The peace of the house. Yet he thought about what she'd said.

'Have you ever considered that it could be vice versa? That it is with you that I flee? Think of what I'm fleeing from – I daren't let the grief in and make room for it. There are people here in the parish who can help me to grieve, because we have a language for it, in the church – and you don't see that. You don't speak that language. You've never been able to, Birgitte.'

Birgitte shook her head. 'You can't be reflexive about grief. It's a feeling. It must be spontaneous, right there in the stomach. It can't be scheduled three times a week to coincide with visits from the pitying, sacrificing parishioners.'

Thorkild shook her off, irritated, and went into the living room, but she followed him.

'When it comes down to it, I think you are afraid. I think you're afraid to admit to yourself that you aren't dying of grief, but that you actually can see that you can move forward. To hell with it, Thorkild. What you need is what you've always dreamed of with me.'

'And what would that be? What do you think I've always dreamed of with you?'

'Don't you know? It's in your eyes, all the time.'

'Stop it, Birgitte. What do you even know about me any more. It's been so many years.'

'You need to have sex. You need to let go of everything and lose that damn control.'

She had maintained her grip on his hand. Now she tugged at him and led him towards his office, where she authoritatively pushed him down on the couch. She held a strong hand against his chest as if to hold him down while she calmly proceeded to undress him. Thorkild buried himself in an intense inner struggle, but quickly surrendered completely. He opened all the pores of his body and mind and allowed himself to be over-powered and invaded. Without loosening the pressure on his chest, she loosened her own clothes and sat astride him.

The feeling that swept over his body as she sank down over him made him dizzy and he gasped for breath, over-whelmed, in a startled cry. It was blissful, and it hurt. He was rock hard in a split second, harder than he had been since adolescence, harder than ever, was how it felt. And it was infinitely long ago since he had felt the inside of a woman.

She paused for a moment, letting him get used to the feeling. Then moved quickly and fiercely, rocking herself into place on him until Thorkild exploded, helpless, surrendering. He bellowed, tears ran from his eyes, and Birgitte lay down behind him and hugged him, with complete naturalness, as if she had known that it was precisely that kind of release she wanted to provoke.

Thorkild cried. For two hours he wept and sobbed. Naked and entwined by Birgitte's naked body, he lived through an ecstasy of grief.

Later, they climbed into the guest bed that had been Birgitte's. They sat under the quilts, naked and with steaming green tea, which Thorkild thought tasted of grass. He was exhausted, hungry, his body felt as if it was on fire as he buried himself in the feeling of the downy, foreign skin against his. The artlessness with which lovers touch each other after sex, the brand-new landscape between two people. It felt a lifetime ago since he had been touched. She caressed his hair. He stroked her collarbone, completely lost in the feeling of her soft skin against his fingertips. His preoccupation seemed to amuse her.

'I've always lived with this big "why" in my life,' he told her. 'When the other boys at school were interested in natural science and had constant light-bulb moments of things that had effects and causes, I would ask myself why? There was a huge contrast in the questions we asked. I could never be satisfied with explanations of how events cause each other with mechanical laws or chemical processes. It never seemed appropriate.'

'You're not a schoolboy any more, Thorkild.'

'It's the same now. I'm haunted by the question of why she was murdered. And I don't know what answer would be worse: that it was an accident, a mistake, or that she had such an influence on another that she had to die.'

Birgitte looked out of the window.

'Whatever meaning lies behind it, it will still be meaningless to you, Thorkild.'

'Well, I have a hard time with the meaningless. It's like a flaw in my brain. I can't see events as meaningless. Everything happens for a specific reason. It's almost a mania with me, everything has a meaning to be found.'

'Manic is exactly the word.' She gave a little laugh. 'I guess it helps you get things in order. To avoid chaos and randomness. You keep everything together – and most of all you keep yourself together. But you can't do that without losing yourself.'

'What do I have to lose? Other than my temper.'

She gathered her blanket around her, hid her entire delightful body beneath the duck down; she was irresistible. Thorkild wanted her again. In the midst of thinking about Karen, the inappropriateness of it caused him to tremble, but the desire did not subside. Birgitte held him with her gaze.

'You could lose access to yourself because your temper is in the way. The ever-rational meaning structures. Imagine if you don't fit into the equation, Thorkild, there was a meaning, but that there was no room for whoever created that meaning?'

'Many things make sense. I fantasise that they find the killer. That everything will be clarified. All the questions. And then, with peace of mind, I can forgive. That's how I preach. That you could face each other, that he openly and honestly would tell me why, that I would not understand it, yet I would forgive so it would no longer count for him and he wouldn't understand it, and then they the two missing understandings would cancel out each other. As a gesture from heaven.'

She smiled at him, a peaceful smile as he recognised from the old days. It made her look young, fresh as when he first got to know her, a lifetime ago. What did he look like in her eyes, just now, at this moment?

'A gesture from the sky. How anointing. What if he will not let you have the option of forgiveness?'

'He's the one who gets it. It lies in the word. It's me who has something to give.'

'And you will have the whole saint effect, and that's worth a lot. Thorkild, you cannot go free of guilt in this life. And that's good. Blame is what makes the real human relationships. That is what makes us commit to each other, we love, we're linked together. If you go free of guilt, then you walk away from the seriousness that gives relationships their depth. In reality, blame is perhaps the meaning of it all. The kit that binds us together. Imagine if I forgave you when you were guilty of doing me right?'

'The blame . . . is the distance between us.'

'The blame, dear, is important. The importance that we have in each other's lives. That's why you're so busy with the damn killer. Now it's a diffuse guilt, because it cannot be directed at anything. And all guilt needs to be directed towards something. That's why you need to find him.'

She slid out of bed, out of his grip and began to get dressed, slowly, piece by piece. She tried to smooth her messy hair.

'It's terrible, what you're saying,' said Thorkild. 'It's the whole mechanism behind scapegoats. This is precisely what drives human cruelty. That we suspect each other, accusing one another, justify ourselves by wiping guilt off on others, if not the entire community. I don't believe in that. We have to fight those mechanisms. There are always other reasons. Man is a product of all possible circumstances: upbringing, surroundings, personal capability. Karen's killer, too, I'm sure.

I just want to see it, understand it, know what excuses him and how a man could go so far because of my Karen.'

'Christ Almighty, Thorkild. Excuses? People are not excused. Not just like that. We're guilty. We all are. And when it becomes unbearable, that's when your god comes into the picture. We must carry the guilt that is there to carry. The idea of human freedom requires that we can actually choose differently in some situations. Otherwise, it makes no sense. And where I incur guilt – and I do, in all my decisions – I must take it upon myself to live with it. But there will always be a residue. Something I'm not guilty of, because I, for various reasons, didn't have a choice.'

'Yes, and what do you do if guilt must always be addressed? What do you do with the rest?'

'I suppose you use your god, my dear vicar. As the creator, He is exactly the personification of all the guilt that cannot be carried by human shoulders. When man can no longer help himself, God will, because He has arranged life itself that way. So, the real guilt is present among us. But only the real one. What we actually have to bear, because we could have acted differently. But God must carry the rest. When they find the murderer, then you must decide for yourself how much you will excuse him. And the rest? Yes, that's where you let God have a piece of the cake. The murderer may atone for what he's actually guilty of. And then you curse God for the rest.'

Thorkild was silent. He stood up and walked into the bathroom. Turned on the shower. Felt surrounded by the two women, Birgitte and Karen, while the warm water knocked against his body. It felt different, Birgitte had rinsed off the showerhead with vinegar. He closed his eyes and saw Karen's dark eyes and Birgitte's white breasts, thinking about the circumstances that had made his life the way it was. All the thoughtful choices stood before him as sheer coincidence. The thought sent a shiver through him, and still he felt pervaded with a feeling of ease, a happy twitching in the body, an erection that would not completely wear off.

He pushed the thoughts away. Got out of the shower, ready to greet a new day, although it could hardly be called morning yet.

Birgitte had begun to clean up the kitchen. There was freshly brewed coffee and bread on the table.

'Why have you come, Birgitte?' said Thorkild.

'Look at us, Thorkild, we're up so early that not even the morning paper has arrived before us.'

28

Over lunch that day, Thorkild repeated his question to Birgitte. She had found an old set of china which had been his grandmother's. Soft and delicate, cream-coloured earthenware with gold edges and painted field flowers.

'I had some vacation saved up. Does it matter why I'm here? I'm here because I want to be here.'

'Last night . . . you were wonderful.'

'Don't, Thorkild. Don't talk it to death. You talk and talk. Look, I've made an omelette, why don't you try some?'

He took a piece, Birgitte brought the pepper mill and poured fresh pepper over the food. He sneezed. The pepper mill had been empty for years, standing in a greasy corner by the stove. She must have discovered it and bought fresh peppercorns in the supermarket.

'It tastes great. Don't you have a boyfriend? You never had children?'

'You would know something about me if you had ever called me back these past years.'

He looked at her in surprise, but there was no trace of reproach in her voice. She smiled disarmingly.

'No, nothing of the sort, Thorkild. I didn't marry, had no children. I married work. I'm a consultant in the personnel department, I deal with arbitration. And now I've had enough and I need a break. We're separated, the job and I, considering a divorce. Is there anything else you want to know?'

'Probably.' He wanted to ask her what she wanted to achieve with her visit. Whether she felt something for him. How long she was going to stay. But it felt trivial, and it was as if she read his thoughts.

'But you could of course choose your questions carefully, Thorkild.'

And just then, the phone rang, and Thea Krogh's voice sounded from another reality.

'Hello, Thorkild, it's Thea. Krogh. How are you?'

The voice sounded fresh, enthusiastic. The image of her appeared on Thorkild's retina, and he looked over at his star map. Confused. They hadn't talked for quite a while, not since he had called to update her on his conversation with Isabella. Back during his days of doing detective work about Karen, something he had gladly shelved for a while. The smell of the new woman was everywhere on him, despite the hot shower. Birgitte at the table, Thea on the line, Karen, who looked into nowhere on the picture on the wall. He quickly took the phone into the living room.

'Thea? Hello, I'm good, thanks. Is there any news?' He could hear his own voice, rushed. Surprised, his mind travelled back a few days when the only thing on his mind had been waiting for one of these calls from Thea Krogh. But now the interruption was unwelcome, he wanted the omelette and peace and quiet and Birgitte's body. His desire for her was omnipresent, impossible to shake off.

'I just wanted to follow up on a few things. A few routine questions. But maybe it's a bad time,' said Thea, and he wondered if she had picked up on his impatience.

'No. It's OK. We're having lunch. But ask away, you surely have lots to do.'

'How are you, Thorkild?' Her tone was compassionate and comfortable, just as he remembered it; he had often thought of her quiet voice when the turmoil in his body had threatened to take over. Now it seemed patronising to him.

'Well, I'm fine. I had a visit from some of the parish council a few days ago. The grocer, among others. And Anton. It would have been nice to know a little about what goes on in the investigation.'

'Yes, I understand. And I'm sure you understand the way we work. Nobody is trying to keep you in the dark. When I know something, you will too.'

Thorkild gave a conciliatory nod at the phone. 'Yes, of course. Sorry. But it was an odd situation. And I feel sorry for Mogens Jepsen, it can't be easy to be him.'

'No, it's probably not.'

'And how are you, Thea?'

She didn't answer. 'We still have no explanation as to how Karen ended up in the grocer's car. The most likely explanation is that it was stolen.'

'But you do have a man in custody? Torben Jepsen?'

'Yes . . .' she sounded hesitant. 'And you still can't think of anything that can tie Karen to him? The very smallest of details could be important here.'

'Again, no. Nor to Mogens and Elisabeth. We've been through this so many times, Thea. Is there really nothing new to go on?'

'Yes, there is. We're investigating all possibilities. And I've looked at the books you sent me, Thorkild. The ones you borrowed from Isabella Munk.'

'And what do you make of them?'

'The same as you, I think,' she said. 'Inspirational books. About meeting your potential.'

'Change your life, leave everything.'

'No, not really. I think Karen's choice of books is a matter of getting in touch with yourself, feeling what it is to be yourself. I see them as being a little more down to earth than you do, Thorkild. Not a revolution, just a change.'

He let the words penetrate him, he liked them.

'As for the therapist Isabella mentioned, we haven't come any closer,' continued Thea. 'I find it odd that you knew nothing about an expenditure of that size. I don't know any therapists who work for free. It's also odd that Isabella Munk doesn't know any more about it, if they were so close. I wonder if Karen could have lied about that part to Isabella Munk. And that's the reason I'm calling. You know her.'

'Do I? Well, I suppose anything is possible. But why would she do that?'

Thea weighed her words carefully.

'Could you imagine that Karen was undergoing a process of self-development, supported and encouraged by Isabella, and that she wanted to give the impression of being further along in the process than she was? To please a friend? Maybe it was all a little too much for Karen.'

'I don't know,' said Thorkild, tired now. 'Honestly, Thea, I simply don't know. Before, I would have said that it was important for Karen to be committed to what she did. And now I think she suppressed so much . . .'

They let the silence last a while, it felt comfortable between them.

'We've learned a little more about the lectures Karen attended,' said Thea. 'And while we're on that: Did Karen talk about the lecture? A man with a brooch, maybe. A writer who calls himself the Århus poet, a lifestyle expert named Bo Zellweger?'

Thorkild sighed.

'I don't understand you, Thea.'

'You don't understand me?'

'Why do you keep asking? I wish you would believe me: if Karen had said anything about anyone, I would have told you. God, I'm tired of this.'

'I do know, Thorkild,' said her quiet voice, and it comforted him to a degree that made him lean against the wall and close his eyes. 'I don't think you're holding anything back. But the human brain's storage of information is such that detail usually draws in more details. It's basic interview technique. When recalling a detail that you thought was unimportant, it triggers an association of new details. A name you might not even remember having been told. A colour, a scent – scent is actually one of the best triggers. Don't let yourself be frustrated, Thorkild. Try to let it work.'

'Yes. I'm sorry.'

'Don't apologise. Let us help each other instead. We want the same thing here.' And then: 'Did your wife have any connection to the south of Jutland? Aabenraa, specifically?'

Thea's voice was suddenly hard to decipher, and Thorkild was curious. Was Thea Krogh tense, moving out on thin ice? He thought a little.

'Not immediately, no. She has an old aunt in Tønder. That's the only link to south Jutland. Why?'

'I don't know if you remember that there was a case there. An old case from '99. There's probably no connection whatsoever. A manslaughter with two women involved. As I said, it's a routine inquiry.'

'Two female homicides?'

'We're just investigating, like we have to.'

Thorkild wouldn't let go. 'What is this, really? Where are you with that guy, Torben Jepsen? I thought you just needed solid evidence. He's in custody. You would surely not keep a man in custody unless you're pretty sure you have the perpetrator?'

'No,' Thea hesitated. 'We don't expect more killings. There was one murder in Aabenraa, and it was probably solved. Most of them are solved, thankfully. There is no link to Torben Jepsen there. It's just a feeling. My call is a routine matter. It's probably not the way to proceed, Thorkild.'

'Which way do we proceed, then?'

'*We* hardly do anything. By we, I mean the police.'

'It doesn't sound like a lot to me. There are no results, and now you're talking about a murder in Aabenraa, over ten years ago. It sounds as if you're grasping at straws.'

'It's probably Torben Jepsen, you know. That's a result.'

'Why do you say probably? Is that not the police's conviction?'

'I cannot tell you any more right now, Thorkild.'

'That's currently the only thing you have to go by – a presumption and an old case from the other end of the country?'

'We have more to go by. I can guarantee you, Thorkild, we're doing everything we can. But Thorkild—'

'Yes?'

'You're not the one who asks the questions, OK? Have a little faith in me.'

This time, Thorkild would not be dismissed.

'Can I get permission to see the report? The one from Aabenraa?'

'Of course not.' She sounded disappointed, as though she had expected more of him. And not so hopeless an enquiry.

'Well, then I'll just sit back and wait to hear from you once again, Thea. Then I can hang around here at your mercy and wait for something to happen. Or for you to decide to tell me something. Or I could just move on with my life.' He was upset, his thoughts were back with Karen.

Birgitte emerged from the kitchen, leaning against the door frame and looking at him.

Thea Krogh hesitated.

'There are newspaper articles from 1999 that deal with the murders in Aabenraa, if you want to know more. Journalists called them *The Shadow Murders*. I cannot tell you any more than that. But now at least you know that something is in fact happening. All the newspapers are publicly available.' She paused and breathed deeply. 'I do care about you, Thorkild.'

The hurt in her voice surprised him.

'Why are you telling me this?' he said, in a low voice.

'I don't know, really. You asked me to. Didn't you? What is it you want me to do?'

'I don't know,' said Thorkild. Fully in line with the truth.

29

Birgitte had rummaged in the house all morning. Made coffee, cake, tidied up. As if something important was about to happen. It was Sunday. It had been five weeks since Karen had been found in the river by the vicarage.

'You are amazing, Birgitte,' Thorkild was standing in his pyjamas, leaning against the stove with a coffee mug in his hand and watching her. 'You're an amazing lover, you're a classic housewife, you are even beautiful.'

'I am, really,' she said.

'But I don't know if I'll ever love you in that way.'

Birgitte looked deliberately hurt and said, slowly:

'You just had to say that? You know what, I'll take it as a challenge. I'm counting on you needing time to recover. Before I leave, I promise you that you'll love me.'

She had moved towards Thorkild and stood looking him in the eye, challenging him. Her final words were spoken with her lips as close to his as they could get without touching them. Then she laughed disarmingly, turned her back on him and walked into the living room. 'Sometimes you say things, Thorkild, that make me feel I'm in one of those old Danish movies. With Paul Reichardt. You talk about love as if you know what it means to love me.'

'We make love all the time.'

'And we could be doing that right now, if you hadn't invited guests.' But she wasn't angry, she was never angry. And never really serious.

'It's just this poor guy I promised to talk to, who's coming,' said Thorkild. 'It's part of my job.'

'It's Frank who's coming, Thorkild. Your new ally, as I understand it. Imagine all the others who come into this house, who have known Karen and think of her. This guy is the first who will see me as the lady of your house.'

'You're not the lady of the house. You're a guest, visiting.'

Birgitte peered around the corner of the door frame.

'From today, I'm the lady of the house. Get dressed, man of the house.'

Thorkild laughed.

'OK, I'll get dressed, and then I'll help with the icing on the cake. You want to choose my clothes as well? Crazy woman.'

When the bell sounded, Birgitte was the first one at the door. She greeted and welcomed Frank in. Frank was halfway inside the living room before Thorkild had time to react.

'Hello, Vicar. Tell me, did she rise from the grave?' Frank nodded his head in the direction of Birgitte, who for once looked baffled at that remark. And Thorkild wasn't free from enjoying it a little.

'No, she's an old friend who is visiting and helping me. Welcome, Frank. The trip went well down here?'

'Yes, yes. It did.' Frank looked around cautiously.

Birgitte had already regained her footing, seized the tray that stood ready in the kitchen, and invited Frank into the living room.

'See, now there is cake and coffee. And do you take milk or sugar, Frank?'

'Uh, no. No, it's OK, just black.'

Frank collected himself and stared at Birgitte. Thorkild was amused by him, Frank was more taciturn than he had been when they first met.

'Welcome, both, to my house.' He put the stress on *my*, while he glanced at Birgitte. 'Have some of Birgitte's wonderful lemon cake. She's the best in a kitchen. And above all, a good friend. It's important to have good friends. Which is also why I'm glad you came, Frank. In many ways, we face the same situation.'

'You're right. Although I've mostly come for the cake.' Frank reached out for the tray. 'And if you've wondered what has befallen me lately, I have not avenged anything yet. The right one to hurt just hasn't shown up.'

'Let's hope the right one never does,' said Birgitte.

'They'll figure it out,' said Thorkild. 'The police know what they're doing. There are so few murder cases they don't solve. I guess it's simply a matter of waiting. And having a little confidence.' He thought he almost sounded like Thea, and felt a twinge of remorse at the thought of the telephone conversation earlier. He had considered calling her up again.

'On what? Waiting for what?' said Birgitte. He thought she sounded challenging, and it irritated Thorkild. They were all sitting at the table in the living room now, and the cake was passed around.

'For them to find him, so we can move on. I have complete faith in the female investigator, Thea Krogh. You've met her, Frank?'

But she went on. 'And what if they don't? Find him?'

'They will, of course, Birgitte.'

Birgitte looked at him.

'My point is that it hardly makes any difference. Life is happening right now. You cannot just wait. Look at your life! Clean it and give it some new clothes. What difference does it make if the murderer is found? Karen is gone, your sister is gone, Frank, and life goes on.'

Thorkild gave her a look that hopefully sent her the message that he was getting tired of her.

'Yes, and they may not find him. You hear stories. Unsolved cases – they're showing a TV series right now,' said Frank.

'Isn't it amazing that you can make a whole series of programmes about cases that have never been solved? There was an interview with a man whose daughter, nine years old, was raped and strangled. That was over fifteen years ago, but his life was completely destroyed. Because justice was never done.'

'You know what, if it's so important to you, then find them!' said Birgitte. 'Both killers, one by one. It will be funny. You can both stand there, one can forgive, the other can take revenge. They'll be terribly confused and surrender to the police immediately. I'm sure.'

Thorkild grabbed the cake tray. Birgitte sounded angry. Frank looked flurried.

'I can just picture it, Sherlock Holmes and Dr Watson. Dalziel and Pascoe, the similarity is indeed striking. You will be beyond compare.'

Frank felt uncertain. He could jump aboard the discussion Birgitte and Thorkild were obviously buried in. But something held him back. He smiled nervously at Thorkild's fiery lady and swallowed the last bite of cake.

'It's better to do something than to do nothing. It's a delicious cake, Birgitte. Is that cheese in the frosting?'

'Mascarpone.'

'What should we do?' said Thorkild.

'I don't know. But if you think of something, then please say so.'

A silence fell over the company. Birgitte tried to engage Frank in conversation, but he didn't bite. Turned suddenly grumpy, introvert. And Thorkild remained silent. Birgitte disappeared into the kitchen.

Thorkild looked around his living room. Stroked a hand over the sofa, the red fabric, where she had been sitting. Suddenly he felt uncomfortable in the silence she left behind. He wondered if she was actually angry, raging underneath all her forthrightness?

He thought of the evening that lay ahead. What would

they do? Would she make the steaks she had promised him, and then take him back to bed? Or constantly poke at him with her silent accusations – he hardly knew what she accused him of. To revel in the murder? His grief, his lack of grief? His lack of interest in her? The idea was exhausting.

'Frank?'

'Yes.'

'You drive a BMW, right?'

'Yes. A two-door coupe. One hundred ninety-two horse-power.'

'It's the kind of car no one in my circle of friends would ever dream of buying. I don't think I've ever sat in one.'

'You're welcome to come out and sit in it if you like.'

The urge to get out, away from the living room overpowered him. He was eager.

'Why don't we go for a drive?'

'You mean right now? Where to?'

'The library. I have something to investigate.'

'Actually I was at the library only last week. And I need to get going, I'm in a bit of a hurry. I'll carry on to Kolding and visit my aunt, then take a short trip across the border. I have a friend who manages one of the Sky Stores in Flensburg, we'll go out and play some paintball. Do you want anything? I'll be coming back this way the day after tomorrow.'

'Could we do it on Tuesday, then, on your way back? We need to find out about a murder in Aabenraa in 1999. A woman was murdered.'

Birgitte returned with the coffee pot, she was standing in the doorway, watching them.

30

'Thea Krogh!'

A blond, middle-aged policeman came to greet Thea with a big smile and an outstretched hand.

'Sorry, have we met before?'

'Andreas Robenhagen. You asked for me. I was head of the investigation into the murder of Rie Møller back in the day. And no, we haven't met before. But I've heard a lot about you.'

'Hopefully not too unfavourable.'

'All good. Praise and flattery.'

Andreas Robenhagen showed Thea around at the police station in Aabenraa, chatting easily with her, apparently relaxed and straightforward. He stopped by his small office and grabbed a thermos, and afterwards they sat in two chairs in a small, stuffy meeting room. Robenhagen asked a receptionist to make sure they weren't disturbed, threw the window wide open and shut the door. Then he looked at her, expectantly.

'I'm really glad you found the time for this meeting,' Thea began. 'As you know, I'm investigating the Karen Simonsen case in Roslinge, and we're stuck, to put it mildly. As of yesterday, it's been five weeks.'

'You're counting?'

'I have people who do that for me.'

He smiled.

'I thought you had a man in custody?'

'Yes, that's right. A man who had the opportunity. There are forensic traces, circumstantial evidence that points to him.

And it may be our man. But we can't establish a motive and conclusive evidence.'

'Has he confessed?'

'No. But it's really not important whether he has. Confessions are very much in the public eye right now. The press and the politicians are sceptical. We need more on the table.'

'You don't have to say another word, Thea. I can tell that you're looking for someone else.'

Thea decided to consent by not answering. She didn't need any rumours that the investigator from Århus was so unsure of Torben Jepsen, the man in custody.

'And your only connection to here is that it's a shooting of a woman?'

'Like I said, I look into the possibilities, whatever they are.'

'Need I tell you how much of a long shot it is? That there would be a connection simply because it's a woman who's been shot? Furthermore, our murder was solved. Murder slash suicide. We have the weapon. There are no more loose ends.'

'Yes, I'm aware of that. Look, Robenhagen, you know what it's like to run out of options. To grasp at straws, if only to be doing something, to be certain that you've done everything you could.'

Andreas Robenhagen looked at her. 'And sometimes it's the thinnest straw that offers the solution. Well, it's true, I do know. It's so often about a gut feeling. In time, we learn to trust our guts. And my gut feeling right now tells me that there's something you're not telling me. An investigator doesn't travel all the way from Århus to ask about a murder that was solved. Is there a link to Roslinge, Krogh? Are you saying that you have heard from The Shadow?' Robenhagen's tone was sarcastic, Thea looked firmly at him.

'Nothing like that. Not at all. I have no hidden agenda. So, could you summarise the case for me?'

Robenhagen nodded.

'OK, it was in '99. We found Rie Møller dead in her home. Shot with a 9mm Luger. She belonged to what Aabenraa has to offer in terms of upper class. Large expensive car, a giant box of a house with hideous marble figurines in the garden. It was her twelve-year-old son who found her. Really nasty. He was supposed to have been in school, but instead he was at home with a cold, up in his room on his PlayStation, didn't hear a thing. The husband's name was Carl Eskild Møller, and he claimed he was at a conference in Vejle. We've never been able to prove that one hundred per cent.'

Robenhagen looked distant, recalling the details. It was obvious that he had retold the case to outsiders and curious dinner guests hundreds of times. He had no papers in front of him.

'Her son, Oliver Møller, dials 112 and we're on the scene ten minutes after the ambulance, but by then, Rie is long dead – she died instantly, shot in the throat. And then we have word that the owner of Hyttefadet – it's one of the local bodegas – says there's some girl down there with blood on her hands, crying and saying she's killed someone. Off we go and pick up Camilla, who is indeed covered in blood and screaming.'

'That must be Camilla Laursen,' said Thea.

'Camilla, yes. Poor girl. Not the sharpest knife in the drawer. She was on welfare, had been for about six months. Pretty blonde. We've never been able to clarify her motive for killing Rie Møller. She was a bit depressed about being unemployed, but her caseworker was sure things were moving in the right direction, they'd found a job for her in a kindergarten. No previous diagnosis. When we got her down to the station, she was incoherent and difficult to understand because of her crying. I wasn't the one who did the interview, but I've seen the footage. What she said made no sense. And the reporters had a field day, running stories about a hypnotised killer and a great big jealousy drama. That's when the media dreamt up *The Shadow*. That someone had hypnotised Camilla Laursen to kill Rie Møller because she had money. And then Camilla would have been the young mistress in an intricate love triangle. But it made no sense.'

Robenhagen looked steadily at Thea.

'Camilla said nothing to indicate anything of the sort. It's true that she repeatedly claimed, "He made me do it." And at some point later on, "I love him." But at completely different times during her interrogation. I have my doubts as to whether the two statements were even connected. And I'd damn well like to know who leaked it to the press. Particularly this one journalist, jeez, he was annoying. Wouldn't stop calling. We had one hell of a situation. Had to set up a hotline for worried housewives who were afraid that the neighbour might suddenly be hypnotised and break in, armed with a kitchen knife.'

'Could I have permission to view the recording of the interrogation?'

'Yep, I'll have it sent to you. But believe me, there's nothing to see there. Is that what this is about? Do you have a hypnosis theory going in Århus?'

Robenhagen looked at her, insistent.

'Please continue. I'll tell you afterwards.'

'There was no indication that Camilla Laursen and Rie Møller knew each other. The bulk of Rie's estate went to her son, and it wasn't a lot, there'd been a prenuptial agreement – certainly nothing worth killing for. The Møller marriage was not a happy one, Carl Eskild had a mistress – a lawyer in Haderslev, we found out – but they no longer see each other. He lives alone in the villa with Oliver and isn't doing so well, or so I hear. If there was a connection between him and Camilla Laursen, we didn't find it. Carl Eskild didn't seem overly heartbroken over Rie's death – I can always tell: most men are lousy actors. And he admitted he had a mistress as soon as we confronted him with it. But he seemed genuinely surprised when we showed him pictures of Camilla. That's my opinion. Coffee?'

Andreas Robenhagen fished a roll of paper cups out of a cupboard by the wall and poured coffee from the thermos he had placed on the window sill. 'I bring it from home. I bloody have to. My wife has this thing about cooking it in a pot with a cinnamon stick. It's really good. Try some.'

The coffee tasted of coffee from a thermos, but Thea smiled appreciatively at Robenhagen.

'Forty-five minutes into our interrogation of Camilla, we decided to stop. She was weeping and wailing and shaking her head and wanted out. She was such a tiny girl, we thought it was wrong to continue like that. Not a word she said made sense. And there was no doubt that she was the perpetrator, was there? So we decided to drive her to a psychiatric hospital. Which meant going all the way to Esbjerg. And since we weren't that well staffed at the time, I offered to take her.'

Robenhagen grimaced.

'It's so trite it makes me want to puke. I find my jacket and car keys, Camilla comes out of the interrogation room with Thorvaldsen, who was in charge, and she's handed over to me. Suddenly, her voice is clear and she says she needs the toilet. Crystal clear. And I wonder if she's been acting the whole time, inside that room with Thorvaldsen. But he is subsequently prepared to lay his head on the block that she wasn't. He's a seasoned old rat, Thorvaldsen. And I'm not an idiot. It's a tiny toilet in the middle of the hallway, there are no windows she can slip out of, no sheets to hang herself in, so I let her go. And I don't know how she did it. I must have turned my back on her. I wrote a text message to Lene that I wouldn't be home for dinner because of the trip to Esbjerg. Next thing I know, Camilla's gone. She must have run like a deer. I turn around, the toilet door is open, I hear her steps down the hall, around the corner. And that's how Andreas Robenhagen ended up with the traffic police.'

Thea had heard about Robenhagen's fate.

'We're all over the city – her home address, she lives in a dorm out south. She's nowhere. And this damn town isn't that big. It's a mystery. I'm thinking she probably took the bus into thin air. And then we screw up again. This time it's not my fault, luckily. The twenty-four-hour surveillance on her home falls apart, I still don't know why. By the time we've corrected the error and sent someone out to the address – this is ten o'clock the following morning – it's already happened. Camilla has come home in the meantime, and she's lying dead in her living room. She's been shot as well. With a damn Luger. It's on the ground beside her. It looks like a suicide and the case will be closed as such. Easy and convenient. No need for trial and so on.'

'You don't sound convinced.'

'What do I know about it. There was a suicide note, written on her computer.'

'But your gut feeling . . .?'

'Yes. We have a technician here, I've always had great respect for him. He's a big fan of that TV show *CSI*. Leaves no stone unturned. He finds Camilla's fingerprints on the gun, and that's what establishes it as a suicide. But he told me afterwards that it was just too obvious.'

'Obvious?'

'It's this classic idea people have about staging a suicide. You shoot someone, wipe the gun down thoroughly with a cloth or handkerchief, press it into the hand of the victim, and it's a home run. But if a skilled technician sees a gun like that, you might as well have written a note that says *I'm trying to fool you, mate*, and stuck it in the hand of the victim. A gun is full of bacteria, gunshot residue and finger-prints. If someone wants to commit suicide, they always fidget with the gun. Thinking for and against, sweating, hands shaking, putting it down and picking it up again. Unless they're in a state of panic – but when you're in a panic, you don't wipe off your gun before putting it to your temple. Nope, you have to be smarter than that to cheat our technical experts. When he gets a clean and polished gun with one single, carefully placed and clear set of fingerprints, he smells trouble. Suicide is unlikely.'

Robenhagen lit up. 'And that's obviously why you're here.

You've heard it through the grapevine. Too bad, they went to a lot of trouble to keep that one in the dark.'

Thea nodded.

'It was tough,' continued Robenhagen. 'A lot of palaver, back and forth. We had the local council election and tons of pressure, the mayor was ringing up every other minute. My boss – thankfully he's retired now, the old asshole – brought in other technicians to make the suicide conclusion cut and dried. It was obvious that we needed the matter closed as quickly as possible. Murder/suicide. They were terrified that someone would tell the reporters that there were doubts within the department. The media were already in a frenzy about the story of poor Camilla, the young, blue-eyed mistress, who was hypnotised to murder, all that *Shadow* rubbish. Was she murdered herself before she could reveal the name of the mysterious hypnotist? It sure as hell wasn't a story my boss wanted out there. So they closed the case. And my ass ended up in Traffic before I could speak up. Due to procedural errors, as they called it. And it was understood that, if I were ever to advance again, I'd better back up the official conclusion. A gag, effectively. And it worked, I've kept my mouth shut. How it has made its way to Århus, I sure would like to know.'

Thea didn't answer.

'I can probably guess. Technicians have professional pride. And they talk. It wouldn't surprise me if some technician's given you the idea of travelling down here.'

It was very close to the truth. Thea's review of previous homicide shootings hadn't offered anything interesting until Alice Caspersen had placed a finger on the *Shadow* case and said that it might well have been filed under solved but that it wasn't necessarily where it belonged. A closer look at the case summary, which also explained the theory of a hypnotist, had aroused Thea's interest.

At the same time, cases that were closed as suicides had also become a political hot potato in the wake of a few instances where relatives had refused to accept police conclusions at face value. There was reason to pay attention.

'And the mysterious *Shadow*,' she asked. 'What do you think, Robenhagen?'

'*The Shadow*. I don't know. If there was such a person, he murdered Camilla. It could be someone who spotted a chance. Had his eye on her. Used her own gun. TV Denmark came down here a few years later and tried to bring the case to life again. The TV team focused almost exclusively on *The Shadow* – it's the most interesting angle. That someone else murdered both Camilla and Rie. But it's hard to say. Camilla said *He made me do it*, but I think it's just as plausible that it refers to some mysterious voice in her head, rather than the only undiscovered hypnotist and star psychopath in Aabenraa.'

'Where did she get the Luger?'

'No idea. We've been unable to trace its origin. Which in itself is not so remarkable. It's not easy to obtain legal firearms in this country without an entire rainforest of paperwork. But she could have bought it from some Polish guy selling them out of the back of a van. That, unfortunately, is becoming more and more common. Maybe not for a little girl on welfare. But if you want to buy a weapon in this country, it requires only a modest effort.'

'And that was it?'

'The hell it was!' said Robenhagen, offended. 'We know the job down here as well, Krogh. And the case bothered me like crazy because she ran away from me, right? I can tell you that we were all over it. There isn't an email address on her computer that we didn't check. Not a call on her mobile that we haven't traced. We've been over her flat a thousand times. Talked to everyone. The only thing that tickled my curiosity was something that the TV team came up with. They had spoken with the municipal caseworker about Camilla, found out she was depressed. I think the caseworker was roughed up a bit by the journalists – Why wasn't she in treatment if she showed signs of depression? and so on – and then she tells them that Camilla was seeing a therapist on her own initiative and was starting to feel better. I mean, for fuck's sake! I can tell you, I was pissed off about that. I'd talked to that caseworker at the time, and she'd said nothing about any damn therapist. I went straight down to her office the day after the broadcast.'

Indignation radiated from Robenhagen.

'I gave her a piece of my mind. She didn't know much, except that Camilla was happy with the therapy. The state didn't pay for it, she paid for it herself. We got him linked to an address that was in her calendar. It didn't make a difference – we had obviously already checked out that address at the time of her murder. An empty apartment. The landlord told us that a man had lived there for a while, he was doing some kind of acupuncture, but he had never seen Camilla there. And that was the closest we came to a mysterious shadow. An acupuncturist. Whom we couldn't find.'

'What do you mean, you couldn't find him?' said Thea.

'Exactly what I'm saying. He had disappeared into thin air.'

'And that doesn't sound an alarm with you?'

'You know what? Of course it does. But you're out in the fucking country now. I don't think it's likely that Camilla's acupuncturist killed her. There was all sorts of weird stuff hanging on the walls in there, creepy posters of people with needles in them. Acupuncture zones, and what have you. And a guy like that doesn't stay long out here. People don't go in for acupuncture. The landlord says that no one ever came. The man hadn't lived there for very long. He gave up and moved. It's obviously tempting to imagine that he's the mysterious shadow. But it's not very realistic.'

'Because?'

'The landlord had a – as it turned out – fictitious name for the man. He paid in cash each month, hand to hand, right into the landlord's pocket. No contract, no credentials, no utilities account, zero kroner in deposits, the Rent Act you can stick up your arse. But that isn't unusual! This is the kind of place people flee to. For all sorts of reasons. The wife has left with the kids. You were fired. A criminal sentence. You committed fraud. Your good reputation in the old neighbourhood has gone up in smoke. It's not unusual to tamper a little with the name, make a fresh start. We have many eccentrics, many outcasts around here.'

Thea nodded slowly, poured herself some more coffee just for show.

'What happened then?'

'Well, what happened. Nothing, I guess. All I had was my gut feelings, and I was out of favour because Camilla escaped. I was off the case, the case was closed. There were no more moves, no more options. Camilla shot Rie, and then she took her own life.'

'It's rare for a woman to shoot someone.'

'Right, TV Denmark also used that angle. But then again, there are so few murders in Denmark, any statistics would give a distorted picture.'

'I wonder about her mental state. Who did you use to assess her?'

'Our usual, Erik Marstrand. He was at the psychiatric hospital then. Now he runs his own practice in town. We still use him. But it wasn't ever a proper assessment. It all happened so quickly. Erik was only presented with the facts after Camilla was dead.'

'What did he say?'

'He said it was probable that she was very depressed, but he obviously had reservations, it could never be more than an educated guess. You're welcome to read his report, it's in the dossier. You can also pop down and have a chat with him.'

'Do you have his address?'

Robenhagen scribbled on a yellow Post-it, and Thea stood up.

'Say hi to Lene and say thanks for the cinnamon coffee. It was an experience.'

The man nodded distantly, far away in his thoughts.

'Robenhagen,' said Thea, 'thanks for your help. I'm sorry about the way you were treated.'

'Treatment and treatment. I don't know quite what to think. And that's the honest answer. Suicide is not unlikely, taking her mental state into account. The technical evidence also pointed in that direction, to the untrained eye.'

'But your gut feeling tells you something else.'

'Feelings,' said Robenhagen with a wry smile. 'They don't necessarily make your job easier.'

31

Thea still had the taste of cinnamon in her mouth as she rang the doorbell. Erik Marstrand's practice was on the third floor of a townhouse in the middle of the pedestrian street in Aabenraa, a yellow-washed building that was nicely maintained, but otherwise didn't stand out in any way.

Across the street, the bells in St Nicolai church were chiming.

When Marstrand opened the door, he was on the phone with Andreas Robenhagen from Aabenraa Police. He opened the door for Thea and invited her inside, while he good-naturedly talked on the phone, obviously reviving the case. She remained standing in the waiting room, decorated in yellow hues like the building, while the psychiatrist's voice could be heard, echoing around the apartment. A window was closed, the flush of a tap. She heard a kettle hissing, then Erik Marstrand appeared in front of her.

'Andreas rang to say you were coming. It soon turns into a long chat, you know. We've worked together for many years. That was in the days when I assisted the police as a consultant,' he explained to Thea when he had finished the phone conversation. He showed her into the consulting room. 'Now I dedicate most of my time to my private practice. It gives me a better night's sleep, being able to follow patients all the way through, and being able to put something together that actually makes a difference in their lives. Prison work is draining after a while. But I'm sure I don't need to tell you that.'

'It was on this occasion you dealt with Camilla Laursen?'

'Yes, sort of. She had never been in the psychiatric ward, so I didn't know her in advance. I just reviewed the case as it was presented to me after her suicide.'

'And the murder.'

'Yes, that too. Both were tragic. It affected the whole town back then. If it hadn't been so tragic, it would have been fascinating. To observe how an entire community becomes a study in mass hysteria and collective paranoia.'

Erik Marstrand invited her to sit in one of the two twin sofas that stood opposite each other on a thick carpet in the middle of the room. It was obviously a luxurious old apartment, the consultating room was one of two en suite. The psychiatrist placed two coffee cups on a stylish table with a glass top and steel legs. On the shelf under the glass were different journals of psychiatry, in English and Danish. The decor was aimed at creating a professional ambience. The pictures on the walls covered a wide spectrum of beliefs, with maps of the brain and the nervous system and the periodic system side by side with Buddhist mandalas. There was a poster featuring small photographs of men. Writers, philosophers, psychologists. Thea recognised names like Freud, Nietzsche, Dostoyevsky, Sartre, Fromm. Underneath, it said *Fifth Congress of the Assembly of Psycho-Existentialism*. Everything was displayed in discreet frames that did not disturb the overall impression of a clean, white, bright room. There were large windows and a door that could be pushed aside, leading to a French balcony that overlooked the pedestrian street. But there was also a television and a bookcase

full of fiction and personal pictures in small frames, of Erik
Marstrand fishing in what looked like a Swedish archipelago.
The man was tall and broad-shouldered, a muscular face with
a masculine covering of grey stubble. He wore a white short-
sleeved shirt, loose-fitting pants and bare feet; even his toes had
a tan.

Having followed her appraising glance around the room,
he surprised her with his question: 'Do you like it?'

'This space? Yes. Definitely. It's very . . .' she was looking
for the appropriate word, 'comfortable.'

'I'm delighted to hear that,' said Marstrand. 'I put a lot
of thought into it. It's hard to decorate a room to make
as diverse a group of people as those that make up my
clientele feel comfortable. I see them all – suburban housewives, bikers, anxious teenagers. More and more children,
unfortunately.'

He poured something black into the cups, which on closer
inspection turned out to be a strong tea.

'It turns out that I've run out of coffee. So I hope the tea
is OK. I can fetch some water too?' Thea shook her head.
'No, thank you. Tea is fine.'

'It's amazing how many people come here and expect a
couch they must lie on,' said Marstrand. 'So decorating has
become quite a science. I have colleagues who decorate as if
it was a living room. Some go so far as to have a basket with
a dog lying in it, a ticking clock or a fire in the fireplace.
Cosiness. Then, there are others who need filing cabinets and
large, dominant desks they can hide behind. Others, again,
where you feel transported into a wellness spa with incense
sticks and bonsai trees. I may have chosen a bit of a mix here.'

Marstrand sat down on the other sofa. He looked at her
expectantly. Thea took a pad and a pen from her bag.

'So you're interested in that old case?'

'It's routine. I'm interested in Roslinge and Vindbygårde.
Women killed with guns. I don't know if you are familiar
with those investigations?'

'Not beyond what I read in the newspaper, unfortunately. There's probably a limit to what insight I can offer you.'

'I'm not planning to use you as a professional witness. I just grabbed the opportunity to pick up some general observations from you, since I'm in town. It was nice of you to make time for me.'

'No problem. That was an interesting case, in many ways. However, the connection isn't quite clear to me. The case down here was solved.'

He looked at her, enquiringly, and Thea wondered how much the psychiatrist knew about the suicide having been called into question. It was hard to read his expression.

'As I said, I'm not looking for anything specific. There is a homicide. I want to understand the mechanisms behind it.'

'It's a tendency you seek?'

Thea shrugged. 'I have a murder, the motives are unclear. I'm looking for anything.'

'And even though it was a long time ago, tendencies in psychiatry have a long range. Do you think you're dealing with a murderer who's suffering from a psychiatric disorder?' The voice was deep and pleasant, the words carefully chosen, the proncunciation precise. She felt comfortable in his presence.

'I try not to think too much. I like to keep the picture completely open, as much as I can, not to miss anything.'

'It sounds like a wise strategy. Ultimately, solutions are never simple. Many people who kill suffer from some mental defect, but they also have a motive and an opportunity. So what's more important? One can also ask, is it even possible to kill without a dysfunction of some sort being present? But that's not the same as the motive for a murder.'

'What you're saying is that it's always ambiguous, complex.'

'It's people we're talking about. The explanation is rarely straightforward.'

Erik gave a knowing laugh. He stood up and took a carafe of water from the refrigerator, which he placed along with a couple of glasses on the table between them. 'Actually, it's too hot for tea.'

Behind him, the draught from the windows pushed the doors into the next room slightly open. She spotted a bed.

'Yes, you're right,' he replied, although she hadn't asked. 'I use this place both privately and professionally. It was a few years ago that I resigned my position at the hospital. I try to make a living giving lectures and writing. I travel around a lot. And I don't have as much money as I had back then.' He smiled at Thea. 'So it makes sense to have a little place that serves several purposes. I still have time for my private practice. And as far as money is concerned, wouldn't want to go back.'

She nodded.

'If we could return to the case you became part of. What was the reason why Camilla Laursen shot Rie Møller? I understood from Andreas Robenhagen that there was never any doubt that she did shoot her.'

'Yes, it's a good question. I just spoke to Robenhagen about it. It's never good for the police when you have a killer but no explanation as to why. The meaning is, of course, important to us all. From the information I got, I posthumously assessed her as criminally insane at the time the crime was committed.'

He looked at her, firmly. '*Assessed* is in this context a very important word. It's not easy to analyse a dead person. However, the information clearly indicated depression, a natural tendency to pessimism, which allegedly was reinforced by her situation. She might have known Rie Møller, even though the police weren't able to establish any connection, and something could have happened in that relationship, perhaps triggered by the difference in social status – if I might use such a loaded term – that has caused Camilla to react. It was probably a crime of passion. This is suggested by the subsequent reaction, at the bodega, where she repents.'

'Is that normal?'

'To act out of passion?'

'We all do.'

'Yes, all the time. But you're right in saying that people whose mental constitution is fragile in some way find it easier to do so. What we sometimes encounter is that it turns into a form of mania. An excited state, which can have many expressions. It's characterised, among other things, by the fact that you cannot sleep. And lack of sleep can manifest itself in the hallucinations Camilla suffered from. Delusions of voices speaking to her. It's also possible that she didn't know Rie Møller at all.'

'Chose her at random?'

'It need not be a coincidence,' said Marstrand. 'The way the murder of Rie Møller was carried out suggests there was a certain amount of planning. The weapon, for example. You buy a weapon, that's an indicator of homicide. There are many indications that she knew when Rie Møller was at home and when her son wasn't – it was pure coincidence that he was off sick on the day of the murder. I would guess that she had followed Rie Møller for a while.'

'Pursued her, in other words. A stalker.'

'Yes. It's mostly a term one associates with Hollywood stars. But actually, it's a widespread problem. I had a woman in therapy who had been subjected to stalking. One day a man suddenly showed up on the other side of the street from her house. And he stayed there. Every night. On average, a stalking lasts two years. Two years! It's scary, right? Two years in which the victim is in a more or less constant state of anxiety. It is profoundly debilitating.'

'But there was nothing to indicate that Rie Møller felt threatened?'

'No. And those situations, where there is no connection between the perpetrator and the victim, are the least frequent. They account for only a third. There are no studies in Denmark that document the phenomenon, so the figures I have are from Germany.'

They sat for a while. Thea decided to ask him straight out.

'Do you see anything suspicious in the case?'

He smiled.

'No, I don't. I know that you are thinking about the doubts Robenhagen has about the technical verdict of suicide. I don't have the expertise, so I can't say anything about that. But from the information I was given, I can see how the girl for one reason or another was provoked, pulled the trigger, regretted it afterwards, had hallucinations and dreams that attempted to defer the blame to dominant figures in her life, and ultimately, not being able to live with what she'd done, she killed herself. Wherever she got the gun from the first time, it would have been right there for the second.'

Erik Marstrand had an air of calm about him. Legs crossed, hands folded, speaking without gestures. Thea bit her lip.

'I had subsequent therapy sessions with the crime technician in question,' said Marstrand. 'To have your professionalism questioned is very stressful.'

'I thought something like that was covered by your confidentiality agreement,' said Thea.

'Not that part, no. The police management made some supervision sessions available to the staff in an attempt to round things off properly. But they're registered, the records are public. Personally, I considered it an unsatisfactory way of working.'

Thea felt her mobile phone buzzing in her bag.

'What kind of lectures do you offer?'

Erik pulled a business card from his wallet. It was made of thick, cream-coloured high-gloss paper.

'Why don't you take my card. It has my website on it, so you can keep up. I often do courses in your auspices. Mostly about my profession. The main one I do is about medicating children. Methylphenidate, better known as Ritalin.'

'Amphetamine.'

'It's a common misconception. In fact, the substance is much more related to cocaine. It elevates the dopamine levels in the brain. It has also proven effective in the treatment of dissocial personality disorder. Psychopaths, in other words. Maybe the police could benefit from knowing more about that.'

'Yes, probably.'

'If you can afford it,' added Marstrand. He was getting to his feet, signalling the end of the meeting. 'I have an appointment here, at half past. But you are welcome to call if you have other questions.'

Instead of going to the door, Thea went over to the French balcony and looked down at the pedestrian street.

'How do you avoid becoming too dominant in a person's life when you are a psychologist or psychiatrist?' she asked. Erik Marstrand collected the glasses.

'It's an important question. Everybody dealing with that area needs to understand how to do that. It's vital to set that person free. Establish a feeling that he's acting on his own, standing on his own two feet. That the development you are working on is based on the person himself.'

'It must be difficult.'

'Yes, but you learn.' He took the glasses into the kitchen, came back and looked at her. 'It's absolutely necessary, and you discover it quickly when it fails. The progress stops immediately. So in a way, it's a given.'

'Thank you. It was good of you to see me.' Thea stopped for a moment. 'One last thing?'

'Please.' There was barely a hint of impatience in the other's voice.

'Can a so-called midlife crisis be brought on by depression?'

Erik Marstrand considered it.

'It's hard to say. What brings on what, I mean. Depression is extremely common, yet difficult to diagnose. Some doctors have very absolute terms for when someone can be said to be depressed. Others, myself among them, are somewhat more cautious with definitions. I've seen people going about their work and commitments to the letter and yet they were very depressed, suicidal. It would be easier to comment if I knew a little more about the context.'

Thea hesitated.

'A woman in her late forties. Lives peacefully, going about her business. Husband and children. Suddenly experiences a need to develop and become someone else. Reading dozens of self-help books, distancing herself from her family, trying therapy, doesn't tell anyone about it.'

'A midlife crisis,' said Eric, 'is usually just a sign that you've looked at your life and don't much like what you see. It becomes clear that, unless you take drastic measures, life will go on as it is. You haven't become rich or famous, you never took that trip or opened your shop, you didn't have the kids you wanted. Last-minute panic.'

Thea took her purse, stretched out her hand. Marstrand squeezed it.

'But when you say woman in her late forties,' he added, 'there's another possible explanation. It's called menopause.'

Thea smiled: 'Menopause? As a symptom?'

'Not as a symptom, no. Just a possible explanation. It can trigger a change of behaviour. The pituitary gland affects a woman's ability to produce certain hormones – oestrogen and progesterone. The woman's hormonal balance is completely altered, she experiences physical discomfort and some changes for the worse, the skin becomes looser due to lack of collagen, she grows visibly old. Many people experience a depression-like state.'

As she stood in the door, Eric Marstrand added:

'It's quite natural and rarely serious. But if you ask me whether a woman in that state might have reason to look more closely at her life, reconsider some things, it would not surprise me at all.'

32

Thea had called a team meeting. She had also asked her boss and senior Anne-Grethe Schalborg to take part. She had arrived early and looked for Kristian, hoping that he had done the same, so they could talk. They used to be so good at it – snatching any opportunity to spend fifteen minutes together, give each other a quick kiss and exchange a few words. But he wasn't there.

One by one the participants dropped in. Tired and with the mandatory stimulant of a steaming coffee mug in their hands. They were taciturn. They sat scattered around the table, so that the late arrivals had to fill in the gaps. The last to arrive was Kristian; he found a seat without looking at her. Thea took her place at the end of the long table. She looked at the people gathered there. They had done a good job, and she wanted to tell Anne-Grethe this in front of them. Many of Thea's colleagues felt intimidated by Anne-Grethe. She took up a lot of room, both because she was a big, tall woman and because she dressed to look imposing. Today, she was wearing a tailored grey suit, pearls in her ears, shoes with heels that made a lot of noise as she crossed the linoleum. Dark-framed glasses, a discreet but stylish makeup that matched her outfit. Anne-Grethe was an elegant woman who looked more like the director of a museum of modern arts than a police chief. Her almost constant smile served only to emphasise any criticism, making it more caustic and hard to take. But Thea had never felt her authority as a threat.

Not even at this moment, as Thea got to her feet and turned

on a projector, which immediately began to hum and spew out hot air.

'Torben Jepsen is still in custody. He remains the prime suspect, although we still need to investigate openly, and widely. Let's start with him.'

Torben's face appeared on screen as a backdrop for a series of bullet points to accompany Thea's summary of the case.

'We know for certain that Karen was transported in the grey Suzuki Grand Vitara belonging to Mogens Jepsen, owner of the supermarket. We found her blood in the car, along with remnants of hair and clothing fibres. Of course, there are also traces of Torben Jepsen in the car. And we've found traces of DNA that isn't a match for anyone in the grocer's family, including his cousin. We found it on the car's steering wheel – a measurable mass of something that could be a mixture of sweat, snot, maybe even tears. And it shows at least that someone else has been in the car. We don't know, but if Torben didn't kill Karen, it may be our murderer we have here.

'Mogens' wife Elisabeth had lent the car to her husband's cousin, Torben Jepsen. When Bjørn found the car and chased it down, it was Torben at the wheel. His explanation was that he had borrowed the car that Friday. After business hours in the supermarket, where Mogens had entrusted him with closing up, he'd invited a friend inside. They had some beers out the back.'

Kristian chipped in:

'This is true, according to Torben's friend, Leif Birkerød. We've talked with him twice. He confirmed Torben's story. And he was almost sober, even. He says that he left the supermarket before Torben, and therefore doesn't know where Torben went afterwards.'

Thea continued.

'Torben, understandably, didn't want to tell Mogens about the beers they'd had on the house, so to speak. He didn't want to drive home drunk, either, which we can either respect or see as a story fabricated to please the police. So he walks home. The grocer's wife confirms that he arrived home. And the next morning he offers to go to the baker's. Instead of driving, he walks into town, buys the bread rolls, and according to him the car is there, sure enough, but it's parked a hundred metres down the street from where he left it. His explanation is that he parked the car there Friday, leaving the keys in – we're in the country – and he was too drunk to remember to take them with him when he went home on Friday night. And then someone took the car sometime between 8 p.m. on Friday evening and 9 a.m. on Saturday morning when he goes to the bakery. He drives it home, leaving his own fingerprints on the steering wheel, the freshest ones there.'

Again, Kristian spoke up:

'We've conducted extensive inquiries in Roslinge, asking about the car. No one can recall having seen it, either parked on the main street or being driven during that period. The fact remains that Torben Jepsen is strongly linked to the car, there is nothing to prove his story, we cannot with complete certainty be sure that he slept at Mogens' all night. But then again, there is nothing to disprove his story, and we still need a motive.'

'The family can cover for him, saying he was home with them all night,' said Anne-Grethe.

'If it's a cover, it's an effective one,' said Kristian. 'They all put their heads on the block, saying that no one left the house after one in the morning, when Jepsen got back. We can't nail them on that, Anne-Grethe. But back to the lack of motive. The missing link to our, to put it mildly, enigmatic victim.'

Thea drank from the bottle of tap water she had in front of her. Most around the table followed her example, sipping from their coffee cups.

'Yes. Now we turn our attention to Karen. Nothing connects her and Torben Jepsen. One might say that nothing connects Karen to anyone.'

The image on the screen switched to a picture of Karen. She had got it from Thorkild. It was a Christmas photo of a grey-clad Karen; in the background was the tree and a table that was covered with wrapping paper and a big bowl of tangerine peel. Behind the table you could just make out Thorkild, who was looking at Karen. And Karen looked at the photographer, but she didn't give the impression that she wanted to be immortalised. There was some reluctance in her smile. She wore white marguerite earrings, her hair was worn shoulder-length in a very comely, motherly pageboy cut that didn't suit her very well.

'I'll spare you the factual details of the case – most of you are familiar with all that. Although you, Anne-Grethe, could perhaps do with an update.'

Anne-Grethe's smile didn't falter.

'The technicians have not gotten much further. We're still searching for the two bullets that passed through the victim. It's a meadow area, and we fear that they may well be lost. Moreover, we don't know the exact place, as you're all aware. Alice Caspersen is working her way through, metre by metre. She's out there as we speak.'

'Yes, all right.' Anne-Grethe's eyes rested on Karen's photograph, piercing and thoughtful.

'As to the victim: we've used various resources to find out what kind of life she lived, who she knew. Karen and Thorkild lived very separate lives,' continued Thea. 'Karen didn't work. She was a vicar's wife and did the things that a small community like this expected of her. Nice and calm. But never truly committed. It's striking that most people refer to her as someone they never got to know. Even Thorkild.'

Anne-Grethe nodded calmly. 'And the children?'

'We've spoken to the children. Michael and Nadia. They live in Copenhagen and rarely came home. Even they speak of their mother as someone they didn't know much about when it comes to the life she lived. But they describe her as a good mother, who never made a fuss about herself.

Neither the children nor Thorkild could suggest any potential enemies. There is also no indication that any of them had a reason to want her dead.'

'It sounds like a stone-dead marriage,' noted Anne-Grethe. 'The vicar may have wanted out of it, didn't want to risk a divorce.'

'He could have, of course,' said Thea slowly. 'But I don't think so. Where's the risk? These days, even vicars get divorced. I think he would rather have risked divorce than murder.'

'Does he have an alibi?' said Anne-Grethe impatiently.

'No one can confirm one, no.'

'So his exclusion from the investigation is based on what, exactly? Your gut feeling?'

'Our gut feeling. I think that everyone here who has met Thorkild Christensen considers him to be of no interest as a suspect. The motive is simply too vague.' People nodded around the table. 'But he's not excluded from the investigation. I would like to make that perfectly clear. We continue to check up on him, just like we check up on everything else. But we're not even close to anything that justifies an arrest.'

'No exaggerated religiosity? Something sectarian?'

Thea sighed.

'You roll your eyes, Thea. But you forget that people can entertain all sorts of wild ideas. Especially vicars. It's been seen before. That's all I'm saying.'

'Like I said, it's not my feeling. May I continue?'

Her boss nodded, aloof.

'Karen Simonsen had a good friend, Asger Jørgensen, whom she saw due to a shared interest in literature. He doesn't know that she saw anyone else. He has an alibi and no motive, as far as we're aware.'

'He could have got somebody else to do it.'

'Yes, but it isn't very likely. Again, we need a motive.'

'What if she didn't want to sleep with him? Sex is always a good motive. The motive of all motives, speaking of religious sects.'

Thea smiled, involuntarily.

'You are so right, Anne-Grethe. And Asger actually has a lover – Elisabeth, the grocer's wife. We've spoken to her. She describes him as a man with no real desire. He comes to seek out a little comfort with her, occasionally. She says that he always spoke highly of Karen and never suggested problems, conflicts or sex. In our view, there's nothing there.'

Anne-Grethe frowned. 'I understood that there had been an identification of this Elisabeth in connection with the crime scene. And the time of the killing.'

'This is correct,' said Bjørn. 'But I don't believe it. It's a crazy old lady, she's unsure of the time. Elisabeth, Mogens and Torben Jepsen are each other's alibi. Her parents were visiting, they've confirmed it. If a woman was seen on the mill path, it wasn't Elisabeth. Unless the conspiracy involves the entire family, including in-laws.'

Anne-Grethe mulled it over. 'There are a few too many coincidences for my taste. The grocer's car is used for transportation. His wife is spotted at the scene . . .'

'True. But they claim the car was stolen. We have foreign DNA in it. It could have happened that way. Another thing is that Anika Svendsen is becoming more uncertain and hesitant every time we talk to her. She's reached the point where she can't distinguish between what she thinks she's seen and what she thinks we want her to say.'

Anne-Grethe nodded.

'Back to Karen. She had a friend in Århus – Isabella Munk,' continued Thea. 'She never told her of any problems with men or her children or anything else. And according to both Isabella and Thorkild, the two women were close. According to Isabella, Karen was going through some personal development, but it wasn't anything dramatic.'

'Let's write down the most obvious opportunities.' Thea grabbed a pen and drew on the whiteboard as she spoke. 'First and foremost, Torben Jepsen. Thorkild Christensen. Her children, Michael and Nadia. Asger Jørgensen. Elisabeth Jepsen.'

She turned back to face the table. 'Apart from Thorkild Christensen, all have alibis, unless someone's covering for them. That's where we stand, Anne-Grethe.'

Her boss nodded again, she didn't take her eyes off the board. Thea turned and began writing again.

'Let's add a couple of unknowns. Isabella Munk spoke of a therapist whom Karen saw as part of her inner journey of discovery. This one's a bit dodgy.'

'Because . . .?' demanded Anne-Grethe.

'Thorkild Christensen says that she didn't pay for any therapy, so maybe she just referred to someone as a therapist. Or maybe someone offered therapy free of charge. The therapist goes on the whiteboard.'

'And Thorkild Christensen can say that with one hundred per cent certainty? That he can account for every krone that his wife spent?'

'He doesn't have to. We've been through her accounts. She was the type who paid everything with her credit card. So we can actually say, very specifically, what she spent her money on. There are no transfers or payments of cash. So unless she paid for a course of therapy with what can be purchased in the local supermarket, no money was spent on anything of the sort,' said Thea, with an approving smile for Søren Edvardsen, who had had the tedious task of reviewing Karen's accounts for the previous year.

'Then there is the belly-dance instructor down at the gym,' said Kristian. 'His alibi checks out. He was hired for a hen party in Holte, and he stayed in town overnight. We've confirmed that he taught a so-called goddess dance and afterwards lectured about tantric sex. Some kundalini-inspired hokum about controlling your orgasm by exercising the diaphragm. It was also the title of his lecture: *The Orgasm Comes from the Stomach*.'

Everyone at the table chuckled. Even Anne-Grethe was forced to surrender and crack a genuine smile. Thea continued.

'OK, finally we have a lecturer. Another one, that is. Nothing to do with tantra. A person who gave a lecture down at the gym that Karen attended. There is nothing mysterious about that. She's probably attended twenty lectures since, in the parish community centre. But the mystery is that we cannot find out anything about this man. His name is Bo Zellweger. There is one person registered with that name, but he's been checked and is not a suspect. It must be an alias, which is confirmed by the fact that no other information can be found on him. The few who attended the lecture describe him as an ordinary-looking man. Tall, blond. All they can really remember was a brooch he wore, on his shirt. I'm putting him on the whiteboard. Name of *Brooch*.'

Kristian interjected:

'Apart from these people, we also believe we should interrogate Anika Svendsen again, our dubious eyewitness. Initially she pointed the finger at Elisabeth Jepsen, and so we've written her off. But I think there's a possibility that parts of her story could be true. She may not have seen Elisabeth, but she saw something. Perhaps we've overlooked this *something*. I'll take care of that.'

Thea ended the meeting. She delegated a few tasks that hadn't already been assigned, and otherwise encouraged the staff to continue the good work, if possible even more zealously. She sent Kristian a look that she hoped he would interpret correctly, telling him that they needed to talk, asking if he would wait for her. Then she remained in the room with Anne-Grethe.

'If everything points to an unknown perpetrator,' said Anne-Grethe, 'then maybe we should bring in professionals. Someone who can draw up a profile of our killer. It's not that I mean to criticise the work you've done thus far, Thea. But it looks as if we could use some new inspiration. Something needs to happen! Is there nothing in the archives?'

Thea shook her head.

'I've studied similar cases,' she said. 'There isn't much to qualify the search, since we don't know the weapon, or much else for that matter. So I've searched for cases where women were killed with guns. Naturally I've checked out Vindbygårde, the latest one. I've been to Aalborg, spoken with a few people up there. And I've been to Aabenraa to familiarise myself with the old case of Rie Møller, you might remember it?'

'Not off the top of my head, no.'

'*The Shadow Murders.*'

'Ah yes, of course. Yes, I remember,' said Anne-Grethe. 'That case was solved, right?'

'Yes, it was. I've spoken with the detective who worked on the investigation, Andreas Robenhagen, and their consultant psychiatrist from back then, Erik Marstrand. And what I can't seem to let go of is that they too found that the victim had been seeing a mysterious therapist who couldn't be traced.'

Anne-Grethe, who had stood up, sat back down, gestured to Thea to do the same.

'I remember that we talked a lot about hypnosis back in '99,' she said. 'It's a sexy angle. The journalists gave it everything they'd got. They dug up some so-called experts who, based on a lot of old cases, supported the theory that it was possible to commit murder under hypnosis. We started getting enquiries from relatives. From lawyers, whose convicted clients wanted to have their cases reopened in light of this new and exciting "evidence". Then the National Commissioner decided to start taking it seriously.' Anne-Grethe smiled wearily.

'We were summoned to attend a series of seminars. Selected journalists were invited to participate. Actually, the Director of Public Prosecutions put pressure on newspaper editors to get their crime reporters to show up. It was a noble idea – that we could learn together. We brought in our own experts. And they unanimously said the same thing I'm going to say to you now, Thea: It doesn't happen. You cannot take control of another person's mind. Hypnosis is a passive state. Skilled hypnotists can make suggestions – that is, choose to guide the subject's focus on to certain things. But it's always the hypnotised individual who's making the journey. The state of trance is, in fact, self-hypnosis. Control can never lie with the hypnotist. It's a myth. And thank goodness for that.'

Thea sat for a while.

'But you can manipulate. A strong will against one less strong.'

'Not to that extent. I don't believe you could succeed.'

'No. The psychiatrist in Aabenraa said the same thing. At the moment when the therapist moves away, leaving the client standing on his own two feet and taking ownership of the process, the therapy fails. The development grinds to a halt.'

Anne-Grethe stood up again, put on her coat. Outside, a harsh autumn rain was thrashing against the windowpanes.

'It's tempting to imagine that you can pin the responsibility somewhere else. Defence lawyers live by it. Hitler constructed a genocide around it. But I don't believe it. We have to operate on the belief that responsibility for the things we do as humans lies within ourselves. If you don't believe that, Thea, you'll have a difficult career. Maybe not right away, but eventually. Because that would mean there are many in prison who don't deserve to be there.'

'No. You're probably right about that.'

'You have to look for one of two things,' said Anne-Grethe. 'A truly insane person. Or a person whose motive was strong enough to kill.'

'I just don't see the motive right now.'

'But it's there. And fortunately, there is a certain poetic justice in that part. People are deeply unpredictable. Motives are the opposite. They're always the same.'

33

For forty-seven-year-old Alice Caspersen, it was especially satisfying to be assigned to investigations like this. To be allowed to delve, uninterrupted, into one case. To work it, completely immerse herself. Normally, her work was so diffuse. Constantly multi-tasking, juggling several cases at the same time, confined to the lab, performing specific tasks like searching for traces of human organic material in a vehicle, identifying what model of firearm fired a bullet, when rigor mortis occurred in a case. But on an investigation like this, she could work on every aspect, draw her own conclusions on the whole process, feel a familiarity, perhaps even a kinship with the victim. Trawl through a crime scene, again and again. And the Roslinge case was difficult to let go of.

What was particularly hard to let go of was the two missing bullets. Two bullets that had caused the death of Karen Simonsen, and now they were gone. She had had several men assisting her in the effort to locate the bullets, they'd spent every hour of daylight searching. But it was an impossible task. Initially, they didn't even know the scene of the crime. They'd been combing the river at the location where Thorkild Christensen had found his wife. Since then, Anika Svendsen had come forward offering vague testimony as to where the crime occured, but it hadn't been specific enough to enable them to find the bullets. Assuming you could rely on *anything* Anika said – Bjørn Devantier's strong doubts had rubbed off on Alice. The body had been moved and transported, it had been left lying in water. Most likely, the bullets had sunk into the spongy bog or had been carried along by the river – although quite shallow at that point, the current was nonetheless powerful. It was possible that she would never find them. It was a hopeless task, nowhere was the water deep enough that you could send out divers. Another possibility, the one she feared the most, was that the offender had had the sense to pick them up and take them with him. Whatever the explanation, the lack of progress was getting on her nerves. Without the bullets, it was hard to come up with anything more than a guess as to the weapon. Without the fatal bullet it would be almost impossible to prosecute. And Alice Caspersen never guessed. She stated. She concluded.

Which was why she had gone back to Roslinge in pouring, icy rain that made her head ache and her horn-rimmed spectacles steam up as she struggled down to the area she wanted to examine once again. The entire area was divided into scanning zones with GPS coordinates, but she was the old-fashioned type who preferred a map and compass. With a red rain jacket, her red hair tied back with a scrunchie, thigh-high rubber boots and the omnipresent Haglofs bag on her back, she was as usual equipped to face any challenge.

'You're not the type who lacks the equipment,' a colleague had once said with a smile, catching sight of her toolbox with its array of torches, tweezers, pliers, magnifying glasses, Swiss Army knives and screwdrivers assembled in different types of multi-tools. He himself carried a black suitcase that reminded Alice of the cases full of torture instruments that modern television dramas revelled in at the moment.

She waded through the stream to the trees on the other side of the water and began systematically evaluating the area. First she took a view of the river from an opening in the bushes between the path to the school and the path by the water. That would be an obvious spot if you wanted to surprise someone walking on the path. As Karen had been shot obliquely from the front, the bullets would have been aimed in the direction of the area she was in now. Which she had already been through at least ten times.

She checked the fallen logs, one by one, with her little metal detector and probing fingers. She worked her way from the hill inwards. Systematically. Left marks with chalk on the trunks as she was finished with them. Methodically.

Ended up at a hunting tower constructed of coarse laths behind a ridge of trees, which she despondently let her detector run over, the signal fluctuating at each nail joint.

She looked at her watch, she had been at it for two hours.

Next she followed the path up towards the vicarage. She didn't have a specific purpose, just wanted to look around to form a picture of the scene she had read so much about.

The vicarage was lit up, and she decided to knock. She needed a toilet, and even though she was the outdoors type, she had her limits.

'Sure, I have enough mirrors and tweezers for all purposes, but taking the ticks out of my own butt I can do without,' she thought to herself, half aloud, and rang the doorbell.

A big, blond man jerked the door open.

'Hey,' he said, astonished. And then, addressed to someone inside: 'We have a robin visiting.'

'Can I use the toilet? My name is Alice Caspersen, I'm with the police.'

'I'll be damned. They've sent out the red flashing siren today. You want to see if we've written the killer's name into our toilet graffiti? I don't think I've seen you before.'

'I'm a technician. We don't often visit with people when they're home – or alive, for that matter. You're not Thorkild Christensen.'

'No, no. I'm Frank. But look, the toilet is the second door on your left. Just give me a shout if you need paper, there are many of us who use it now.'

Alice took care of business and then warmed her hands under the hot-water tap. She heard voices from the kitchen and went out there to say thanks. In the kitchen, Thorkild Christensen came to greet her.

'Hi, yes, I'm Thorkild. Would you like a cup of coffee? You must need something warm, if you're investigating outside in this autumn weather.'

Without waiting for a reply he poured coffee into a mug.

Alice would have declined – she had coffee in her McKinley thermos – but it was nice and warm in the kitchen, and outside the rain was gaining strength and lashing the windows.

'What's your name? We haven't seen you before. Yes, and sorry, here's Frank, who you met before, and that's Birgitte sitting at the table.'

Frank mumbled a hello. The blonde woman at the table got up and stretched a hearty hand towards Alice.

'Alice. Alice Caspersen. I'm with the technical branch of the police investigation—'

'Into the death of my wife,' helped Thorkild.

Alice looked at the company, confused. 'You all live here?'

Birgitte took over. 'Sit down, yes, we're all living here at the moment, Frank here has chosen to stay a few days, it has become a complex little collective. We should get a sign on the wall that says *The Conglomerate*. Wouldn't that be an appropriate name?'

There was no bitterness in Birgitte's voice over the crowded household. It was as if she found it funny that Frank and Thorkild had anything to do with each other.

'Come, sit down, Alice,' said Thorkild. 'We would like to ask you a few things, now that you're here, if that's OK.'

Alice sat down at the table. Thorkild, committed, leaned towards her. Frank sat half a chair length behind them. Birgitte perched on the backrest of a chair with her legs on the seat, both present and absent.

'Ask all you like, but I'm not going to answer anything relating to the investigation,' said Alice emphatically, slurping the hot coffee.

'Yes, that limits the possibilities a bit,' smiled Thorkild. 'How are you getting on?'

'Forget it. I don't mean to be rude. But you're wasting your time. Don't you have a liaison officer at Århus Police you can talk to? If you want my advice, let the police work and mind your own business.'

'OK. I understand. I just thought that it might be nice to be updated. You can tell Thea Krogh that I said that. It's been five weeks.'

They sat for a while.

'What do you hunt out here?' said Alice.

'Hunt? What do you mean?' The vicar was confused.

'The hunting tower back there by the path. I just wondered what it's doing there. It's in a strange place.'

'You think maybe someone was up there looking for someone to shoot?'

'No. That's not what I think. It's too far away from the path for that. I just think it's too close to a residential area to have such a tower.'

Thorkild smiled. 'I don't suppose it will remain standing. Anton Svendsen built it, not more than a few months ago. He hunts deer, but I can't remember him catching anything for years. And since then he's quarrelled with the local police officer, who wants it removed. You can't have it that close to people's houses. There are regulations.'

'One hundred and thirty metres away from buildings and at least half a hectare of forest,' Alice announced.

Frank nodded appreciatively. 'The technician masters the technique.'

Thorkild poured more coffee. 'No one gets to tell old Anton where he can build his hochstand. His father, grandfather and great-grandfather have apparently been hunting here since absolute monarchy came to an end. He applied, was refused, and so he built it anyway. Bjørn said he would come over and take it down – told me to call him if I ever saw Anton armed near that stupid tower. But then all that business with Karen happened. Bjørn has hardly had time to go out and take it down.'

Alice set down her cup.

'You know what, thanks for coffee. It was really nice of you.'

'Do you have a phone number? A card? One or the other?'

Alice hesitated, then fished out a crumpled card from a side pocket in her backpack.

'Here you go. But like I said: I'm not the person to call.'

She put on her soaking wet raincoat and hurried out into the rain and back to the hunting tower, where she once again took her detector out of the backpack. With quick movements she let her fingers slide over the muddy pine bark. In a joint, the detector went off with a high beep. The nails. Still, she checked again, this time with her fingers, scratching at the stiff bark until she noticed the crack where a single bullet had penetrated. Heroic.

She got her tools out. Tried her collection of pliers until she found one the right size to prise out the bullet. She took the chisel and hammer and struck twice into the side of the hole. That's how she got to it. She got the spirit level and protractor out. Drew up the horizontal lines she needed. Measured the angles. Finally she turned around and placed her digital rangefinder pointing in the direction where the shot would have been fired. She wrote all the data down in her notebook.

She didn't find the second bullet.

She carefully packed up her gear, gave the pliers a drop of oil, dried everything off with a cloth she had brought for the purpose, and placed each item of equipment in its allocated slot in the toolbox and backpack.

She noted the exact locations on the path and the bushes, where, respectively, victim and murderer would have been standing to fit with the angle of the shots and the idea she had about the perfect hiding place for an assassin.

Then she called Thea Krogh.

'How the hell is that possible?' said Thea, who otherwise

never swore. The excitement in her voice was as rewarding as if she'd pinned a medal on Alice. Here was a bona fide breakthrough. 'We've combed the entire area! The bullets were lost. That's what you said.'

'That's what we thought,' said Alice. 'But they cheated us. When the joints made the detector go off we obviously carried out a visual double-check – but we had forgotten to account for the fact the hunting tower was newly built. The laths it was made of were undressed stems of freshly cut forest pine. And they contract themselves.'

'Contract themselves? Around the bullet?'

'Yes. I should have thought of it. There's plenty of water in fresh wood. The free water, which transports water from the roots to the leaves. And the bound water, which sits in the wood's cell membranes. When the tree is cut down, all that water begins to evaporate. But the wood doesn't shrink evenly like a balloon. It's a very complicated process, especially when there are lesions on the tree, like from a cut or a bullet hole. This is what makes planks curl over time. Long treatises have been written on the subject of tangential shrinkage. I recommend "Understanding Wood" from 2000.'

'Alice, what exactly happened?'

'The bullet got sucked into the wood, the wood contracted and twisted around it. The conditions were optimal, the wood was fresh and humidity was high. We were also unfortunate in that it entered right by one of the joints. The nails accounted for result on the detector, cheating us. It's an easy thing to overlook. A blessing in disguise. But now we have a bullet, Thea.'

'What does it tell us about the weapon?'

'Not much, unfortunately. It's a common classic type of ammunition: 9 x 19 mm Luger Parabellum. Originally developed for Luger weapons, but now it's used in all kinds of guns. The Italian Beretta, the US Colt, the German Walther . . . just to name a few. There are many weapons we can exclude, but unfortunately, also many weapons it could be.

Still, we will be able to tell whether the bullet was fired from a gun we already have in the system. Guns are unique, as you know. They put a useful little fingerprint on the bullets.'

Alice patted the plastic bag in her pocket, feeling the hardness of the bullet against her dirty fingertips. She was as excited as a child at the prospect of getting it back to the lab and extracting its secrets.

34

'It's a fast car, but it drinks like an alcoholic.'

Thorkild went into the service station while Frank bought petrol. That morning, Birgitte had babbled away in her perpetual good mood. She seemed to get a kick out of their expedition, even offering to make them a packed lunch. Sausage rolls, perhaps? Thorkild had refused, but he still felt like a little boy when she kissed him goodbye, on the nose.

He enjoyed the bustle of the service station and a surprisingly good cup of coffee, made by a petrol station attendant with a badge that read, optimistically, *Barista*. A lovely moment of peace, watching the travellers who came and went, armed with French hot dogs, fizzy drinks and windscreen washer. He was seized by a desire to become a petrol station attendant, just stand here in glorious anonymity day in and day out and sell fuel to passers-by. No responsibility he couldn't handle. No real hardships. A robbery, at most, or that the deep fryer stopped working. Maybe it was having the vicarage invaded by both Birgitte and Frank that made him look upon a petrol station, of all places, as a refuge.

Then Frank roared up in the silver streamlined 530, jerking open the passenger-side door. The BMW hardly stopped before it was speeding up again, with Thorkild sinking into the rocking, light grey seat. While Thorkild leaned back and enjoyed the comfort of the car, Frank began pushing buttons that automatically adjusted the seat height and headrest.

'It's fantastic, Frank. How much does it cost you?'

'Too much. But I love it. I've dreamed of having such a car all my life.'

Thorkild smiled graciously. 'I probably have, too.'

'Why don't you get one? Isn't there enough money in the church collection fund? Why don't you just do it? Realise a few dreams, now that you're on your own?'

'We had the children soon after we got married, and this kind of car just wouldn't have been practical. You need room for all sorts of equipment. And you can't be too fussy about your car when you have children. Michael once discovered that you can write on cars if you have a stone. He was very young.'

'Holy shit! Glad I don't have kids.'

'Have you never wanted children, then?'

Frank changed the subject.

'So you need to visit the library. The Central Library in Århus, nothing less. Very fancy. I've always liked Århus. There's a really good ice cream shop in Vestergade. I'll probably have time to try all the flavours while you sit and read newspapers and chase shadows.'

Thorkild smiled, knowing that Frank was every bit as curious as he was.

'Sanne and I went to the Århus Festival together,' continued Frank. 'Sanne got so drunk, we had to stay an extra day because she couldn't sit in the car to go home. She only had to smell the cap of a bottle and she'd be drunk. It's damn cheap to take her out. Not counting the hotel bill, though.'

He corrected himself: 'It *was* cheap to take her out. Doesn't matter now, does it?'

'I've started going out as well. I was at an oriental belly dance the other day,' said Thorkild.

For once, Frank took his eyes off the road and sent a puzzled glance at Thorkild to see whether it was appropriate to laugh. But when Thorkild didn't twitch a muscle, his incipient belly laugh turned into an embarrassed grimace.

'Karen. She went out, almost every Tuesday evening. I thought she went to the gym. But when I got there, I found out that she hadn't been for almost a year. All the same, she disappeared out of the house every Tuesday after we had dinner. She even brought gym clothes and paid a fee. As if to show me that she went.' He hesitated, came upon a thought that stung. 'She even hung her gym clothes out to dry when she came home.'

Frank shook his head.

'Thorkild, I'm sorry to say this, but she's been seeing someone else, surely. It happens, you know.'

He bit his tongue. This intimacy was getting a little uncomfortable.

'No, I don't think so, Frank. I had thought the same, except . . . I know it sounds like something everyone would say about their wives, but she wasn't the type.'

Frank shrugged. 'They never are. If you knew how many men I've heard say exactly that.'

'And I called one of her good friends. Or maybe her only friend. I think she would have told me, if it was the case.'

'Her friend? Doubt it. They lie through their teeth to protect each other. Just like men. Women and men are equally full of lies.'

Thorkild wondered if that was true.

'To think, you can be that close, as husband and wife, and not see the changes in one another,' he said.

'I wouldn't know. I've never been married. Or lived with anyone, seriously. So maybe you're right.'

There was silence in the car. There wasn't much to say.

'Why have you never married, Frank?' said Thorkild.

'My sister, Sanne, she was always home,' said Frank, ignoring the question. 'Obviously I can't know for sure that she was, it's not like I stood outside her door every day and checked. But she was always home whenever I dropped by. And at the times of day when you turn the lights on inside, there was always light when I walked past. I can really only remember one exception. And it was a Tuesday night. A few times, actually. Peculiar, huh?'

Thorkild glared at him. Frank laughed out loud.

'Tuesday is apparently the night for women to go out on their own. And keep secrets from their husbands and brothers.'

Thorkild shook his head. 'Honestly, it's too far-fetched. And I think you're driving a little too fast. You can only go eighty here. Surely you don't want to end up in the clutches of Thea Krogh?'

'Yes. Or no, why not? Do you believe it's possible that Sanne and your Karen knew each other?'

Thorkild replied, somewhat disillusioned. 'I think, by now everything is possible.'

35

'I hope old Anton lets us talk with Anika alone.' Kristian was talking to himself. Thea turned down the car radio. It was the first thing Kristian had said to her since they set out on the journey to Roslinge. The first thing he had said to her in a long time, actually. She was familiar with his silences, his need to pull away from her when he was angry. But this time, the silence had been long. And total. No calls, no emails, just a few short and concise text messages.

'Haven't you told them what we want?'

'Yes, yes. I'm just not sure it sunk in.'

'Then we'll ask him to leave. Otherwise, it's not going to work. He's a belligerent old fogey.'

They pulled up in front of the mill house where Anika and Anton Svendsen lived. In the old days the mill, driven by Roslinge River, would have supplied the villagers with flour. The mill wheel had long since been lost. What remained was a thatched idyll of half-timbering and peonies, bulging windows and a flagpole in the garden with the paint peeling off, which would have been a romantic dream if a young couple had moved in to fix it up, but was currently a ramshackle home, inhabited by the Svendsens for the last forty-seven years.

They sat there for a while without getting out of the car.

'This is just the sort of place you would love to live,' he said.

She looked at him.

'Me? I'm a city girl. I've grown into my apartment, they'll have to cut me free the day I die,' she said lightly.

'No. Basically you're a girl who would have lived here.' He looked straight ahead, it was hard to decipher his face.

Anton opened the door after they had let the door knocker drop twice. 'Can I see some identification?'

'Kristian Videbæk from Århus Police.' Kristian showed his badge. 'And this is my colleague, Thea Krogh. We talked on the phone. Can we speak to your wife?'

'You can talk to me and my wife. And that's how it's going to be.'

Thea sighed. 'Is she in?'

Anton showed them across the corridor's yellow and crooked tiles. On a rack of deer antlers was his shotgun, side by side with her yellow raincoat. It smelled of old clothes and camphor. In the kitchen, where they were shown in, it smelled of coffee. There were four cups on the kitchen table, and Anika Svendsen was sitting ready with a troubled look on her face.

'Anika –' Kristian began while Anton, scowling, positioned himself beside Anika's chair '– we've asked to have a chat with you. You remember that you spoke with our colleague Bjørn Devantier before?' He looked at Thea, who had placed herself at the kitchen sink with a reserved expression on her face.

Not having been offered a chair, Kristian was squatting opposite Anika, so he came eye to eye with the little woman. He probably couldn't have stood upright in the low-ceilinged kitchen without taking down the cobwebs between the beams. He fished out the tape recorder from his pocket and put it on the table in what was meant to be an understated motion. It failed; the couple jumped visibly, Anika stiffened. Kristian maintained Anika's gaze until she seemed to have recovered.

'Please sit down. You can't sit on the floor. You, too,' said Anton.

Thea remained standing. She wanted Anton Svendsen out. He didn't look as if he was going anywhere, though.

'Yes, the officer was here,' he said with a disdainful sniff. 'It must have been a festive occasion for Devantier, actually having valid business at the mill. I'm not the least bit surprised you've had to come for a second visit. The man simply will not listen.'

'I know who did it,' said Anika with a rusty voice. Anton rolled his eyes.

'You can forget it. They don't listen to old women. Especially not when they've already made themselves look completely ridiculous, Mrs Svendsen.'

Anika looked down at the table. Then it came, stubbornly: 'When a crime is committed, one must do her duty. People can say what they will, Mr Svendsen.'

'The whole town is talking.'

'We know you told Bjørn Devantier about Elisabeth,' said Kristian. 'But, Anika, it's not her. It couldn't have been her. Is it possible that you were mistaken?'

'Yes,' came the prompt answer. 'I was wrong.'

'Do you hear that!' snorted Anton. 'You have squeezed everything that you can out of my wife. How do you think she will handle all the things you make her say? Now you say she was wrong, and immediately she agrees with you. It's no wonder people confess all sorts of things when they talk to police. What Gestapo methods!'

Thea had had enough. 'Mr Svendsen, we're here also to talk with you. Is that a büchsflint rifle you have hanging out in the hallway?'

Anton turned red with rage. 'Devantier again! Unbelievable! Do you hear that, Anika? You can tell that pathetic excuse for a police officer that my rifle has remained hanging in its place ever since he and I had our little talk.'

'Calibre 12?'

'Calibre 20. That goes without saying. Not büchsflint, but a common double-barrel. *Side by side* it's called, in modern Danish. It's a genuine antique. And I have a permit!'

Thea waved him into the hall.

'I believe you. But show me anyway. I need to inform you of the requirement to keep that kind of weapon in a secure locker.'

Anton stormed out into the hallway with Thea following. She had trouble shutting the crooked kitchen door until Anton, unfazed, helped her.

Kristian quickly continued. 'Tell me—'

Anika interrupted him. 'It's the girl from Aalborg.'

'What do you mean?'

'I saw the posters. That girl who was killed in Aalborg. She was the one I met down by the river. Not Elisabeth. I was wrong. You must excuse me. Maybe you could apologise to Elisabeth on my behalf.'

Kristian sighed.

'But now you're sure? You know it's a serious business, accusing someone of murder. Twice.'

'Quite sure. And you don't have to lecture me. I'm ninety-two years old. I smuggled propaganda sheets in my laundry basket during the war. I bought the newspaper, it's in the living room. I'm sure it's her.'

'And how can you be so sure this time? They weren't very good pictures in the newspaper.'

'She has a wart on the side of the nose, right?'

Kristian thought. He hadn't noticed. Maybe.

'It's not common, well, to have a wart next to the nose. Not many have that. I saw it instantly and I thought: That's her.'

Kristian sighed again.

'And Elisabeth?'

'It's a freckle. It's something else.'

Kristian nodded. 'Yes, I suppose that is something else.'

He excused himself and left the house. Outside, he caught Alice Caspersen on the phone and gave her a task.

'Alice, tell Anne-Grethe Schalborg that we're not getting anywhere with the Svendsens. It's impossible to get Anika Svendsen to say something useful. Now she's given a second identification – this time it's the murder victim from Vindbygårde. But please try to call Aalborg Police, will you? It's only fair to mention it to them. And could you send me a picture of her?'

By the time Kristian had received the picture on his phone, Thea and Anton had both returned to the kitchen. The conversation was still about weapons. Kristian showed Anika the picture.

'Yes, that's it. The wart. It is absolutely her.'

Thea looked at Kristian, surprised. He almost imperceptibly shook his head. He put the tape recorder down and indicated for Thea to follow him. They thanked Anton and Anika Svendsen for the talk and left.

'Who was that in the picture?' said Thea, as they headed

out of Roslinge. Kristian drove quickly but safely, she had always felt very comfortable driving with him.

'That,' said Kristian, 'was none other than Sanne Andersen, the murder victim from Vindbygårde.'

'Oh no. OK. So, I guess there was nothing more to learn from Svendsens. What a waste of time. If it's any consolation, I think Roslinge is a safer place anyway. Now that Anton has promised to buy a gun locker.'

He smiled. She took his hand.

'Do you have time to come home with me?'

Kristian looked at his watch. Then Thea's phone rang.

'We have our killer!'

Anne-Grethe Schalborg had a big smile on her face. It had only taken a few hours to get the whole team together for a quick briefing. There was an expectant anxiety in the room, everyone delighted to hear the good news, but at the same time fretting about the need to get home on time, pick up the kids and prepare dinner. It was late afternoon, they were standing around with coffee mugs or resting on the armrests of the red conference chairs, ready to make a quick getaway.

'Anika has identified a new murderer, believe it or not,' said Thea. 'Sanne Andersen, who was later killed in Vindbygårde. Anika recognised her from the posters. And this time it checks out.'

There was a murmur of disbelief in the room.

'It was a strange process. She made the identification, described the clothes she had seen Sanne Andersen wearing. So we rang Aalborg. Clothing matching the description was found in Sanne's wardrobe. Wrapped in a black plastic bag. Splattered with mud, even. And they'd run dozens of tests but had nothing to match it with.'

'So you had to go out and dig up mud,' said Bjørn Devantier.

'It wasn't necessary. Alice Caspersen volunteered her red rubber boots, the ones she was wearing when she trudged out there only yesterday. Exactly the same area.' Kristian smiled, a sight that Thea always enjoyed. He had a lovely, generous smile when things were going the way he wanted.

'The mud matched. It's from Roslinge River. So we've identified a very unlikely suspect in connection with the murder of Karen. It's certainly a surprise. Sanne Andersen, the recently deceased victim from Vindbygårde, was seen in the vicinity of Roslinge River immediately after the shots were fired. Clothes recovered from her wardrobe have soil from Roslinge on them. And as if that weren't enough, we've just heard there are traces of gunpowder residue on the right sleeve of the jacket.'

Kristian nodded appreciatively at the fast-working forensics department. The gunpowder was the trump card.

'Moreover – and this is news to everyone here – the ballistic tests that we've just run on the bullet found in Roslinge prove that it was fired from the same weapon as the bullets found in Vindbygårde. A nine-millimetre firearm of some kind. We still have no weapon, but we now know both crimes were committed with the same weapon. There's no doubt in my mind that we have two coherent cases to investigate. Sanne Andersen shot Karen Simonsen. And afterwards Sanne Andersen was shot with the same weapon. Now it's all a matter of establishing Sanne's motive, finding interdependencies between the two women, how they knew each other . . .'

Jørgen Schmidt stuck a hand in the air.

'And what about Torben Jepsen?'

'Torben Jepsen is no longer of interest in this investigation,' said Thea. 'We have two murders with what looks to be a much more cryptic context than anything we've considered up to now. In the course of a month and a half's investigation into every aspect of Karen Simonsen's life, we have not come across a single connection to Sanne Andersen, to Vindbygårde – nothing. We're looking at a whole new investigation. There's no evidence of Torben Jepsen's guilt. There's no reason to reject his version of events. And, to be blunt, he doesn't fit the profile, based on what we now know. We're not looking for a small-time crook, an alcoholic on benefits. So he'll be released tomorrow. Any questions?'

Thea packed up her papers and was the first to leave the conference room.

PART 3

36

Frank found a vending machine while Thorkild tracked down a librarian who volunteered to show him how to access the library's own databases, as well as InfoMedia, the online database of Danish print media. She pulled a long face when Thorkild asked her to help him the good old-fashioned way and go into the library's physical archives to retrieve a stack of *Jyllands Posten* newspapers from October 1999.

It took quite a while, and her face was crimson and sweating when she returned with a pile of dusty newspapers and threw them on the table in the library's reading area. Thorkild settled down and made a start. He gave a bunch of newspapers to Frank, who began to flip through them sporadically.

'Wouldn't it be easier just to talk to police? You could call your friend Thea.'

'They can't divulge the information. We can only find out what information was made public at the time.'

'I don't read the papers much, but I reckon you've got the wrong one there. You might want to choose one with bigger headlines.'

'No, look here. This fits the dates.'

Thorkild spread some newspapers on the table and studied the headlines:

42-year-old found shot in her home.

He began to read, while Frank disappeared and came back with more newspapers.

'I don't know anything about newspapers, but I think this is a little more exciting,' he said, adding his papers to the top of the pile.

Thorkild had to agree with him. Three of the covers were almost full-page head-and-shoulder shots of two very different women. One was a sleek-looking woman in her early forties with curly black hair and pale pink lip gloss that made her lips look like sticky candy. The other was young, blonde, with the looks of your average Danish high school student. Pretty, but nothing outstanding. Happy eyes that looked straight into the camera. It wasn't a grainy photo like the other one; she was of a generation that made sure high-resolution photos were always available online.

He saw in his mind's eye the picture of Karen that reporters had unearthed when it was her turn to adorn the front pages. He'd refused to hand over a photo to the officious editorial manager who had contacted him. So they had gone to the university archives and found an old, unexciting image.

He lost himself for a moment in the blonde's cheerful gaze, then went on to the headlines. They started out modestly enough: 'Shot in her own home – 12-year-old son found Rie'. Then turned into: 'Jealousy Drama: Young Girl Murdered Rie', 'The Camilla Case: Hypnotised to Murder', 'The Shadow made Camilla a Killer' and 'The Shadow Case: Camilla Laursen found Dead'. Frank was right – there was more juice in the tabloid press.

'Are you planning to read them all?' said Frank impatiently. 'Do I have time for a hot dog? This all happened years ago, Thorkild. I don't know what connection you're hoping to find.'

'There might not be a connection,' said Thorkild. 'But now we've come all this way, it doesn't hurt to look. Besides, it's always nice to have a day out, don't you think? We can go up the pedestrian street afterwards, if you like.'

'No, I don't like.'

Thorkild smiled.

'Let's go, then. Just a hot dog, and then we'll come back here and get stuck in.'

'Tidy up after yourselves,' the librarian barked after them.

37

Back at the Central Library, the librarian stared sceptically at Thorkild and Frank as they re-entered the warm library.

'I've just packed it all away,' she said. 'You'll simply have to look it up on the computer.'

'That's also easier if we want transcripts,' said Frank.

They were directed to a computer station, where the librarian overcame her impatience. 'Everything is catalogued – you can search by year, month, day, subject, the personal names in the articles, media types, etc. You can go in from multiple ports, simultaneously. First a wide search, and then you work your way in, systematically, in depth,' she explained.

Thorkild nodded and took over the keyboard, then the librarian rushed off.

'One of the gates is the time – the articles written just after the murders. Another is the actual case – here we get everything that was written, even later on. I'd like to take as much as possible back home to read. Which one will you take, Frank?'

'Why don't you go ahead, Vicar. If I can't get the newspapers in physical form it doesn't matter.'

'Are you not the least bit interested?'

'Yes, I am. But if I know you, you'll tell me all about it when you've finished reading. And as I said, I'm not a big reader. Knock yourself out.'

Frank trudged away, sat down at the opposite end of the room. It a typical modern library, with a vast open area in the midst of the bookcases equipped with café tables, sofas for readers, seating for three to four people at each computer terminal, and sloping display shelves with the latest editions of a selection of newspapers and magazines.

After waving Frank off with an amicable laugh, Thorkild buried his head in research. In a short time, he trawled through a lot of material. He skimmed, jotted notes on a pad and printed reams of copies. From time to time Frank wandered by and peered over his shoulder.

'Take it easy, Thorkild, that's a krone per print. You're not going to ruin me, are you? It would make a lovely obituary: Frank never read a book, but went bankrupt on newspapers.'

'If you want to help me instead of complaining, you could perhaps pick up some coffee for us?'

Frank clicked his heels and strode away.

It was near closing time. The young guys who had been sitting in the middle of the room playing World of Warcraft or some other noisy game had now home, and the library was quiet at last.

Thorkild enjoyed the silence. To immerse himself and work his way methodically through a project, alone, all alone, that was something he felt comfortable with.

The coffee didn't arrive. Thorkild completed the thread he had followed by pressing print and got up to stretch his legs. He'd been at it for over an hour now. He was in the mood for a cup of coffee and wondered what had become of Frank.

Thorkild looked around the library. Went out to the vending

machine at the entrance, looked in the Gents', checked the various departments and nooks.

'I'd better look over by the comics,' he said to himself and smiled. But in vain. Frank was nowhere to be seen.

'Have you seen the man I came in with?' he asked the librarian. She shook her head.

'We're closing in five minutes.'

Thorkild wondered whether Frank had set out to get decent coffee from a café in town. Then his eyes fell on the computer terminals where the young men had been playing. Stunned, he looked at the monitor and felt the heat rising in his cheeks. It was the *Jyllands Posten* website, and there was a news update emblazoned across the screen:

Aalborg victim was a murderer: Sanne killed Karen.

Thorkild leaned on the table. There was the horrible picture of Karen. And there was one of Sanne. She shared the same facial features as Frank, it was easy to see that they were siblings. The two images were side by side, unsightly. Thorkild breathed deep and tried to comprehend what he read. It was a short article, set in large type.

New evidence suggests that there is a connection between the two recent female homicides. Apparently, shortly before her own death, the murder victim from Aalborg, Sanne Louise Andersen, killed Karen Simonsen, the vicar's wife from Roslinge, north of Århus. Both the Århus and Aalborg police forces have refused to comment, but Chief of Århus Police Anne-Grethe Schalborg confirms that they are now investigating new information in the two murder cases.

'It's true that we're working on a new theory, but we have yet to determine definitively that Sanne Andersen is the perpetrator. The motive is not clear and I have nothing further to say at this time,' says Anne-Grethe Schalborg.

'It is, as I see it, a natural evolution of our society that we now see women behind violent crimes, including murder. But it really is a strange case,' says journalist Andreas Møller, an expert in criminal cases.

The murder of Sanne Louise Andersen has been dubbed the Stigmata Murder because the victim was shot through both hands. The reason is still unclear to the police.

We will continue to follow the case.

'Shit!' said Thorkild hoarsely and pulled out his mobile. 'Shit, shit, shit.'

There were eleven missed calls to his phone from Thea Krogh. Three calls from Birgitte. And four messages on the answering machine. He didn't take the time to call back, but quickly packed up and ran into the street.

Frank had probably seen the news. He could be anywhere. What was he doing now?

Thorkild didn't know what to do. He tried calling Frank, but there was no answer.

He walked around the streets. First along the canal, Immervad, the small square, the large square, the harbour and up to the station, Bruun's Gallery, down the pedestrian street, along the narrow streets back to the library and then the same circuit all over again, this time peering into back-yards, restaurants, cafés, pubs and shops, criss-crossing the immense harbour at random. No Frank. And no Frank on the phone. His own phone rang several times, but it wasn't Frank. Suddenly finding Frank was the most important thing, the only important thing he had to do. Moreover, he didn't have the energy to talk to anyone else. Not the kids, not Birgitte and certainly not journalists. Thea Krogh, perhaps? He needed to know what had happened. How could this happen so suddenly, out of nowhere, an internet headline exploding in his head and Frank's, turning the world upside down?

Thorkild stopped and took the time to call Thea.

'Thorkild. I'm so glad you called.' There was relief in her voice. 'Have you seen it? Heard my messages?'

'I've seen it, yes. Haven't listened to the messages yet.'

'I deeply regret that the news got out before we'd spoken to you. I don't know who leaked it to the press. It's possible that it was Anton Svendsen.'

'Anton? That crazy old man from town? What's he got to do with it?'

'It was Anika who delivered the breakthrough. She saw the suspect, Sanne Andersen, that morning and identified her. I'm afraid it checks out. Anton was present at the questioning and had his nose put out of joint a bit.'

Her voice was trembling.

'Thorkild, where are you? I was worried. I called several times.'

Thorkild felt tired, didn't have the energy to explain and didn't answer.

Thea cleared her throat.

'We've been working flat out ever since. There was a pair of boots in Sanne's closet that had traces of mud on them; Alice Caspersen has confirmed that the mud originates from Roslinge River – something to do with the unique composition of the local limestone, I think. Apparently mud is as good as a fingerprint. Anika gave a detailed description of the clothes Sanne was wearing, so detailed that we were able to find the items among her belongings. She wasn't wearing them in any of the pictures that were shown of her in the media. We already had traces of Karen's DNA in the blood found in the Suzuki, but now we've also matched samples taken from the car to Sanne. We knew the DNA we'd found belonged to someone other than Torben, Mogens and Karen or any of the others Mogens told us had been in the car. Now we've identified it as belonging to Sanne Andersen.'

'I thought Sanne Andersen's possessions had been packed away,' said Thorkild, because he vaguely remembered that

Frank had told him about it. Luckily, Thea Krogh didn't ask how he knew that.

'As part of their investigation into Sanne's murder, Aalborg Police took some of her clothes with them. I've talked with a detective from up there, he's on the case. They tried to trace where she had been, given the mud. But there was no, absolutely no indication whatsoever that the two murders were linked, Thorkild. No reason to suspect that she had committed a crime. No one dreamed of comparing. It's an absolutely remarkable development. Do you have any information that might help? Did Karen ever talk about Sanne Andersen, or about Aalborg or Vindbygårde? It's important, Thorkild. We've been in contact with Sanne Andersen's brother to see if we can establish a connection that way.'

'You had contact with her brother? Where is he?'

'I don't know. It wasn't me who spoke to him. Why?'

'. . . I've been trying to find him. Without luck.'

'I don't understand. What do you want with him?'

Thorkild didn't answer. Instead, he kept walking, increasing the pace, feeling on the verge of panic. And angry as hell.

'How can it be on the news before we've been informed? That's simply not good enough.'

'As I said, we don't know where they got the story. But there's money to be made, tipping off the media. And like I said, Anton Svendsen wasn't too happy with the police. At least not at first, when we came to interview Anika. We believe it's most likely that the tip came from him. We're dealing with it, believe me. But frankly, Thorkild, it's not what you should concern yourself with right now.'

'What do you mean?'

'I think you should talk to your family. And don't discuss this with reporters. I'll come out and see you. Are you at home?'

'No. I'm not. I'm in Århus, dammit! At the library. You said it yourself – that I should check the newspapers!' His voice was accusing, she was practically the reason why he was there. 'And I'm with Frank Andersen right now! Or rather, I was. He's gone. He saw the news and took off, and now I don't know what to do.'

She held a long pause. 'OK.'

'OK? What do you mean, OK? What do I do? I've been all over town, several times.'

'I didn't think you would be *hanging out* with Frank Andersen. What in heaven's name are you doing with him?'

'What did you think, then?'

She didn't answer. Instead, her voice became matter-of-fact:

'Was Frank Andersen driving? Have you checked whether he's taken the car?'

'What? No, it's still here. It doesn't look as if he's been back to it.'

'I'll tell the police in Århus to look out for him. Why don't you keep looking, then we'll see if he shows up within the next few hours. Call me if you need help. But for Christ's sake, Thorkild – do you know Frank Andersen?'

'No. I only met him after Karen was shot. He sought me out. I don't know him, Thea! I don't understand what's happening.'

He hung up and carried on walking. Not so much searching now as trotting around aimlessly, following the same route along the pedestrian street in one direction and along the harbour in the other, preoccupied with his own thoughts.

Why would a woman from Aalborg travel to Roslinge to murder Karen? It seemed absolutely absurd. The connection between the two unthinkable. He'd imagined some hardened criminal, a man with a problem, someone who Karen had somehow gotten in the way of. Or a dropout, like Torben. He realised this was the first time he'd conjured the image of Karen's killer in his mind's eye. Now the photograph of Frank's pale, blonde sister stood in the way and blocked everything. This didn't fit, not at all.

He found a café on Storegade and bought a tuna sandwich.

Then he continued to walk. When he had completed the same round again, he went in the same café and got a cup of coffee. On the next lap, he bought a pint. He was sitting in the café after another lap and another beer when the phone rang.

'This is Søren Edvardsen, Århus Police. I understand you're looking for Frank Andersen?'

'Yes. Yes, I am. Have you found him?'

'Thea Krogh asked me to inform you. We picked him up about half an hour ago at a tavern. They called us in because he was drunk and had become . . . somewhat unpleasant. It's not serious, but we brought him in.'

'I'll come and get him.'

'I would not recommend that. He's asleep, and he probably will be for several hours. Thea said to tell you to just go home. She'll call you.'

Thorkild didn't answer, but closed the phone and left the café.

At the police station, he asked to see Frank. There was a young officer at the reception desk. Thorkild tried to sound composed, telling them he needed the car key. He succeeded against all expectations. He was led to a cell where Frank lay on a couch and slept quietly, like a small child, curled up in a heavy stench of smoke and whisky. With the young policeman's help, he got the car keys from Frank's pocket and trudged off again.

Uncomfortable, he sat behind the wheel of Frank's BMW and fiddled uncertainly with the keys. He managed to get it started, then he spent another ten minutes adjusting mirrors, seat, steering wheel and switching off the navigation. He drove very slowly back to police headquarters and parked just outside the entrance. He walked into the reception again, asking to speak to Thea Krogh and was told she was busy.

After he got back into the car, there was a knock on the window. Edvardsen stood there, looking grave. Thorkild rolled down the window.

'My young colleague told me that you reeked of beer. That

can't be right. Do you mind?' He asked Thorkild to breathe into a little apparatus.

Thorkild gestured with his hand, deprecating. 'Forget it, I'm guilty. Can I sleep here with my friend until tomorrow?'

Edvardsen laughed, one of his rare laughs.

'The bus station is right up there. But it won't be long before Thea shows up. I've told her you're here. Won't you take a seat?'

Thorkild sat down in the reception area to wait.

38

Frank hadn't uttered a word since he woke up in jail, rubbed his eyes, took stock of the situation, found that his car keys were gone, looked up and saw Thorkild standing there, ready to take him home.

'Come on, Frank,' Thorkild had said, and Frank followed him. No questions or explanations, they had just walked out.

And now they were sitting in the silver BMW, which Frank had carefully inspected for damage. With a snort, he turned back the settings to suit him. And off they went, at breakneck speed and in an icy silence that Thorkild several times tried to break. Frank's face was closed, the stench from him overwhelming. Thorkild succeeded only when they approached the ring road.

'How are you, Frank?'

'Like hell, what do you expect?'

Frank's tone was searing, and it hit home – burrowing deep into Thorkild's compassion, his empathy for Frank. He felt liberated and wonderfully angry. It was a magnificent feeling.

'You can stop that right there. Don't even think about being mad at me. I've been running all over Århus, searching for you everywhere, because you just disappear and go drinking. And then you end up in jail, and I have to take the bus home and then back in again at an ungodly hour. I'm well aware of the fact that you're upset, and I am too, make no mistake about it. But you left me at the damn library, running away like a little child because you're afraid. And even for that, I can muster up a little understanding . . .' Thorkild raised his voice, he was shouting now: But I'll be damned if I'm going to sit here and have you snap at me. As if it's all my fault. Grow up, man!'

Frank turned his head and looked at him with a fury that faded and turned into a look of dawning respect.

'Fair enough, Thorkild.'

'Fair enough? What does that mean?'

'It means fair enough. I'm sorry, dammit. It wasn't cool to abandon you. I just lost it.'

'Yes, I did, too.'

'What happened?'

'They called and said you were sleeping in the holding cells. I drove the car up there – I wanted to take you with me, but no dice. So I waited for three hours for Thea, and then I went home. This morning she called and said you could come back to Roslinge and get your bag, so you can take a shower and put on some clean clothes and stuff. They're coming out later to talk to you.'

They sat for a while. Then Frank turned on the radio. Thorkild reached in, turned it off and stared at him incredulously.

'You don't want music? Seriously, Thorkild, I don't know what to *say*. OK? What the hell do I say to you? Do I have to say something?'

'No, you don't have to say anything But dammit, Frank. Won't you tell me what you think about all this? Don't you *feel* anything?'

'Fuck you! Of course I *feel* something,' sneered Frank.

'What are you, a psychologist all of a sudden, so I have to tell you my feelings? Is there something you think I should apologise for?'

'Does it really matter *what* I am? And I don't want you to apologise, don't be stupid. But I'm a part of this now, in a whole new way. I think, in a way, you owe it to me to say something.'

'I *feel* that my sister has become a murderer. What am I supposed to feel? What would be right?'

Thorkild sighed, couldn't find an answer. Frank continued:

'It's going to sound stupid, what I have to say to you. But I don't believe that Sanne has done it, has killed your wife. I can't for the life of me figure out why she would have done it. You must believe me, Thorkild, I didn't know that she even knew your Karen.'

He sounded earnest, and it dawned on Thorkild that Frank was afraid, seriously afraid.

39

An organ chorale by Buxtehude sounded out in church.

Dietrich Buxtehude. One of the young substitute organist's favourites, beside the obvious Bach. Baroque heavyweights. They suited the church and the organ's fifteen ranks. The organ was new. A Frobenius. It had a much lighter tone than the heavy old organ, as Thorkild remembered it. Jakob, the new substitute organist who commuted from Århus, where he attended the music academy, had come to the church after the organ had been replaced. He had not been involved in the process and often complained that they should have made sure to get the ranks that allowed you to play the romantic organ music. A nasal pipe of some sort for César Franck and perhaps a velvety celeste. Unbelievable that they hadn't thought of a little spice.

The organ chorale by Buxtehude was the service prelude. Thorkild looked out over the church from his seat in the choir. He liked the look of the congregation. A good mix of young and old. It had become a cliché, Thorkild thought, that churches were close to extinction, attended only by a few elderly ladies wearing hats. In Roslinge, every Sunday, more people attended church than the football match. And the young families turned out too. If an age group was missing, it was those in their mid-forties to sixty; 1970s youth.

The congregation had its eccentrics, those who didn't fit in elsewhere. Then there were the trusty regulars who came Sunday after Sunday, most of them with young families; they were the most responsive, offering opinions on the choice of hymns, praise and questions about his sermon. There were the members of the parish council. There were the remnants of the inner mission, dating back to the time when it had been a strong movement among farmers. Anton and Anika Svendsen belonged to that category; Anika, who had chosen the church as a natural place to confide crucial evidence to the police. There were politicians, out to boost their profile in readiness for the town council elections. There were always a couple of scouts present in their green uniforms. And finally there were the ones you would in the past have called the Grundtvigians – avid followers of the nineteenth-century spiritual leader who believed citizens should be educated to participate in the new-born democracy, resulting in a colourful movement of free folk high schools throughout Denmark that endured to this day.

Years ago, the cantor had entered the church as a member of the parish council for the Grundtvigian contingent. The Grundtvigians' belief that people should be people first and

Christians second annoyed pietists in parish councils all over the country. But the cantor had fallen down from his reaper, developed a limp and been forced to switch career. So he wound up in the church as a sacristan and cantor, probably more because of his insistence on accuracy in the service than his singing voice. He was notorious, for example, for throwing out candidates for confirmation in the middle of the service if they giggled too much.

Now it was Thorkild's turn to perform. It always took for ever to get the service going. Prelude, petition, a hymn. He thought about his youth, when he played the trumpet in the town orchestra. You could sit for half the concert and become flaccid and lazy before you suddenly had to put in an effort. That was what this reminded him of.

The first hymn of the service was 'The Church is an Old House'. Dorian tonality, three beats to a measure. When the hymn finished, the organist intoned properly to G major in preparation for the choir's response.

Thorkild cleared his throat and went to stand before the altar: 'The Lord be with you.' The cantor, who had a cold, led the way in the response: 'And the Lord be with you.' The polite greeting which begins any service.

Conducting a service is all about timing. You must be able to time things, like a musician or an actor, to get the service flowing. Thorkild was annoyed with the organist, who always started playing a fraction too early, as if he was nervous about not making it in time. It ruined the flow.

He was half aware that there was something lacking in the congregation's response. A voice was missing. The congregation had its own sound. He was so familiar with it. Without being able to tell exactly which church-goers contributed what, he knew the overall sound. And a voice was missing from that sound today. It was also missing when the congregation recited the prayers for the baptism. And suddenly, it was there again: 'Lead us not into temptation.' Thorkild could hear it now. It was Anton Svendsen, who only occasionally contributed with his deep, slightly rusty voice. He was sitting there in his usual place, but he wasn't singing along. His face was closed, dark.

Thorkild had split the hymn before the sermon in two. First, they would sing verse one through four, afterwards the final four. When they had sung the first four, the organ ceased to play and Thorkild took his place in the pulpit. Anton meanwhile continued with verse five in a high, squeaky voice that sounded lonely in the empty space.

He even stood up when he sang: '*The grass is like every sinner, ends before he begins, withering in its spring.*' He stopped there, in the middle of the verse, at the height of the melody's climax. It was as if Anton had asked a question. Then he sat down. There was an excited rush through the church, an almost audible exchange of glances and the obligatory fit of giggles from the confirmation candidates.

Thorkild began his sermon, undaunted.

'There is an old word called mercy. We know the word knowledge. Mercy doesn't. It is the word used to describe the very quality of God: that he knows no man's sin.'

'You should hope so.' It was Anton who responded from the audience. People shushed.

'God does not see our mistakes and shortcomings,' continued Thorkild, uncomfortable.

'That doesn't mean you can't behave properly,' said Anton, his voice thin and angry, an old man's voice.

Thorkild bit his lip, not knowing what to do. In his first year as a vicar, he had often written about the sad monologue-based service. Knew it had an essence to it. Once inside the church, the word is, in principle, indisputable. Disagreements and disputes belong outside. But even if he wanted more dialogue, this was not what he'd had in mind. Resolutely, Thorkild stepped down from the pulpit and moved to the middle of the aisle.

'Anton, whatever's on your mind, I would like to invite you over to the vicarage to discuss it after the service.'

Anton sat silent and looked down. Anika, who sat beside him, curled up her face in a horrified grimace. Then Anton muttered something Thorkild couldn't hear. 'What was that, Anton?'

After a while, Anton looked up at Thorkild and said, clearly:

'I'm not entering that den of iniquity.'

'Excuse me?'

'Your house. A den of vice, a whore house. It's not dignified for a vicar to behave like that.'

'No! Anton,' shrieked the woman.

'I don't know what you mean.'

'You should be a role model for the congregation. This is what a vicar is. But you live with a woman, out of wedlock, disrespectful to your wife's memory. Is that other man part of it too?'

Thorkild didn't answer, but stood bewildered in front of the congregation.

He saw the cantor walk up the aisle and enter Anton's pew. Anton stood up. The cantor threatened Anton with a clenched fist, which caused Anton to hastily climb the back of the pew to the row behind. The cantor walked out of the one row and into another. The congregation stood up and began moving around the church to get away from the curious dance. Anika yelled, cried and pleaded for Anton to stop. Anton climbed from pew to pew. The cantor ran in and out between the rows. Neither said a word. The organist was trying to save the situation and resume the service by starting to play the next hymn. It was Grundtvig. This reminder of his ideological model apparently emboldened the cantor: he picked up the pace. Anton fled all the way down the rows to the bottom of the church, terrified of the big cantor whose limping march made him seem almost inhuman. The escape was accompanied by organ music, the people cried out because it was the only way they dared to interfere, while Thorkild walked insecurely down the aisle for the sake of at least doing something. The confirmation candidates laughed and cheered.

The organist switched to Brorson. Anton, recognising the pietist anthem, changed direction and ascended pew after pew, heading towards to the choir. The cantor followed. In the choir, Anton defended himself from behind the baptismal font. The cantor struck some blows across it, but without being able to hit Anton. The Romanesque granite stone of the baptismal font had become a true front between the two combatants.

The cantor went left of the baptismal font, leaving the aisle free. Taking advantage of this, Anton ran past the baptismal font and down the aisle, toppling Thorkild who collapsed bewildered in the middle of it all, and disappeared out of the church.

The cantor ran down and closed the massive wooden doors behind Anton, turned and looked towards Thorkild. 'The vicar may continue.'

The organ stopped. The candidates clapped appreciatively. People sat down in the new places they had fled to in the church corners. In the midst of it all was Thorkild, conscious of all eyes upon him.

He sat down on the cold tiles on the floor and composed himself. Then he got to his feet and gathered his thoughts. Clearing his throat loudly, it suddenly came to him what he should do next. Something he had wanted to do for a long time.

'If you don't mind, I would like to end the service here.' He paused. To see the reactions and to gather courage for the next step. 'Instead, I would like to invite you to my home tonight. The vicarage, say at eight? All are equally welcome.' He stressed the word *equally*, while he looked at poor Anika, who had remained sitting in her place, face buried in her hands, sobbing.

That evening, the congregation quietly showed up. Thorkild had been excited at the prospect. Now they had begun to arrive. Then even more came. Most of the morning's church-goers, as far as Thorkild could tell. Even a couple of the confirmation candidates, three girls and one boy. Not Anton, of course, but Anika came sneaking in. She gave a shy greeting to Thorkild, who stood at the door to welcome people. There were others: Lily, Asger Jørgensen. The grocer and his wife had the unfortunate cousin with them, now released from custody. Torben Jepsen looked pale and tired; his dark hair had grown long at the back, his arm rested on Elisabeth's shoulders as if he was leaning on her for support. The grocer marched into the house, but Elisabeth and Torben stopped, uncertain. Torben didn't look up as he stood in front of Thorkild.

'Christensen . . .' he said, nothing more.

Thorkild reached out a hand towards him.

'Torben. You are welcome here. I'm infinitely sorry for what you have been through. Come inside.'

Jepsen shook his head.

'I won't come in. Thanks, anyway. I don't belong here. I just wanted . . . I don't know. I'm going home now, Elisabeth.'

'I'm sorry to hear that,' said Thorkild. 'I'd like it if you came in. Don't you think belonging can also be a decision?'

'Maybe. But not here. It's too much. For them and for me.' He nodded towards the living room, where chit-chat and the clinking of coffee cups could be heard. 'I appreciate the invitation, Vicar, but I just want to go home and watch television. I have a splitting headache. Text me when you're on the way home, Elisabeth.' And then he disappeared into the twilight.

'That's to make sure he can be in bed and out of the way when Mogens comes home,' said Elisabeth softly, as if she owed him an explanation. 'That's why I should text. He hasn't said a word to Mogens since he came out of prison. And he has nowhere to go. I have no idea what will become of him.' Tears formed a shiny film over her eyes, her voice was stifled like someone who needs to cry for several hours.

'Maybe he'll return to Copenhagen,' suggested Thorkild.

'I don't know what he'd do there. No job, no money. No family. Nothing. On the other hand, he doesn't have anything here either. Except for someone who loves him and wants to help. Do you understand, Thorkild, why I'm the one he hates most of all? All I wanted was to help him. Give him shelter, a hot meal every day. I wanted him to feel that he has a family. My sons adore him. I got Mogens to give him the job at the store. And yet it's me he detests. He never says so. He tries to hide it. He doesn't like Mogens, he hates the town here. But I'm the one he despises most of all. Why is that?'

She was crying very quietly.

'I don't know. I think you're wrong.'

'I'm not wrong.'

Elisabeth disappeared into the house and into the bathroom.

Bjørn Devantier came trotting along with Moos on a leash, which he tied firmly to Karen's clothes drier in the garden. They all showed up: most of the parish council, the cantor and the organist, the janitor and the manager of the gym, an enthusiastic squad of scouts, the chairman of the Chamber of Commerce and the chairman of the utility plan.

The next person who entered was not from Roslinge. Bjørn must have made her aware of the event. It was Thea Krogh.

'Thea. It's nice to see you.' There was an unspoken question in Thorkild's eyes that she decided to answer immediately.

'I don't know why I came.'

Thorkild would have said something other than welcome, but he was interrupted by new arrivals. Thea slipped around him and dived into the vicarage, where the woman who apparently lived here now took her coat and gave her a brilliant smile.

Birgitte acted as waitress. Neatly dressed in a very deliberate and very comely manner, she served coffee and tea and cake. There were folding chairs from the parish community centre for people to sit on. People were sitting close to each other in the living room, some in the hallway and kitchen with a view into the living room. Thorkild walked around like the good host and tried to talk to everyone.

In the middle of it all, he tapped his glass to get their attention. Speaking slowly and carefully, he moved around making eye contact with everyone.

'Some of you were cheated out of a sermon this morning. You won't have one now. But there are some things I want to say anyway.'

They looked up expectantly and stopped chewing. One of the confirmation candidates quickly turned off his iPod.

'I have lived in this town for many years. All these years together with Karen. We didn't come from Roslinge. I will never be from Roslinge. But I love the town very much. I've learned a lot from it. I've learned a lot from you. Above all, I learned the importance of *belonging*. I don't belong anywhere. I left my hometown. I've moved around to educate myself and to work. I'm not one of the mission people, I don't belong to the Grundtvigians, I'm no scout, I'm not a member of a political party, and I'm not in the Chamber of Commerce. It made me believe, mistakenly, that I didn't belong anywhere. That I didn't stand for anything.'

He was agitated, his voice slightly hoarse.

'Some of you know my sermons. They are . . . ironic. Some say I'm good at impaling people with words. It's easy to impale when you do not yourself stand for something that can be impaled. But I stand for something. There is also a place I belong. I belong as a human being with feelings. I feel pain and sorrow over Karen's death. There are no correct ways to mourn. But the feeling is there. And I'm experiencing all its manifestations. Sometimes in ways that are difficult for others to look at.'

He looked around, caught first Birgitte's bright eyes and then Thea's gaze. She was leaning against the doorframe to the kitchen, watching attentively.

'I believe in love,' he continued. 'That people spontaneously wish others well without thinking of themselves first. And that we need other people. I've been helped by good friends. I will love and live the best I can. I will not let standards and respectability stand in the way.'

He looked again at Thea. Searched for recognition in her eyes, but it was hard to decipher. He got it from Birgitte though. She seemed moved.

'I'm an educated person,' he continued. 'That's how I know myself. This means two things. This means that I am in fact educated. I've learned something I can use externally. To do my work. But I'm also emotional. I believe that we should live our lives based on our own experience as well as our education. Here, there is no contradiction between reason and emotion. It is only by knowing our feelings that we can navigate and adjust our lives so it makes sense. It's the way we can seek joy, love, sincerity. It requires action to continue to rediscover joy, love, sincerity. We should be emotional when we can. I will not compromise on that. Therefore, friends are welcome in my house. Therefore, lovers of all kinds are welcome. This is what I stand for. This is where I belong.' People clapped at Thorkild's speech, enthusiastically led by Birgitte, her smile radiant. The coffee machine in the kitchen gurgled and hissed as someone poured more water into it.

As the congregation left, many smiled and said polite thanks. Bjørn slipped out to the barking dog.

Anika Svendsen said nothing when she left, but warmly took Thorkild's hand between hers, cautiously daring to look at him.

The grocer's Elisabeth had smudges of mascara under her eyes.

40

There was slush and mud. The sun had not been seen for several days. Now, at least, it was there like a large white disc, just visible behind the transparent clouds. White grace.

Fallen leaves, soaked and half-decayed, littered the roads and sidewalks. Thea's tyres ploughed into a thick sticky mass of leaves mixed with apples that had fallen some time ago from the Elstar tree in the front yard. It smelled sweet and rich and strong as she opened the car door. There was a lull in the rain, which had been pouring all day, so she left the umbrella behind. Spying an apple on the wet lawn that was still firm enough to eat, she walked across the grass to get it. Then she leaned against the car and took a bite of the tart fruit, while gazing thoughtfully at the vicarage.

Thorkild came out on the steps.

'What a nice surprise,' he beamed. 'This is proper community policing, when you patrol people's front yards.'

He laughed. Thea was quite surprised.

When she was out in uniform, she tended to park the car more discreetly in order not to alert the neighbours to the fact that the police had called at an address. Today, she wanted to be informal. It irritated her, always to be seen only for her profession and not for the person she was. The vicar probably felt the same way.

So why had she gone to Roslinge? She had gone to Roslinge to see Thorkild Christensen. If she was honest with herself, it was the closest she could come to an explanation. Even though the case was still an open mystery, they had in fact found his wife's murderer. Not that she deserved thanks, but in all that time they'd worked the case with nothing to show for it she had experienced a pang of guilt every time she came in contact with Thorkild. Maybe now she was hoping for a little recognition. And she was curious, too, what it had meant to Thorkild, finally knowing the identity of his wife's murderer.

'Come inside, won't you? You can watch out for burglars from my kitchen window.'

He was obviously in a good mood. Thea went in, took off the sturdy boots and commented on the music that sounded throughout the house.

'Yes, you probably know the song. "Dark is November, the leaves have fallen".' Thorkild could not say the words without accentuating the triple rhythm. 'A wonderful piece for choir, this arrangement brings out the Middle Ages and the strong rhythm of the song. Listen here. I think it's called hemiola, when two bars are divided into three beats.'

Thorkild began to drum hemiola on the door frame as he walked in front of her, into the kitchen. Drummed upon the things he walked past. The kitchen table, refrigerator, the hard plastic of the kettle while he poured water into it. Thea could not help but laugh at the vicar's almost flamboyant erudition.

'You're amused?'

'Hemiola. I'd no idea. There is much to learn. Music has always been mostly background noise for me.' She sat down and took the steaming cup the vicar handed to her. 'In my childhood, the radio was always on at home. Non-stop. My mother used to listen to it. She stayed at home all the years I went to school.'

Thea saw puzzlement in the vicar's eyes. One moment she was uncertain of what it was. Then it dawned on her. Her childhood home in Viborg was not what he expected to hear about now. She felt a pang of regret that surprised her.

Instead, she met his expectant gaze and found another voice. It should have been factual, but sounded strangely familiar and wrong somehow. Really, who was she, here, with this person?

'Well, Thorkild. So we found Karen's killer.'

He threw out his arms.

'Yes. Not that it makes a difference.'

'No difference?'

He nodded. She pondered.

'No, there are still many loose ends.'

The vicar rubbed his eyes, nodded, slightly absent. She felt sorry for him, felt a real desire to get through to him.

'You look uncomfortable. Is there no satisfaction in it for you? To know who Karen's killer is. And that she suffered the same fate? If I may say so.' She cleared her throat, wondering if the sentence was inappropriate.

'No, honestly. There's not much of an explanation in it for me. It's the opposite, actually. It's deeply unsatisfactory.'

'You were in Århus with Sanne Andersen's brother? Why?'

'Yes. I haven't talked to Frank since. What is there to say? Right, why were we together, he sought me out, he thought we had something in common.'

'How is he handling it?'

'How do you handle something like that? He's shaken up, of course, just as I am. And baffled. And now you're probably telling me that you don't intend to give any explanation.'

Thorkild's mood had immediately changed. Thea regretted that she had gone straight to the point. She had naively thought that now they could move on, stop discussing the case and actually talk about something else. Feeling incredibly stupid, she gave a little sneer at her reflection in the surface of the black tea.

'I mean, why did they know each other? What had Karen done? What was that life I didn't know about? It really is . . . disturbing.'

Thorkild could not sit still. He tried, but he'd already stood up and sat down again three times, opened the window, cleared things away from the table, closed the window.

'And it doesn't help with a dead murderer. What can she tell? It's not justice I need, it's an explanation.'

He looked at her. The music stopped, leaving a noisy vacuum. He seemed desperate, a complete contrast to the smiling man he had been minutes earlier.

'Thorkild, we're doing everything we can. Nobody wishes more than I that we could find the solution to everything.' She spoke quietly. Looked at him, appealing, hoping for his understanding of her work. And the understanding of her that she hoped he possessed.

'What did you want here?'

He almost cried it out, it resounded in the room, and she felt his frustration right to the marrow.

'You're right, it was probably a mistake to come out here.'

She searched for the words and felt exposed, clumsy, misunderstood. And so she continued with more words.

'I don't know quite what to say to you, Thorkild. Let alone what to do. In fact, I thought we might try to talk about something else?'

Thorkild was silent for a moment, looking out the window. Then he turned to Thea and exploded:

'What is this? Yes, that would be lovely. The vicar and the cop. Then you could catch the culprits and drag them into church on Sunday morning and I could forgive them in a row. That would be interesting, more so than my congregation, whose greatest crime is the many things that they fail to do.'

'This is totally uncalled for.' She stood up.

He continued, undaunted, his voice rising:

'Then we could get rid of the altar wine, and the murals could be supplemented with graffiti, and during the service the children could go to the waiting room and learn about the three wise bank robbers, while the organist played the theme from *The Godfather*!'

Thea stopped in her tracks, dumbfounded. Thorkild paused mid-tirade, as if there was more to say. When he didn't say anything else, Thea took her coat and went out to the car. Without a word.

On the way out of the driveway she passed a small light blue VW polo, which was just entering. She caught a glimpse of the woman behind the wheel, whose mouth was open. For a moment Thea thought that she was screaming or crying. Until it dawned on her that the other woman was singing behind her steering wheel. Then they passed each other.

The clouds had gathered into a thick darkness, and shut out the sun. No mercy.

Thorkild stood behind his kitchen curtain and watched Thea as she climbed into the car. He was seething, yet at the same time he was struck by a sense of having wronged her. An orchestra of constantly changing emotions. As soon as he felt happy and uplifted, frustration and sadness punched him in the stomach with a vehemence that surprised him. The way he had parted from Frank with the new rift between them, all of Birgitte's chirping and planning, and then suddenly Thea, whom he'd hoped was coming with news when he saw her standing outside his home with an apple in her hand. She had seemed so resolved, and he had almost pictured the final scene in a film, with soft background music playing as the policewoman, the one person he felt really understood him, would offer a plausible explanation and complete the circle. Instead she turned up here with empty hands, with nothing. He could not understand why.

Still he was sorry to see her go, her steps heavy and dejected as she made her way towards her car. She would leave him, mistreated. And that wasn't right, no matter what.

She might have come empty-handed, but at least she had come.

Feeling guilty, he was about to run after her when Birgitte's car swung into the yard. He could hear the music from the kitchen, and he was both happy to see her and tired to his very core at the thought of all her chatter, all the food that was to be made of the groceries in the shopping bags she was carrying. She demanded so much from him, requiring his attention and presence, his energy and libido, his appetite for everything. And always with a big question mark hanging over them. What were the two of them going to do with one another – that was a decision that could not be postponed for much longer. If he knew Birgitte, she would just come straight out with it. In principle, she could step into his kitchen tonight, put the bags down, ruffle her hair, fix him with her eyes and ask.

So a profound relief washed over him when he was saved by the ringing of the phone.

A spontaneous joy when he saw that it was Frank.

And a brand-new overwhelming sense of enterprise that grabbed him when Frank said:

'Thorkild? It's Frank. I need to talk to you. I got an email from a woman who says that she murdered my sister.'

41

'I'm going to Århus. I need to buy a few things. Is there anything you need? I'll probably go to Bruun's Gallery, pop into the pharmacy. It's easy to park there.'

Thorkild and Frank didn't answer Birgitte. They barely looked up from the computer screen on the dining table. She tried again:

'I'll probably not be home before tonight. There's leftovers from yesterday in the refrigerator. Chicken breast. You could make a pasta salad.'

This time she didn't wait for a reply but marched out to

the Polo, switched on the engine and reversed out, dangerously close to Frank's shiny silver car.

Frank had rushed down to Roslinge almost immediately,
after he saw the email. He'd phoned Thorkild while he was
on the road, and now they were sitting side by side at the
dining table. When the portable altar, the medium for communication across space and time and the object of their attention
had finished with its ritual of demanding passwords and
loading software, Thorkild logged in to Frank's Hotmail
address.

'It's called frankieboy, at, hotmail, dot, com. And the code
is kissmyass. There are two s's in that. Jesus, it's slow, man.
Get yourself a new one.'

Thorkild laughed, his mind suddenly at ease again.

'There it is,' continued Frank, strangely unmoved. 'It's the
first one.'

The subject was Sanne. The sender: *TheGoldenGun*.

'Holy shit,' Thorkild muttered when he opened it and the
words in all their incomprehensibility appeared on the screen.

To Frank Andersen
   You don't know me. I know you, because your sister told me
about you.
   Your sister is no more. I shot her.
   Your sister deserved to die. You need to know that.
   I knew your sister well. We were like sisters.
   Secretly. Nobody knew we met. Besides those we met with.
   I knew it, the day she made herself a murderer.
   She took a life, and had her life taken. Now it is I who is
guilty. And because of that, I will also die. Naturally or intention-
ally. None of us know our destiny, do we?
   I have a question for you: Is life ever anything other than
people struggling to survive and turning off the light for others
along the way? Therefore, death is always just, and therefore
we all find it, one way or another.
   I don't write this to hurt you.

You must understand why your sister died. It is my gift to you.

Her death is as fair as everyone else's death.

Do not tell anyone about this, nothing will come from that. Do not respond to this mail.

You will never find me, so don't try.

M

Thorkild read the email. He didn't have to, because Frank was looking over his shoulder and reading aloud. Very loud indeed. He could feel Frank trembling even from a distance, it was practically in the airwaves all around him. Shivering, quivering, sputtering, furious. His calm was gone.

'I'll get her. I'll fucking kill her. Once I find her . . .'

'We need to show this to the police, Frank. Have you sent it to them? Did you answer the email? What have you done?'

'I haven't done anything. I've done fucking nothing. Nobody has. Sanne has not done anything. It's this psychopath, this crazy person who's behind it all!'

Thorkild remained silent, trying to keep up. Stunned that the big man was crying. Frank was standing as if nailed to the spot. He sobbed and howled and raged, all the while bending over Thorkild's shoulder, looking at the screen. It was awkward and too intimate, so Thorkild slipped out from underneath Frank's arm. He could not bring himself to go and hug Frank, so he went to the sink, turned his back on Frank, aware of the rejection, and looked out the window.

Frank continued his rampage, his sobbing, his protests. It was too much for Thorkild. This was too invasive.

'Now, Sanne wasn't without fault,' he tried.

'What do you mean?' Frank stopped his tears immediately and straightened up.

'You know what I mean.'

'She didn't kill anyone, it wasn't like that, there must be some explanation, Sanne hasn't bloody killed someone, she could not even . . .'

'Frank,' Thorkild interrupted, 'stop that. I don't think this is the place for you to seek solace and compassion, do you? My wife was murdered, wasn't she? Pull yourself together, man, and let us look at this.'

'Holy shit, Vicar. You're not saying . . .?'

'Frank, according to the police there's no doubt that Sanne shot my wife. There is evidence, crystal-clear forensic evidence and a bloody eyewitness. It's time for you to accept it. And don't stand here and waste my time with prevarications and conspiracy theories. If I hadn't known you first, and if Sanne hadn't been murdered, I'd feel compassion for you and her, yes, and I'd probably hate her too. If we're going to continue with this, that's the premise: Sanne killed someone, and that someone was Karen. But maybe this will tell us why.'

'Give me a fucking break,' Frank went a few steps to the left, cleared the table, came within two arms' lengths of Thorkild. Threatening.

'Frank, stop it. I think you should go home, and I think you should talk to the police about this.' Thorkild pointed at the computer while he turned back towards the door, the door that led into the living room, not out towards the hall. He took a few steps backwards.

Frank hesitated, then pulled himself together and moved towards the other door. He turned in the doorway.

'Thorkild, I thought you were my friend. I guess I was wrong.'

Thorkild stood there for a while, until he heard Frank start the engine. Then he went into the hall and locked the door. Back in the kitchen, he took a glass of water. He had a dry mouth. Then he sat down at the computer.

He copied the email into a text document and shut the browser down. Then he read the message again, slowly, while he wondered about the choice of words, trying to comprehend what he was reading.

Someone had murdered her, Sanne, as an act of justice? And sent Frank the email as a sort of redemption. They used the word *gift*.

I know you, because your sister told me about you. Sanne had known her killer. And there had been others. Secretly. Had Karen been one of these others?

He tasted the final initial, *M.* He noted the return address *Thegoldengun.* Then he opened a new browser and searched to find out whether it was possible to discover the IP address from an email. He gave up. Logged into his own email and sent his question to one of his old schoolmates, Emil, who had a management position at TDC and was an avid computer geek. Sat for a while, restless. Then he reserved the James Bond film of the same name as the email address from the library, and sent another email.

> Frank, can't we help each other instead of fighting? Sorry I was angry. Call me if you hear more from M. And don't do anything stupid.

When Birgitte came home early that evening, Thorkild was gone. There was no message for her. Late in the evening, when she went to bed, he still hadn't come home.

42

'I've called this meeting because we have to put the pieces together again. There isn't any fresh information that you don't already know. To put it bluntly, we're stuck. We have to see if we can find something new together, hidden in the pieces we already know.'

Thea's hands were trembling as she poured herself a glass of water. Exhausted, disillusioned, the case had been dragging on too long, and they were getting nowhere.

'You've all done a great job. There isn't a tile in Roslinge that hasn't been turned over, or an individual who hasn't been questioned,' she looked at Bjørn and Jorgen. 'There's hardly a hair that hasn't been scrutinised with a magnifying glass and microscope,' she looked at Alice. 'And everything that could have been analysed or checked out or compared against the databases has been taken care of, and I want to say thanks.' She looked at Søren and Kristian.

When Anne-Grethe Schalborg wasn't mentioned in the praise, she stood up herself.

'I'm here to keep abreast of your efforts. I have to say, I'm not as impressed as Thea, to say the least. We cannot live with the reputation this case is giving us. In order to get a fresh pair of eyes on this, I've brought in my young nephew, Janus Schalborg. Janus is twenty-six years old and fresh out of the academy. His PG2-internship was in Aalborg, so he knows the area well.' Janus stood up, a lanky young blond with slightly nervous eyes that sent glances in all directions. He stammered a hello and sat down again quickly.

'I expect that you will welcome him and use his expertise on North Jutland conditions. It may well prove useful now.' With this, Anne-Grethe left the floor to Thea.

'It was fourteen days ago that we became aware of the connection between Roslinge and Vindbygårde. There was no doubt it was a breakthrough and we were full of optimism. Sanne Andersen shot and killed Karen Simonsen with two shots. We succeeded in locating the scene of Karen's murder. We even found one of the bullets. Ballistic tests proved that the same gun was used in both killings. But we don't know anything else about the gun. And unfortunately, that is the hallmark of the investigation as things stand. Two weeks on, we don't know anything else. We've found no connection between Karen and Sanne. Nobody had any idea that they knew each other, or even so much as travelled to the area where the other one lived, not in the past several years. Both were loners – but there the comparison ends. They moved in different circles. No common relationships whatsoever. Think of all the times we meet new people and find we have acquaintances in common. Denmark is a small country. But these two women did not have a single acquaintance in common, as far as we know anyway. Perhaps because they were both shy. But what have they used each other for? And how did two shy people who preferred to stay at home get together?'

'The internet,' Jørgen Schmidt suggested.

'According to Thorkild, Karen Simonsen never used a computer. All we know about Sanne is that she had an email address. She apparently had no computer. None found, no ISP registration, no network at the address besides an open network at the neighbour's – she may have logged on to that. But you're right, Jørgen, it cannot be excluded. Neither has been in contact with the police before. Nobody in either of their social circles has given us anything more to go on than a speeding ticket. We have now accounted for every trace of DNA in the Vitara that Karen was transported in. We know every one of those people. They have all been eliminated from our investigation. Except for Sanne, of course. She in turn has been murdered and yet there is nothing in her apartment to help us find her slayer. Not a thing.'

'At the last meeting, we wrote *Brooch* on the blackboard,' said Søren.

'Yes, that remains the only unknown phenomenon in Karen's life. But we cannot connect it to anything in Sanne's. There's nothing to indicate that she attended lectures, it's reported that she never set foot outside her door. As a result, that lead is less interesting now.'

'The murder in Roslinge was planned,' said Kristian. 'Sanne targetted Karen specifically. Most murderers know their victim. We haven't been able yet to establish how they knew each other, who provided the link between them. But it's there, it must be. We're just missing the connection.'

'There's nothing to indicate that Karen was ever in Vindbygårde. Aalborg Police showed pictures of her to almost the entire town of Vindbygårde – the residents in Sanne's apartment building, staff on trains and buses along the route – no joy. And it's the same with Sanne,' said Bjørn. 'Nobody can recall ever having seen her in Roslinge. Except for Anika, the old kook, and that was in connection with the murder. We've looked at her GPS: no mention of Roslinge on there. According to her brother Frank, she hasn't travelled much. There are 100,000 kilometres on the mileometer, and she'd had the car for six years.'

'But there's a GPS,' said Kristian. 'Why have a GPS, if you never go anywhere? And it doesn't tell us anything about her whereabouts?'

'It's an old GPS. She got it from her brother for Christmas the year she bought the car. It doesn't show lists of past routes, but it does make suggestions as presets from memory when you enter the street name again. I've entered every street name in Roslinge and the surrounding areas. Nothing popped up as a preset. But of course we could enter every street name in Denmark if you want.' Bjørn sounded frustrated. It irritated Thea, not least because she shared the frustration. In these days, with GPS coordinates attached to almost every human activity, they had to be chasing the only woman in the country who left no electronic trail behind.

'No need for sarcasm, Bjørn,' she said. 'We'll do what it takes. Simple as that.'

'What about the phone?'

'You mean Sanne's mobile? It's gone and we can't trace it. It's simply disappeared from the radar. We've checked with the telephone companies for both Sanne's mobile, Karen's mobile and the vicarage landline. Those are the only phones we know they had. All calls have been traced. Nothing unusual. Which is saying something. It merely confirms the picture that we have of very introverted individuals. Sanne has called a total of seven different people within the last six years. The vicarage phone obviously has more numbers listed. But Thorkild has marked the numbers he knows, and for the rest, we're down to an equally small portion. All of them have been checked. It's got us nowhere. Karen's mobile phone was found at home on her bedside table in the vicarage. She called Thorkild and her children and a few friends. No one else.'

Søren Edvardsen looked thoughtful.

'We have a new face among us. Our young companion. Maybe he's the solution?' He spoke in the direction of Janus Schalborg. 'Perhaps we should hear a little more about you, so we know what you do?'

Janus got to his feet, stood awkwardly in front of the crowd like a candidate for confirmation about to deliver the long-dreaded speech. He scratched his bright hair. His aunt looked at him, expectantly. Thea felt a little sorry for him.

'Right, er, I was trained in the Funen police district. My last internship was in Aalborg. Traffic. But I've also been in the emergency section of the Copenhagen Police. It was like an internship, before the academy.'

He said no more. An expectant, impatient mood hung over the room.

Schalborg gathered her papers together. 'You are trained investigators. You know what to do.'

Thea followed up on Anne-Grethe's final words:

'We need to concentrate our efforts on Sanne Andersen. As things stand, it's her killer we need to find. I'm going to Vindbygårde to see if I can get a little further. I'll be in Århus the rest of this week. From Saturday I'm in Northern Jutland.'

On the way out of the conference room, Anne-Grethe held Thea back. She whispered: 'I expect you to take care of Janus. I don't suppose it'll be a problem.'

'What do you mean, Anne-Grethe?'

'He's nervous, inexperienced. I won't have these seasoned investigators using him as a whipping boy because he doesn't know how to say no. I realise he's my nephew, and yes, I'm giving him his big chance. I expect your full support.'

Thea nodded, too weary to speak, and gathered up her belongings. She was wondering whether it would be possible to stay in Vindbygårde or whether she should book a hotel in Aalborg, when an arm was placed on hers. Kristian. Whom she hadn't really spoken with in a long time. The anger she felt towards him ran through her. It was he who had been distant, not her. She had phoned. She had sent messages. She didn't realise what it was he was punishing her for.

'Can I see you, Thea? I miss you.'

She shook his arm off.

'You miss me! Well, how about that. You have use for me now?'

'Thea, it was never like that. It just seemed like you needed some air.'

She smiled, wryly.

'Some air? Are you sure you're not transferring your own needs on to me? It's nice to hear that you know what I need, Kristian. Very reassuring. I've had plenty of air, so thanks for that.'

'Sorry I haven't called. Can't we skip the whole explanation, Thea? All the justifications? Maybe we should just see each other. Try to find each other again.'

'I don't know, Kristian.'

'What don't you know? Thea, we're not teenagers, there's no reason to be so dramatic. You know everything about me.'

'No. For example, I don't know what's going on with you at the moment. I think it's strange. And there's so much going on now. We're stuck in this investigation, I'm stuck with you.'

'You're not. We are as we have always been.'

'I don't know what to do, Kristian. It's driving me crazy.'

'Yes, I realise that. I'll help you. Thea, I miss you.'

'I miss you too.'

'So let's get together. Can't we? A few hours tonight, perhaps?'

She shook her head slowly.

'I have to work. Give me a few days. By then, I hope we'll have gotten the investigation going. I'll let you know. I will. Can you wait for that?'

'You're going up north?'

'Not until Saturday.'

He put his arms around her and felt safe again.

'We've always been able to wait for each other. Of course, Thea.'

43

'Hi, Vicar, friends again?'

Frank had phoned Thorkild, his voice as happy and cheerful as if he had just gotten out of the shower and was ready for a day's work.

Thorkild, sitting in front of his computer in the vicarage, shook his head irritably at Frank's teenage phraseology. On the other hand, it was somewhat more straightforward than the long rant he had rehearsed for when Frank next called. He decided that simple was best.

'Yes, Frank, friends again. How are you?'

Frank paused.

'I sent an email to the mysterious Miss M.'

'You did what? You weren't supposed to. And the police?'

'I got a reply.'

'Frank, I asked you something. Does Thea Krogh know about this?'

Frank ignored him.

'I asked M what she had gotten out of killing my sister.'

'You wrote that?'

'Yes, and also of course that Sanne isn't a murderer, and that it's all a mistake. I know you don't believe that, but I'm certain of it, dammit.'

He held a tense pause, and then broke it, abruptly.

'Thorkild, I *know* about your wife. I *accept*, if you will, that something happened there, that every indication says that it was Sanne. But we can sure as hell agree that there must have been a *reason*, right? And until we know the reason, it's too early to judge her. Isn't it?' His voice was pleading.

'Well, Sanne has, without a shadow of doubt—'

'And you'll stop that, Vicar, else I'll hang up.'

'Easy, Frank. Friends again, right?'

Frank snorted.

'Why must you always . . . wallow in everything? Leave it alone, OK? You talk and talk. Jesus Christ.'

'Frank, I'll let it go. So tell me, what did M reply?'

'I can send it to you if you're by the computer.' Frank clicked on buttons, and Thorkild looked in amazement as the email *re: Sanne* popped up on his screen as easy as anything. He opened it eagerly.

First, he read Frank's brief tirade, written in capitals:

FUCK YOU. MY SISTER WAS NOT A MURDERER. YOU ARE SICK IN THE HEAD. SANNE WOULD NEVER HURT A FLY. I HAVE NO IDEA WHAT YOU ARE TALKING ABOUT. LOOK ME IN THE EYES WITH YOUR ACCUSATIONS YOU SICK BITCH OR SHUT THE FUCK UP. BUT YOU WOULDN'T DARE AND I CAN UNDERSTAND THAT CAUSE I'LL SMASH YOUR FUCKING HEAD IN. YOU HAVE MURDERED MY SISTER? ANYONE CAN SAY THAT, WHY WOULD I BELIEVE YOU? BUT IF YOU DID, THEN START LOOKING FOR A TOMBSTONE.

And then the response from M.

I didn't want to answer you, but I feel sorry for you. You are full of hate.

The day will come when you will understand that my revelation was a gift. It is necessary to let go of hatred. I understand you are angry.

I forgive you.

You must realise that Sanne was ill. As sick as we all are. A murderer was she, like I am. We all kill life. Every time we want another man dead, we kill. Like you, Frank. I stand by my fault. Imagine if we all did. Don't you think life could blossom again, freely and openly?

So your accusations mean nothing to me. I would like to look you in the eye. It is you who dare not face something. The truth.

M

Thorkild sat for a while.

'Frank, the most likely explanation is that somebody's taking the piss out of you here. An unusually cruel joke. M may well have read all this in the newspaper, right? And found out that Sanne had a brother. There are many crazy people who would pull a stunt like that.'

'Write and pretend to be a murderer to mess with me?'

'Exactly. I know it sounds far-fetched, but it happens. More than you might think. All kinds of harassment between people. It's so easy to write something anonymously in a letter, even easier through email. Communication has become so . . . so noncommittal. And those who resort to such things may not necessarily realise the harm they do.'

'Yes, but this isn't a joke.'

'How can you know that, Frank, explain it, please?'

Frank hesitated. 'She wrote something in another email.'

'Another? There's more?'

'You'd better read for yourself.'

Several keyboard clicks at the other end of the line. And several emails ticked in.

'Frank, you're crazy,' said Thorkild, really upset. 'You can't be corresponding with such a madwoman. You shouldn't even dignify that sort of thing with an answer. And what if she actually is Sanne's killer!'

'Yes, I can. It feels good, Thorkild. I've also written to that guy Steffen Hou.'

'Who the hell is Steffen Hou?'

'It doesn't matter. Someone I don't like. You can write anything and get rid of all your aggressions. It's probably healthy. Don't you think, Thorkild?'

'No, I certainly don't. I can assure you, I don't.'

'You're so easy, Thorkild. Of course I'm not chatting away with murderers and sex offenders, do you think I'm an idiot? Irony, get it?'

'I get that this correspondence is idiotic.'

'Relax. You've got everything I have. Read on. There was a picture in the last mail.'

Thorkild took a deep breath.

'OK, just give me a moment to read this and maybe see if I can grasp it.'

He opened Frank's response to M. This time he had refrained from using capitals.

Why did you do it? Was it because of Karen?
Frank

As Thorkild read it, he realised that it was the first time Frank had said directly that Sanne was guilty of Karen's death. It gave him a strange feeling of relief.

Dear Frank
  I don't know why I'm telling you this.
  Maybe I just want someone to know my story.
  We all fight our battles to belong in his world. For 23 years, I lived with a man who beat me. Do you know what repeated violence and aggression does to a human? Do you know what

you become when you live in anxiety and fear? Crooked, invisible, gone. Nervous, calculating your every action. Eventually you start to depend on what you so fervently dream of escaping. Your whole measuring scale is this: whether what you do triggers him or not. There is suddenly no other measure. And you can no longer live without it. Then, how do you know what's up and down. You disappear without it. It is the worst. To live in a dependent relationship with what you hate and want gone. Can you even imagine the paradox?

But I was lucky. I had the opportunity to escape.

But the journey I had to make meant that I too – with violence and power – had to take my god-given right to exist, to force it through. Even when what I did made others into victims. It's life's harsh law. You do not get life without taking life. I took life, when I got the chance. I now live freely and openly. Your sister was in many ways a fateful meeting. She was not just a random woman. When I finally managed to escape from my husband, it was she who told him where I was.

I don't know why she did it. I will ask myself why she did it for the rest of my life.

He found me. Just as I breathed out, free at last, he found me. He broke down the door. I don't know how I managed to escape alive.

We all have guilt. But now maybe you understand why Sanne was infinitely guilty when it came to me. Now she's dead. A revenge death, a justice death, a liberating death to me. But her fate is better than mine was. Better to be dead and not know that you're dead, than to live with your personality imprisoned and knowing it.

Do you understand that?

I don't expect you to be happy on my behalf.

But perhaps this explanation will satisfy you. One day.

Frank, clearly not satisfied with her explanation, had written back.

You know nothing. You're making it all up. You could be anyone, and you are nothing. Do not write me again. You don't know Sanne. You are sick in the head.

'Good answer, Frank. It's about what I would have done.'
'Read on,' said Frank drily. Thorkild opened the third mail.

When I'd fired the gun for the last time, I saw her just lying there. It was a feeling of being finished. I did myself a favour. Finally, it was just about me. She was lying on the kitchen floor. I put the gun to her hands and shot twice. Once in each hand. To kill the hands, which as everyone's hands, bear guilt.

I'm telling you the truth.

She wore jeans and a grey cardigan. A ladybird in silver around the neck. Check the police report. I also took her phone, a Nokia. Here is a picture of it attached. You called her that morning at 9.32. You spoke for 3.52 minutes. You sent a message after I'd shot her. 22.08. 'Hi Sis, phoned this morning to ask if you want to join me. Speak to you later.' The phone is taken apart and thrown into the sea, do not try to trace it. Do you believe me now?

I understand that it is hard to read. I'm writing this for your own sake. One day you'll be grateful.

M

Thorkild sighed.
'That explains all the stigmata nonsense. But, Frank, is the part about the phone true?'
'Yes, it's true. The image, it's her phone.'
Thorkild opened the image that was attached. Stelephone. jpg. Thorkild quickly closed the picture again. As if something came too close.
'So I wrote her back,' announced Frank. Thorkild opened the last email from him.

I will find you. All the police officers in the country are looking for you. You have nowhere to hide. You will pay for this.

And M's laconic reply.

Do not go to police. You will make it worse on yourself. I know where you live, even though it sounds trite.

I am sometimes outside your window. I see how you stand in front of the mirror at night before you go to bed, flexing your muscles like a big strong man. Pathetic. Watch out, I might put a bullet in you.

The truth will set you free if you allow it.

If you go to the police, you will never hear from me again.

M

'Frank, I have to ask you again. You've told Thea Krogh about this?'

'No, dammit. M says I shouldn't go to the police.'

'You have to! It's the first thing you do in a situation like that!'

'I won't risk not hearing from her again, for fuck's sake. Think, Thorkild! She's the key to it all! She has to tell me what it is she thinks Sanne has done. And then perhaps we can also find out why Karen had to die. This is the way, can't you see it? I'll tell the police in time. I just want as much from her as possible first.'

'If we fail to tell them this, we're obstructing the police investigation. It's a criminal offence, Frank! Do you want to go to prison?'

'Just a few days, Thorkild. I'm begging you. Wait a few days. Wouldn't you like to know the truth? It's about Karen too. Once the police find out, they'll put you on the other side of the crime-scene strips again, I can guarantee you. Is that what you want, Thorkild? So you can shuffle around in your vicarage and wait for someone to call you with whatever little piece of information they'll throw you?'

Thorkild was writhing.

'But she threatens you. Threatens you your life! You cannot stay at home with some sick person looking in through your windows.'

Frank was silent for a while. When he spoke, he sounded tearful.

'Can I stay with you for a couple of nights?'

Thorkild prepared food for them both. Seventy-five minutes later Frank was standing in his kitchen, unshaven and with dark circles under his eyes, but ready to eat. Birgitte always kept the fridge full, so there was plenty to work with. He made a stew, which was allowed to stand and simmer for so long that the air in the kitchen was dense. The doors were closed, the blind rolled down. Thorkild had lit candles and Frank sat on the bench that stood along the wall. He had a blanket around him and looked sadder and more pale than when Thorkild had picked him up from detention.

'You look like a third-day drunk, Frank. Do you want a beer with your meal?'

Frank didn't answer. Poked at the food that Thorkild had put on his plate and drank the beer from the bottle, although Thorkild had poured some into a glass.

When they had finished dinner, Thorkild put the plates aside and invited Frank into the living room. 'I've got this old James Bond movie from the library. Want to watch it?'

Frank smiled without a twinkle in his eyes when he saw the title, but accepted the odd movie choice, *Man with the Golden Gun*.

'Britt Ekland,' said Frank, while they watched the movie. 'She's cute. Those big blue eyes. Really cute.'

'Cute? I didn't think Bond girls were supposed to be cute,' said Thorkild. 'Although I haven't seen that many Bond movies.'

'I've seen them all,' said Frank. 'I have a box set. You can borrow it, if you want. Lots of hot girls. But Britt Ekland, she's my favourite Bond girl. She reminds me of Sanne.'

Thorkild looked at the woman on the screen, a flawless body in a colourful bikini, full lips, the dark blonde, shiny hair that swirled around the Swede's shoulders, well groomed. A seventies dreamgirl who, most of all, looked infuriating, he thought. As if she was about to speak out any Bond girl cliché. He didn't see any similarity to Sanne Andersen.

'I don't mean physically. But the character, right? Mary Goodnight really tries to get something going with Bond, but he's totally indifferent. Not to give it all away, but at some point they're at his hotel room, and then there's a knock on the door, it's a woman Bond would rather have. So he pushes Britt Ekland into his closet, where she gets to sit and listen as he bangs another woman.'

'I see. Yes, that isn't very sympathetic.'

'She sits in there for so long that she falls asleep. And what does he do, after the other woman is gone? He wakes her up and doesn't apologise for pushing her into his closet, or that she had to listen to them having sex. Oh, no. He just says *I promise, your turn will come*. Really cold, as if he knows that, whenever he wants her, she'll be ready. Then he can have her. Who's your favourite Bond girl?'

'Uh. I haven't seen that many of them, I can never remember what they're called. The one with the name, maybe. Pussy Galore.'

'Honor Blackman. A classic. It's from *Goldfinger*. Maybe she reminds you of your wife?'

'Not exactly. But, Frank, you say that this one –' he pointed towards the screen '– reminds you of Sanne. Yet you've never mentioned anything about any men in Sanne's life. Was there someone who treated her badly?'

Frank hesitated. For a long time.

'No,' he said. 'Not that I know of. One might say that Sanne also just sat in a closet and waited for whenever it suited life to give her something.'

Thorkild smiled distantly.

'It's not easy to find someone who sits in a closet.'

'Yes. If you're the one who threw her in there, then you know damn well where she is.'

On his way to bed after the movie, Thorkild got his computer and checked his email while Frank was slouching on the couch. A thought had struck him.

'Frank, this picture? I've emailed a guy who knows a lot about computers. It's one of my old friends. He's all right. He says that in order to locate an IP address, you must have access to police resources. I think, frankly, you should go to Thea Krogh with this. She can help us. And perhaps they can use the picture. Do you remember Alice Caspersen? She left her business card. We'll call her tomorrow, right? Ask her how to use a picture to trace someone.'

Frank didn't hear anything. He was asleep on the couch, which was only just wide enough to accommodate the big man.

44

Local news, parish of Vilå
The World According to Men of Letters

A night on the street.
What has the murder of Karen Simonsen done to Roslinge? There are many who ask us. Is there still life in the town? Something must surely be different now? The answer is probably yes and no.

Autumn evenings still have their occasional peak. Shortly before half past seven, people set off to meetings in the parish council, the central heating committee, the trade association, Roslinge internet supply, the board of the sports hall. The activities have split the week in a manner that everyone is familiar with: the hall has Mondays and Tuesdays, Thursdays are for church, while the old scouts and the new role-playing games club fight over Wednesday evenings. You all heard the rumble at the beginning of the autumn season. When one group accused the other group of stealing its members, and it culminated in a battle in the woods by the old scout hut, where the green halberdiers charged with sticks into crowds of heavily armoured orcs and uruk hai'. Yes, life goes on, the activities that preoccupy us continue as if nothing had happened. At half past nine, people return to their homes. In the interim, the streets are deserted. We know the picture.

But this autumn, a new association has emerged. Some of our fellow citizens have come together to ensure law and order in Roslinge. But the numerous meetings have so far not resulted in anything other than discussions about who is the town's enemy. Some believe it is the youth we must act against; they want to establish a parents' association that will man a border control on the alcohol run to Vilå's Crazy Daisy and confiscate the youngsters' stock of booze, knives and condoms.

Others believe it is neo-Nazis who have chosen to target Roslinge, and that Karen was merely the first victim in an eradication manoeuvre. The only evidence they can point to is Sanne Andersen, with her bright Aryan looks.

And others suspect there is a local mafia lurking in the old part of Roslinge. Allegedly, they were the ones behind the thefts last July. With their drug-trafficking and gun-smuggling connections they would have had no difficulty procuring the murder weapon. The Association for Roslinge Law and Order meets on Wednesday evenings, and it's obviously prevented a new bloodletting between the scouts and the role-playing games club. If nothing else, the association has made peace in the woods for a while.

So, yes, something is happening in Rosling. And it's something new.

At half past nine every evening, people meet on their way

home. Some stop, talk, report on what is being said one place or another, alliances across the town's organised structures are developed. Others barely greet each other, distrust having planted itself among the inhabitants.

And that is how Roslinge has changed over the autumn.

Asger Jørgensen

45

Three spotlights illuminated the small stage. Black-painted wooden boxes made up the stage floor and the surrounding walls were black. A small piece of theatre. A void in the world until someone stood up, stole the light and stepped forward from the black background. Filled the space which before had been darkness. Palpable expectation from the café chairs and tables; even in their empty state they were turned to face the performance. Towards the dark void. Like a flower that senses dawn and nods to the east.

The hall was filling up with people. The small library offered lecture evenings as one of their windows for the suburb dwellers into the busy world outside. The evenings, admittedly, rarely attracted anyone new; those women of fifty-plus who attended such lectures to have something to discuss with their educated daughters were already members of the library. The hall was small, so it felt crowded when thirty visitors had passed by the librarian in the doorway and dropped twenty kroner into the saucer at the entrance. 'There's coffee and a biscuit later, included in the price,' said the librarian, reluctant to be seen taking money. Seeing as it was a public place.

Tonight's attraction was, as the somewhat frisky and spirited poster on the door proclaimed, an evening with *Happiness and Life Coach Ivan Geertsen.* Isabella sighed as she read the description of the lecture. So bloated. The contrast between the inflated title and the provincial name. But she felt the same way about the people who read self-help books and attended lectures by gurus. The very thought of it made her tired.

She was at that age where most of her friends had begun to develop obscure interests. The children had left home and the emptiness had to be filled. Isabella saw it mostly as a new emptiness with a veneer of meaning over the top. Like an illusion. It was an entire industry of perverted culture, and using public funds. Those old symbols of education, lectures and books, might still exist in the modern age, but the contents had grown thin, Isabella thought. All the trappings of yesteryear on the outside. But the content? So puritan. The monologue running through Isabella's mind had been rehearsed many times before, the tart, pithy observations honed over the years of wrestling with the self-help industry, whether engaging in her own quests or those of her friends.

It had become predictable in a way. And she was tired of it. As if she, with her lifestyle – still single in her late forties and living in the same apartment in the Øgade quarter – had suddenly turned into a role model for her friends. They all seemed to beat a path to her door, turning up exhausted after their divorces, their depressions, their affairs. One after another they would sink into her sofa, drink her tea and gaze around the quiet apartment appreciatively as if here was the embodiment of their dreams of freedom and independence.

She always listened. Firmly but kindly rebuffed their proposals that perhaps they might move in for a while so they could taste her life. Sent them on their way with words of encouragement, invitations, books. Followed their emancipation process with loyal interest.

Karen had been as predictable as the rest in her search for new meaning. Yet Isabella had enjoyed being with her and thought a lot about Karen when they didn't see each other. Because Karen had never once condemned or pitied her, the way so many of her other female friends had done when they married and had children. Karen had simply accepted that Isabella had chosen a different road in life; she had remained a friend, a quiet constant in her life. Not someone to be dug out of a closet and dusted off because married life had suddenly lost its appeal.

Isabella had turned up this evening because Karen had talked about being inspired by a lecture she'd attended by a life coach or somesuch. Isabella had forgotten the name, but it certainly wasn't Ivan Geertsen. A name like that she would have remembered, and the arrogant title *happiness coach* would have stuck in her mind too. Nevertheless Karen's enthusiasm had piqued her curiosity enough to brave the rain and her worst prejudices in order to hear what a happiness coach might have to say. At the sight of the poster, however, she almost turned around and went straight back out into the rain again. *Poor things. Poor bastards*, she said half aloud, eyeing the expectant audience. Nevertheless she dropped her coin into the saucer and joined the late arrivals taking their seats as the librarian announced tonight's guest.

She had hung her wet rain coat in the library's 'at your own risk' closet. She was apparently the only one who had. Damp coats were strewn over the remaining chairs, and she had to ask for no less than three ladies' coats to be removed before she could sit on the only vacant chair in the hall.

The three other women, who were squeezed together around the small coffee table, were talking about a lecture they had attended a week ago. *Oh God,* thought Isabella. *They attend lectures like it was badminton or target shooting or embroidery.* She rolled her eyes while they continued talking about astral therapy and energy fields as well as the standard of acoustics and speaker systems in the city's lecture halls.

'This guy should be worth looking at too,' said one of the

women, giggling. At that moment, the houselights grew dim and all eyes turned to the stage.

Lectures are an archaic discipline, primitive and dignified. Stepping on to a stage to fill and occupy the space with words and gestures. To capture the audience by affirming what they want to hear while you tell them something different and new, something they didn't know they wanted to hear. To balance the tone, articulation and tempo to both space and audience. Being able to entertain without it being fun and therefore frivolous, and to be able to teach without it being didactic and therefore boring. It's a close and intimate communication with a public space.

When Ivan Geertsen stepped up on the black boxes and into the spotlight, everyone in the hall knew he had mastered the art. The movements were calm, yet with a clear commitment. When he opened his mouth, the voice was deep and the tone one that made his audience feel cared for and secure. Isabella felt torn immediately. Seduced, and therefore reluctant.

She watched the man. It was hard. The lighting over-exposed his skin, making it white and shiny. He wore a beret. He was big and imposing, yet relaxed in his movements like a man who feels comfortable in his own body. Was he worth watching? Definitely. There was no denying it. Much as it annoyed her to admit it, she was enjoying the sensation he aroused in her body. That little tense feeling in the diaphragm we feel when we meet a really attractive person.

'What are we?' was his opening line. 'We're humans. Yes, that's what we are. Humans.'

Then came the pause for effect, followed by: 'But what is that? What does it mean?'

Another pause. Clearly the dramatic pause was a device he used often. Too often, Isabella suspected.

'To live, to exist, to be human. That's *becoming* human. You're not. Not yet. You sip coffee and listen to lectures. Why? It's pacifying. Why have you come?'

And then he softened, laughed and said, 'But I'm glad that you come to lectures. Otherwise I would not earn my money.' People laughed and he used the break to take a chair, similar to the ones the audience were sitting on, that stood in the wings. He sat on it, the wrong way round, on the edge of the stage. Established a more intimate setting as he continued, calmly and with his forearms resting on the backrest and the hands in explanatory gestures.

'You see, I will make sure that when you leave the hall tonight, you are new people. You will experience a rebirth. One of the big ones. A true rebirth. All religions have it. The church baptises people to their new life, Buddhists are enlightened, Jews are reborn in Jerusalem. But it's just pictures. Metaphors for that which all peoples in all times experience, and you are going to experience it tonight. Now the time has come for you. You must experience the real thing. The true rebirth.'

There was a scattered, somewhat strained chuckle in the hall.

Isabella already hated every word. But she had to give him credit for the way his whole appearance worked on her. He captivated her with his confidence and natural ease. He took the stage so perfectly.

Ivan Geertsen rose again, pushed the chair aside with a firm foot and rolled up the sleeves of his white shirt. He stood on the stage with slightly spread legs and arms at his sides, solid and firm.

'You will rise. When you leave here – when you stand up and leave, you will rise to a new life. As you begin to live for yourselves.' Ivan Geertsen looked into the thirty pairs of eyes watching him before he continued.

'The world is full of considerations. They go by different names. Care, courtesy, friendliness. The correctness of suburban ladies. You know it, I can tell. Don't you? You show consideration, you make sure things get done. That the house is vacuumed before the guests arrive. That the kids bring a gift to other kids' birthday parties. You wash your husband's football shorts. You make sure the family eat a varied diet and not just pasta Bolognese. Subscriptions and TV packages, right? That's your domain. Your life. I can hardly say the words.'

They were nodding, some giggled again.

'Do you feel insulted? Does it tickle? It shouldn't. I'm not a stand-up comedian who pokes fun, gets in a few cheap shots. A little loving satire. Forget it. It bores me. I'm bored. So very bored.'

Now there was silence. The harsh words lingered. Meanwhile, the man's gaze was tender, almost loving.

'Love is the worst of words. Not because there is no love. But there is primarily one law of love: Love yourself. That's where everything starts. No one can love without loving himself. You must live. Live yourself, stand up, take responsibility. Seize the power of will. The power over your own life.'

Isabella forgot about common sense and surrendered, surprised.

'Listen to me now.' Ivan Geertsen started moving back and forth on stage. 'My mother. That is where it begins for us all.' He laughed at the cliché. 'My mother was never there. She was there, but she wasn't *there*. She was invisible, a ghost. Apologetic, vague, cautious. You know it, don't you, when uncertainty gets the better of you. After all, we're all insecure sometimes. But you can choose not to be. Uncertainty is the worst. You float through life, bobbing up and down on the ocean waves like driftwood. You have to shape yourself. Grow sharp edges so you can punch your way into life. Become. My mother lived before you could choose to be anorexic. She was fat and blubbery. Her body was so blurred, you couldn't see where the world ended and she began. It became one. There was no difference. That's why girls today make themselves skinny. It's because then they get an edge. Your bones make your shape, so you stand out clearly from the outside world.'

Ivan paused: 'I'm not asking you to become anorexics.'

The audience laughed again. This time, more polite and a bit scared.

'And why not? Well, because that's nothing but an empty image of what it's really about. Like religion. It's just imagery. What's real is when you begin to live. Firmly, with conviction. Stand by yourself, love yourself, hate your enemy. That is power. It sounds awful, right? Power. It isn't. Power over your life means that you begin to act, stand by yourself, *create* yourself. But first, you must have the will. The will to power. That is what you'll get tonight, ladies and . . . Right, sorry, just ladies.'

The audience laughed again. Now more relaxed. He'd won them back, and even Isabella enjoyed his style.

'Let me give you an example. It's obviously an anonymous example. Take this woman.'

He pointed and looked at the air beside him to imagine that she was standing there. 'A woman who was with me for a long time for what I call life therapy. She understood it all. She was clever, gifted, even beautiful.' He turned towards the hall. 'She reminded me of you.'

People smiled, and Ivan Geertsen continued: 'But I hope that you won't continue to be like her.'

After an artistic pause where he focused on the audience, he looked to the imaginary woman again. 'This woman came to me many times. It was an intense course. We got to know each other for better or worse. Let's say she was from one of the suburbs around Århus. Like many of you. Children, families, she was on top of things. But why did she come to me? She didn't feel she was alive. She didn't *feel* it. I told her that she wasn't. She wasn't living. There was no life. Her husband, her children, her life had stolen it from her. Isn't that a paradox. Her *life* had stolen her *life*?'

The audience nodded, spellbound.

'I became obsessed with helping her. And why? Well, because

she was like my mother. She was equally indistinct, floating away with the world. I desperately wanted to help her. It was just like that thing which my mother never discovered, but fortunately I discovered for her: a second chance.' Ivan Geertsen spoke with pathos, his eyes shining.

'I gave her exercises – they were about sensing and feeling. She completed them, dutifully. She never felt herself. The exercises were simple to begin with. She had to smash a plate on purpose and feel both the pain and joy of chaos. She had to yell at someone. She had to kiss a stranger on the street, perhaps to feel the joy and freedom, or perhaps to feel disgust, to feel something at least. None of it worked. Her feelings were so deeply buried. Can you imagine that? Do you know the feeling? Could you kiss a stranger?'

The audience wondered.

'I paired her with another woman. The idea was that they would use each other. Fall in love, kissing, touching. I know this sounds forward. But what is it that holds us back? The truth is that it took tougher methods. And what happened? After hours of intense work, all my effort in trying to help her. She dared nothing. Can you imagine that? She refused. She wouldn't. And she did it in front of the other woman. Right there, she spoke against me.'

The audience sat with open mouths. There was absolute silence. Isabella thought that for an audience as uptight and cultured as this one, it was heavy stuff, crossing a few boundaries.

'She wouldn't,' he repeated. 'That's the word for it. Would not. She had no will. She never came to life. She *was* dead. And she *remained* dead.'

Dramatic pause. That must have been the five hundredth, thought Isabella. Talk about exaggerated rhetoric.

'I could have been disappointed. But disappointment is for the weak. Those without their own lives. I had to look at myself, manage the shame and defy the humiliation. She remained dead because I couldn't do more. Her whole world had become like her. The children had moved far away, driven away, for she couldn't handle them just as she couldn't handle life. Her husband had drifted away, at least mentally. No will, no power, no life. In order not to harm each other, we stop making something of each other. So she and her unworldly vicar of a husband did nothing to each other. It sounds awful and it is, too. I'm not saying this to scare you, but to awaken you. There is hope for you yet.'

Isabella didn't hear the rest.

Something dawned on her. She began to hear the whole lecture again in her head. Everything changed, the meaning changed. She sat for a long time in her own thoughts. Saw the man on stage moving around with his well-coordinated movements, but there was no sound. And there was no longer any charm in his movements. She got herself together, raised her hand.

Ivan Geertsen pointed at her while he jokingly said to the others that there was obviously someone who hadn't understood what he said. Isabella asked:

'The woman you're talking about – what happened to her when you left her?'

The next pause was not a well-coordinated artistic break. When Ivan Geertsen spoke again, he answered slowly, almost fiercely, eyes locked on Isabella with a force she would remember long afterwards.

'Remember, that was an example. An example not to follow. In her case, she lived neither before nor after. I hope you don't follow.' He continued to hold her gaze for several long seconds. Then he turned to the others, smiled and continued: 'For all of us, it's about life. How are we to live?'

Isabella stood up, fumbling, bumped into the table. People stared at her. She walked out of the hall. Out in the closet, she took out the phone she had trustingly left in her coat pocket. She phoned Thorkild, asked for and got a number from him, which she then dialled.

'Thea Krogh,' said the voice at the other end.

'It's Isabella Munk. I was friends with Karen Simonsen, I got your number from her husband, Thorkild. I understand that you're working on the case?'

'That's correct. How can I help you?'

'I've previously spoken with someone named Edvardsen. I don't know . . . I think I have to move fast here. Perhaps this is a little crazy. But I'm standing in a library in Vilå. I'm at a lecture with this man Ivan Geertsen, and I think he knew Karen.'

The voice on the phone was quiet and attentive.

'What are you thinking?'

'I knew that Karen had been to a lecture with someone who called himself a life coach. And this guy stood here just now and talked about a woman he had known in therapy. A therapy that failed. And he said some very unpleasant things about her. He refers to her as dead, both before and after therapy. I know it sounds crazy. But there is something about him. He is both very seductive in his rhetoric. And very very scary.'

'Did he use Karen's name? What made you think he was talking about her?'

Isabella thought.

'No. He didn't. He mentioned a suburban lady who was married to a vicar. Nothing more specific than that. I just think . . . I have a feeling. Is that too weird for the police . . . intuition?'

'No,' said Thea Krogh. 'It's not too weird. I'm coming to Vilå now. I can be there in twenty minutes.'

Isabella went back to the hall. The crowd was breaking up. The women had risen, they were standing at the tables and chatting while they put on their coats.

'Has he already finished?' she asked her table mates.

'Yes,' said a stout woman with small jingling curls, who struggled with a damp anorak. 'He had no time for more questions. It was a shame, really, I thought he was quite good. A little over the top, maybe.'

'Damn right,' muttered Isabella.

She made her way through the bulky overcoats up to the stage, where the librarian was hastily tipping Karen Wolff biscuits on to a plate. Having promised the audience that refreshments were included in the entrance fee, she was belatedly making an effort to serve them. 'You're welcome to stay,' she called half-heartedly after the departing ladies. 'The coffee's brewing. It'll be maybe ten minutes. Yes?' She turned to Isabella with flushed red cheeks.

'The lecturer – Geertsen, where'd he go?'

'He's just gone out to get a cup of coffee. He'll be back in a moment, I haven't paid him yet – he insists on cash.' The librarian shook her head wearily. 'It meant I had to run down to Nordea at the last minute, so I didn't have time to get everything sorted properly. Cash – in this day and age. But a man like that sure knows what he wants, doesn't he? Did you enjoy the lecture?'

Isabella shook her head. 'He didn't leave a card or anything?'

'Actually, no. But ask him yourself.' She pointed: 'Our kitchen is out there. Would you be a doll and bring back the cream for the coffee, it's on the table.'

Out the back, the kitchen was empty. Isabella saw an open door. It was a rear entrance leading to the car park.

When she went to look, she caught sight of the rear of a car quietly driving away, gravel licking the tyres.

46

Towards Roslinge once again.

In the car, Thea tried dutifully to create a comfortable atmosphere for the boss's nephew, Janus Schalborg, who had insisted on driving. She felt sorry for the lad: thrusting him into an investigation he was obviously not qualified or prepared for might be Anne-Grethe's idea of boosting his career, but it wasn't going to make it easy for him to find his feet within the department. All the same, she was reluctantly impressed by the fact Anne-Grethe made no attempt to disguise her nepotism.

So Thea asked about his family, if he had a girlfriend, why he wanted to join the police. She'd undergone years of training in the art of questioning suspects and coaxing timid witnesses to open up. The skills she'd mastered had often proved useful in her private life. At family celebrations, she would always end up talking with the new boyfriends or spouses who seemed to find the rest of her family a bit too daunting. It was a role she'd grown tired of. It would have been different if she'd been dealing with her own children's boyfriends – she'd have done her best to be the perfect mother-in-law. But here she was with no children, stuck with the task of putting her nieces' leftover partners at ease.

Janus reminded her of one of those awkward overgrown teenagers. Handsome in a slightly bland way with blond hair hanging down over his forehead. And that abundance of energy, so typical in the young, like they're always in such a hurry to justify themselves.

'I chose to become a policeman because I wanted a job

that's physical but useful and intellectual at the same time. I'm a real all-rounder. Fastest in class on the hundred-metre track, and top on my written assignments. Plus, it's a good cause, the police, right? A job with meaning.'

Janus's legs couldn't seem to stop twitching. Almost like nervous tics that made his long-limbed body seem wobbly and almost dangerous to be close to. The car gave a dissatisfied hop as he made the clutch jump.

'How is it a good cause?'

'To catch criminals and cage them up so they don't make any more trouble.' Janus had kicked twice into the panel in the time it took him to complete that one sentence. He smiled disarmingly at her. 'It may well sound easy, when you say it that way. But basically that is what it's all about, right?'

'I'm not sure. You really believe that?'

'It may sound strange, but Aunt Anne-Grethe says that when all the layers are peeled away, it's really that simple. They need to get off the streets, she says. That way, you protect the law-abiding citizens. It's no use having laws if no one follows them. My aunt has talked like that ever since I was a boy. That's why I wanted to join the police, even though my mum didn't think it was a good idea. But there aren't many jobs out there where you can say that you work for the good guys. That's what I like about the police. We're the good guys.'

Thea looked straight ahead. Janus continued.

'All the stuff about preventive action, it sounds fine. But someone has to do the hard work, right?' He was eager. 'Someone has to be prepared to take down those who fall through the net and live in the wrong way, do the wrong things. It's honest work. Like a kind of garbage disposal man.'

'And if you see a car on the road here with someone who hasn't fastened his seat belt, what do you do, Janus?'

'Take the number and call our colleagues in Traffic.'

'Are we to decide what everyone else has to do? Be their guardians?'

'Yes. It's not everyone who is able to take care of themselves. It's an unpopular viewpoint, I know, but there it is. Otherwise, there wouldn't be so many problems in society. It's up to the police to educate people.'

'What do you think it does to society if you are watching people's every move?'

'Hopefully, they will eventually learn.' He studied her questioningly. 'Surely you must be thinking along the same lines? Why else have you chosen the police?'

Thea sighed. It would be strange to have this young man as a protégé, Anne-Grethe's self-proclaimed garbage man. The image amused her. As did the thought of *Aunt Anne-Grethe*.

'OK, Janus. Let me tell you about Asger Jørgensen, the man we're heading out to see.'

'You don't have to, I've obviously read Bjørn Devantier's report. The man can't spell to save his life.'

'It could well be that there was more to tell.'

'Anne-Grethe has told me what I need to know.' He looked at her in astonishment.

They were silent the rest of the way. Thea noticed that the light was out in the Roslinge vicarage.

When they arrived at the bungalow, Thea led the way up the garden path to the front door and rang the bell. Smiled at the man who opened the door.

'Asger, hello, my name is Thea Krogh. You have previously spoken with my colleague, Bjørn Devantier, but since you contacted us again we agreed that I would do this interview with you. It was something about a book?'

Asger nodded. 'Thanks for coming. I don't know if it's worth your time. That's for you to decide. Come in.'

Janus stuck out his hand: 'I'm Detective Janus Schalborg. I'm with Thea Krogh.'

Asger shook his hand and showed them inside. Found a book in the overloaded bookcase in the living room. *Behind the Mask*, said the title. The cover featured an illustration of an ornate carnival half-mask that was sliding away from a pair of staring eyes.

'You already know that Karen and I met and talked about books now and then. Last time we met, she gave me this book. It's a crime story – the English title is *The Pellicle*, which apparently means some kind of cell membrane. The Danish translation is not terribly impressive, I'm afraid. Karen didn't read crime novels, but had gotten it from a friend.'

'Who was this friend?' said Janus.

'I don't know. But since I like a good crime novel, she gave it to me. I didn't read it right away, but then last week I went up to visit the vicar, Thorkild, to talk to him. He said that he wanted to know more about what his wife was reading, and I told him what little I knew about her. And then I went back and started the novel. It's perhaps a bit far-fetched. But halfway through the book I found an underlined paragraph. Shall I read aloud?'

'Please do,' said Thea.

'We need to take the book in for technical evidence,' said Janus.

'Yes, by all means do that. The connection is that it's about a wealthy Englishwoman with a diagnosis that manifests itself in obsessions and delusions. She goes, on her family's insistence, to see a highly recommended therapist, whom she falls in love with. Apparently it's not unusual for such a fascination to develop between patient and therapist. But this is group therapy, and there is another woman in the group, who is an undercover journalist trying to expose the man's alternative method. In what I'm about to read, it's the patient's thoughts we're following:

They're right. For the first time, I think they're right.

I really am crazy.

Is this reality? Or all inside my head? Can you see a membrane covering me, a coat of thin, milky water?

I think about him constantly. Do not sleep. Feel his hands on my naked body, as real as it can be. At all times. Can lay in bed or sit on the underground, lots of people around me and suddenly I can feel his hands.

Inside of me. It shudders throughout my body and I quiver, so I think everyone around me must be able to feel it.

I look for him constantly. Can feel his breath as real as if he's standing behind me, in front of me, beside me. Waking up at night and have him everywhere on me. Like a membrane.

You can do everything with sex, he says. It's in the sessions.

He talks about how important it is for me to take control over things. All things. He says that it's like sex. That's where I can practise it. Take control, decide. When he talks about it, it's as if he pushes himself into me, through the membrane, and it hurts.

He thrusts into me with his words. Hits me all the way inside. I sit there and smile while he speaks.

And I imagine how he takes me. Firmly and determined. That there's no one else he wants. He says that sex is a mirror of life. I can control, I can hold on, I can decide everything, pace, intensity, everything. I can take power. He says I should do it. That it would be a good exercise for me.

He says anything is possible in sex. You give life with sex and you kill with sex. It's metaphors. But a metaphor for what? I cannot take him. We're not alone. I look through my milky white membrane, look at him. And at her. The membrane makes her face white and luminous.

I can tell how she wants him. It's so obvious, it's embarrassing. I hide my face because I don't want to look at him in the mirror of her eyes.

When he talks about control, he speaks directly to me, but it's like it's about something else. I think he's asking me to get rid of her. I think he says that she stands in our way, and that I must take control so we can happen. I think he says I can only get him if I remove her.

He says it will be good for me to take control. The ultimate control. And that's justified, I know. For he and I, there is a meaning to us. It's like hiding a deep secret there, to be redeemed. And for deep truths to be redeemed, there must be sacrifices. He knows what he's talking about. If that's what he wants from me, it's the truth. How can I not do what he asks me? So that's what I must do. He demands it of me. I have to be adult and mature. That I can act when it comes down to it.

I've found the weapon. For his sake. For my own sake. Because it is good for me, because he demands it, because it is meant to be. I take my membrane off, let it slide down my face, so she can see who I am.

She will meet death in the water.

Asger stopped reading. Janus looked at Thea, hesitant. There was silence for a while. It was Asger, who broke it:

'Now I've had time to think about it, and I don't like it at all. It's a spicy read. And I think you should find this friend who has given her the book. This is what it's about. Maybe. Do you follow?'

Thea nodded thoughtfully. 'Karen met her death in the water. In a way. Roslinge River.'

And we know that she saw a therapist, she thought to herself, and pictured in her mind's eye Isabella Munk who had stood there, freezing and determined outside the Vilå Library and told her about a captivating speaker, whose name was Ivan Geertsen, and who had been talking about power. A speaker, no one knew who he was. Who was to be paid in cash. And there were no pictures.

'It's a tremendously unpleasant thought,' said Asger. 'But is it possible that someone has played a sick game where he wanted Karen to know what lay in store for her? To read this book and realise the connection when she met her killer by Roslinge River?'

He thumped the book down on the table in front of Janus. Janus stood up. 'What were you doing that Saturday morning?'

Thea broke in:

'Janus, that's not the way! Asger, thank you for contacting us. You did the right thing. This could be very important. Have you no idea about who this friend might be?'

Asger looked confused, eyes darting between the two people in front of him. Then he replied to Thea's question:

'No, I've tried really hard to recall whether Karen ever said anything about a friend. But she was so taciturn about her life, so I don't think so. But what really made me think the book might be important is –' Asger took the book out of Janus' hands '– there is a dedication here in the front. See, it says:

To Karen – there are many ways of doing it.'

Thea nodded to herself, thoughtful. The book seemed to describe some bizarre form of therapy. Could Karen's therapist have given her the book? Like some form of vision or as a cruel joke?

There was a smiley, painted with black magic marker after the dedication, a big, cheeky smile.

47

While Frank and Birgitte were still asleep, Thorkild dug out the crumpled card and phoned Alice Caspersen on her mobile. She answered after only two rings, even though it was seven a.m., as if she always had it close to her. The voice sounded cheerful, but was immediately a little reluctant when Thorkild introduced himself. He had opened the computer, and was looking at the email from M and the picture she had taken of Sanne's phone on the day of the murder. He wondered what and how much he should tell Alice Caspersen. He hadn't quite thought his strategy through, and it was obvious now that he had no reasonable answer to her question about what she could do for him.

'If you have a digital image,' said Thorkild slowly, 'what options do you have to see where it was taken?'

'Why do you ask, Thorkild? If it is of interest to the investigation, I would very much like the picture. You know that, I'm sure.'

'To the investigation,' he did his best to sound disoriented. 'Right, I don't think it is. Otherwise you would have it, obviously.'

She was silent, clearly not impressed by his explanation. Thorkild improvised as best he could. 'I'm looking at some pictures of Karen that my daughter sent me. There's nothing exciting about them. I'm just having doubts about where they were taken. And I thought if I could think of it, it would perhaps be helpful to . . . I don't know. Your picture of her. So I don't know whether it would be useful yet. Was hoping you could help me figure it out.'

'Email me the picture, OK, I'll find out.'

'You can't just answer me? I would like to continue with it, now I'm getting started.'

'I'm not near a computer screen.'

'So you can't help me?'

'You know what, just send me the picture, I'll look at it as soon as I can. I'd like you to do that.'

'OK. I will. But can't you tell me a little about what the potential is? It's a digital image. I was wondering if it's possible to find out where it was taken.'

She thought.

'But it probably can't be done,' he coaxed, and it had the desired effect. Alice's professional pride took over.

'Everything can be done,' she said, firmly. 'But it's a tough question. There are many possibilities, but it requires certain things in the image. Are there any buildings or any other characteristics one can find? Signs are also good. We always look for whether there is a clock somewhere in the picture. With digital images these days, you can magnify even something as small as a wristwatch in the background and make out the time. The time may help us to analyse the light. We can analyse the colour spectrum in the image – compare the date with the weather and time of day and assess whether the colours are warm or cold, whether there is water nearby which reflects, things like that. But if it's flash-images, we're screwed. A few pictures have a geotag, and then you're good.'

'What is a geotag?'

'A GPS coordinate attached to the image, in the same way the date is attached. With smartphones and advanced digital cameras, it's more and more common that images have a kind of digital profile that can tell you where it was taken. But some people disconnect that kind of feature. How old is your picture?'

'It's at least six years old,' Thorkild lied. 'That much I can see from Karen's hairdo. It must have been taken with Michael's first digital camera. It was the size of a shoebox and used common triple-A batteries. I don't think it's realistic to find a digital profile. But it's very advanced what people can do these days.'

'There's nothing you can't do,' snorted Alice. 'The people who buy smartphones better not commit crimes. Modern GPS systems mean that you can virtually follow people's doings step by step. But it's also a mentality. People document everything. Facebook has become a digital testament, a testament to people's lives in an adequately edited form. I don't understand the desire to indulge in that sort of thing. Do you?'

'No,' said Thorkild, a statement entirely consistent with the truth.

'There have been cases in the States and in England where idiots forget that their digital rhetoric is open for public view. A gang member brags about a murder on Facebook. A woman who receives single mum benefits posts her wedding picture online. And bang, say hello to the police and the authorities. And they don't understand how it happened. The same with those geotags. You only geotag a photo if it's OK for the world to know where you've been.'

'What kind of people geotag their photos?' said Thorkild. Alice Caspersen chuckled a bit.

'A few years ago I would have said technical fetishists who had expensive phones through work or some other expensive device that had both GPS and a camera built in the same unit. But now these devices have become commonplace. Even my eleven-year-old niece is running around with an iPhone that is more advanced than the equipment I've spent most of my career using. But you think we need go to back a few years with your picture?'

Thorkild confirmed, uncomfortable with lying to Alice. But she didn't sound as if she had any objection to educating him a little.

'Six years ago it would have been the technical nerds. Today it's everybody. Not that it's my specialty,' Alice said, modestly. 'If you don't have the equipment to do it automatically, anyone can do it manually with free online photo programs like Picasa, which links to Google Earth. If you travel a lot, for example, it's a fun way to visualise where you've been. It's a big job with photos,' she continued, 'it's not my specialty. I'm more into crime scenes. But there are many who make it a specialty today. I know that a lot of research goes into seeing if we can restore the proportions of people's faces. If the picture is taken up close, for example, and with improper use of the lens, then the picture is difficult to use, for example in a newspaper when you need the help of the public. But you can take it into account when analysing the image. Fascinating, no?'

'Definitely. Thanks for the help. I'll look into it.'

'And Thorkild . . .' Alice Caspersen held a long pause. It dawned on Thorkild that it was supposed to be significant.

'I'll let you know if I find something interesting. Of course.'

'Even the uninteresting. Send me the picture, OK?'

'I will,' said Thorkild and knew that he wouldn't. Instead, he called Emil at TDC and welcomed the fact that his old school friend answered his mobile, without asking what on earth he was doing at quarter past seven in the morning, or worse, ask about Karen and the investigation.

Emil was one of the people who had stayed in the background, aware that they had neither more in common or greater need for each other now that Karen was dead. Other old friends he hadn't seen for years had snuck up in the form of well-intentioned letters, emails or telephone calls. And although Thorkild had sincerely appreciated the effort, it had not had the desired impact: that he wouldn't feel alone. Most of these inquiries had given him the opposite feeling. A loneliness that was evident in the distance between him and the old acquaintances, a common discomfort over the circumstances that made the contact necessary.

'Right, hello, Thorkild,' said Emil, almost businesslike. 'A geotag. Is it a physical image you have there? Then you'll need a standard scanner, they can usually decipher geotags.'

'No. I have it digitally.'

'On the camera itself? If you open the image on a digital camera, you are looking for image metadata. It's called EXIF. Alternatively, XMP.'

'It's an attachment to an email. I don't think I can find metadata. But dammit, Emil, I wouldn't know what it was if it was right before my eyes.'

'No worries, Thorkild. You need a program. I'll send you the link. It's open source, completely legal. Here you go.'

Thorkild nervously opened the email from Emil. 'How do I know if it . . . fits my computer? It's really old.'

Emil laughed. 'Don't worry, Thorkild, it's a cross platform. It'll work. Now simply press "run", and then you're golden.'

The small decipher program popped up on Thorkild's screen, and with a beating heart he opened the picture of Sanne's phone using the software.

'I don't understand. Has it worked? I get a lot of numbers. It could be anything.'

'What are the numbers?'

Thorkild read from the screen's blue flashes.

'56.1903,10.2351.'

He could hear Emil slap his desk at the other end of the line, thrilled.

'Congratulations, old man. That's a geotag, no question.'

'I don't understand. It's coordinates?'

'Exactly. Converted to decimal places. It's easy to figure out. No, you know what, I'll send you a converter.'

Another email from Emil ticked in, Thorkild was impressed with the rapidity of the way Emil fished information out of his searches. 'Do you have it? Fine. Then you simply enter the decimals. And voila.'

Sure enough, the entries resulted in a neat little series of numbers, which immediately made more sense to Thorkild.

N 56° 11' 41'' E 10° 14' 06''

'Coordinates. This is unbelievable.'

'And do you know what to do with the coordinates, Thorkild,' said Emil's happy voice. 'I have a meeting here, at quarter to eight. You're on your own.'

'Yes, I think so. Thank you, Emil. There is a kind of map program, isn't there?'

'Google Earth. Enjoy.' Emil hung up, and Thorkild was tired at the thought of again having to download and install. But when it was done, the rest was incredibly easily. An address, even a grainy image that appeared on the screen.

Stalakitvej 15, 1.tv. Located in the southern part of Risskov.

A search on the address laconically stated the name Matthiesen.

This was where the picture of the phone was taken. He looked at the date. The day after Sanne's murder, if he wasn't mistaken.

He sat for a while, puzzled.

Upstairs there was a trickle of water in the pipes, Birgitte was in the bathroom. And the couch in the living room was starting to creak under the weight of Frank, who was about to wake up. And here he sat with an address, a possible address of Frank's sister's murderer.

Thorkild put on his windcheater and walked out into the garden. As always, when he needed to think, he went out on the grass, looked at the trees, the garden, down at the river. Like the Sunday morning when he saw Karen's dead arm sticking out of the water without being aware that that was what he saw. He looked at autumn. He looked at the trees, the leaves lying in heaps on the thick grass, the rose petals that had withered and sat on the stalks up against the house wall, the shine of the blue sky, reflected off the river. He tried to picture Karen's calm face, but she didn't come. Instead, he saw Thea Krogh's reproachful eyes, Thea whom he hadn't seen since the day he had almost driven her out of his house. And who probably didn't see it as her first priority right now to keep him updated on anything.

When he came back, Birgitte and Frank were up. Birgitte was rummaging in the kitchen, baking buns, brewing coffee and setting out portions of vegetables and cheese and finely chopped yellow peppers on small plates while she kept Frank busy setting the table. The steam from the hot oven was like a thick fog in the kitchen.

'You're outside? It looks cold. There's frost? Come and sit down. Careful, the buns are hot,' said Birgitte, and he smiled at her, for once grateful for her chattiness.

He sat down and buttered a bun, saw it melt into the bread and wanted to ask her to stay in his house forever and take care of him. He ate while he hid his head in a web of thoughts, Frank was barely awake and Birgitte was twittering.

'If it's freezing, I'll be in the garden today. We need to bring in the flower pots so they won't break. And pick up the last apples, we can make juice from them, you can rent an apple press at the co-op. Maybe Frank will help me take up the Georgia onions. And Thorkild, I thought we could drive into the woods for some spruce?'

'You're going to make Christmas decorations,' said Frank, annoyed.

'I'm going to cover up the spice garden. There's laurel and sage and two French tarragons and the most beautiful rosemary bush I've ever seen outside of Tuscany. Are you aware,' she said, turning to Thorkild '– how much work has gone into that spice garden?'

Birgitte ate quickly and left the kitchen at a brisk trot. Thorkild and Frank lingered over coffee, while they listened to her put on her coat and wellies and disappear out the door. Then they followed her progress from the kitchen window, marching towards the spice garden with a wheelbarrow filled with clattering garden tools, a rake, a pair of secateurs. Thorkild buried his head in his hands and prayed that she would soon be out of sight and that Frank would just keep quiet. He didn't.

'I think it's strange how that woman reigns around here. One minute she pulls you upstairs, giggling and playful, the next she's marching around the garden, honouring your wife's memory. I don't understand—'

'I have the address, Frank,' interrupted Thorkild. 'I have the address of Sanne's murderer.'

That made Frank shut up. But only briefly.

'What do you mean, you have an address?'

'I looked at the picture. It had GPS coordinates, it's in Risskov.'

'Holy shit, Thorkild. An address!'

Thorkild enjoyed the surprised expression in Frank's face. The old vicar was good for something.

'And before you get started, Frank, I think we should call Thea Krogh. We need to tell her about the email.'

'Yes, we do, but—'

'But?'

'It's too weird, Thorkild. So I say we just jump in the car and take a look at the place. I know you really want to call Thea, but I don't want to hang around. We're—'

Thorkild held up a deprecating hand.

'Frank, we said a few days, and then we would call. You've had a few days.'

'It was yesterday, Thorkild. It was only yesterday. I'll have a look before the police come and fuck it up. I'm going, regardless of what you say. We can make the call afterwards, I promise. Right after.'

'If you're going no matter what I say, why are you even telling me?'

'Because I don't want you to call the police before I've had a look. And because you're coming, too. I promise you that we're not going in, OK? We'll just drive by.'

'And why am I going?'

Frank took a while to answer. 'Because I thought we could take your car. Or Birgitte's little Polo. If M was actually lurking around my house, she probably knows my car, right? It's not exactly discreet.'

They said nothing to Birgitte.

Frank instructed Thorkild to put on shoes with rubber soles, and something that covered most of his face and hair. Clad in black hats, a black jacket with an upright collar for Thorkild and a black hooded sweatshirt for Frank, and dark blue jeans and sneakers, they resembled a couple of bank robbers on their way to commit a crime. Thorkild caught a glimpse of himself in the big full-length mirror in the hall and didn't recognise what he saw. But he was excited, elated. In fact, he discovered, he was in high spirits as they sat behind the wheel of his old car and rattled off towards the fashionable quarter of Risskov.

48

'Where the hell is Kristian?' Thea was irritated. 'I asked everyone to be here, and then he's missing.'

Yet another team meeting at police headquarters. It was 8.30 am. Thea was wondering if Kristian was angry with her and obstructing her meeting, although it wouldn't be like him.

'Why don't you just begin, Thea. We're all busy,' said Jørgen Schmidt.

'And you and Kristian will probably keep each other informed anyway,' commented Søren quietly. Thea sent him a sharp look.

'We need to focus our attention on Karen Simonsen again,' she insisted.

'I thought the focus was Sanne Andersen and you were just about to travel up North,' said Bjørn. 'So this is a tad confusing.'

'Maybe you were just hoping that the solution would lie outside your district,' mumbled Søren.

'That's enough, dammit. Listen – there've been some new developments,' said Thea. She told them about the lecture Isabella had attended and how she had summoned Thea in vain, and about Asger, who had called in with information about the book that Karen had received from an unnamed friend.

'Janus went with me out to Asger's.' And in light of Anne-Grethe's admonition: 'He did a good job.'

'What about the book's author. Could he be the one? Has he written a recipe for murder and published it?' It was Søren who asked.

'He's English. What's more, he's dead.'

Thea had the book in her hand. Every now and then her teenage nephews, both avid fans of American movies and TV series, would persuade her to join them in watching one. Invariably the plot seemed to involve a murderer engaged in some game of hide and seek with the police, leaving taunting messages at the scenes of his crimes or a trail of intricate clues they were intended to follow. The film-makers obviously found the concept irresistible, but it amused Thea no end – such arrogance, such hubris in a killer was almost unheard of. The few real-life cases where a murderer had displayed such self-confidence had occurred in America, and even there they represented an anomaly in an otherwise bullet-proof pattern. The vast majority of criminals were intent on erasing all traces of their crime, making themselves invisible, preventing the police tracking them down.

But here she stood with the book in her hand, looking at the dedication, the smiley and the underlined section.

Then, Janus spoke:

'Personally, I think it's too obvious. I'm sure this Asger knows more than he told us. It's a well-known fact –' he looked around him '– that criminals of this calibre often return to the scene.'

'How do you suppose Asger Jørgensen, in contacting us, has returned to the scene?' said Thea, her irritation fast turning into full-blooded anger.

'Not in a literal but a figurative sense,' said Janus, as if addressing a particularly dull student. 'He needs to stay close to the investigation. Perhaps he believes it's going too slow and he's trying to put us back on track, playing with us. I once saw this movie—'

Thea sighed loudly and cut him off:

'Maybe you can tell us about that movie during your lunch break, Janus. For now, let's concentrate on arriving at a profile of the suspect. I believe we need to focus on the image that is slowly evolving of this person who gave a lecture at the gym in Roslinge under the name Bo Zellweger, and at the library in Vilå under the name Ivan Geertsen. It was possibly in connection with the lecture in Roslinge that Karen made contact with him. Could he also be the mysterious therapist that Karen was seeing? According to Isabella, last night's lecture was a discourse on power that concluded with some unpleasant insinuations about a woman who was married to a vicar and who had disappointed him. The set-up was the same in Vilå as it was in Roslinge: he had approached the organisers offering his services, there was no contract, no signature, no social security number, no bank details – he insisted on being paid in cash.'

'And they accepted that?' said Søren.

'Apparently so,' said Thea calmly. 'According to the librarian, there's a demand for these sorts of events – the local community want the library to function as a place they can gather, where the public can be informed and educated not just by books but by experts showing up to talk about their specialist subject. Trouble is, decent speakers charge several thousand kroner, and the libraries are starved of resources. So they leapt at the chance when Ivan Geertsen contacted them saying he wanted to do the library a favour, because he was originally from Vilå. He told them his fee would be 800 kroner, cash in hand, for a lecture that would otherwise cost 15,000. He referred the librarian to a website that was crammed with references to articles published in reputable journals, book jackets and rave reviews of his lectures. The website no longer exists – it was obviously a fake. But it served its purpose: the librarian naturally thought she had a bit of a scoop on her hands.

'Both Isabella Munk and the librarian have provided us with physical description,' said Thea. 'Unfortunately, it's average at best. Though it is consistent with descriptions of the Roslinge lecturer. He is remembered as a tall and very attractive man. Isabella Munk is sure that he was wearing pancake makeup, the heavy foundation stage performers use.

And it seems our guy has a predilection for items that draw the eye, distracting attention from everything else – for example, in Roslinge he wore a distinctive brooch. And in Vilå, the guy wore a beret.'

'There are no pictures of this illusionary lecturer?' asked Bjørn.

'We're contacting as many of the attendees as we can track down. So far we have two women who took pictures with a mobile phone. Unfortunately you can't see anything on them.'

'A vampire, obviously!' Bjørn laughed.

'No. Just a very clever use of light sources. According to the lecture organisers, Bo Zellweger and Ivan Geertsen insisted on setting up their own lights. Both times the speaker was surrounded by a square of dazzling fluorescent lights; combined with the auto flash photography on the mobile phone cameras, it effectively sabotaged the images. It's that simple.'

'Sounds far-fetched to me.' Bjørn shook his head.

'It is,' smiled Thea. 'Nevertheless, it worked on the two pictures that were taken. According to the organisers, he also declined to have his photo taken beforehand, and asked that they go up on stage at the start of the lecture and warn people not to take pictures. In Roslinge, he told the audience this was because flash photography would distract him, interfering with his concentration, and that the atmosphere he was hoping to create would be ruined if people were constantly fidgeting with their cameras. He assured them he'd be available for photographs afterwards, but instead he disappeared before they had a chance. It's no coincidence.'

'I still don't understand your reprioritisation,' said Jørgen. 'We know Karen's killer.'

'Yes, but not Sanne's. Sanne *must* have known this individual. She must have. This is the connection we've been looking for, to explain why Karen was killed, to help us close this case. It's the only thing we have to go on.'

Alice looked out over her horn-rimmed glasses.

'In Vindbygårde we've analysed the angles at which the

shots penetrated the kitchen doors. The shots were fired by a person of average height, 180 to 185 centimetres. We can be certain of that because there are traces of gunpowder on Sanne Andersen indicating that the shooter was standing right next to her. Thus, we have the distance to the kitchen doors, and the rest is trigonometry.'

Thea continued: 'We know Karen Simonsen had recently had contact with someone involved in therapy, life coaching, self-development, or whatever you want to call it. The same topic that Ivan Geertsen and Bo Zellweger lectured about. It's also the theme that we encounter in Asger's book. And there's another possible connection too. There was a murder case in Aabenraa in 1999 that also featured a mysterious unnamed therapist. A woman shot another woman and then allegedly committed suicide. Officially, the case was closed. But some of those involved in the investigation have expressed doubts. Perhaps, in time, we will see a coherent pattern emerge, one that goes back even further. There's no record of Karen having paid for whatever therapy she received. Perhaps the payment consisted of something other than money. These "therapy sessions" may have taken place every Tuesday evening. Perhaps this was where she encountered Sanne, who also seems to have gone out on Tuesday nights. We have that information from her brother Frank, but he's not sure that it was every Tuesday. Perhaps it was just the one. It's all guesswork at this stage. As to that whole stigmata-angle to Sanne's murder – I'm not sure what to make of that.'

'If this therapist was able to drive Sanne to commit murder, the way it's done in the book,' Bjørn said pensively, 'we're looking for someone with extraordinary power over others. He'd have to be a charismatic figure of immense power and persuasiveness. And she must have been very much in love, almost obsessed with him.'

'So this is our theory now,' concluded Thea. 'We must find out where they met this man. Perhaps together, maybe separately, maybe Tuesday evenings. It must be possible.' She gestured to end the meeting.

At that moment, Kristian stuck his head in the door:

'I have the address. I have the fucking address!'

49

'I know where both Karen and Sanne went!'

Kristian stood breathless in the doorway, waving a piece of paper. His face was tense, his cheeks red and his eyes had a spark Thea could not recall having seen in a long time.

'Do you remember that I asked about Sanne's GPS? I was working on the assumption that they could have gone to the same place. A place that was neither in Roslinge or Vindbygårde. So I looked at it again.'

Alice frowned. 'I thought that GPS was down in the lab.'

'It was, and they bloody well wouldn't part with it, so I had to stay down in their smelly lab – sorry, Alice – while I cross-checked. It's possible that Karen went on the bus route 123 from Roslinge to Århus on Friday night, the night before she was murdered. We know she was seen at the bus stop, at least. I assumed that it was the bus that she took at other times. But where did she go? She could have changed bus, but we have the bus pass from her purse, it was stamped on three Tuesdays this past spring. It was a multi-ride ticket, valid for only five zones. The bus station in Århus is six zones away, so she's certainly not gone there and changed. Of course she could have changed after five zones, but I had to start somewhere. So I took all the possible street names within walking distance of the relevant bus stops in the fifth zone from Roslinge.'

Bjørn exhaled, impressed. 'That must have been a hell of a lot of work.'

Kristian nodded. 'There were loads of them. Anyway, I typed the street names into Sanne's GPS, which suggests previously entered addresses as presets when you start with letters it has seen before. At one point it suggested Rødkildevej – a road in the northern part of Risskov. It suggested Rødkildevej 8.'

There was an excited buzz around the table. Finally.

'Who lives there?' said Thea, trying to keep the adrenalin from taking possession of her voice.

'Someone's renting it, naturally. The landlord claims to know nothing more than the name on the contract. Has never seen or spoken to the tenant, who's always paid on time. No problems.'

'And the name?'

'Carlo Collodi. False name, like all the other data he's listed on the lease. It's incredible how easily it can be done. But I know the landlord. Quite well, actually. It's Little Per.'

The Århus officers nodded, the two country policemen looked confused.

'Little Per, a.k.a Per Thorning, owns a lot of properties around Århus and he's not fussy about who he rents them to. It's all done on a 'don't ask, don't tell' basis. Itinerants, gypsies, illegal immigrants, people who've been smuggled in so they can work illegally in restaurants and hotels. Little Per crams them in – six men in a one-bedroom apartment. Among other things, he owns two of the five known biker properties around these parts, and he's completely indifferent to protests from the neighbours and letters to the editor and enquiries from the Enterprise and Construction authorities. He buys, and he rents. It's well known here in town that if you need a place to live and don't want anyone to know about it, Little Per's your guy. Whether your business is human trafficking or you just need a place to live within a one-kilometre radius of your ex-wife to have visiting rights with your children, the rule's the same. You pay a deposit and three months' rent in advance, and then you multiply that amount by three, stick the cash in an envelope and hand it to Per. Then you get the key.'

Jørgen looked sceptical.

'Multiplied by three? That's a lot of money for an apartment.'

Kristian glared at him. 'You're not just paying for an apartment, you're paying for secrecy. If you're involved in trafficking, the hundreds of thousands you have to fork out will soon be recouped. You can run four or five women out of that kind of place.'

Thea shook off the thought.

'OK. Do we have anything on Carlo Collodi? Anything?'

Kristian smiled at her, it made her feel warm, she was happy to see him like this.

'Nothing, but that's pretty much what I'd expected. Except for the symbolism, maybe. Carlo Collodi was the Italian author who wrote Pinocchio. The puppet who escaped from his strings. A story of becoming a real person. Achieving freedom.'

'I think we're beginning to see a pattern. But Pinocchio couldn't lie without it being obvious. So let's see how he does now that we have an address for him,' said Søren, satisfied.

People got to their feet, the energy in the room was palpable.

'Right. We'll hit the address immediately.' Thea's hands were sweating as she gathered her papers together. 'We'll give it everything we've got. Briefing here in twenty minutes. Nine thirty sharp.'

50

From Århus Police Headquarters, four cars set off at exactly 10 a.m. Two vans, each loaded eight officers equipped with bulletproof vests and loaded pistols, and two Ford Mondeos. Into these were crammed Thea, Søren, Kristian and Janus, along with Alice and one of her assistants, as well as two dog handlers, who kept their dogs in the back of the car.

From the vicarage in Roslinge, Thorkild and Frank set off in Thorkild's clattering car, which according to Frank was more discreet than his sleek silver model, except for its squeeling brakes. Both men in dark clothing, both excited.

The police sped off to Rødkildevej 8, the address that had been entered in Sanne's GPS and was within reach of Karen's bus route. If the two women had been seeing the same therapist during the same period, this could well be the place where they met.

Frank and Thorkild were heading for Stalakitvej 15, the address the geotag from the photo in M's email had pointed to.

From Grenåvej north came a noisy car with two men who looked like criminals. From Grenåvej south came a police convoy.

When they arrived at the junction, the lights were red.

The police vehicles stopped. The old car stopped.

They were on opposite sides of the junction, as if they

searched each other out. They were close to their respective targets. They sat in their vehicles summoning their strength and courage for the missions that lay ahead of them, missions that would culminate tonight.

But a junction of this type is not a meeting place. You never really see each other. Enclosed within bubbles of bodywork, panels and paint, you catch only a glimpse as you pass each other by. We look upon others as obstacles with whom we have only the highway code in common.

This was the case at the junction today: the police on one side and Frank and Thorkild on the other. When the light turned green, they passed each other and proceeded towards their destinations.

The police stood in formation outside the house on Rødkildevej 8, a stately brick villa hidden behind tall, weathered elm trees. The house was almost completely covered with ivy and had definitely seen better days. Two officers patrolled with dogs in a 200-metre radius. The other officers crept alongside the house wall, and took up positions underneath the windows with their visors down, communication devices in their ears and hands poised on their weapons. The passengers remained at a safe distance. From the front seats, with binoculars, they were able to follow the deployment, as were the neighbours, who discreetly peeked out under their blinds.

Frank and Thorkild parked at the kerb outside Stalakitvej 15. They looked at the house. An ordinary three-storey yellow-brick house, built in the eighties. There were no hedges. There was no lock on the front door and no intercom. The windows in the apartment to the left on the first floor were empty. A couple of lonely light bulbs hung from the ceiling.

There was no trace of life in the house on Rødkildevej 8. The police officers stuck close to the wall like black parasites on a large, dead rhino. The head of the police task force spoke into their earpieces.

Frank and Thorkild got out of the car after waiting for five minutes. There had been no signs of life in the house. They went up the weed-filled garden path. For once, Thorkild hadn't even opened his mouth to warn Frank of how unwise the expedition was, he just silently stepped out of the car and followed Frank. The half-landing in front of the apartment was empty. No door mat with a *Welcome* in green print, no clogs or boots or other items, not even a name on the door.

The police officers launched a coordinated attack.

Frank and Thorkild rang the doorbell.

The air was filled with the sound of stomping boots, officers shouting, the splintering of the front-door frame as it was bashed in, and the leader of the task force shouting commands to his colleagues and to any residents in the house:
    'This is the police! Get out now!'

When no one answered, Frank opened the unlocked door and called out *Hello?*

The officers covered each other with their weapons as they rapidly and efficiently cleared room after room.

No one answered Frank's call. They walked into the house.

The officers' conquest of the property was over in no time. There were no hiding places, no furniture, no cupboards, no nooks or crannies. The house was empty. Completely deserted.

Frank and Thorkild found no one at home. The home was undoubtedly inhabited. As desolate as it had looked from the outside, it was teeming with personal belongings on the inside. But no people. Whoever had lived in it must have left in a hurry – and some time ago, judging by state of the kitchen; there were dishes on the table with mould growing on them.

The police secured the house. Then they sent in Alice and her assistant to secure any evidence. There was nothing much for them to examine. No papers, no books, nothing at all. Bare, cold, unfurnished rooms. It was immediately apparent that any finds they might make would be under the microscope – clothing fibres or fingerprints. They left behind a police car, parked outside with two officers standing by to receive any visitors, though it was hard to imagine that anyone would come on an errand to a house that had been so thoroughly emptied. Two more officers were given the task of interviewing neighbours. Alice and her assistant grabbed their leather suitcase and Haglofs backpack filled with forceps and lenses and tweezers and began their tedious silent and coordinated trawl through Rødkildevej 8.

Frank and Thorkild tried to find out whose house they were in. They trudged from room to room, kicking the heaps of clothes to one side. 'This is turning out to be quite an illicit affair,' remarked Thorkild, rummaging in a pile of papers on a cluttered desk.

'Now that we're inside anyway,' said Frank, 'it's not as if the crime's all that much worse, just because we're checking a couple of folders and having a nose around.'

They put some empty bottles by the front door, cleared a window sill and opened a window. The sound of falling bottles would give them a few seconds of warning to flee out the window, in the event someone suddenly came home.

Together, they started to look for M.

51

The murder investigation team was back at police headquarters right before lunchtime. Tired, they convened in the meeting room, armed with coffee. It had seemed they were so close, with the address. One step ahead for a change. But now resentment was plain on their faces. They might yet be on the verge of a breakthrough, but they wouldn't know until the forensic examinations were complete. The immediate feeling was one of disappointment.

'Fooled,' said Søren Edvardsen laconically. 'It was probably too much to ask: an address where our guy was still living. Actually, we shouldn't have been surprised. If both Sanne Andersen and Karen Simonsen had visited that address in therapy, they could have easily told someone about it. It's no wonder he's long gone.'

'We're still a step forward,' said Thea firmly. 'We're going to track him down. There must be something in the house. It's not possible that there's nothing there. And maybe the neighbours have seen people coming and going. The address is a breakthrough.'

'I doubt it,' said Kristian. 'The house was deserted. It's unlikely we'll find anything we can use.'

'Nevertheless, we must continue. There are opportunities, good opportunities – we just need to put our minds to it, do some creative thinking. No matter how much you want to erase all signs of your existence, some tracks will always remain,' said Thea, determined, and opened her computer screen.

*

They were now looking to see if the house held any other clues. They called craftsmen throughout the area to find out whether anyone had ever done some work in the house. They called furniture shops and freight companies to investigate whether anyone had delivered things to the address – or perhaps, more relevant, considering the emptiness of the house, removed items *from* the address.

No joy there.

Kristian Videbæk phoned the insurance companies, refusing to give up. He had luck with Tryg, who insured the house. But the trail immediately went cold again because the insurance had been taken out in the owner's name, not the tenant's, even though the owner knew nothing about it. There had also been a car registered to the address. It was a black Citroën CX from 1986. Kristian felt a glimmer of hope, but the car too had been registered in the owner's name – and it had been scrapped the previous year. Irritated, Little Per had announced over the phone that he knew nothing about any car; and as usual where Little Per was concerned, it was impossible to say whether he was telling the truth.

It was a tiresome job.

They were all on the phone. It took time to make the calls. Normally, they'd have been able to draft in helpers to deal with such routine chores, but it hadn't been agreed in advance, so there wasn't anyone available. Besides, Anne-Grethe was adamant that they must pursue the case only with the available resources.

Thea was fuming as she dialled the number of yet another carpenter. So close, and yet the police force couldn't release a single assistant man-hour to assist their inquiries. And now they'd had to extend their search for craftsmen all the way to Lystrup, having drawn a blank with the locals.

The neighbours, predictably, had been no help. The privet hedges were obviously very high in Risskov, and discretion between neighbours was the norm. Some had been downright amazed that the police thought they might have something to contribute. In Risskov, neighbours wouldn't dream of 'prying into one anothers' affairs'.

'The comings and goings of one's neighbours,' explained a friendly, heavily made-up, villa owner decked out in jewellery and designer clothes, 'sometimes the less one knows of these things, the better.'

Frank and Thorkild were dealing with an apartment which, on the face of it, was teeming with information. If they'd had the trained eyes of the police, it would certainly have been the case.

But Frank insisted that they could not wait.

'Once the police move in, we'll be denied access to all this,' he argued. 'And you heard her – the redhead, Alice – we won't get to know a damn thing. We'll be kicked out and sent home to wait by the phone, while Birgitte chirps away telling us how ridiculous we are. Is that what you want, Thorkild?'

Again, Thorkild hesitated long enough that Frank took it as consent and rummaged further into things.

The small apartment might have been teeming with stuff, but it was all pretty makeshift. New purchases from Jydsk Linen mixed with tattered furniture picked up from flea markets. Cheap teak alongside scratched mahogany. There was a vast TV cabinet containing a big silver grey television, a DVD, a PlayStation and a bunch of DVDs on the shelves. A built-in glass cabinet displayed six wine glasses and a bottle of half-decent whisky. A sofa and a chaise longue in faux leather. On the walls were posters in glass frames, one of New York's skyline and one of the figure of Christ in Rio de Janeiro.

There was a small bathroom with a red-tile floor, and a drying rack over the bath with a couple of T-shirts and two pairs of white panties hanging from it. The shower had a shelf with shampoo and conditioner, both of an ordinary, inexpensive brand. In the kitchen stood a bowl with a couple of mouldy oranges. The refrigerator was empty except for a carton of milk that Thorkild had no desire to sniff. And the bedroom floor was covered in great heaps of what looked like menswear, a few boxes and two old desktop computers. The apartment gave the impression of both a junk attic and a bachelor pad, apart from the bed in the guest room. This was a futon that unfolded, and on it lay a blanket and pillow in soft, cream-coloured cotton sateen, a folded flowered bedspread and one decorative pillow. A beer crate next to the futon functioned as a bedside table; on it was a jar of lotion and two small scented candles in a candlestick.

'What kind of place is this?' said Frank. 'Those panties are the only sign that there was ever a woman here.'

Thorkild pointed to the futon.

'Apart from that.'

'And what is that?'

'It's a nest, I think,' said Thorkild. Somehow the tiny bed in the middle of the mess grabbed his heart. 'It's a place where a woman is huddled together, and tries to have a little bit of luxury, perhaps for the first time.'

'You mean M. This is where she fled to, from her husband? It seems so . . . random. Impersonal. Full of cheap tat,' said Frank.

'Yes, I would imagine it's the kind of place you live in temporarily or borrow from a friend who is travelling. I don't think any of the things here are hers. And she must have left in a hurry. I could easily imagine that her husband found her here.'

'Sanne wasn't involved in it. I can tell you that,' said Frank, determined. 'She can smell conflict from miles away and her first instinct is to run. I cannot for the life of me understand why Sanne would have had anything to do with a woman like that. Or why she would ever show a violent man where to find his wife. Sanne is the most peaceful person.'

'If M fled from here, she obviously managed to take some stuff with her. Or else, someone has been here since and removed it. Where are her papers – all the personal things like her passport, driver's licence? There must be something with her name on it, at least.'

'Again, no computer. Do you see, it was there –' Frank pointed to an empty space on the desk, where a large black spot without dust revealed that something had sat there. 'And she definitely had access to a computer. That much we know.'

'You can get access in any library.'

'Hardly, given the times of day she wrote to me. I think she has a computer with her. Maybe one of those very small ones.'

'Look here, Frank.'

Thorkild stood with a photo album in his hands.

'Where did you find that?'

'It was under the futon. It might belong to M. Or it could just be part of all the other crap here. It's hard to tell,' said Thorkild, leafing through the album.

There weren't many pictures in it. Occasionally, there were empty spaces. As if someone had cleared out her life, removed the things she didn't want to think about. Frank looked at the one woman who kept appearing the pictures. A woman who looked shyly away from the camera. But she smiled. She had dark hair, a slender body and tired dark circles under hazel eyes. She was skinny. Pretty, in an evasive manner. She looked to be in her mid-thirties. Frank studied her with a mystified wrinkle of his forehead.

'She looks small and harmless, doesn't she? Appearances deceive, if it is in fact her. The one who sent these nasty emails and murdered Sanne. Nice to know what she looks like,' said Frank brusquely. Then he went into the adjacent room to open more drawers and cupboards. Something that sounded like a stack of cassette tapes fell to the floor with a loud noise.

'I don't think it's her. It's impossible to imagine, in a way, right?' Thorkild looked at the woman's pale smile. She looked like so many other small, slender women. The dark hair, the anonymous blue jeans and black, long-sleeved top, facial features which were slowly beginning to show wrinkles. One picture showed her in a bikini, sitting on the lap of a stocky but otherwise handsome man wearing colourful swimwear. On the plastic table in front of them stood two red drinks with umbrellas and a sparkler, in the background was a big, blue swimming pool.

They looked happy – average happiness, posing in an isn't-this-great way, Mr and Mrs Townhouse on a package holiday. Thorkild looked at the man's tanned hand resting on the woman's hip, his thumb wrapped lovingly around the side of the bikini bottom.

Was this M? Was this her husband? Were those the hands that hit her when things were not as nice as on their package holidays? He looked for any sign in her eyes of uncertainty, watchfulness, but found nothing. And he recalled her words. *Crooked, invisible, gone . . . you start to depend on what you so fervently dream of escaping . . . Can you even imagine the paradox?*

No, he thought to himself. I can't. The thought of hitting a woman was beyond him, beating Karen would have been unthinkable, and he had neither wanted to nor had any reason to.

'Why do men hit?' he enquired into the air. Frank heard it.

'Because they're stronger,' came the reply from the living room. Frank was breathing heavily, he was struggling with the moving boxes.

'Have you ever hit a woman?'

Frank put the box down with a thud and appeared in the doorway.

'Hell no. You don't hit women.'

'So it's about chivalry?'

'It's about behaving properly. But chivalry isn't interesting to talk about any more, right? There are plenty of women who hit their men. Were you aware of that, Thorkild?'

Frank lifted the box up again and emptied the contents out on the floor. Old toys.

'We're stopping this now, Frank. Nothing's coming from this. Nothing good. The police have a lot of other resources. We risk doing more harm than good.'

'Thorkild, come on. You say A, you must also say B. We can't stop now, we're so close. I'll look after you, Thorkild.'

Thorkild was touched by the brotherhood shining from Frank's serious eyes.

'I'm sorry, Frank, this is fundamentally wrong. I don't like being here. And I don't know what it is you think we're close to. There's nothing here we can use. Let's go now, leave the police to do their work. For all we know, M could show up, armed. Or her violent husband.'

'What are you so afraid of? Have you ever known me to leave little Thorkild all by himself?'

'Yes, as a matter of fact. Have you forgotten our excursion to Århus? If we can find this address, so can Alice Caspersen. The police could be here any minute, in theory.'

'Listen, this has been damn wrong from the beginning. Just keep the gloves and hat on, so you don't leave tracks. And enough with the holier-than-thou attitude. You wanted to come in here as much as I did.'

'I'm not just worried about getting caught,' objected Thorkild.

'The police will get bogged down in procedures and writing reports and what have you. And by then the trail will be as cold as a well-digger's ass.'

'Like a what?'

'Allan Olsen, right? The singer? We like him up north.' Frank took a deep breath. 'Dammit, Thorkild, ten more minutes, then we're leaving, OK? Then you can call your beloved Thea. And if they find it themselves, we don't have to tell them what we've done, right?'

Back at police headquarters, the hunt continued. Kristian had given up on the insurance trail. He was standing in the foyer, taking a cup of coffee from a vending machine, when Thea came out of her office to grab some late lunch from the cafeteria. His good mood was gone, and he looked grumpy. It surprised Thea, and even though she had enjoyed the sparkle in his eyes before, she now missed Kristian's calmness and professionalism at a time when they had yet to produce any concrete results. Or maybe just someone to lean on.

'Anything new?' she asked.

'No, we're getting nowhere. We're looking for a man with

brooches and introverted women, a master of the art of keeping one step ahead. It's certainly not a description you can look up in the yellow pages.'

She stood looking at him, trying to muster some energy.

'It'll come, Kristian. Remember, we have an address and the basis of a description. You know how it is with this kind of case, all of a sudden the link's there. It can go from absolutely nothing to a breakthrough in a split second, once you find the right angle to attack it from.'

'Damn—'

'Seriously. Are you OK?'

'No, I'm not, since you ask, Thea Krogh. I'm tired, I'm frustrated. And I really thought it was a breakthrough with the house. I need something to go right for once.'

She felt a hint of irritation. It was rare for Kristian to whine, but she didn't like having to deal with this side of him.

She grabbed his arm. 'We'll figure it out. Come on, Kristian. Help me out here.'

'Yes, but how long are we supposed to go on like this?'

'I wasn't talking about the investigation. I was talking about us.'

'So was I, Thea.' Kristian shrugged off her hand.

Then Thea's phone rang.

Thorkild looked out the window. The world was grey and lifeless under a veil of drizzle. The whole neighbourhood seemed dead. A car drove slowly past the house with sticky tyres, Thorkild jumped. And suddenly he wanted out.

'This is it, Frank, your ten minutes are up.'

'Yes, yes. One last drawer. I'll just check it, and then I guess there's nothing more we can do.'

He rummaged frantically through the desk drawers.

'It was a long time ago that there was nothing more we could do.'

'You haven't fucking done anything yet,' Frank mumbled.

'Excuse me, what was that, Frank? For a moment I thought

I heard you accuse me of not doing anything. And if I remember correctly, it was me who took the initiative to do anything at all. Go to Århus, check out the damn picture and get things going. While you were out and about in Vindbygårde, beating people up.'

'Oh, forget it. I just don't think it would kill you to be a little more involved in this. You've always got one leg out the door,' Frank replied with his head buried in the desk's bottom drawer. Then he gave up and disappeared again into the small bedroom where Thorkild could hear him kicking a pile of books.

'Yes, I have, Frank. For the tenth time: there's nothing we can do here.'

'Whatever you say. Can't you keep your mouth shut for just a moment.'

'Are we going?'

'One moment—'

'Frank!'

'Here it is!' Frank held a triumphant piece of paper into the air.

'What?'

'Now we're going. Hurry up. Remember all your stuff and let's split.'

'Excuse me, could you just tell me? What is that thing?'

'Weren't you the one who wanted to go? Come on, believe me, we're going.'

Frank left everything as it was and ran out to the car.

'Frank, we have to clean up after ourselves. The window sill and the bottles, even the drawers in the desk, you've left everything open. And what about all the boxes you've emptied? Any idiot can see that someone was here,' Thorkild shouted after him, shrill with frustration.

'Come on, Thorkild. We need to get out of here. There's no time for that.'

'But—'

'I have an address. The person or persons who lived here

have a summer house. I've got the papers right here. I'll be damned!'

Thorkild broke the seventh commandment, stuck the photo album under his arm and ran after Frank out into the drizzling rain.

Thea put her phone back in her pocket and looked at Kristian.

'That was from Rødkildevej – they've just completed round two of the door-to-door inquiries. One of the neighbours remembered seeing the Citroën you were talking about. That it was parked outside for a while. He can remember it because it was trashed. Otherwise, there was nothing. Never any sounds from inside, no one can recall ever having seen anyone.'

Kristian looked up.

'Just a moment, Thea. There's something I need to follow up on.' He ran into his office and started dialling.

Thea looked after him, questioningly. Then her phone rang again.

Alice and her assistant sat on the floor of the villa at Rødkildevej and enjoyed their shared sense of anticipation. The officers who had been around the neighbourhood were shivering and had red noses. But the two technicians had come prepared for any situation. Sensibly dressed in thick fleece and each with a well-padded cushion, hot coffee in thermos and a KitKat for sharing, they sat and took a well-deserved afternoon break. They had worked well, coordinated and effective, and the silence between them was effortless and comfortable. Until a woman stuck her head through the door.

'Are you with the police?'

She was small and round, dressed in a colourful yet tasteful robe. One of those women who knows how to dress according to her figure instead of fighting it. Accustomed to speaking with a natural authority.

'I have something for you. It concerns Andy, my son. He's six years old, and he's been playing over here, in the garden, ever since the house has been empty.'

Alice swallowed her KitKat.

'And who are you?'

'Merethe. Sidenius. Our garden is adjacent to this one. We share a hedge. Well, sharing is probably exaggerating. We've kept it.'

'No officers have been by to talk with you?' asked Alice.

'Yes, they have,' said the woman. 'And as I told them, we didn't know the people who lived here. It's been empty since we moved in. But then I got to thinking – Andy sometimes used to crawl through the hole in the hedge and play in the garden here. I was so scared the first time he went. I was straight on the phone to the police. What with all these paedophiles about, you just want to know where your kids are at all times of the day, right? But he'd only crawled in here.'

'I see. And . . .?'

'And he did it several times after that. And then I remembered that I found this in his pocket when I washed his clothes. It's possible that he picked it up in here. Unfortunately, it's been washed at sixty degrees.'

She stretched out her hand to Alice, who took the little key.

Leaving Merethe Sidenius standing there, she immediately called Thea.

'Off the top of my head, it looks like a summer house key. It's a DaniTrio, they usually produce that type of key. But God knows what it's for.'

'Nothing on it? Summer house keys—'

'—usually have such a nice orange keychain with the address written on and a sticker from Dansommer, yes,' interrupted Alice. 'And the keychain is here, but the address is missing. Otherwise, it would have been a little too easy, huh? We need to go out and test keys, as if it was another Blekingegade case.

How many summer houses are there here in this country, do you suppose?'

She sounded carefree, and it gave Thea a pleasant, calm feeling in the stomach. At that moment, Kristian emerged from his office, breathless with excitement.

'I got hold of Tryg again. They said the trashed Citroën the neighbour saw outside the house had been involved in an accident – it was torpedoed by another car. The incident was reported to the police. Thea – we forgot to check our own system!'

'Yes, but what's the point? It's unlikely he would have filed an accident report using his real name.'

'Of course not. It's still the false name. And it was never pursued, so there are no details on file of the other party involved or any witnesses. What's interesting is the location where the accident occurred. I've checked it on Krak – it's a summer house area by the coast up in northern Djursland. It's not that far from Roslinge, Thea.'

She stopped.

'Did you say summer house area?'

They immediately sent out a patrol car with an officer. Then they called Jørgen Schmidt in Vilå and told him that he would be picked up in half an hour by a patrol car from Århus, which had stopped by Risskov and retrieved a key for a summer house.

Jørgen and the police officer were to try the key on every summer house in the coastal area. Whatever it took, they were going to find the door that matched that key.

52

Jørgen Schmidt spent the half hour before the patrol car from Århus was due to arrive visiting the local locksmith in Vilå. The locksmith was a man of property. He bought old houses in the countryside and restored them himself, with a little help from his friends. Or rather, when the town's craftsmen were short of work, they came and worked cash in hand for the locksmith. He always had something for them – an hour or a day or a week. It wasn't that important. He used their time, which would have otherwise been wasted, and in return they quoted him a favourable price. Jørgen was aware of the arrangement and didn't feel called upon to do anything about it. It was an excellent system for the small community. On top of that, houses that would otherwise have remained abandoned were renovated and sold. Jørgen hated the decay he saw in neighbouring villages; when you let rubbish pile up and things get run down, it had a tendency to rub off on the surroundings. So the locksmith was performing a service for the community in a way, but it meant that you always had to call in advance and get him to come down to the shop if you had an errand there.

By the time the patrol car arrived, Jørgen had summoned the locksmith to the shop and had him cut four extra keys. Afterwards they picked up Jørgen's two reluctant teenage sons when they finished school at 3pm.

'Frank,' insisted Thorkild, tired of constantly stalling and making objections. 'This isn't working. We have to go home first. We need to think things through.'

'That's exactly what I've said all along – you think too much, Vicar. We have the address: Mågevej 7, Pynten, Glesborg. It's not the North Sea, for fuck's sake. It's not far from here and we'll just do it the same way we did the last place, right? Just take a look.'

'Is that what you think we did in Risskov? We just looked?'

'You've gone into overdrive, Thorkild. Want me to pull over so you can take the bus home?'

'No, just go. But listen, this address you found – you don't know that it has anything to do with M.'

'It has. I can feel it. Think about how I found it, right?'

'You didn't actually tell me where you found it.'

'It was under the futon. Wedged between the slats. Right underneath her little nest, as you called it. There's a good chance that it's her. The address means something to her. Enough that she wanted to keep it close, save it under her bed.'

Thorkild felt an indefinable anxiety rise within him.

'It makes no sense. There's not a single personal document in the apartment, no trace of her. And then suddenly an address, all nice and convenient?'

'It was with the photo album, if you remember? Oh, I guess you do, because you've nicked the album, Your Holiness. Take a look at it. That's not personal?'

Thorkild hesitated.

'So what now? We run out and grab her?'

'No,' said Frank wearily. 'We go out and see what kind of place it is. If there's a mailbox, if there's a name on it, anything.'

'I don't know, Frank, honestly. What will you do if you run into Sanne's killer? Am I going to stand there with you, intent on revenge all of a sudden, and some deranged killer, without being able to call the police because we've set off in pursuit of some mad idea and let things get out of hand? Don't you understand? This, what we're doing, is a criminal offence.'

'Not as much of a criminal offence as murder, for crying out loud. Don't you have a right to defend your own?'

'Frank, for the love of God, Sanne is dead! She cannot be defended any more.'

Frank was silent.

'Besides, we need to check the address. Let's go home and find a map, OK? You've had your way, Frank. Now I get to decide this one thing. In any case, it's out in the north of Djursland, so Roslinge is on the way, right?'

He thought, hoped that if he could just get Frank home, he could perhaps, with Birgitte's help, persuade him to stay there.

'OK, we'll check the address,' Frank agreed reluctantly. 'And then we'll head off again? I need to take a piss as well.'

Thorkild consented, reluctantly. He'd gained time, but he had nevertheless promised Frank that they would go out and visit another address. And right now it was not curiosity that plagued Thorkild but a longing – for the first time in quite a while – for Birgitte's arms, her home-made rolls and chitchat.

The idea of telling Thea Krogh about their impromptu visit to the apartment in Risskov seemed completely insuperable.

The summer house area in Norddjurs was desolate and empty. There was a harsh wind, which was cooled further by the icy water. Only a few places had lights on, the majority of the houses were empty and dark, their terraces drenched and the water heaters switched off. It was an area with impressive amounts of scrubland, impenetrable, wild blackberry hedges separated the properties, the few trees were windswept like on the west coast.

'What the hell makes people buy a holiday home here?' said the Århus police officer. 'Three-quarters of the year they're just paying for it, and in summer they use it only because they have to come and mow the lawn.'

Jørgen felt offended on the area's behalf, but remained

silent. He didn't want to get into a stupid patriotic defence of the locality with his children sitting in the backseat. They had switched to Jørgen's civilian car in order not to attract attention.

'Here we are,' said Jørgen, steering into a small alley. 'If you two go in that direction,' he told the Århus officer, 'we'll take the other.' He didn't want to let his boys go alone, and he'd had about all he could stand of the Århus officer, so he sent the eldest of his two sons to accompany him. First though he asked the officer to lose his jacket and instead wear the anonymous oilskin coat that Jørgen fished out of his trunk.

'You'll just walk around, discreetly, get it, Kasper,' he admonished his son, who was obviously excited at the prospect of taking part in an investigation. 'If there's light, you drop it and you don't go near the house. If someone's coming you just say that you've gone to the wrong house. Then you just smile politely and take off again.'

He himself went in the opposite direction with Emil, whose bouncy, youthful steps forced him to speed up. There was no teenage laziness where his two were concerned. And they both wanted to be policemen like their dad. Something Inger wouldn't hear of. She thought she had sacrificed enough anxious hours on the police force, had begun to talk about an art school for Emil. Jørgen thought how angry she would be if she knew the boys were out here with him, trying keys in the hunt for a murderer.

'And you don't say anything to Mum when we get home,' he yelled after Kasper. 'That goes for you too, pal.'

Emil shrugged. And so father and son began the laborious work of walking up the sloping, moss-covered driveways and inserting keys into rusty keyholes.

A silent hour went by, then Jørgen's mobile rang, startling both him and Emil.

It was the oldest kid. They had found a lock that the key fitted.

'You don't go in until we're there,' yelled Jørgen. 'Get away from the house now, Kasper.' Then he hung up and hurried to fetch the younger boy, who was kicking a football that had been left in someone's overgrown garden. Emil smashed the ball into a rosehip bush and was ready to go.

When they arrived at the address, the Århus officer and Kasper had entered the house anyway.

'Honestly –' said the boy, when Jørgen rushed in and looked reproachfully at him '– the house was completely dark. It was obvious that no one was here. And it's actually pretty cold, Dad.'

Jørgen was not so easily appeased, but he said nothing and began to look around. It was he himself who had taken the boys. The Århus officer remained silent, but he was smiling. They had a look around.

'Kasper and Emil – you do not touch anything,' Jørgen told his boys. He would like to have sent them out, but they were right, it was freezing cold. 'Sit down and shut up.'

The house was furnished sparingly and anonymously, as are most holiday homes. Cheap teak furniture, a well-padded leather corner sofa, reproductions of Monet's works on the walls and the compulsory cross-stitch embroidered wall hangings with hearts and little sayings. A shelf made from untreated pine contained oversized books and paperback novels, a game of ludo and a deck of playing cards. Two rooms had bunk beds and empty cupboards, a duvet and pillow without covers neatly stacked on each bed. There was a drawer in the kitchen with papers that looked promising, but it turned out they were just pizza menus, tourist brochures, a worn phone directory and a few manuals on electrical items. But the third bedroom and the kitchen clearly showed that the house was inhabited. The kitchen had plenty of food in the cupboards and dirty dishes. In the bedroom they found a big bag of clothes. It was as if the occupant had packed all their personal belongings, ready for a quick exit, Jørgen thought. He quickly surveyed the items in the bag. Women's clothing in sizes small and medium. Socks, underwear, a pair of narrow-legged jeans, a few sweaters and a big, snug fleece jacket. A toilet bag with a toothbrush and some other gear. Jørgen didn't want to go through it without gloves on.

Whoever she was, she had lived there for some days judging by the stash of food and the rubbish bin. Had she been alone? He looked closely at the dirty dishes. Several plates bore traces of the same leftovers, but it might just mean that she had eaten the same meal several times. That was for the techs to decide.

On the refrigerator door, a solitary picture was hanging. Jørgen looked closer. It showed a man holding up a large cod, which he apparently had caught in the ocean behind him. Jørgen took the picture down and studied it. The man had dark clothes on, and the image was blurred because it was focused on the cod. It seemed so provocative to Jørgen, he blushed. Here was perhaps the man they were looking for, blurred and impossible to identify. As if that lone image had been left there just to emphasise that they would never find out who he was. That it was him, Jørgen, who was the cod, held up by the tail, helplessly squirming and immortalised on film.

He took his phone out and called Thea, who sounded tense when she picked up.

'Hello, Thea? Jørgen Schmidt here.'

'What's up, Jørgen, have you found the place?'

'We sure have.'

'Tell me! Tell me you have something to go on.'

'The place is empty, we've searched it,' declared Jørgen.

'You what! You were asked to locate the spot and wait! I thought I made myself clear: you were to wait outside,' said her excited voice.

'We'll go outside now, Thea, and wait. Don't worry. Maybe you would like to hear what we found?'

'Yes, tell me, Jørgen. There wasn't anyone there, I take it?'

'Someone's been living in the house. Possibly, more than

one person has been here. Judging by the clothes, whoever lives here is female. Small.'

'You went through the clothes? You're not the least sorry, are you?'

'I haven't gone through anything, I've only used my eyes. What do we do now?'

'You wait. Hide the car somewhere where you can see the entrance to the house, so you can tell us if she returns.'

Jørgen didn't bother to tell Thea that his two sons were there, she was upset enough already. He decided the best thing to do would be to rush them back to Vilå before it was getting too dark, while the Århus cop waited in the bushes in front of the house.

53

Jørgen Schmidt had just dropped off his two sons and was passing the town sign on the way out of Vilå when his phone rang. The Århus officer sounded excited, his words was whispered and rapid:

'Jørgen! There's a car here. An old piece of crap. It's coming down the road here. They can't see me. The strange thing is that the driver has switched off his lights. It's getting pretty dark out here, so it's moving like a shadow. Certainly not normal.'

'A car. Is it the woman?'

'Don't know. It's stopping. God, it's noisy, they need to check their brakes. Nobody's getting out. It's as if it's hiding. Behind some bushes on the other side of the driveway.'

'Have they seen you?'

'Don't know. It's getting dark. I don't think she can see me, but hurry up and get back out here.'

'I'm on the road. Twenty minutes, OK.'

'Twenty minutes! Better run a little faster, pal. Hey, hang on, the interior light's just gone on in the car, there are two people in there. Men, by the look of it.'

'For crying out loud! I'll report it in. Stay hidden and wait for me. Are you listening? You're not to go after them yourself!'

Back at Århus police headquarters, the detectives investigating the women's murders were experiencing that familiar tension that always precedes a raid.

For the second time that day they were full of hope and anticipation. A surprising number of criminal investigations arrive at this peak early on: the leads quickly emerge, the task force is sent out, and there's an instant bonus. In the Roslinge and Vindbygårde cases, things had been exceptionally slow in getting under way. Weeks had passed before the call came to turn the blue flashing lights on and send out the task force, only to get to Risskov and find nothing but an empty house. That had been a massive let-down. Not least for Thea.

She had a friend who suffered severe allergies. To counter the risk of anaphylactic shock, she never went out without her adrenaline pen – a disposable syringe that delivered a shot of adrenaline to stabilise the blood pressure and cause the blood vessels to contract. Thea was thinking that she could use a shot of adrenaline right now. The disappointment that had settled into her body after the outing to Risskov had left her drained of energy.

But then this new opportunity had presented itself. From a coincidence. The discovery of a summer house key. Not forgetting Kristian's discovery of the insurance claim, which had told them where to start looking. And now Jørgen had found the house and reported that someone appeared to be living there.

Thea's thoughts turned to the Blekingegade case, which

was on the curriculum at the police academy. The police in that case knew that there was an apartment somewhere belonging to Denmark's only real terrorist group, and they had gotten hold of the keys. They unsuccessfully tried the keys in staircase after staircase in Copenhagen. A laborious, endless job. Until one of the group members, Carsten Nielsen, crashed his car on Kongevejen, and in the car the police found the address of an apartment in Blekingegade. A strange coincidence, like so many things in life.

Right now Thea wasn't fussy – coincidence or not, all she cared about was solving this case. When Jørgen's call came in, the surge of adrenalin hit her with such force it was like getting drunk.

The communication with Jørgen was being transmitted over the police radio. It crackled from the loudspeakers. The process of being filtered through various wireless devices had removed all traces of timbre or individuality, rendering Jørgen's bright squeamish voice without colour. The language was always pared down and precise with this form of communication. He swore that he would wait with his colleague outside the summer house. They would remain, hiding and waiting, until the squad arrived.

Thea switched off the microphone to Jørgen and gave the task force a collective message to go to the cars. She would remain at the headquarters. She had established herself in one of the conference rooms where there was room for any necessary personnel – such as Søren and herself – a large screen and the speakers transmitting activity on the police radio. It was all set to go. Kristian gave her a long look before he left the room to join the first cars.

'Get the GPS coordinate to all cars, keep the lines open so we can inform on the way. The address is Mågevej 7, Gjerrild. A black wooden cottage. One floor, two doors, both facing the road. Corner property. And the property is densely vegetated,' she told Søren.

Alice stuck her head into the conference room.

'Before I go, I've been meaning to tell you that Thorkild Christensen called me this morning. I've been so damn busy, I haven't had time to take care of it. It sounded as if he had gotten wind of something. He talked about a photo with a geotag. I've simply not had enough time to do anything more about it, but I thought you'd want to know. We're going now.'

Alice disappeared again, heading down to the cars to get ready for the big ride.

Thea thought for two seconds about what that might mean, then Jørgen was on the radio again:

'When can we expect reinforcement?'

'Fifteen minutes, twenty minutes max, I expect. Won't be until then. The techs are just leaving now.'

'And we're to stay put?'

'Thank you, you'll stay where you are. Look at the GPS, see if you can locate possible hiding places for our vehicles on the road around the site. There are two roads around the corner. And my map says that there are parallel roads we can use the other sides. Can you get an idea of whether they can be used?'

Thea had projected a map up on the big screen. There was a report from the cars, they were ten minutes away.

Søren Edvardsen came in, breathless, with notes in hand.

'An ordinary rental house. The rental office is local, they've confirmed it. So far, it's a fourteen-day rental in the name of a woman: Pernille Matthiesen, address Stalakitvej in Risskov. With an option for two more weeks, two thousand five hundred a week because it's low season. According to the rental agency, she told them she's an author on a writing retreat.'

'Oh, God,' said Thea. 'Not more women murderers.'

'No, it's atypical. She's not in our registry. Do we know her from the case?'

Thea shook her head. The police radio crackled.

'Jørgen here. Another car's just arrived. Such traffic. A Silver

Audi, I can't read the registration plate, either it's too dark and I'm too old, or it's all muddy. They drove up in front of the house. So we've got two unidentified cars here now. The first one with the two men inside seem to be hiding.'

'OK, Jørgen. What's happening?'

'They're getting out, there are two of them. A woman and a man. He's tall. They're locking themselves in now, I can't see their faces. Hang on.'

There was a rattling, Thea swore she heard a car door open. She sat with her heart in her throat until Jørgen returned.

'Have you got a pen? AW65441.'

Søren scribbled down the number and disappeared.

'You suddenly have better vision? It's a miracle,' she said drily.

'It was about getting maybe five steps closer. They're too far away to hear anything. Just go and run the numbers.'

'Jørgen, how does it look with the parallel roads?'

'Moment, Thea.'

Another voice took over, breathless.

'Thea Krogh, this is Allan Vang. From Århus Police. I've just been out to scout a little.'

'Hopefully you're kidding me, Vang. Otherwise, it's directly contrary to the instructions you received,' she said grimly.

'Sorry, Krogh. I got the impression from Schmidt that we were to check the area for possible escape routes.'

Then the connection went. Thea hit her hand on the table, frustrated. Alice's assistant, who had stayed put, started pressing buttons.

A moment later Vang was back on the line. Calmer now. He described the layout of the parallel roads and the general terrain. Thea called up satellite pictures of the area and copied them into a program that allowed her to draw directly on to the map. She expertly drew six circles on the roads around the house. The officers were divided into two teams. She quickly wrote names in each circle – three from each team. Then she sent the picture off to Kristian, so he could pass it around. Now everyone knew where to take up position upon arrival. They were five minutes away.

Then, Jørgen's voice.

'The first car! They're getting out! We have two men going up to the house, they're dressed in black. There's something very wrong here.'

Thea held her breath.

'They're sneaking around the house. Should we move?'

'Don't do anything, do you hear me? Sit tight, help is minutes away from you. Let them go into the house. Then we'll take them as we enter.'

'But they're not going into the house! They're sneaking around. They're not with the people from the house, I think. What the hell do we do? They're not exactly subtle, they're bound to attract attention. We can't have that now, we're so close. I can easily take them! It's just a matter of getting out of the car.'

Thea hesitated a moment. Then she thought of Alice, who had popped her head in with a message.

'Can you get a video shot of the two and send it to me?'

The radio was silent, then it rattled again.

'But it's dark, they're wearing black clothes, it's impossible to see anything.'

'Try anyway.'

A minute later, a ten-second clip ticked in. Thea had no doubt. She could not see faces, but the movements and the body types were all too familiar. She buried her head in her hands.

'That's Frank Andersen and Thorkild Christensen. I'm one hundred per cent sure of it.'

'What are they doing there?' said Søren, nonplussed and irritated.

'Get them out of the way, Jørgen – if you are in any way able to. It's Thorkild Christensen and Frank Andersen.'

'They're involved? Both of them! That's incredible.'

'That's not certain. They could have found their own way

here, God knows how. Arrest them if need be and get them into the car so they don't get caught up in our action.'

Then there was silence. It was unbearable. Two men out to overpower another two in an unknown wilderness, trusting only Thea's word that they were harmless. And a few metres away, inside a house, was a potential murderer, maybe two. And there was still a while to go before reinforcements would get there.

The worst part was always the waiting. The famous and magical silence before the storm. The time when all decisions have been made and there's nothing left to do but wait.

Then the radio crackled:

'We've taken the two without any drama. They're in their car now, Frank Andersen and Thorkild Christensen. Allan's in the car with them, and I'm getting back in my own car. He wasn't happy about it, the big one.'

Thea was relieved. She breathed with a deep, gasping sigh. They were safe in the car. She realised that she had been frightened. Was it Thorkild she'd been anxious for? At the same time she was happy because she had been able to deliver a crucial insight. Because she had observed the two so carefully that she could recognise them only by their movements. But then the worries came creeping back. What had created this alliance between Frank and Thorkild, how had they found their way there?

Her train of thought was interrupted by Søren Edvardsen, who burst into the room.

'The car—'

'Yes?'

'The silver Audi. It belongs to an Erik Marstrand, I just got it confirmed. We don't have him in our registry. Residence in Aabenraa, as far as I can see.'

'You're joking? Erik Marstrand?'

'Do we know him?'

But before Thea could say anything, Jørgen interrupted her over the radio.

'A shot! There was a shot from the house. What should we do?'

'Nothing, for God's sake, do nothing. Wait, wait, our cars will be with you any moment.'

'Yep,' replied Jørgen. 'I can hear them. Your supermen are on the way.'

Thea looked at her watch. 6.30 pm.

Thorkild sat slumped in the back seat, beside himself with emotion. Embarrassed at finding himself arrested and with such a feeble excuse. Angry. At Frank, but mostly at himself for letting things go so far. Afraid. Grabbed by a police officer he didn't know, and bundled into the back seat of a car that was hidden in a thicket on the opposite side of the road from the house.

There were other cars arriving, taking up positions around the house. The cars were in darkness, but he could see the outline of police lights and sirens on the roofs. Then Thorkild saw officers rush out of the cars. The officer who had arrested them sat with his radio in hand, but it was silent. Before, there had been plenty of activity, but now there was complete silence. Apparently they all knew what they had to do. They were standing out there now, some sheltering behind the cars, some in the middle ground, hidden behind trees and bushes, and some right up at the house, pressed against the wall between the windows. Then came the three words over the radio: 'We're going in.'

And the officers who stood by the house moved in. Thorkild could see them simultaneously bashing in the two doors. A moment later, the windows were shattered by other officers. They stood frozen for a few minutes with their weapons aimed at the windows; the rest of the squad had already entered through the doors.

Thea held her breath and listened intently. She glanced at her watch, counting seconds. Team One had to be inside now. She waited for the clear signal. Why wasn't it coming?

After two minutes, Kristian's words sounded on the radio: 'Clear. Team One goes into the house with me. Team Two: form a chain and search the area with Jørgen Schmidt. He knows the terrain.'

Thea drew a breath again. But only for a moment, as another voice spoke.

'Thea, send an ambulance. We have a man in here, shot. There's so much blood!'

54

The panic was immediate and made her dizzy.

In a moment, the world vanished around her and all that remained was her throbbing pulse and the image of the man she belonged with, alone in a dark house with an armed killer.

'Kristian,' she called over the radio. 'Kristian! What's happening! Are you clear?'

'Thea—' the connection broke with a snap. Angrily, she slammed the radio down on the table. 'What's happening? Where's the connection? Get it up and running again!'

The technician played with buttons. The radio hissed.

'All units, I need a report now! Is there a man down? Where is Videbæk? Jørgen!'

Jørgen's voice cackled, she could hear that he was running, panting.

'Kristian Videbæk went inside. He has two men with him. There is one reported injured. I'm going in now!'

Thea grabbed her jacket. Rushed down the stairs with the radio pressed against her ear. 'Kristian, where are you? Kristian!'

In the garage, the connection went altogether. She jumped

into her official car and took off with screeching tyres. Was considering switching on the siren when Jørgen's voice came through.

'Krogh? It's OK. We have a man down in the house, it was the one who went in with the woman. There's no one else at the address, we have an initial clear.' And then: 'Kristian Videbæk is OK. He put his radio down to help the injured man. We've called an ambulance.'

Thea bit her lip hard. Squinted to prevent the tears from falling, cleared her throat.

'There were two in the house. What about the other person, the woman?'

'No trace of her. A window at the back of the house is open. The man has so far only told us that they were two, himself and a woman. She fled from the house after she shot him. She could have brushed right past us in the confusion.'

'What the hell! Were our people not in place?'

'Yes, but it's pitch black out here and there's lots of shrubbery. Wait till you come out here, see for yourself.'

'She shot him?'

'We haven't questioned him yet. He's lying on the couch. A couple of the boys are giving him first aid. But yes, he's told us that she shot him, it's her summer house.'

'Jørgen? Get me Kristian. Say it's important. No, tell him to call on my mobile.'

Kristian's voice was surprisingly calm, almost laughing when he rang her up a few minutes later.

'You're driving and talking on the phone at the same time?'

'Damn you, Kristian,' she began to cry anyway.

'Stop. There's no time. I'm OK. Take it easy. Now let me tell you what we know so far.'

His voice was quiet and rock solid. How she loved him when he spoke that way.

'OK. Tell me. Goddammit, man, if something had happened to you.'

'The guy in here is bleeding violently. We wrapped him up well. He says it's not his house, but the woman's. She's renting it.'

'We know, Søren found her through the rental agency. She lives in Risskov.'

'At Rødkildevej, I guess.'

'No, Kristian, Stalakitvej. An apartment. We found no connection.'

'But she shot him, he says. The gun's still here, thrown on the floor. And then she fled. I think we need to move fast here.'

'The ambulance is coming, Kristian.'

'What about you, Thea. You're not coming out here?'

'Yes, I'm coming. On my way out of Århus now. Get Alice started on the gun and the house. And get some people to go after the woman. She can't get far without the Audi, it's dark.'

'Yes, it's infernally dark. North of Djursland, you know. I've got people following her. We have a dog patrol coming. We'll get her.'

Thea sped up when she reached the motorway.

'Kristian, this is important. Postpone the interview until I get there.'

'There's plenty of people here.' He sounded offended. 'Don't you trust me to do it?'

'Kristian, I know him.'

'You know him?'

'Aabenraa, remember? I spoke with the police down there, and afterwards with their psychiatric counsellor – Erik Marstrand. I think it's him you have lying there. And I think he's our therapist.'

'But how do you know his name?'

'The car. That's his Audi out front. Søren ran the licence plate. I'm on my way.'

She squirmed her way into the tiny summer house plot with screeching brakes, almost ploughing into the ambulance. At the last moment she managed to angle her Mondeo around it instead. Her face had a frantic shine to it when she entered the summer house and saw Kristian standing in the doorway to the living room. Suppressing the urge to throw herself into his arms, she pulled herself together and contented herself with squeezing him hard on the arm as she tried to take in the scene.

Three paramedics were doing their best to stop the bleeding. There was a lot of blood. It lay in pools on the living-room floor, one wall had vertical burgundy stripes running down it, while the other walls had splashes, and the couch where he lay was soaked. A few police officers stood and watched, they too were covered in blood. It was hard to believe so much blood could come from one person.

One of the paramedics came up to Thea. 'One bullet straight through the leg – there's an entry wound and an exit wound. The exit wound is usually the largest, as in this case. Shot from the front and at close range. Often, shots at close range and from small firearms cause massive internal damage due to the shockwave, so we can't say for sure how much blood he has lost. There may be internal bleeding too. He's passed out a few times due to the blood loss, but the bullet didn't hit any vital organs or major arteries. We've performed a tamponade, elevated him and tied up the wound. In the ambulance, we can give a blood transfusion.'

The paramedic started to manoeuvre the groaning man on the sofa on to a stretcher. With clenched faces, they moved around the blood-soaked body, adjusting bandages and putting in a drip. A couple of times the victim wailed out loud. One of the paramedics was preparing a shot of morphine.

'The ambulance was quick to get here,' said Kristian. 'It's impressive. Jørgen says it was called as soon as the man was reported injured. And they got here perhaps ten minutes later. All the way out here.'

The paramedics carried out the stretcher and loaded it on to the ambulance. One of them turned to Thea.

'Are you coming?'

'We both are. We have a shooter on the run somewhere in the woods. We need something from the victim now.'

The paramedic nodded and gave her a hand so she could pull herself up into the vehicle.

'When did the call come?' said Kristian, who looked thoughtful.

'At 6.35 p.m.'

'Man or woman?'

The paramedic checked his report.

'It doesn't say. The station gave us an address and said that there was a shot. That's all we know.'

Thea looked at Kristian.

'She phoned it in? Does it fit with the time?'

'We'll get it checked. Right now, let's do this,' said Kristian, taking out his digital recorder.

'Careful,' said the paramedic. 'He's lost some blood. You know the drill. If he becomes ill, you stop. Right away.'

When the ambulance started to move, the paramedic settled on a bench at the victim's left side. Kristian took the chair reserved for relatives, and Thea sat down next to the paramedic, by the man's head. It was hard to recognise the man on the stretcher. There was blood all over his body, he must have been lying in a pool of it and tried to stop the bleeding in the leg with his hands. His face had red fingermarks swiped across the cheeks, the hair was a tangled mass and looked grotesque because of the clotted blood. Yet she knew that it was him.

'Erik Marstrand,' said the man on the stretcher. The voice was hoarse and strained. 'But we know each other.'

Thea studied him in silence for a moment.

'How did you end up here, Marstrand?'

'Long story. Very long story.'

'Believe me, I would like to hear it.'

'I'm a therapist, as you may remember. I was treating a woman with some violent disorders. Pernille. I tried to help.

She was in an extremely violent marriage. I helped her escape from the husband. That's why we were in the summer house.'

'Together?'

'Together. Help is help. Sometimes it's not enough to sit and talk about things, right?' He sent her a fearful look. 'Sometimes it's not professional help that's needed but specific help. Human to human.'

'But she shot you?'

Kristian interrupted.

'What was her name? We need to have her full name so we can get the search underway.'

'Pernille Matthiesen. She lives in Risskov, a temporary apartment. She's originally from Skanderborg, her husband still lives in their house.'

Kristian fished out his radio, made a call. Erik Marstrand grimaced with pain, the paramedic adjusted his drip.

'Marstrand, this is important. Why did she shoot you?'

There were tears in the man's eyes.

'It got out of hand. She was on the run, desperate. We had been out to meet with a lawyer in Randers, and afterwards we called by her apartment for some things. We had just arrived back to the summer house. Suddenly she became frightened, saying she could see men out in the front yard. And that she was wanted by the police. I ask her why, of course, but she wouldn't tell me. Just kept saying that this was the end, he'd beat her to death.'

'Did you see anyone in the garden?' said Thea, and thought of Thorkild and Frank, sneaking around the house.

'No. And no one knew where she was. But she was sure it was her husband and one of his cronies who had found her. They had found the last apartment where she was hiding. That was the place she fled from.'

'Stalakitvej, Risskov?'

'Yes? Yes, that's right. They beat her up so badly. I'll never forget it, Pernille called me the same night, I couldn't understand a word she said. Her tongue was swollen and they had knocked out two of her teeth. It was then that I decided that the help Pernille really needed was to get away from that man. So I told her to calm down. I grabbed her. That was probably a mistake.'

He sank back and closed his eyes. The paramedic glanced at Thea.

'Marstrand, focus – what happened then?'

'Pernille started to scream, she became hysterical. She said I'd betrayed her, that I'd told her husband where to find her. That I'm the only one who knew her hiding place. I tried to tell her she was wrong, that there was no one outside. But she was crazy with anxiety. And a rage I've never seen before. Suddenly, she pulled a gun, her hands were shaking, she was out of control. I don't know if she meant to shoot or if the gun just went off.'

'How did she get the gun?'

'Don't know. Haven't seen it before. She must have bought it because she felt threatened. She knew that I would ask her to get rid of it, so she must have hidden it.'

Marstrand coughed, the paramedic gave him some water in a paper cup.

'Why did she feel she was being followed by the police,' continued Thea.

'I don't know. She only said it once, just before she shot me. That the police were after her, that I shouldn't call them, that they had been in her apartment and gone through everything.'

'Her apartment had been ransacked? You say you came straight from there.'

'I never went inside. Pernille insisted that I should sit in the car and look out for her husband. When she came back, she had a bag with some things. At the time, she said nothing about the state of the apartment. Can't we stop? I would like to talk with you, but I have these terrible pains.'

Thea shook her head.

'Pernille is gone, we need to find her. How long have you lived in the house?'

Marstrand looked tired.

'I wasn't living there. She was. I just brought her food a couple of times. I know you probably think I've exceeded all professional boundaries, but I didn't live with Pernille in that house. We don't have a relationship with one another, physically or otherwise. She needed help. You would have probably done the same if you'd met a woman in that situation.'

Thea nodded. Kristian, however, looked as though he was running out of patience.

'Erik Marstrand, we found this summer house. We showed up here, in time to save you from dying of blood loss, because we were investigating a murder. We weren't following the trail of Pernille Matthiesen – it was your trail that led us there.'

'What do you mean?'

'Two women have been killed, both allegedly engaged in a course of therapy with a psychologist, therapist or psychiatrist.'

Thea thought it best not to interrupt and point out that this applied only to Karen Simonsen.

'They met. The two women met somewhere. Two lectures with a happiness coach with a fake name. A house with a fake name on the lease. In the house a key to this summer house, and in the summer house we find nothing less than a psychologist, a therapist. What are the odds, Marstrand?'

The man on the stretcher rolled his eyes.

'She shot me, does that count? I might well have died from blood loss, as you yourself pointed out, if you hadn't arrived. How come I'm the one who must prove my innocence? I know nothing about your case. And I wouldn't hurt a fly.'

He rose up on his elbows, his anger made his eyes look hazy and shifty.

'Listen, I work with people who have serious illnesses. Often, they exhibit a significant degree of social dysfunction.

Of course they fall into conflict with other people. You need me to tell you that? I've been involved in hundreds of cases. Thea Krogh can confirm it, I hope. Andreas Robenhagen from Aabenraa definitely will. The police have always had confidence in my work. I've tried to help these people instead of locking them up. This time I'm involved. So much that I've come close to sacrificing my life for the cause. Who are you to cast doubt on my reputation?'

His breath was coming in gasps, his head hit the stretcher's base with a thud.

The paramedic interrupted.

'I'll have to ask you to stop this. The patient mustn't become agitated or the bleeding could worsen. He needs to be stabilised now.'

Evidently the paramedic was right. Erik Marstrand's eyes were closed. His eyelids flickered, he sank into unconsciousness.

Thea and Kristian sat in silence for a moment. Then they asked the ambulance to stop and they got out. Thea called Jørgen, but he didn't answer. Instead, she caught Janus Schalborg.

'Janus. Is there anything new?'

The kid hesitated. 'I think it would be a good idea if you came back here. We've sent a car after the ambulance.'

When they arrived back at the summer house at Mågevej 7, they found Janus standing outside, waiting for them.

'We haven't found Pernille Matthiesen – for good reason. She took Jørgen's car, it was standing by the road with the keys in.'

'You're kidding,' said Kristian.

Jørgen came trotting up to them.

'Lose the tone, Schallborg Junior. There was a shooting, I ran into the house. If I'm not mistaken, I was following Thea's instructions.' He looked at Thea, who nodded. 'I'm sorry. She obviously spotted her chance.'

'But surely you've traced it,' said Kristian.

'We're all over it, but nothing so far. She's long gone. We've tipped off all surrounding police forces. It can't take long. We have people running patrols on the motorway, more are to come.'

'But Alice has made good progress with the gun,' said Janus.

Hearing her name mentioned, Alice Caspersen appeared in front of them. She looked comfortable and confident in wellies and with the backpack over her shoulder.

'The gun is a Luger. A common type of handgun. No registered ownership in Denmark. Probably bought in the Eastern bloc – it's quite common.'

'It was a Luger in Aabenraa as well,' commented Thea. 'There are many coincidences here.'

'As I said, a regular weapon,' continued Alice, well pleased. 'There are fingerprints on it, the same fingerprints as on most of the dishes in the house and on the panel for the Audi's passenger side. I have a colleague working on Stalakitvej, where she supposedly lived. He sent me scanned images. It seems to be the same fingerprints there. So, in all likelihood, it's the woman who lived in the house and who lived in the apartment, and who Jørgen spotted getting out of the car, who is the shooter. Pernille Matthiesen. This fits with Marstrand's explanation?'

Thea nodded. 'That's what he says, yes.'

'Furthermore—' said Janus, eager to get to the next bit. Alice didn't look as if she appreciated the interruption. She cut in before he could finish:

'Furthermore, we examined the bullet fired here in the summer house. It has the same characteristics as the bullets that both Karen Simonsen and Sanne Andersen were shot with. In other words, the murder weapon we've been looking for.'

'And you're certain that only the woman's fingerprints are on it?'

'One hundred per cent certain.'

'So we have our killer,' Kristian concluded. 'Pernille Matthiesen, murderer, almost a double murderer if she had succeeded with Erik Marstrand.'

'Why did she shoot him?' said Søren Edvardsen.

'She panicked,' said Thea, suddenly remembering why Pernille Matthiesen had panicked. She broke into a brisk trot towards Thorkild Christensen's car, opened the door, slid into the back seat and demanded an explanation.

Thorkild told their story. He was visibly affected, his voice was breaking up on him and his eyes were shifty and uncomfortable. Frank sat silently beside him.

Thorkild told her about the apartment on Stalakitvej. About the emails from M. Her intimidating husband. Thea nodded as the story progressed. Everything was consistent with what Erik Marstrand had told them. Thorkild told how M had admitted the murder of Sanne Andersen. Claiming it was because Sanne had leaked her apartment's address to the husband.

Frank gave a start when his sister's name was mentioned. 'Like hell she did,' he said softly, staring out the window.

'You don't think she did, Frank?' said Thea.

'I know she didn't. Why would she do such a thing?'

Thorkild looked at him, jaws clenched.

'Damned if I understand, Frank,' he said, seething with anger, 'how you can still cling to the idea that you know anything about what your sister has done. You are so . . . so naive! Good heavens, if you could just hear yourself. You can't defend someone you don't know a damn thing about.'

Thorkild hid his face in his hands and sat for a while. Thea left him alone until he'd collected himself and was ready to resume.

'The photo showed that M had been in Sanne's apartment. There was a detailed description of how Sanne looked when she was shot. Frank said there were details that had never been published.'

Thea nodded, it was consistent with the report from Vindbygårde. And it explained why the police in Aalborg hadn't found Sanne's phone.

'I can't do this, Thea,' said Thorkild. 'I don't have the energy to sit here and apologise and justify. We never intended that it would come to this. We did something, we needed to do something. And now you're telling me that this Marstrand is possibly mortally wounded because of our foolishness. That the woman who is responsible for it all got away.'

'Not to mention that you might have obstructed the police investigation and handled potential evidence,' said Thea, and smiled to herself.

'Which is probably a criminal offence,' said Thorkild, exhausted.

'It probably is,' said Thea. 'If someone decides to press charges.'

55

Birgitte woke up feeling dazed. Rubbed her eyes, protecting them from the glare of the TV in the otherwise dark room. She had fallen asleep. When she could focus, she looked at her watch. It was seven in the evening. She had slept soundly, she felt it in her heavy head and gritty eyes. To her regret, she noted that Thorkild hadn't come home. Neither had Frank. She was alone in the vicarage. She listened for them, but heard only silence.

Then her whole body gave a start. The sound of a loud knock on the door hit her. That was what had woken her up, she realised. Now it was repeated, someone was hammering at the front door.

Had she bolted the door? Hesitantly, Birgitte got up off the couch, wrapped a blanket around her shoulders and walked towards the insistent knocking. She swore to herself because the lack of a peephole in the solid oak door meant she would have to open it. She undid the latch and opened the door carefully, slightly ajar, then quickly stepped back. Partly out of fear, partly because of the weight of the dark-clad figure who shoved the door and entered the vicarage.

Birgitte was knocked down. She rummaged around on the carpet to get up. Meanwhile the door was shut and locked, she could hear it. She saw the figure run into the living room. Her heart was racing like runaway horses, her mouth went instantly dry, and she was about to fall over again when she got up on her shaky legs. Suddenly, she could not hear anything. Should she run out the front door? Get away, call for help? Then came the plea from inside the living room.

'You gotta help me.'

A frail woman's voice. Birgitte froze on the spot, didn't respond. Couldn't get out a sound even if she had dared. Her legs found that they could stand, but not move. The slender voice repeated its plea, but it broke on the last word. Birgitte could hardly hear it because of her own pounding heart.

After an eternity of waiting Birgitte convinced herself that the girl would have probably already hurt her if that was her objective. Calmer now, she took a few steps forwards and peeked into the living room.

On the sofa where she had just been was a terrified woman, shivering with cold. She was hiding in the plaid blanket. Just a little face poking out, distorted, with every muscle visibly tense and a pair of eyes looking in all directions. Her hair was messy, woolly, there was debris of some sort in it.

Birgitte went in and sat on the edge of an armchair opposite her. The woman on the sofa coughed, cleared her throat.

'Sorry I knocked you over.'

'Who are you?'

'This is where Thorkild Christensen lives?'

'Yes. It is.'

'Is he home?'

'No. He's gone to a summer house.'

'Who are you? Are there any others here?'

'I'm a good friend of Thorkild. There's no one other than me. Who are you?'

'He doesn't know me.'

Silence. Birgitte let a few minutes pass to give the woman time to calm down. Still tense, she spoke.

'I need a place. I've nowhere to go. There is a man after me.'

'Why did you come here?'

'Thorkild is . . . a vicar, right? I knew his wife, Karen.'

The woman was silent, as if that was explanation enough. Her eyes scanned the room. A branch struck hard against the window, she jumped up and buried her head in her hands. 'I've no more strength. I can't run any more.'

'We'll figure it out,' said Birgitte, without knowing how. 'I'm sure you can stay here tonight. Thorkild will be home soon, and we'll see about everything tomorrow. But what did you say your name was?'

'Pernille,' the woman said, resigned.

'How did you know Karen?'

Silence again. Pernille's muscles began to relax, and then the tears rolled down her cheeks leaving black traces. Soon she was sobbing like a small child.

'I think you should go to the bathroom and wash up a little,' Birgitte said gently. 'You have branches and leaves in your hair. Calm down. I'll make some tea. Do you need something to eat?'

'Promise you won't call the police. I'll tell you everything.'

'It's the second door on your left. I have some leftovers on the stove, I'll just heat it up. Take your time. Are your clothes wet?'

Pernille stood up slowly, nodded.

'Nobody's coming in here. I'm not letting anyone in.'

The woman went into the bathroom and shut the door behind her. Birgitte could hear the hot water tap being turned on. It ran for a long time. Maybe she was holding her hands under the water. Birgitte tiptoed upstairs, took out her mobile and rang Thorkild. He didn't answer. Instead, she sent him a text message asking him to call her as soon as he could. Or come home.

Then she found two large towels and a tracksuit in Karen's closet and went down and knocked on the bathroom door.

She was small in size, Birgitte could tell. But not a girl. A woman in her mid-thirties, she figured. Just small in size. Maybe she seemed extra small because she never looked up. So far she had only seen Pernille's eyes in quick glances. She had taken a shower and put Karen's tracksuit on, it was too big and sagged on the slender body. Her eyes were red and her cheeks swollen with tears. She was all cried out and tired. When they sat down in the kitchen she just poked at the food in front of her. Birgitte had taken the wet clothes from the bathroom and hung them out to dry in the pantry: jeans and a white shirt. She'd stuck her hand in the pockets to see if there was anything there, a weapon, some ID, whatever. Nothing. It didn't seem as though Pernille had anything with her, not even a phone or a purse. She'd been wearing a pair of leather boots with a low heel; they were muddy and damp. Birgitte placed them under one of the hot water pipes in the pantry and stuffed them full of newspaper. Then she went back into the kitchen where Pernille still hadn't eaten, but was about to pour more hot tea.

'How did you get here, Pernille?'

'I ran. Most of the way. I had a car, but it ran out of petrol.'

'Where did you come from?'

Pernille was silent. 'Does it matter?'

'I don't know if it does. Why don't you tell me what happened?'

Pernille stared blankly at nothing. Her voice was colourless.

'I need help. But the police can't be the ones who help me. Please don't ask why. Will Thorkild be home soon?'

'I hope so. What do you need him for?'

'I must go back.'

'Where to?'

Pernille didn't answer. Her jaws were tense, seemed to be struggling to think of the words to say but unable to find them. Birgitte let her wait, but eventually she just sat and looked down at the table with the teacup in her hands, resigned and defeated.

'Where did you know Karen from?' tried Birgitte.

'We met. We were three. Three women. Seen sometimes alone and sometimes all together.'

'You saw each other alone?'

'Alone with him. My friend. He has helped me so much. That's what we had in common, Karen and me. He helped us with things.'

'He's the one chasing you?'

'No! He helps me. He's the one I must go back and help. It's my husband who's after me. My former husband. He doesn't know where I am. Or—' She looked confused. 'I didn't think he knew where I was. But he found me. He always finds me. He'll find me here as well.'

'And he hurt you? Your husband?'

'Yes. But no more. I want it to stop.'

'Have you been to the police? Got a restraining order? There are places, centres.'

Pernille didn't even look up.

'Yes. And yes. Police and restraining orders. And places and centres. Tell me, when do you get help? One can easily terrorise a person anyway. A restraining order is a piece of paper. A centre is a few quiet nights in the eye of the hurricane. I've done it all. Except what needs to be done. I'm learning it. Karen was learning it.'

Birgitte didn't take her eyes off the woman. In her pocket she fumbled with the phone, kept it in her hand.

'Where did you meet with Karen?'

'We met in his house. In Risskov. He had a kind of practice there. At least until recently. He said he had to leave it.'

'Who is he?'

'He's good,' the woman looked up. 'Psychiatrist.'

'And the name?'

'Does it matter? Names are just empty words to lock our identity into being one and the same. In reality, we move. And therefore, we're never the same. That's what he taught me.'

'But he must have a name?'

'Every time we met he insisted that we would all be called something new.'

'But Karen?'

'That's what she called herself the first time she came. The other two of us were already in session at the time.'

'What did the other woman call herself the first time,' said Birgitte, even though she knew the answer.

And with a slender voice:

'Sanne.'

'You know that they're both dead.'

'Yes. I know.'

'You know?'

Pernille suddenly started to eat the hot food that had cooled off. She drank greedily from the water glass. Birgitte filled it up.

'We were just together. Out in a summer house. *Pynten*. He and I.' She made a gesture with her head as if to signal to the north. 'I rented it after my husband found my last hiding place. My therapist helped me.' Suddenly her voice was factual, calm. 'He has been an invaluable help. A friend. There were so many practical things to sort out. My husband has the car. So how do I get around? I can take the bus, of course, or I'm cycling. But take today, for instance. I needed some things. He came and drove me.'

'Drove you where? Pernille, I don't follow.'

She continued as if she hadn't heard:

'We come back to the summer house. I invite him in for a cup of coffee.' She smiled, a crooked grin. 'It's funny, isn't it? For the first time, after living for several weeks in a state of continuous alert, I feel a glimmer of confidence. That moment where I invite him in for coffee and he says yes, and I walk into the kitchen to put the kettle on, and he walks into the living room and turns on the lights. And then off again, right away. And I know, I know instantly that I'm being punished. To let my guard down for just a few minutes, for thinking I could have sat down and drank a cup of coffee with my friend. For all the terrible things I've done to get rid of him. The punishment is here, there was never any way around it, everything I've done has been in vain.'

'He turns off the light? I don't understand.'

'Yes. He turns off the light. Rushes into the kitchen and turns off the light in here, too. The only light is the small red-eye of the kettle. He says I must be quiet. That there's someone in the garden. Just at that moment, I see it too. Shadows outside the window. I ask him if he saw who it is. He nods, I can see it in his eyes. They've come for me. And they will kill me this time.'

'They? Your husband?'

She nods.

'My friend pulls me back into the bedroom. He opens the window, says that I must run. He helps me out, I turn around to give him a hand. He says he'll stay. That now it must end. And that I must run. And I do. Into the darkness.'

'Out in the woods?'

'Yes, at first. Just frantically running into the darkness. I don't know how long I'm running, or in what direction. Then I hear the shot. And I know I must get help. That my friend can no longer help me. That I can't run around blindly in a forest, while my husband can quietly go out into the darkness and listen for my steps, the branches that break. He's

374

armed. He'll just follow the sound. I realise that I must return to the road. Stop a car, see if there's someone in any one of the houses, anything. I run back to where the sound came from. Trying to understand where the house is. Trying to remember the plot, where the road runs, which is next door? And then I bump into the car – there is a car with the key in it. I don't even think about it. I drive, look for lights in the houses, there aren't any. I don't know what to do. Then I see the signs for Roslinge. That's when the car stops. I get out and run.'

She gasps for breath.

'I must go back. I'm afraid to, but I must. I must help my friend. Oh God, maybe he got killed.'

Birgitte looked at her, determined.

'We'll call the police. It's the only thing to do. Can't you see that?'

'No. You can't. You can't call them. I'll take off again. Can't you lend me some money, just to buy a little petrol?'

'But why, Pernille? They can help you. Get you to safety, drive out to the address and help your friend.'

'I stole a car.'

Birgitte shrugged.

'I'm sure they'll forgive you for that when they find out what danger you were in. That can't be what worries you.'

'No. I shot Sanne. It was me.'

The calmness in her voice was total, she looked at Birgitte, colourless, as if she saw right through her. Birgitte clutched the phone in her pocket, made her voice calm.

'You shot Sanne.'

It wasn't phrased like a question. Birgitte sat with a murderer in front of her and wondered why she wasn't more scared than she was. But Pernille seemed no threat to anyone. Her small stature, her restless eyes.

'Yes.'

'Why?'

She looked calm, confident.

'It was a part of our development. Taking power, he called it.'

'Your friend?'

'Sanne's development went off track. She was insane, she became obsessed with our therapist. Suddenly, she saw Karen as a threat. And me. She betrayed me. We had such confidence in each other within the group. And then suddenly she stabbed me in the back. I could have been killed. It was her plan that I should have died that day.'

'What day?'

'The apartment I lived in. It was just a transitional phase until I found something else. A hiding place. Nobody knew where it was, not even my therapy group. And then one day he was there. My ex-husband. He had a pal with him. And a croquet mallet.' She pulled up her upper lip. 'You see? Two teeth. These are temporary crowns, I had to borrow money to get them. He lent me the money, although he knows I can never pay him back. I ended up jumping out the window, I landed on the balcony downstairs, the woman who lives there opened the door for me. Then they disappeared.'

'And it was Sanne's fault?'

'I know it was Sanne. I know this because my therapist told me when we next saw each other. That he was stuck in an ethical dilemma and had to tell me something that meant he would breach his confidentiality. Because we were friends. *Are* friends,' she corrected herself. 'Sanne's therapy sessions worried him already. She was obsessed with him, said she loved him. And then she told him not to count on me any more. That I might not come to therapy again. That she had followed me, knew where the apartment was. And that I should get home to my husband where I belonged.'

She looked at Birgitte. 'Do you understand? Do you understand why I had to do it? No. You don't understand. How could you? I can see it in you. Nobody's ever laid a hand on you. Am I right? So well groomed, so much faith in your eyes. Confidence and trust in the world. That it holds good things for you. Do you understand what it means when you know the world has nothing good in store for you? That the fear you live in will be with you always? That the violence, you'll carry it with you, with him or without him. It will dwell in you. You become one with the violence. Someone like you cannot understand what that means.'

'I know, Pernille. I get it. Thorkild will understand it as well. And Frank.'

'Frank?'

'Frank. Sanne's brother, whom you wrote to. I'm sure they will understand it. Not forgive it, maybe. But understand what drove you to act. And you've also had the need to tell them, obviously.'

Pernille's eyes were dark with renewed fear.

'Whom I wrote to?'

'You wrote emails to Frank. Told him about it. The violence. The murder. You may not know this, but Thorkild and I both know Frank. He drove down to us just after he got the email from you. Have you forgotten about that, Pernille?'

'I've not written any emails. Don't say things like that. Stop it!'

'I've read them. You explained everything. The details of the murder. A picture of Sanne's phone. You signed them with the letter *M*.'

Pernille wrapped her arms firmly around her upper body, rocked back and forth.

'Oh, God. That isn't true. It's him! He took her phone. He said he would get rid of it. I don't understand.'

'Are you sure, Pernille? Is it possible that you have repressed a lot of things here?'

The woman stood up with a jolt.

'But then I'm not safe here. I thought that because my crime was against Sanne, I would be safe here. Here with those who must hate her. Tell me –' she grabbed Birgitte by the arm, 'you hate her, right? Does Thorkild? Will I find allies here? Is there no room for hatred in this world?'

Her eyes were feverish, she looked as if she was hallucinating. Birgitte took her by the shoulders.

'Take it easy, Pernille. I haven't phoned the police. I promised you a bed, and we'll sort out the rest tomorrow. I stand by my promise, of course.'

Birgitte wasn't convinced she was doing the right thing. But she would not go back on her promise to Pernille before she was sure what to do. All her talks with Thorkild and Frank about revenge and meaning and all those things, now she suddenly held the key to it all and had to find out what she thought. Or rather, whether she could pursue and stand by what she had always thought to herself when Thorkild talked about finding the sense in it all, finding *closure*, and Frank had talked about revenge.

She helped Pernille sit down again.

'Tell me a little more. The therapy. What was it he did with you?'

Pernille hesitated.

'He was always talking about power. About taking power. A way of becoming. We were all, in our different ways, cowed. I was the most obvious. But also the others. They hid in their homes, Sanne behind her phobias, Karen behind her husband, oppressing their dreams, he said. He had the power we needed. Can you imagine that? To have power over others so you can empower them. The power to kill, even. It was the greatest test we had to pass. He called it an exam.'

'So you had to kill? For him?'

'No, no. No, nothing like that. He has nothing against people as such. It was all symbolism. A theoretical exercise. What is death? Death is just absence. It's a nothingness, as nothingness it is not conscious of itself. The dead don't know that they're dead. Therefore, death is not miserable. It doesn't matter. That's how he said it. I've learned it by heart.'

'I don't understand,' said Birgitte. 'Why kill?'

'Because he who kills experiences the greatest feeling. He called it an earthly Elysium. The dead get their afterlife – Elysium. But he who kills gets his earthly Elysium. Blessedness. But you misunderstand. It was not to be taken literally. It's just a way to talk about it.'

'How is it blissful to kill?'

'You take life. In another sense, you give life. When choosing who should die, you also choose who will live. It's like being God. And after all, everybody deserves it in some way. No? That's why, ultimately, we must all die. Everybody has something on their conscience. Sanne betrayed me, she betrayed my trust, she basically just wanted to possess. Him. And I took his words and translated them into action. Killing Sanne was the most blessed thing I've done in my life. And I don't regret it, not for a second.'

'What did Karen have on her conscience?'

'That she couldn't. Couldn't do what he asked of her. Take power, grow, evolve, become human.'

'I still don't understand. What did you do, exactly?'

'He gave us the gun. Said it was easy. Encouraged us to fire it. We had to feel the intoxication of holding a loaded gun in your hand, the power converted into a small weapon. And it was intoxicating. Believe me. All the times I've laid bleeding on a floor and fantasised about shooting him. The feeling of the power in my hand made me dizzy.'

'Was it easy?'

'Yes. More than you might think.'

'And you regret nothing? You say it should not be taken literally, that it was just a way to stage a theory.'

She shook her head. 'I did something extreme. She did something extreme. The extremes give extreme results.'

'Did you tell your therapist what you had done?'

She didn't answer that.

'Answer me, Pernille.'

'I don't want him involved. The only thing he has ever done is try to help me.'

'And you still think it was Sanne who betrayed you.'

'Yes. He said so.'

But she began to cry, a pathetic and childish sobbing, Birgitte took her hand.

'Why are you crying?'

'The emails. I don't understand the emails. Will you not show them to me?'

Birgitte fetched Thorkild's laptop and found the document where Thorkild had saved them all. The document was stored on the desktop and was simply called *M*.

Pernille read in silence.

'I don't understand this,' she said. 'I have not written these.'

Birgitte stroke her hair.

'You know what, I think? I think you've been the victim of a very, very rough manipulation. A man who has played his own game. Wanted to prove he had power over other people. He used Karen, Sanne and you as his puppets. It makes me infinitely sad.'

Pernille looked at her, her eyes were pleading.

'I have something I want to show you. A video clip. It's in my email. He sent it to me before . . . I drove to Vindbygårde. To show me what Sanne was capable of, to let me know why I needed to be careful. Maybe you can watch it and see that he was right. That he was good. You know these things, don't you?'

'Are you sure you can stand showing it to me?'

Pernille didn't answer, her fingers were fast as lightning on the keys, opening a browser and finding an email account.

56

Thea made a quick decision and told Frank and Thorkild about her interrogation of Erik.

A brief report in curt language to the two 'private investigators', as Kristian had dubbed them with thinly veiled sarcasm.

'Marstrand insists that Pernille Matthiesen panicked because she was chased by her husband. And our studies so far show that she was responsible for Sanne's death. I need hardly explain to you how nice it might have been to confront Marstrand with the emails that you've told me about, the information about Sanne's murder. He's the one who has the best connection to Pernille now, and can help us track her down.'

'No,' Frank said angrily. 'I think we got the message, OK?'

Nobody said anything for a while. Thea took the floor again.

'Well, I guess that's it, then. I'd better go back.' She was a little unsure of the words. Couldn't bring herself to say goodbye to the two of them, it felt so unfinished, but she knew she had to, sooner or later.

'What's the latest on Erik Marstrand?' said Thorkild. 'You said you didn't finish the interview because he was in a bad shape.'

'Yes. I'll head along to the hospital now to make sure that everything goes as it should. Erik Marstrand will be checked at Skejby. He has lost a lot of blood. We'll resume the interrogation when it's safe to do so.'

Thorkild still looked down.

'Let me know how he's doing, Thea – will you promise me that? Just a text, so I know whether he's going to be OK.'

She nodded. 'Goodbye then. Maybe I'll see you around. And

remember what you promised me. The very first thing you do when you get home is to forward all of those emails to Alice and myself. It has top priority. We might be able to get something out of them that you couldn't.'

'Hardly. Bye-bye, then,' Frank snapped.

On the trip home to the vicarage in Roslinge, Thorkild and Frank stopped by the water. They didn't say much. Sat and looked at the pale winter moon. Their bodies were fighting to stay warm beneath the winter coats, hats and mittens. Thorkild reached out to turn on the engine to get a little heat. Then his phone rang and he struggled with mittens and coat-tails to answer it.

'It's Birgitte. I've called you like a hundred times. Where are you?'

'Out by a summer house somewhere. I told you, remember? On the way home now.'

Birgitte was silent. Thorkild's senses were awakened. It was unusual that she rang him. Especially not several times in a row.

'Has something happened?'

She was breathing heavily, as if she didn't know where to begin.

'Thorkild, I need to talk to you. Where are you, exactly?'

'I'm out by the water, you know, the old ferry site. You want to come out here? We're just leaving, actually.'

He felt Frank's judgmental eyes on him and was glad that he hadn't said yes to rushing back to the vicarage.

'I think it's best that I come out there.' She hung up.

'Birgitte's going to stop by,' he said, hoping he sounded more casual than he felt. He got out of the car.

The water was glassy, ice had gathered at the water's edge, forming small flakes of frost around the reeds. The sharpness of the winter air stung his eyes, the cold stung his cheeks. He looked down at the silent water, the dark brown mud on the bottom and a few sticklebacks that moved in tiny jolts. And suddenly felt that nothing in the world could compare with this heartbreaking beauty, this screensaver in the winter's decay. Everything was quiet around him and in him. Not a sound. At least not until Frank turned on the radio inside the car, and a lousy pop rhythm penetrated the closed doors. And then the sound of Birgitte's little Polo arriving, going way too fast.

She got out of the car. She ran along the beach and out on the remnants of what was once a pier where Thorkild stood in the moonlight. She threw herself into his arms.

'Where on earth have you been? What's happening, Thorkild?'

'What's happening? We were a little stupid. We're just getting in the way of police. But they knew what they were doing, and we were lucky. They even saved a man who was wounded inside. The killer, Sanne's murderer, fled, but they are close to catching her – M, who I told you about, from the emails. So I suppose that's it, I think.'

She stared at him, and suddenly he started to giggle nervously at the thought of the explanation he had just offered her.

'How are you?' she asked.

The words stood in a funny contrast to her expression. She had flushed red cheeks and unruly hair.

'I don't know.' Thorkild looked up for the first time. 'I honestly don't. Guess I'd better find out.' He smiled at her, wryly, disarmingly. She waved him off.

'Thorkild, listen. I don't know what happened down here. About an hour ago, a woman came to visit. At your house. She wanted to talk to you. But you weren't there, so I let her in. She was breathless and dirty, as if she had run through a forest to get there, and she looked frightened.'

'What are you saying, Birgitte?'

'She said she had fled from a summer house. Her husband wanted to kill her. She had been with her therapist. I think she's been subjected to manipulation of the worst kind. I think it's clear that the therapist has sent emails to Frank about it all, using her name. As a confession, an explanation, so that he would go free. But she told me everything. He's the one who's behind it!'

Suddenly Thorkild could not feel his body. He was so numb he could barely control his voice.

'What about the police?' he managed to ask. Birgitte snorted and spat.

'She wouldn't go to them. She's guilty herself, she said. Oh, Thorkild, she was crying and totally out of it!'

'Birgitte, this isn't right. It can't be right. It simply can't! A man's been shot. Shot by that insane murderer. Think, Birgitte!'

'Thorkild, she described the summer house. Mågevej?'

Thorkild nodded.

'She's a tiny woman, slender as a thirteen-year-old. The victim of an insane impostor.'

'But, Birgitte, he was shot. Dying before our very eyes. He's the one who's the victim! Where is she now, Birgitte? Birgitte!'

'Home. She's in bed. She's not going anywhere. Has nowhere to go.'

'But . . . I don't understand.'

'Thorkild, you must talk to that Thea person. You're on very good speaking terms with each other. You may be able to get her to do something without sacrificing Pernille.'

'Hell no, it's too weird. There are so many maniacs in this town. They always come to me. The vicar, you know.'

'Thorkild, that's not true. You know it's not a coincidence. She came straight from that summer house, dirty, frightened, she's told me everything. Her name's Pernille. She's the refugee. Of course she is.'

'Birgitte . . .' He shook his head, wanted to look out over the water again, sink back into the emptiness. She grabbed him roughly by the shoulders and shook him urgently.

'Thorkild! Listen, do you remember that story you told me one night? We talked about evil. You said that all evil is rooted in the great love triangle. A father and two sons. The fact that all human evil comes from envy. A father must always bless the one, and thus curse the other. The second will be belittled. Do you remember? Cain and Abel and their father. Isaac and Ishmael and their father. And what was the third example?'

'Esau and Jacob.'

'Yes, yes. Right, Thorkild. How did that go again?'

Grateful, Thorkild retreated into the familiar history:

'Esau was the firstborn. The one who was to inherit. But he sold his birthright to his twin brother for a bowl of lentils. The mother witnessed it, and she loved Jacob best, she helped him win back that which she thought he was entitled to from his father.'

'Yes, by cheating.'

'By dressing in goatskin, so the father, who was almost blind, thought that Jacob was Esau. He was hairy.'

'Who was belittled, then?'

'Jacob remained so. He was afraid of Esau's revenge and fled.'

'Yes, Thorkild, yes. It's a deception. He made himself out to be the victim. He makes himself appear the victim by shooting himself. *He shot himself*. It's amazing. He has awakened all your pity, so you automatically have to see him as a victim and the other one as the culprit. But I'm the one, Thorkild, who has sat and drank coffee with the true victim. That story came into my mind while she was speaking. This is why. Thorkild, dammit, stop staring out at the water like a fool. Deal with what I'm saying!'

'I'm trying, Birgitte, dammit, I'm trying! But you're not making it easy for me. I can't keep up.'

'Then let me show you something.'

She took his hand and pulled him to the car and let him in the back seat, where his old laptop was whirring as if the battery was running low. He heard Birgitte call for Frank while he focused on the screen, trying to understand what it was he saw. Frank pushed himself on to the seat beside him, Birgitte went in the front.

'Start the film, Thorkild.' She turned towards Frank. 'It's not like you think, Frank. I had a visit from the woman you call M tonight. I think she's the scapegoat in some sort of game.'

Suddenly Thorkild wouldn't, dared not look.

'What is it you want us to see?'

'Pernille showed me the film. To show me why Sanne was dangerous for her, that she was insane.'

The two men in the back seat stared at the screen as Birgitte reached over and pressed play.

The first thing that happened was that the film quickly zoomed out. Away from a face. The image shook, back and forth, until it focused on Sanne's face. She was sitting in a wicker chair with a burgundy cushion and looked as though she had just sat down. Behind her, a matte white wall. The light wasn't good, the recording amateurish, that much they could at least see. One could not sense the room. As if the picture was not important. The sound, however, was sharp throughout, the wicker chair creaked underneath Sanne. She was probably five feet from the camera, which shook and settled down, probably because it was located on a plain surface. A tripod, maybe. And a shadow slid in front of the lens and became a figure in the front. Another creaking of a wicker chair, and the figure became a black shoulder that filled a portion of the picture's left side. And they heard Sanne say, with a crisp, thin voice: 'It's good to be here again. I missed you, really missed you.'

And the black shoulder answered, 'How are you, my girl?'

The man's voice was altered, presumably when the film was edited, so you couldn't hear it clearly. It wasn't really scary, just blurred, as if he was drunk.

Sanne, however, was crystal clear, gentle. 'You look great.'

'You don't look so good, I think.' They could see the man leaning towards Sanne. 'How is she, my girl?'

Sanne simply nodded in reply.

'Tell me. That's what we're here for. Remember, Sanne: I'm your husband, your father, your friend, your only one.'

Sanne looked down at the floor, repeating the words: 'You are my husband, my father, my friend, my only one.'

'That's right, Sanne. That's how it should be. You need to have someone who takes care of you.'

'I'm so lonely.' Sanne spoke slowly and lifted the opaque blue eyes to face the man in front of her. 'I'm lonely. There is no one. No one else anyway. It's as if people see right through me. Everyone can see it: "She's a loser, that one,"' Sanne sneered. It was the first subtle difference in her voice. 'It's like a big wall around me that says stop, warning, do not enter. Do you remember the comics? You know, Uncle Scrooge's money bin with all the signs out the front?' She smiled slightly at the recollection. 'I've probably got this hot-headed person inside of me running and jumping around and scaring people away with cries and weapons and landmines and everything. You just can't tell. It's inside. There's only you who have seen it.'

Sanne looked down again, she looked at her fingers, frantically searching for nails and loose skin she could tear off.

'I only have you,' she said quietly. The nervousness of her hands had not found its way into her voice. 'All day long, I think of you only. You must promise me that you won't leave me. I can't do it without you.'

There was a long pause.

'Sanne, it's quite natural that you feel abandoned. You're about to do away with all your ghosts. You get lonely when the ghosts leave you.'

'But you're not a ghost.'

'No, I'm not a ghost. I'm real. I'm your husband, your father, your friend, your only one.'

Sanne's lips moved along with the last sentence.

'Say it out loud, Sanne. When you say things, they become reality. You know that.'

'You are my husband, my father, my friend, my only one.' Monotonous and ritual. 'What do you want me to do now?'

'Tell me first about the exercise I gave you last time. How did it go?'

Sanne smiled to herself, dreaming. 'Yes, that's right. You told me to get angry. It was a strange thing.'

'Not angry. I asked you to get really mad and scold someone, maybe even for no reason. Can you remember why?'

She nodded.

'Because I need to find myself, step into character, take power and things like that.'

'Can you remember that we called it creating the will to power?'

Sanne nodded again.

'Tell me how it went.'

She thought about it. For a long time, almost coy. Creating suspense, aware of its effects.

'Yes, there was this lady with her dog, who came to collect for the Red Cross. I scolded her, yelled at her. It was really uncomfortable. But it also helped a little.'

'Yes? That's fine, Sanne. I thought so. How did it help?'

'It was as if . . . everything was no longer just my own fault. Like that, you know. Strange. She hadn't done anything. But it was as if she had anyway, when I gave her the blame for everything.'

The man clapped his hands.

'That's great, Sanne. Right. Just how it should be. Did you feel that you were strong?'

'Yes. Yes, it made me . . . it drove the feeling of loneliness away.'

'But, Sanne, you didn't entirely do what we had agreed on.'

'No.'

'You were supposed to find someone who meant something to you. That was actually what we had agreed. I'm not completely satisfied with you.'

'But I couldn't. Sorry. I'm not ready.'

'This is important, Sanne, you have to conquer what has a hold of you. That's not random individuals.'

'No, it's my mother, I must kill.' Sanne sounded tired and exasperated, almost defiant.

'Yes, Sanne, it's your mother. The one who's to blame for solitude. Your mum. Everyone must, in order to free the self, get rid of the mother.' His voice sounded impatient.

'But I can't . . .' Sanne had the same ritual voice as when she repeated the man's words before.

'But you can't, because she's already dead.'

'I can't, because she's already dead, so . . .'

'So . . .', the man helped her along.

'So I have to kill something that resembles her.' The same monotone voice.

'Yes. That's what I'm talking about, Sanne. You know this. That's what will make you strong. That's what will get you to live. Do you not have a right to live?'

'Yes, I have a right to live.'

'Isn't that why your mother gave birth to you. So that you could live?'

'Yes, that's why my mother gave birth to me.'

'So it's only fair that you get to live?'

'It's only fair that I get to live.'

'It's your mother's wish. Power. The power to live. You must act. You must have the will to power.'

The man slapped his chest, Thorkild could tell.

'The will to power,' repeated Sanne.

'So what should you do?' the man asked rhetorically. Sanne was silent. After a while, she said:

'But I can't.'

'Sanne, you need to stop this. You know how it is. If you can't do what I ask you, we won't achieve anything from seeing each other. It makes no sense. Then I have to say goodbye.'

Sanne's face crumpled at this. She began to weep like a child, while her hands searched everywhere on her body for something to tug at, something to contain herself with. His voice became soothing.

'But, Sanne, I won't leave you. Provided you do what we agree. It's not that difficult.'

'You won't leave me, it's not that difficult.' Sanne settled down while she repeated the words back to him.

'Who is like your mother? Who is it that stands in the way and is a threat that I must leave you?'

'It is . . .' Sanne's teary eyes were fixed on the man. 'I know. I know.'

'Who is it, Sanne? Who is like your mother?'

'She resembles my mother because she's so correct. I'm completely wrong and she's right.'

'She's your *super ego*. Do you remember we talked about it? As long as you're not free of it, you don't develop your own *self*. Then you live in the shadow. Humiliated and ashamed. Isn't that true, Sanne? You must take control of it.'

'And as long as she's my *super ego*, I can't be with you, right?' The blue eyes sparkled.

The man in front of her sighed.

'If you can't make yourself free, eventually we must stop seeing each other.'

'Then our love can't exist?'

'Only those who are free can love. You know that, Sanne.'

'But I can't live without you.'

'You can't live without *you*. You can't be a parasite on others because you can't master living by yourself.'

'Am I a parasite on you?'

'You're a parasite on the world, right up until the day . . .' He waited for her to make the sentence complete.

'When I kill my mother.'

'When you free yourself of what represents your mother,' he corrected her.

'When she's sitting there with you and me . . . When we're both here . . .' Sanne's breathing had become laboured, her chest rose and fell heavily, she grabbed the wicker chair. The woman on the screen, the man behind the screen, both clung to an armrest and waited for the continuation.

'When you are both here . . .' He paused, because Sanne reacted with visible displeasure. 'Take it easy, Sanne. Remember that I'm your husband, your father, your friend, your only one.'

'You are my husband, my father, my friend, my only one.'

'Yes.'

'When she's here, there's no place for me. I can't breathe. She stands in the way.'

'She stands in the way.' The voice was sober and matter-of-fact.

'Yes, she's in the way.'

'Of what, Sanne. What's she standing in the way of?'

'Of you and me.'

'Sanne . . .' The man leaned forward again. 'Now I'm going to tell you something that maybe I shouldn't. But you have to understand what can sometimes happen when we're working the way we do. What has happened is what often happens when you're together like we three are. One girl falls in love. She's fallen in love with me. And it's wrong. But it's actually quite common.'

'But I've also fallen in love!' Sanne got up quickly and stepped towards the man, who halted her with a sudden gesture.

'Shh, Sanne. Sit down. This is something else, you know that. We've talked about it. It was a mistake that she was allowed to come between us. But it's her fault. Only her.'

'Yes, it's her fault.'

'But that's why she can pay to make amends.'

'Yes, she can pay.'

'She may be the example that you can practise in order to be free. Isn't it fair, Sanne? Don't you think?'

'Yes, it's fair.'

'You know, Sanne. You're smart. I can see it in you. You understand and see everything. It's so clear to you. Don't worry about it any more. Just do it. Set yourself free.'

Sanne nodded quietly. The man reached out a hand towards the camera, and a second later, the file stopped playing.

Frank hissed. 'What the hell was that?'

'That,' said Thorkild, quietly, 'explains why Karen had to die.'

Birgitte took his hand.

'Why did she run from the house?' said Frank.

'She was hiding from her husband in the summer house. She probably thought he was coming when she heard the two of you sneak up outside. Hiding from both him and the police.

Good lord, Thorkild, she killed Sanne. Do you think she would ever call the police? Besides, she doesn't have a phone.'

It dawned on Thorkild. As they walked around the house, they'd heard a car start and noticed an open window at the back of the house. This was before the gunshot. The police didn't have that information. Pernille must have escaped beforehand.

'Think, man! Get hold of Thea. I'm going back to Pernille. I'm afraid what she might do.'

Thorkild took out the phone. Hesitated. But then he dialled Thea's number. There was no connection. Thorkild looked helplessly at Birgitte.

'Thorkild, find her. You simply must find her.'

'But . . .'

'Thorkild, damn it, pull yourself together.'

Birgitte turned and walked away.

'Birgitte,' he called after her. 'I'm going after her. I know where she is.'

Thorkild got into the by now well-heated car, Frank followed suit. Turned down the heat and drove off. For once, Frank didn't have much to say, just sat and nodded to himself and blushed, Thorkild didn't know if it was with excitement or rage. He took the lead completely.

'Frank, you should try to call Thea. Keep on trying. I'll drive us to Skejby.'

'Skejby?'

'Yes – get it together, Frank. That's where Thea is. Yes, and the other guy for that matter, whoever he is.'

'Bloody hell. He could be dangerous.'

'Yes. Call her, Frank. We need to move quickly. And please turn down the horrid music, I can't hear myself think.'

Frank rang and rang, in vain, and sighed, despondent.

Heading down the motorway at 125 kilometres an hour, Thorkild caught himself fretting over the loud expressions Frank used to express his emotions. Yet the accompaniment of sighs and moans seemed strangely appropriate.

*

Skejby Hospital is an impressive size. A labyrinth if you don't know exactly where you're going. At 8.30 p.m., Thorkild screeched to a halt at Main Entrance 6, ran in and incoherently explained himself to the woman at the information desk.

'Man in ambulance. Shot. Police found him – they're there, too. Tell us where we're going.'

'I don't understand. You must be a little more clear and speak slowly,' admonished the receptionist.

Thorkild took a deep breath and was about to try again. Then he saw Frank's smiling face reflect in the receptionist's glass cage. He turned around.

'What the hell is there to laugh at?'

'I found the department,' Frank waved his phone. 'Thea has her visiting hours now.'

'Christ, Frank, give me the phone. Is she still there? Thea, are you there?' Thorkild yelled into the phone. Thea confirmed that she was; she sounded surprised. Thorkild began to explain.

'We were there, Thea. We saw the back window open. It was open before we heard the shot. It's a detail, but it's important. I only remembered when Birgitte told me what M had said. It all fits: M didn't pull the trigger, he did.'

While Thorkild explained, he and Frank followed her directions and ran as fast as they could. By the time Thea had finally understood the point of the breathless and frantic flow of speech, they were there. She met them at the stairs, closing her phone.

'Come on,' she said. 'He's in here. We need more police immediately, and we need Kristian to come out here. You two don't do anything right now.' Thea fumbled with the keys on the phone while they ran down the corridor. From a distance, they could see what room it was. Outside stood two policemen, keeping watch.

Thea shouted to the officers, while she was instructing Kristian over the phone. The two officers opened the door.

The room was empty.

57

There was no one. Simply no one there. The two officers feverishly searched all corners of the room, convinced that their prisoner must be hiding, their search becoming increasingly manic as hope dwindled. He wasn't there.

Erik Marstrand had disappeared.

They thought they had rescued a victim. A victim who had been shot and therefore needed to be hospitalised immediately. The doctor in the reception had assured them that Erik was not in danger. Shot in a place where the immediate bleeding was profuse but not life-threatening. Now the indications were that Erik had only lost blood for a few seconds, after he heard the police outside and shot himself, before they kicked in the door. A risk, admittedly, to get them to believe that he was a victim in the case. But he got away with it. And now? Now he had really gotten away. He was a different calibre than the victim they thought they were protecting. Hardened and with everything at stake. He'd simply jumped out of the window. A leap from the first floor was only the second time that day he'd risked his life, but less risky than the first.

Erik wasn't there.

Neither was Frank. Not until he came running into the room.

'He's taken a fucking ambulance!'

Frank had gone over to the nurses' glass cage to find out if they had seen anything. But he never got to ask, because through the window he saw an ambulance parked in front of the entrance, and a man who forced the ambulance driver out on to the asphalt and jumped in himself.

Thea and the officers and Frank and Thorkild ran down the hallway towards the stairs, knocking over trolleys of sterile equipment, drip stands and a single physician who had the misfortune to step out of a room as Frank was sprinting past.

'Look out, dammit,' he shouted over his shoulder to her.

Down in the car park, the officers jumped in their car, while Frank and Thorkild, without thinking how irrational it was that they should engage in a police car chase, threw themselves into Thea's civilian car. Frank rummaged through the glove compartment like a movie cliché.

'Thea, dammit, where are your flashlights for the roof?'

Thea cut the corner over the grass to get out of the parking section. And Thorkild buckled the seat belt in the back seat.

They were lucky. Erik must have had a little trouble getting used to the ambulance, so they could see him at the end of the road before he turned left and headed north.

Thea's was the first of the two pursuing cars, but without her siren and lights she soon became hopelessly stuck at the junction with Randersvej, and it took some time before the police car behind her could make its way past and use its lights to clear a path for them on the motorway.

'Bloody hell!' cried Thea. She stayed close to her colleagues' bumper to follow the flashing lights.

Frank shouted, 'Time to say your prayers, Vicar.'

Thea didn't say a word, just clenched her teeth.

They drove fast and she was almost touching the car in front of her. Across its roof, she could see the ambulance. It was in the outer lane, swaying from side to side as it travelled at high speed.

The police radio crackled. The colleagues had called headquarters for help, and now there was an urgent burst of communication on how to proceed. Thea stayed silent and let her colleagues plan.

The ambulance took the motorway east. Here, there was

more space. Thea could get rid of the car in front of her. They had gained on the ambulance. Thea's colleagues were sometimes close and tried to run alongside of the ambulance. But Erik steered from side to side, almost forcing the police into the guard rails. The officer on the passenger side opened his window and fired three shots at the ambulance tyres, but without success.

'They're shooting,' yelled Frank, exuberant. Thorkild murmured in the back seat, Thea wondered whether the vicar was praying.

Just before the exit to Lystrup, Erik suddenly hit the brakes in the inside lane. Thea was in the outer lane and sailed past the ambulance, unable to do anything. Her colleagues, however, were trapped behind the ambulance and had to brake, so they skidded, did a U-turn and crashed into the barrier. Erik drove on, coming right up behind Thea. Frightened by the situation with the heavy car behind her, she accelerated, only to look in her rear-view mirror and see the ambulance turn right, taking the exit that Thea had just passed.

'Bloody hell,' was the second sentence Thea said on the trip. Blood trickled from her mouth where she had bit her tongue.

Then the radio crackled again. Bjørn Devantier reporting for duty. He advised Thea to ignore the traffic, drive back using the emergency lane and block the exit from below. The next thing that happened was that they heard a big crash. The ambulance had gone straight into another car. It was Bjørn's car, parked on the exit above.

Caught.

But where was Bjørn Devantier? Thea hissed into her radio, they saw the smoke rise from Bjørn's car where it had been rammed by the ambulance.

'Devantier! I don't see him. The ambulance hit him right in the middle! We need to call an ambulance.'

Thea drove up the ramp. Then they saw Bjørn. He was

standing with his legs apart and both hands on the outstretched gun while shouting at the ambulance. His car was a total wreck, but it had served to checkmate the ambulance. Thea jumped out of her car, pulled her gun and surrounded the ambulance together with Bjørn. Thea approached it from behind. A voice sounded from within, desperately calm:

'I have a man on a stretcher. I'll kill him. Pull back now!'

Thea was suddenly face to face with Erik, only the ambulance's rear window between them. He saw her. Then he spoke.

'Drop your weapon. I have a scalpel. I'll kill him.'

A body under a blanket on the ambulance stretcher was writhing, one hand held up helplessly towards her.

Thea bent down slowly and put the gun on the asphalt.

Then she said out loud: 'Let me come in. Talk to you. We'll find a solution.'

She nearly choked on the complete banality of the lie, but suddenly the back door opened with a metallic clink.

Thorkild and Frank were still in the car. They were parked behind the ambulance and had a clear view when Erik, after what seemed a long period of consideration, allowed Thea to enter.

'Holy crap, she's tough, your copper,' said Frank, admiringly.

'My copper will soon be a dead copper,' said Thorkild drily and reconsidered a prayer. The words escaped him, he laid his hands helplessly in his lap, waiting.

Then they saw Thea kick out twice, followed by a blow with her right hand. She surprised Erik, who was thrown to the floor by the first kick. And while he was down, she picked up the scalpel. She had taken Erik completely by surprise. He came to his feet and appeared to be preparing to jump her, but Thea had taken up a solid attack stance with every nerve tense, ready to receive him. Thorkild could see how her carotid artery was standing out against her skin. She yelled to Erik, insisted that he spread his arms against the ambulance interior wall. He hesitated, slowly came to his feet, glanced at the terrified patient cowering away from him in the cramped space of the ambulance. Then he looked back at Thea, who stood motionless before him.

And then he capitulated, his posture visibly acknowledging defeat. He stood up against the wall with his arms behind his back. Thea handcuffed him. Bjørn came and grabbed hold of her, she tried in vain and half-heartedly to get rid of his hands. Her lip was bleeding, she licked away the blood.

'Holy shit, Thea! Good job.'

She gathered herself. 'Thanks – you too. Jesus, Bjørn, I thought you were sitting in that car. And how in heaven's name can you even be here already?'

'I was heading back to headquarters from the summer house. When you reported the chase over the radio, I took the exit to wait and see if you'd come by this way. So I was on the bridge here –' Bjørn nodded towards the bridge over the motorway '– and I could see him make that manoeuvre, taking you out of the game. I drove over and blocked the exit, got out of the car with my radio to contact you. And you know the rest.'

Bjørn smiled at Thea. Then he gave her a proper hug. Held her in an arm's length and looked at her as he shook his head, pleased. 'Thea, dammit. You're bleeding, you know that?'

Meanwhile, more police cars had arrived. Erik Marstrand was led to one of the cars, heavily escorted. It was hard to see him for all the bustle, but he was tall and walked along calmly and majestically, although the officers grabbed his handcuffed arms and roughly ushered him on. He limped, but only slightly. Two female officers took care of the unfortunate and rather hysterical elderly patient who had been on his way to dialysis when his ambulance was hijacked. And others coordinated the traffic so no more cars would drive up the ramp. Among them was Jørgen Schmidt. As Bjørn walked by, he said:

'Guess you lived up to your name today?'

'What do you mean?'

'It takes a bear to stop a Mercedes Sprinter. That ambulance has a catalogue weight of 2.8 tons. Plus equipment, one patient and one criminal.'

Bjørn laughed. 'It's been a pleasure working with you.'

'You too. I think I'll send an application to Århus. What about you?'

'Oh, you know what, I think Roslinge needs a bit of law and order still.'

Thea stepped into her car. Frank cheered her aboard, happy as a schoolboy.

Thea smiled and looked at Thorkild, excited at what he might have to say. Again, the words forsook him and what came out was something inferior.

'How could you?'

Thea was embarrassed and looked down. 'I know I took a risk. But he said something when we questioned him – that he couldn't hurt a fly.'

Then she looked into Thorkild's eyes:

'I took him at his word.'

58

Thorkild thought for a moment while Thea was getting ready to go. She tried to get her pulse down first, and wiped the blood from her mouth with the handkerchief the vicar had handed her. Frank was busy with his mobile. It sounded as if he was calling everyone he knew to tell them that he had been in a car chase.

Kristian Videbæk approached the car at a quick trot. Thea rolled down the window.

'Are you OK?'

She looked down at the bloody handkerchief.

'I'm OK. Just a scratch.'

'Anne-Grethe can't ignore this. Well done, Thea.'

'Thank you,' she smiled. She felt very tired.

'See you later?'

'Sure, I'll see you. I'll probably have to stick around the next few days to finish all of this.'

'Let me know if you need any help, right?'

Thea followed him with her eyes as he left the car and disappeared into the darkness.

Thorkild made a decision, reached over and grabbed Thea gingerly, almost paternally on the shoulder, turned her head. Looked into her eyes with all the determination he could mobilise. The prayer that had failed him, while the drama was in progress, was in his eyes and, he hoped, filled his voice.

'Thea, I have to get permission to talk to this Erik person. I'll walk over and get into the back of the second police car, so I can ride with them to the station.'

Thorkild had slammed the door before Thea could react. She rolled down the window and yelled at him.

'Thorkild, don't do this!'

Thorkild didn't reply, Frank did it for him.

'You might as well give up. Once he's made up his mind to do something, there's nothing you can do about it.'

Thea jumped out of the car and ran after Thorkild, stopped him. Her voice pleading.

'Thorkild, I have to go after Pernille Matthiesen. We need to bring her in. I don't want you in that car.'

Thorkild hesitated, then said:

'This is important, give me half an hour. Birgitte will take care of her. Half an hour, then we'll meet at the police station in Århus around 10. At the entrance, just half an hour, then we'll go. Thea, I've come this far. I'm asking you for this. I will never come near him again. He's sitting in the car, surrounded by police. We can discuss this, or you can go get Pernille.'

And he was right, of course he was right.

'Thorkild, this is already a slippery slope, you shouldn't be here. Now let me drive you home.'

But she knew it wouldn't end up like that, of course she knew.

'I'm not going home. So I'm asking for a ride to Århus. Half an hour, I'll see you.'

Thorkild ran. Thea knew she had to go after Pernille Matthiesen. She called a couple of officers over to give instructions.

Thorkild knocked on the side window of the car where Erik Marstrand was sitting. Two policemen were in the front, and behind them Janus was flanking Erik.

'Janus, I've been given permission to come with you. Thea said it's all right.'

He didn't wait for an answer, but got in the back, on Janus' side of the car. Janus protested.

'You can't do that. It's not by the book. What if something happens?'

But he was put in his place from the driver's seat.

'Just relax, Janus, if it's on Thea's orders, it's fine. If you just sit in the middle, you can probably control things with the muscles you're carrying around. If not, there are two of us back here.'

Janus grumbled.

The officer grinned to his colleague in the passenger seat.

Thorkild watched Erik. He got a different impression than the one Thea had described after questioning Erik in the summer house earlier. She had talked of a pathetic, apologetic and insecure man. This was not how Erik appeared.

He sat up straight in his seat, steadfast, calmly gazing around, and when his eyes rested on Thorkild, Erik looked him straight in the eyes. Possibly with a hint of a smile on his face. Either way, a calmness and complacency about him. Erik looked like a man of about fifty, a receding hairline and greying hair that had grown long enough so that it could be combed back over the crown and down the back of his neck. He was dressed in a tight black sweater, black leather shoes and a big, expensive watch graced his wrist. He had tight, well maintained and suntanned skin. Only the messy blood-soaked hair and the hospital pants someone had pulled over the dressing gave any hint of what he had been through. He looked like a mix of a business consultant and a runaway patient from the psychiatric hospital.

Thorkild found a certain calmness within himself.

'I was married to Karen Simonsen. I would really like to understand what this is all about. Can you help me?'

Erik smiled quietly, didn't look at Thorkild, but carried on staring straight ahead.

'Glad to. How can I help?'

'You don't talk to him,' said Janus, nervously.

'Why was Karen killed? Why were the other women?' Thorkild said, calm, controlled and ignoring Janus.

'Wrong question.'

'What do you mean?'

'It's not relevant.'

'I don't understand.'

The man smiled, almost graciously. 'Death is not relevant. It's nothing. That's why it does nothing. Has no relevance.'

Thorkild, who had also been looking straight ahead, turned, stunned, and looked at Erik. He quickly regathered. 'What would be a relevant question?'

'Why it makes sense for anyone to kill. That's a good question.'

'Then that's my question. Will you answer it?'

'No. You must ask those who have killed.'

'But you have killed.'

Erik looked at Thorkild for the first time and replied, calm, laid back and slow. 'Have I?'

'I know you got Sanne Andersen to kill Karen. I have proof.'

Erik smiled. 'Have you? The thing that you are so boringly eager to prove cannot be proved.'

Thorkild composed himself again.

'Now, Sanne or this Pernille person cannot speak for themselves right now. Maybe you can tell me, as a – yes, what are you, really? A therapist, some have called you. Can you tell me what sense it makes to kill? It really would help me a lot. A lot.'

Erik looked serious, nodded.

'I'm a therapist. Not a psychotherapist, not gestalt, not cognitive, not a psychologist. I'm my own. And unlike everybody else, I help people.'

'You help people!' spluttered Janus. 'You kill people. That's not a great help.'

Erik looked directly at Thorkild.

'I have responsibility for the people I have in therapy. I help them. You have no idea how empowering it is when you take power into your own hands. I get them to take power into their own hands. Take responsibility.'

'What power, Erik?'

'Power. Just power. Power can take many forms. You find the one that suits the occasion. It's that simple.' Erik sighed, satisfied. 'You cannot imagine how many women need to learn it. All the self-effacing, self-forgetting, self-sacrificing women. Those who have never learned to grab life, because they grew up in a sacrificial culture. So tell me, Thorkild, who is it really that kill most life?'

Thorkild was surprised. 'You know my name?'

'I know a lot about you, Thorkild. I had Karen in therapy. She did well, shared a lot with me.'

'What kind of a sacrificial culture are you talking about?

Karen was a part of it, too? Before you decided to make her a victim, have you conveniently forgotten that? The hypocrisy cries to high heavens, don't you think?'

The therapist shook his head.

'This culture. This social democratic, Christian culture, where you feel sorry for the poor, where it's a sin to be strong and powerful. It has thrown a curse on growing as a person. But that's the true sin: to prevent growth, to prevent the power, to prevent the creation. It's the modern scourge of humanity.'

Janus rolled his eyes. Thorkild resisted the temptation to do the same. Instead, he drew a deep breath.

'There is much sin and it has many forms. But it's not the final postulate. There is forgiveness, even for you.'

'But I don't need your forgiveness. At all.'

'Are they allowed to talk to each other?' said Janus, addressing the officers in the front seat, but they waved him off.

'Without forgiveness, people never move on. We never remove the gaps between us, the gaps between ourselves and the lives we want to live,' said Thorkild with all the fervour he could muster.

'What a delusion!' It was the first time Erik showed any real sign of involvement. He laughed. Then he looked back at Thorkild.

'What an illusion that you and I need to move on with each other. Why on earth would we do that?'

'So that we can move forward,' said Thorkild impatiently. 'It's not that I'm going to save your soul. There won't be a Christmas card in jail, don't worry. But we need to move on ourselves.'

'I'm not going anywhere. I have no problem. You have a problem, but is that my responsibility? Understand, Vicar, it's your wish to forgive. It's not my wish that you do so. I don't care. I really don't care.'

'About anything other than yourself.' Thorkild finished

his sentence, indignant tears threatening to run from his eyes.

'Other than myself, yes. That is precisely the point. Certainly, I do things for others. But what I do is teach people to look after themselves. Can't you see that?'

Janus realised something. '*You* could have killed the women. They got the gun from you. You might as well have been the one who pulled the trigger.'

Erik shrugged. 'You will never know, and it really doesn't matter.' He looked at Thorkild, 'Does it matter?'

Thorkild was silent.

Janus tried another way.

'It's clear that you're guilty. Otherwise, you wouldn't have had to flee.'

Erik looked at the young detective for the first time, he moved appreciably over towards Thorkild.

'I'm guilty. The question is, of what. I confess to having caused a lot of people's happiness. But to answer the question that you don't ask: It's a pleasure for me to show how incompetent you are.'

Janus pulled an uncertain smile. Erik continued, blithely. 'You guys make everything so difficult. You think you know the truth – just like the vicar there – but when will you understand that no one can prove the truth? I'll probably have to waste a few years of my life on litigations and hearings now, simply because our culture demands a scapegoat. What primitiveness. Mankind has never really moved out of its caveman mentality.' He sighed.

'Maybe we know more than you think,' Janus said, with forced calm.

'Do you, now?'

'You shot yourself. In a place where it wouldn't be life-threatening. You used the gun Pernille used to shoot Sanne – she probably came to give it back to you, after you provided it in the first place. While you avoid leaving your own fingerprints on it.'

'You will never know. But yes, because a man has been shot, he must be a victim. Can't you see it? It's the whole point, right in front of you: You think you know who the true victims are, who are the true heroes and who are the true villains. You assign blame and honours for a simplified and imbecile idea of what's true. But what do you know? Let me ask you now, is a man a victim because he was shot?'

'You are certainly not a victim,' Janus yelled.

'You know, that is the greatest praise you could give me. But do you see how close you came? How close you were to giving me victim status, how wrong it was?'

Thorkild shook his head furiously.

'Erik, people sacrifice themselves all the time. For the good. The world is full of people who lean towards each other. A condition of coexistence.'

'But not a condition of *existence*. What do we need each other for?'

'For everything! Therein is life. In love. In intimacy. In the presence.'

'You speak like you must, Vicar. You're a slave to your fear of loneliness. Do you understand it? We're alone. You are doomed to live this life alone.'

Janus was stuck between the two arguing men in more ways than one. He'd given up trying to interfere. He carried out a rare inner dialogue, asking himself whether he was failing, or were they just playing to the gallery with their intellects? He decided that it was probably the latter, sighed and forced himself to focus on what was to come. He would receive the honour of bringing Erik in. It couldn't go wrong, he was to be delivered and he needed to file the necessary paperwork to apply for a remand in custody for the time being.

But another question had taken possession of him: Did they have enough evidence for trial? Could the man be right that they had nothing concrete?

Meanwhile Thorkild continued, his voice high and shrill in his desperate attempt to get through to the man who sat there, on the other side of Janus, and who was responsible for Karen's death.

'However we do it, we live. We live with our anxiety. We live with our fear. The worst is probably our fear of death. The final sentence. I would think most people live their lives with their backs turned against death. You can't look it in the eyes, so it comes as a shock to everyone. But the greatest courage is not to declare everything meaningless because of it. The bravest man is the one who can face death and yet live a life full of meaning.'

Erik smiled, a friendly smile.

'Is that what you do, Vicar?'

'I practise. It's about doing your best. I have my doubts. But I don't postulate the ultimate truths you assign to me. I try to stay open. Responsive to how life speaks to me. Curious. That, Mr Therapist, is something you wouldn't dare risk. You get others to act for you. You hide behind others. Me, I dare to stay open.'

'And the rest of humanity? What should they do? Humans cannot live next to open people. They must define, lock things down, in order to stand side by side. To protect themselves.'

'Must they? Dare you not think bigger?'

'That's just your religion talking.'

'It's also yours,' spluttered Thorkild. 'If you want people to grow and develop, you'll want movement. People can grow apart, people can move each other. The main reason for people growing is other people.'

'Yes, when we put up resistance to each other. Just look at the development you've undergone, since your wife was shot.'

'Erik, listen to me. The largest and most important developments don't happen through resistance. They happen through love. When we actually feel attracted to a person, deep inside, because we dare to look with the eyes of love, dare to open up, dare to set each other free, dare to ask open questions and assign value to what other people represent. That is what it means to stand in the open.'

'What if there isn't a single person worthy of love?'

Thorkild looked at the man, for the first time with genuine compassion.

'Then you are a deeply unhappy person. You are also a restricted person because you don't see. See for real. I pity you more than I've ever pitied another human being.'

'So what is love? Other than a reproductive instrument?'

'It's an approach. It's about loving life itself. It's more than . . . It's a gift. There is no better word for it.'

'Sorry, Vicar, I don't believe it. And that is the proof that it doesn't exist. For you and I will not move on together. Can't you see that?' Erik's voice was urgent for the first time. 'This is your big admission of failure. You can't reach me. No one reaches you. You aren't able to stand in the open, as you call it, here with me. Understand it, because right here is where you face loneliness. The ultimate.'

Erik was silent. Thorkild was silent. The others in the car had been silent for a long time.

Janus brooded in silence. As they approached the police station, he said: 'Say, Erik? You forget Pernille. Pernille is our proof against you.'

'Pernille,' said Erik, dreamily. 'You'll never find her.'

'We already have her.'

Erik turned his head and looked straight into Janus' eyes: 'Do you, Janus?'

59

They dropped Thorkild off outside police headquarters.

'You just needed a ride, didn't you? If you want to continue your conversation with Erik, you'll have to rob a bank first, so we can throw you in jail with him. You sure had a lot to talk about.' The driver of the police car laughed and rolled up the window.

Thorkild thanked him for the ride. A ride, which in every sense had only led him further away from home. He felt tired, infinitely tired. He longed for his bed.

He turned around to walk over to the bus station and find a connection home. He didn't usually take the bus. What line was it Karen had used? But he quickly dismissed the idea. It was hard to think of Karen and Erik. Difficult to even broach the task that lay before him, the processing of what Erik had said. His head grew heavy as he imagined that job. How he would sit in a chair, walk out into the grey weather, out into nowhere and just think, think, think. A daunting, but necessary process. Which he didn't have the energy to embark on right now. He barely had the energy to open that door even a little bit.

Which was why he was both relieved and surprised when he saw Thea Krogh further down the sidewalk. She was walking towards him. It was ten o'clock, just like they'd said.

'What are you doing here?'

'In a strange way, Thorkild, you get me to do things differently than I intended. I sent a couple of colleagues out to get Pernille Matthiesen until I can make it out there.'

'Not that I mind. It's nice to see you.'

'You think so?' said Thea.

Was she turning pale?

Thorkild was a bit embarrassed. Didn't know quite what he had meant. But frankly, he thought it was nice. 'Yes, I do.'

Thea smiled, shrugged. 'Can't have you doing something stupid, can I? Just for once. Come on now, I'll drive you home.'

Thea and Thorkild talked all the way to Roslinge. Easy and effortlessly. Sometimes they laughed, a little exuberant, went through what had happened. Thorkild listened, completely absorbed by Thea's report and her calm words. Let her version of the story sink in so that it could form the basis for the story he himself was to make peace with. He felt helped and relieved, as if she laid the foundation for a not yet erected monument over everything, over Karen.

'It's a small world in itself, the police,' she explained, encouraged by his full attention. 'You must commit yourself to find your place in the hierarchy and constantly fight for it. It's like a mini-community. Its own laws and rules. We know the stories about each other and we aren't afraid to laugh at each other's mistakes. You become strong together, when you're constantly understanding yourselves in relation to external enemies.'

She asked him about his job: 'Isn't it weird to be a vicar?' She asked about Roslinge: 'Isn't it strange to live in such a small town?' And he replied that it was like a little world of its own and that it was about finding your place and sometimes fighting for it. They laughed again.

'What's your external enemy?' she asked.

Thorkild pondered. 'Indifference,' he replied, full of thoughts.

Now they had put it all to rest, there were only a few loose ends to be tied together. For that they needed Pernille, who was waiting for them in Roslinge. And Thea wondered silently about this woman, Pernille. Who she was, why she had suddenly decided to capitulate, interrupting her senseless escape? She thought of the man they had in custody. And she was looking forward to taking this misguided woman, Pernille, under her wing and telling her that there was nothing more to fear. Aside from her own legal aftermath. But she had, assuming Pernille knew to behave herself, every reason to hope for a light sentence for murdering Sanne Andersen. She told Thorkild about it.

'I hope that as well,' he said. 'That she won't get too hard a sentence. A poor woman, manipulated. I'll send the file on to Alice as soon as I get home. It's on my computer.'

'Yes, there are certainly extenuating circumstances,' nodded Thea. 'At least, I hope, a treatment sentence.'

'I'd like to know what Frank has to say about that,' Thorkild thought out loud.

As they drove into Roslinge it was late evening. They drove up the main street. It was teeming with people. The trade association had decided that in order to rectify Roslinge's reputation, it might be better to arrange an open-by-night event, as in the surrounding towns.

The pizzeria and the inn were doing a roaring trade in bottled beer and kebabs and deep fried French fries and, in honour of the occasion, roasted almonds. The cantor's wife manned the fryer, while Anton and Anika, keeping a safe distance from the smog and everything else walked arm in arm, on their way home to the house by the mill.

The store, with Mogens Jepsen in his Sunday best, was selling flowers and toys, while a number of market stalls had been set up selling everything from ornaments, books, utensils for the kitchen, carpets and old clothes in the glow of their coloured lanterns.

Everyone was beginning to pack up. It was 10.30 p.m.

Thorkild saw Elisabeth, the grocer's wife, looking at books with Asger Jørgensen behind the flea market's shelves. The fitness centre had a booth selling magnetic sheets – an old fitness trend that had come all the way to Roslinge, and which a young salesman was coaxing Lily to buy. And the cantor, to everyone's surprise, was entertaining onlookers with cabaret show tunes accompanied by the young organist, seated at the piano from the inn, which had been brought out for the occasion.

Thea laughed openly at the provincial enterprise. 'Have you had a PR manager to schedule this for you?'

Thorkild laughed with her. 'You know what, they even asked if I would deliver a speech at the grand opening. Thankfully, I was smart enough to say no.'

Thea thought about it. Then she said: 'Why, Thorkild, why is that?'

60

They turned from the square, drove past the church and on to the vicarage. In the driveway was the police car with the two officers Thea had sent in advance, and Frank's BMW. 'Honestly,' one of them complained when he got out of the car, 'why didn't you just send Bjørn out here? Then we could sit and drink beer, while he took one for the team.'

'Thank you,' said Thea. 'I know it's late. But you'll be off the hook in a moment. There's probably still time for beer and horn music if you want to party in Roslinge.'

She went ahead to the door and rang the doorbell with energetic steps. Thorkild was about to ask her to just go in when Birgitte opened the door quickly, as if she had been waiting on the other side.

'Come inside,' she said, sounding tired.

Thea and Thorkild went with Birgitte into the kitchen, where Frank was also sat.

Birgitte looked expectantly at Thea, who had a big question in her eyes.

'Where is—'

'Your woman, Pernille – she left an hour ago.' The gaze was challenging. Thea frowned, Thorkild smacked his hands on the tabletop, hard.

'What are you saying? Why didn't you keep her here?' he shouted.

'That's not in my power,' said Birgitte, surprised.

'She knew we were coming?' said Thea.

'Yes. That's why she left.'

'You sent her away?'

'It would probably be illegal if I had.'

'But where is she?' Thorkild interfered.

Birgitte shrugged, didn't budge an inch. 'She could be anywhere. She took the Polo, promised to leave it somewhere when she was at a safe distance.'

'Birgitte, dammit,' said Thorkild and fell into a chair.

'What difference does it make?'

'It makes all the difference,' Thea replied, coolly. 'Without her, it's doubtful if we can get a conviction. Erik stole an ambulance and drove away, he lied and put our lives at stake. But the murders . . . For that, we need Pernille's testimony.'

'Dammit, Birgitte,' repeated Thorkild.

Thea thought aloud.

'We'll have to go to trial with everything we have and get him arrested,' she said slowly. 'Then we must do everything to find Pernille in the meantime. Damn! I took it for granted that she was here and wanted to wait for us. What happened?'

'I have not promised anything on this woman's behalf,' stated Birgitte authoritatively.

'What about you, Frank? Did you see her?' said Thorkild.

'Nope. I had nothing to do with it. You're on your own. Do you think I would have let her go?' He gestured deprecatingly with his hand.

'But we know everything.'

'Yes, that's the damn problem,' said Thea. 'We know it all. But from her mouth. And where is she? How far has she gone? Damn, one hour in a car, she could be anywhere in the country.' Thea grabbed her phone and dialled.

'Thea, you can have an arrest warrant issued,' said Thorkild, hopefully.

'Birgitte, you have to describe her, so we can make an image. And the licence plate on the car, what is it? Where did she go, do you know, Birgitte?'

'Maybe I wouldn't tell you if I knew. But no, I don't know. Haven't a clue. Hasn't she suffered enough?'

Thorkild gave Thea a piece of paper with the car's registration number. Thea hurried to make the call, gave the short message to Kristian Videbæk at the other end of the line. Then she called Anne-Grethe Schalborg and told it like it was.

'You're joking, Thea. You have got to be kidding. Pernille is our only witness. You are aware of that?' said Anne-Grethe, quietly furious.

'I'm fully aware, yes. It's very unfortunate. She had left the vicarage in Roslinge when I arrived. The residents in the vicarage were either unwilling or unable to hold her back.'

'But I got the impression that she was waiting for us. Wanted to turn herself in?'

'So did I. But it has not been the case. Or she changed her mind.'

'You just had to pick her up! Jesus, Thea, how could it go wrong?'

It would have been easy to lie. Or just to omit the information. But Thea told it like it was.

'I was delayed. I went to headquarters first, to pick up Thorkild Christensen. The fault is mine. And I'm sorry, Anne-Grethe. I sent a couple of policemen out here. They sat and waited. She'd fled just before they arrived.'

'You understand that there will be consequences?' Anne-Grethe sounded exasperated.

'I understand, of course. You must do as you see fit.'

In the kitchen, Birgitte and Thorkild continued to fight.

'But what difference does it make?' repeated Birgitte, when Thea came back in the room.

'She's right.' It was Frank, who for the first time said something unsolicited. 'I think she's right. Honestly. When I saw him in the ambulance – Erik. I didn't feel a damn thing. Didn't want to take him out even if I could. There's nothing to do, Thorkild. We just have to forget it and move on.'

'But, Frank, it's not about that. It's the entire community. Crime doesn't pay. That's what this is about.'

'So this woman is to forsake her entire future in an effort to serve as an example? I understand the argument. But can you really ask that much of someone?' Birgitte said calmly.

'It's more than that,' appealed Thorkild. 'It's about owning up to what you have done, accepting the penalty – finding closure, for everyone's sake.'

Thorkild glared at her fiercely.

'I'm thinking more of what will become of her,' said Thea quiet. 'This woman has nowhere to go.'

It was Birgitte who interrupted the discussion, her voice frantic.

'Enough, everybody. This is a home. Now we'll make it a home. Have a midnight meal. Tomorrow I'll go back to Copenhagen, and the rest of you will probably also prefer to leave the sweet, nice Thorkild to his own devices. So let's say goodbye tonight. Properly. I've bought some wine.' She pointed to two bottles on the kitchen table. 'Listen, you men can go out and have a beer. I've bought more of those, too, they're in the shed. Then I'll make some food. Right? And Thea, you'll stay. You must be off work by now, surely.'

She shooed the two men out, while she chatted with Thea. 'Are all your days this hectic?'

Thorkild tried hard to hear Thea's answers to Birgitte's question, but the door was slammed in his face.

'It makes no damn sense, Thorkild,' said Frank, out under the carport roof when he finally met Thorkild's accusatory gaze.

'It doesn't?'

'Naw.'

'No. You're probably right. I talked with Erik in the car when they brought him in.'

'Stop it, Thorkild, you're starting to sound like the police.' Frank laughed and sneered: '*Brought him in.*'

Thorkild felt offended. To be corrected in his native language had always been a soft spot. And by Frank, of all people.

'What I meant to say was that it didn't make much sense.'

'No, there's damn little that makes sense. I just want to forget it all.' Frank drank his beer.

'Everything he told me, Erik. Are you not interested in what he offered as justification for his actions?'

'Nah. He's a nasty psychopath.'

'No. Not like that. Well, maybe. But it must make sense to him somehow.'

'It did. Didn't it, Thorkild? But not in your way, I suppose?'

'No.'

'So can you call that making sense?' Frank chugged down his beer.

Thorkild silently shook his head. Breathed in the damp evening air and sighed.

'I don't know,' Frank continued. 'I always thought of Sanne that she was, you know, a *nutcase*. She never saw anyone. She was a weirdo. Actually, I thought that I protected her, living nearby. So I did. But I'm also a bit of a nutcase, right?' Frank looked almost questioningly at Thorkild. 'And then she suddenly changed. You know what, it makes me really happy in a way. That she fell in love. I wish it hadn't been with that guy Erik. Frankly, I'd have preferred fucking Steffen Hou,' Frank snorted.

'But she did it. Fell in love. Right? That's probably the point.'

'Yes. Maybe it was mostly in my eyes that she was a nutcase.'

'But now you can't protect her any more.'

'No. I should fall in love, right? Or move.'

'So you could get some more geotags on your photos.' Thorkild smiled.

'Damn right.'

'Maybe you held each other back.'

'I don't understand.'

'You may have looked at each other like – like nutcases. But now there's no one to look at you that way.'

'You don't?'

'Oh, no. No, Frank.'

'So I can stop being a nutcase?'

'Yes.'

'That's something to think about. Think I'll try falling in love.'

'Just check her mental state first, right.'

'Yes, that would probably be a good idea. I'm not going to end up like Sanne.'

Frank was thoughtful.

'See you around, OK, Frank?'

'Oh yes, now you have a festival here in Roslinge.' Frank lit up and laughed.

'But she's all right,' Frank then said.

'Who?'

'Thea. Yeah? She's all right.'

'Yep. She's all right.'

61

After the roast, marinated and roasted, the cream potatoes, two different kinds of salad, oil and vinaigrette, baked root vegetables and a dessert with ice cream and fruit and chocolate, the strange atmosphere in the vicarage's formal dining room became even more apparent. The meal was sumptuous, and in a nice enough way. Frank told stories and entertained, he was clearly relieved and seemed happy and full of energy. Birgitte was chatting, singing and laughing and, Thorkild thought, hectic. He tried several times to catch her eye to read if she had meant what she'd said. She would go back to Copenhagen tomorrow. Was she angry? Disappointed? Finished with him? And was he finished with her?

With equal parts physical longing and anger he looked at her. Thought of *M*, who was now running into the night until she ran out of petrol or the money he didn't for a moment doubt that Birgitte had given her. But Birgitte avoided his gaze, adroitly and with almost aggressive movements, she urged them to eat more, eat up.

Thea had sat in her own thoughts, but consumed the meal with a ravenous appetite.

When they were done, Frank and Birgitte went into the kitchen to smoke and do the washing up, leaving Thea and Thorkild alone in the darkened room, he in the easy chair, she on the sofa, each with a steaming cup of coffee.

'How to end a good story?'

'What do you mean, Thorkild?'

'You studied literature in your day, right? You must know how a good story ends.'

'Open, I think. The open ending.'

'And what about reality? That has an open ending as well?'

'Well . . .'

'Or is this case just a one-off affair?'

'No, you're right.' Thea looked at Thorkild. 'Reality has an open ending. The court may condemn and underline the result. Then it's over. A case has been completed. A murder. One life is finished. But only if you think it's the whole truth.'

'It's not?'

'No.'

'No?'

'No. Reality is always bigger, always more open.'

'Pluralism?'

'No. No, not really. It's not just a matter of the eyes that see.'

He could not make out her face clearly in the dark.

'What then?'

'Possibilities. Guess that's the word.' Thea thought a little. 'The future is open. In a positive sense – with unlimited possibilities. That's how it is. Reality is a great mentor. Stories about people never end, life never ends, right? That's the way it is, I think. Even in the police world.'

'With endless possibilities? It sounds nice and positive. That, I would like to believe.'

'You do.'

'Yes. I do.'

There was a merry atmosphere in the kitchen. Birgitte and Frank had turned up the little kitchen radio, playing party music. The living room was quiet. A filled silence. It wasn't the words that made the difference. The fullness and silence continued when Thea spoke again.

'The way a person dies, is it casting a glance back at the life that was lived?'

'Yes. It's true for Karen. I've hardly learned so much about her as in the last three months. It's not unimportant how someone dies.'

She could hear that he smiled softly.

'So she's still alive?'

'No. No, she's not. Not any more.'

'What's alive, then?'

He got up and looked out into the dark garden. He put his hand against the pane's condensation drops, and his fingers left a trail in which the drops began to assemble and run.

'The depth, I think. Life is beautiful, and serious and relevant, when you live upright and face death, instead of not looking it in the eye.'

He looked out into the garden, through the darkness. At the bottom of the garden, the water trickled away. The eternal movement towards the bay.

'That's what it's about? That's why you said that your external enemy is indifference?'

'Yes.'

She laughed lightly.

'It makes sense.'

'It makes sense.'

'Even if it doesn't make sense to everyone?'

He sighed. Turned towards her. 'Maybe we're wrong to think that opinions are something that we produce within ourselves, when we're forced to try and fit all loose ends together like an equation, and subsequently we need to get others to think the way same, too. All of our doings – are they just manifestations? Creations to fight the reality of death? A tyranny of opinions that allow someone and something to die so that I can create my meaning, thus avoiding my own existential death? Maybe there *are* just different opinions, and then it's important to find the one you can live with.'

'I can live with that,' she said.

And darkness descended further. They heard laughter from the kitchen, where Frank had dropped something with a loud crash.

'It's strange. Actually, it's strange. Why is it so good to live with others?' said Thorkild into the air. Thea chuckled, Birgitte's loud, chirping laughter was contagious.

'What do you mean?'

'Loneliness. It probably has the same qualities as death. The fear of death and loneliness are similar.'

'You're definitely not alone here.'

'No. No, you're right. But now both Frank and Birgitte are leaving.'

'I thought you were with Birgitte?'

'But I'm not. That's not what I mean, either. Sometimes you can feel incredibly alone when you're with others.' Thorkild looked at her in the darkness.

'She meant it, you think? Birgitte. She's leaving?'

'Yes. I think she is.'

'You could try to stop her.'

'Yes. But I don't want to. Although I'm afraid . . . to be alone here.'

'So you fear loneliness?'

'Yes. I do.'

Thorkild sat down again and poured more coffee for them both. He handed her the cup, she burned her fingers on it.

'Then you need to face it.'

'Loneliness? How?'

She sat up, straightened her back a bit. Pulled her legs up underneath her on the couch.

'Live with it as you do with death. Upright. Let the threat of loneliness give greater depth to the relationships,' she explained.

'It's hard. I want to put things back in place, explain, create meaning to reduce the power of things.'

'But you can't.'

'No, I can't.'

'Then you must live.' Her voice was velvety.

'Then I'll live. Openly. Stand in the open.' His intonation struck a chord with hers.

'Live in the open.'
'Yes, live in the open.'
'Then that's what we'll do.'
'Then that's what we'll do.'

Acknowledgements

This book would not have been possible without our wonderful agent Ali Gunn, who tragically passed away earlier this year. She was a whirlwind experience and offered us one as well; she was inspiring to work with, fought like a lion, exuded glamour and kindness. She made our dreams come true. Thank you for believing in us.

Thank you also to the hard-working, dedicated people at Little, Brown and Sphere; first and foremost our gifted editor, Hannah Green, whose capable hands made the story better. Thank you all for taking a chance on us.

So many friends and co-workers have read and re-read *The Preacher*, offering their constructive criticism, their support and words of encouragement. We are grateful for every minute they have spent helping us with our novel, or hearing us go on about it.

We would like to thank our families for their patience and encouragement. Thank you, Tony, the most patient one of all.

Most of all, we thank each other. None of this would have happened without you.

As well as writing *The Preacher* in their native Danish, authors Dagmar Winther and Kenneth Degnbol also translated their book into English themselves.

Read on for a fascinating interview with them on the themes and inspirations behind their debut and on the experience of writing and translating their novel.

A discussion with Dagmar Winther & Kenneth Degnbol a.k.a. Sander Jakobsen

Tell us about how the idea for *The Preacher* began. And how do the two of you write together so successfully?

The idea emerged on a trip to Romania we both went on as colleagues. We were sat in a bus for hours, looking out at this foreign territory. Sometimes a change of scene can alter the way you think, bringing new perspectives, and the idea of writing together came up. Then, magically, the idea survived coming home to Denmark and our usual settings.

We always agreed that we wanted to write about something real – in the sense that most crimes are not committed by insane mass murderers, but by normal people under unusual pressure, manipulated or momentarily insane because of something they feel passionate about: love, power, fear, the search for a meaningful life. And isn't that what is truly scary, when you think about it? What people are capable of when they're under enough pressure?

We've been very lucky that we both bring something completely different to the table – so you feel that your writing is being improved by someone else. It can be compared to making music: you can play the most beautiful tune on a piano, and then maybe someone will pick up a drum and join in. It will no longer be a solo performance – but it'll be something new and exciting. Working with someone else can sometimes bring out the best in you.

The characters in *The Preacher* are wonderfully drawn, with all of their quirks and certain ways of expressing themselves.

Do you have a favourite? Were any of them particularly easy or difficult to write?

I think Thorkild was our favourite to write – somehow he immediately had a voice of his own. He's a complex character, flawed and emotionally unavailable in many ways but also genuinely vulnerable in his hunt for truth and meaning. It's always inspiring to write about characters that undergo change – especially if it's a change most people can relate to.

The trick when two people are writing together is obviously to draw a character together. I remember we had written Frank with two different hair colours. A detail, yes, but it led to an interesting discussions about who he was. And it's a challenge to write a character like Frank. He needs to be different from Thorkild in almost every way – but he mustn't be crass or clichéd.

The idea of living with someone for so long, but growing steadily further apart from them – as Karen and Thorkild do – is distressingly believable; do you think this is something that is only going to get worse as the digital age progresses?

We're certainly afraid so. And we hope *The Preacher* will be a wake-up call in that sense. We live in a world where every distraction imaginable is right there in your hands; your laptop, phone, tablet. You no longer have to actively seek things out or wait for anything – press a button and it's there, customised and discreet, at your disposal. But it's also about presence. We feel it in our everyday lives; always online, reachable, interacting, creating narratives on social media. Is it a danger that we only see our partner with one eye, or create completely different narratives? Absolutely.

Birgitte and Thorkild's relationship is delightfully bemusing and challenging – did any part of you want to let Birgitte win him over by the end?

A part of us did, yes. But we also really liked the idea of a person who could enter our lives at a point when we're raw and exposed, generating nervous energy, before exiting our lives again. She was in many ways just what he needed at that point in his life, but she probably would have driven him insane in the long run.

Similarly, Thea and Kristian's relationship is fascinating – how do you think this adds to the detective story?

We live in a world where people live and love in many strange constructions. We think it makes them more relatable – the way they do things is not as unusual as one might expect. But their relationship also illustrates one of the biggest challenges we face today when dreaming of a life with a partner: how do we accept the sacrifices we have to make? As we become more individual and basically no longer depend on a partner in any other way than emotionally, we are less inclined to make sacrifices. They love each other very much but are also uncompromising; the issue of having children was too big of a challenge for them to choose each other fully. It's what makes Thea good at her job, but also makes her lonely.

How did you come up with the centrepiece of the novel – the bewitching villain himself?

It amazes me how easy it is to manipulate. Emotionally, politically, so many aspects of our lives are so easily influenced by the agendas of others. And I'm constantly fascinated by the damage we can do to each other, applying just the right amount of pressure at a vulnerable point. We are fragile as a species; hugely dependent on the approval of others and subject to so many life changes and crisis scenarios where we want something completely different out of life than what we've got. Our villain understands this basic challenge of modern life and manages to steer his victims towards the rocks, driven by their desire for change.

One of our favourite parts in *The Preacher* is the brilliant set piece where Thorkild and Frank blunder their way into the police investigation of the summer houses, both narrations running alongside each other: the plotting is masterful. Is the plotting and pace something you thought very hard about from the start?

It was, actually. Knowing that at times *The Preacher* moves at a steadier pace than some crime novels, it was important to us to up the tempo at certain points. But it's also true that most police investigations take time, and we had set out to create a certain realism in this – there will be times when an investigation is frustratingly slow. And then all of a sudden, it takes flight.

We leave Thorkild and Thea at quite a challenging, but uplifting, point: a pledge to live in loneliness and in the open, facing life head-on. Why did you want to leave your readers with this?

Because there are no happy endings, really, just good intentions. We have followed Thorkild on his journey towards answers, but it was also important to somehow show that no answers are final. He has a lot of work ahead of him to put his life back together. And Thea has some soul-searching to do as well – her career has taken a beating and her relationship with Kristian has some built-in dilemmas that are starting to show.

Your publishing story has been very eventful! How did it feel to get picked up in your home country after securing a publishing deal in the UK?

I remember the day after our release party in Denmark, feeling tired after a late night with lots of champagne and flowers, signings and words of praise, I decided to just walk down the high street of Aarhus and that's when I first saw it on the shelf of a bookshop. It felt like a turning point – a sense of accomplishment like nothing else. In my life, there's a before and an after that moment.

Does it feel empowering to have translated your own novel yourselves? Would you worry about someone else doing it?

It does. It's an amazing thing to be able to do – although we have had tremendous help from the skilled editors who have worked on it with us. My time as a journalist in England made it possible for me to feel confident enough to do it, and I'm extremely grateful for that time.

I don't know that I would have been worried about someone else doing it, but it does feel extremely good to know that, to my knowledge, nothing has been lost in translation.

How would you describe *The Preacher* in one sentence to someone you were recommending it to?

Less of a standard crime novel and more of a psychological drama, ambitious with its characters and a genuine look at Danish village life.

Which writers and books inspire you – crime and otherwise?

We're inspired by many authors and genres and are constantly reading: if you want to be a writer, read! Peter Høeg (*Smilla's Sense of Snow*) is a huge source of inspiration – his sentences are like quality chocolate. Fred Vargas for setting a tone so unmistakably French and getting away with the strangest ideas. Stephen King for the sheer joy of writing. Michael Connelly for realism and complexity.

Crime dramas on television have become so strong now – are you addicted to anything at the moment?

Oh, yes. It is amazing to live in a time where so much quality TV is being created. We've recently discovered the brilliant

Sherlock and are eagerly awaiting more *House of Cards*. *Breaking Bad* also left a void in our lives. UK crime shows are hugely popular in Denmark, so a Friday night in often includes *Midsomer Murders*, *A Touch of Frost* or *Prime Suspect*.

Finally, what is next for Sander Jakobsen?

We're working on our next novel which follows some of the characters from *The Preacher*. It will be a thriller and a bit more fast-paced, dealing with powerful dilemmas of violence, journalism, parenthood, love, commitment and betrayal. And then we're looking forward to seeing our words translated into Japanese when *The Preacher* is published across the globe!

A true Danish Night In
is a sacred thing indeed.

Turn the page for Dagmar's
explanation of how to achieve the
perfect state of 'hygge' . . .

Hygge! A Danish Night In, by Dagmar

I once read an article about words that only have meaning in the country from which they originate. Like *biritululo*, a New Guinean word for comparing potatoes to settle a dispute – the largest one wins. Or *tingo* – a person from Easter Island who keeps borrowing things from your home, never to return them. In Italy, if you don't care about politics, you'd be a *qualunquismo*. The French term *esprit d'escalier* means a sentence you wish you'd thought of in a given situation, but it only came to you later.

In Denmark, we have our own word. That word is *hygge*. It's very hard to describe, but it's a crucial part of Danish mentality and a must if you're having a night in.

Hygge is a very individual phenomenon as it varies between what people find to be 'hyggeligt'. But certain common denominators can be deducted: it often involves candles, good company, food or snacks, a roaring fire, quiet conversation. It can mean reading with a cup of tea, snuggled up in a blanket, or it can describe a delightful evening with your friends playing board games. Some have tried to translate it as 'cosy' but that doesn't quite cut it. Hygge is a state of mind which can be contagious. Hygge is something we strive for, or use as a headline for what we have in mind: 'Come on over and let's hygge'. It can be a compliment, used to describe a lovely time being had, or even a person's character. Your living room décor is successful if others call it hyggelig. Hygge can be brought along to cafés and social events.

For me, it is a definition of home. The typical hygge night in in Denmark will involve food of sorts, often a traditional meal consisting of *frikadeller* (Danish meatballs) with potatoes and parsley sauce with a Carlsberg to go with it. Beer equals hygge. Dessert is a given, and Danes enjoy their *rødgrød med fløde* – a red berry pudding with lots of cream on it. Funnily enough, that dessert is considered to be the ultimate test for foreigners trying to speak Danish: once you can correctly pronounce *rødgrød med fløde*, you're getting there.

Hygge involves coffee or tea, candles are lit, the TV is on. We watch a film, a TV series or one of the big game shows that will make up next week's talking points. Two main channels compete for the viewers' attention with their ongoing battle of the TV series: *Borgen* and *The Killing* are products of this epic and healthy battle to create quality shows. We bring out bowls of sweets, including the delightful Danish liquorice that an English colleague of mine spat out in horror, claiming 'it's like eating salt!' And it is; I know of no other country that takes such pleasure in these small ammonium chloride treats.

Maybe we have people over, maybe we pay others a visit. A trip to the pub is not a common thing, best left to the young who drink beer in their rooms with their friends and then head to clubs. If young people describe a night out with their friends as very 'hyggelig' you can be sure it wasn't all they had expected it to be.

But for the children and those of us no longer in our twenties, hygge is sublime; it is the core of Danish life itself.

Find out more about **Sander Jakobsen's** books at

www.sanderjakobsen.com

Or you can follow them on Twitter

@SanderJakobsen

And keep up to date with

@LittleBrownUK
@TheCrimeVault

To buy any Sander Jakobsen books and to find out more
about all other Little, Brown titles go to our website

www.littlebrown.co.uk

To order any Sphere titles p & p free in the UK,
please contact our mail order supplier on:
+ 44 (0)1832 737525

Customers not based in the UK should contact the same
number for appropriate postage and packing costs.